In praise of Sus

Susan Emshwiller's new n   ) its
stellar title in every facet   nase
caper, jammed with rich ch   ) the
human condition. *All My Ancestors* ---   fully
inventive cross-country thrill ride loaded with surprises and
PTSD.

RICHARD KRAUSS editor/publisher of
The Digest Enthusiast

Susan Emshwiller's riveting novel, *All My Ancestors Had Sex*,
exploits genealogy as a springboard for a wild, funny, fast-paced
tale of misfortune, mayhem, and unlikely redemption.
Emshwiller unfolds Izzy's story with such credibility that the
reader never doubts the preposterous premises about this 'ugly
duckling' daughter of disappointed privileged-class parents. Is
this a thriller, a mystery, a romance, a historical novel? Like Izzy
herself, it's a little bit of everything. An exhilarating read!!

ANNE ANTHONY, author of
A Blue Moon & Other Murmurs of the Heart

If you are holding this book in your hand, congratulations. If you
have chosen to buy this book, chosen from all the books you
could have chosen to buy, HUGE CONGRATULATIONS. You are in
for a wild and heartfelt ride. What can I say about Susan
Emshwiller's writing, except that there is no one like her. She is
truly an original.

NANCY PEACOCK, Piedmont Laureate, author of
The Life and Times of Persimmon Wilson

Susan is afraid of nothing in her writing...Full stop. Hilarious! A
mother/son fiasco/journey wrapped in love, grit, and
impossibility-be- damned!! I promise you will love this wild ride
into the inner workings of one whale and one mother.

AMY MADIGAN, actor, producer

Brush Strokes engages with wit and warmth. Emshwiller sensitively
establishes the mystery of a situation, and knows precisely when to
sever the action— realizing what needs to be revealed and what
doesn't.

Pick of the Week, *LAWeekly*

ALL MY ANCESTORS HAD SEX

Also by Susan Emshwiller

Dominoes - a play
(Dramatists Play Service)

Defrosting Popsicles - a play
(Playscripts)

Thar She Blows - a novel

ALL MY ANCESTORS HAD SEX

a novel by

susan emshwiller

PINEHEAD PRESS

ALL MY ANCESTORS HAD SEX
© 2024 by Susan Emshwiller
Santa Fe, NM

www.susanemshwiller.com

PINEHEAD PRESS
www.pineheadpress.com
ISBN-13: 978-0-9894236-5-6 (paperback)
ISBN: 978-0-9894236-6-3 (ePub)
Library of Congress Control Number: 2024903263

Cover sculpture and design and family tree illustration
© 2024 by Susan Emshwiller

Author photo by Chris Coulson

for all my ancestors

ALL MY ANCESTORS HAD SEX

VEGETABLE PLAN

AS I VOMIT MY MEDS on the sprouting vegetables, I wonder if this plan will work. So far, the plants seem happy. Little leaves reach toward the glass roof in a prayerful gesture as I hydrate them. No matter that the hydration is via stomach acid tinged with a cocktail of drugs I can't name except for Lithium.

I'm told, "Working in the greenhouse is a privilege liable to be rescinded at any time for behavioral infractions." I intend to keep this privilege by acting pliant and pleasing, thus getting good marks on my daily evaluation.

Early on, I learned that it's impossible to hide four pills tucked in the gums or under the tongue. My keepers are used to that subterfuge. Nurse Blinky repeats the song for each of us. "Lift tongue, to the side, other side, thank you."

Swallowing is the best option.

That day I was strong-armed up the wide steps and into the Institution was the day I succumbed to the effects of my meds—a squirt of bile in my brain that led to confusion, lethargy, dizziness, and dull contentment. I'm not sure how many months I was in this state but as I floundered, part of me, many parts, swarmed to my rescue. My right hand had its finger down my throat when I finally came to. Now I pretend to be confused, lethargic, dizzy, and dully content—all the while keeping this garden fertilized with meds. I intend to stay awake and aware. Mine is a serious sentence and it's up to me to extricate us from this situation. Up to Me. Us. Me/Us. You'll get it.

But I'm charging ahead of myself. You want the low-down on how I came to be in this nuthouse. Reckon I'll start at the beginning.

1

PAINT BY NUMBERS — BORN

I'M NOT COGNIZANT of what went on before I was born or immediately after, so you'll have to give me license to speculate. Although much of what I'll recount is fact, other moments are informed extrapolation.

I do know mine was to be a paint-by-numbers life. My course was set and the outcome expected to be magnificent.

When I was not even a twinkle in Evelyn and Philip's eyes, they made plans. Perhaps you've heard of Vision Boards where people paste images and words on a surface, creating a collage of what they want to manifest in their lives. My parents didn't do that. My parents made Vision *Books*. They (Mother) cut pictures from periodicals: Architectural Digest, The New Yorker, The Atlantic, Prestige, Town and Country. From clippings of beaming babies in bassinets to well-dressed young professionals in well-appointed homes.

My parents planned each milestone of my projected journey and created thirty-one leather-bound Vision Books. One volume for each anticipated year of my life. Babyhood onward to thirty.

Being members of the super-rich and used to outsourcing everything, they opted to forgo the muss and fuss of pregnancy and implanted their fertilized egg into a surrogate womb. Yasmina was already known as a reliable and hardworking housekeeper and was amenable to the incubation payout.

In a Petri dish, Father's sperm was injected into Mother's egg and presto-chango I was created. The parental chromosomes mingled, set about sorting which parts of the Deoxyribonucleic acid to keep or discard, and I was concocted of these randomly selected strands. Millions of bits of countless generations. I was made entirely of the past. But whoever did the fertilization procedure got a text or notification on their phone and didn't give me a stir. At least, that's my theory. I wasn't stirred and all that DNA didn't get homogenized.

After five days in an incubator, I graduated from a multi-celled embryo to a blastocyst. A syringe sucked me up and squirted me into my new home—Yasmina's insides.

In our Central Park West building, Yasmina was moved from her housekeeper quarters off the kitchen to the suite of rooms that was to become the nursery. She was fed nutritious meals, our chauffeur Alberto took her to weekly checkups and ultrasounds, and Mother brought her to the Upper West Side Yoga Center as a guest member to keep the blood and amniotic fluid moving—and to show off. My parents did not ask to know the sex of this growing fetus, yet they had the baby clothes, silver spoon, and silk sheets monogrammed with E.G.G. in anticipation of Edward Gregor Gaston. As I grew, Philip and Evelyn counted the days and set aside Tuesday the 4th of April in their schedules. They pre-enrolled me in pre-school at Sebastian's and, with a generous gift, secured me a place in Rothschild's Academy for my high school years. My life was in place.

My first crime:

On April Fool's Day, during downward-facing-dog, Yasmina groaned and I popped my head out, my features stretching the crotch of her yoga pants. I hollered, Yasmina screamed, and Mother yelled, "Shove it back in!"

Yasmina didn't. She lowered her pants and I slid out, landing face-first on the yoga mat. Yasmina gently turned me over, and Mother gasped.

My second crime:

I was female.

Unaware of the horror of this infraction, all the ladies in the yoga session curdled around me, cooing.

They say all babies come out a red-faced, scrunched, wrinkly mess that fairly quickly evolves into the cutest button you ever saw.

I didn't.

My third crime:

I was ugly.

FIRST DAY

THERE, ON THE YOGA MAT, Yasmina couldn't help but lift me to her breast. Mother balked. The yoga ladies pulled her aside. "It's just the first drink that's important. All those good nutrients. After that, you can use formula."

And so I was allowed to nurse. Yasmina's eyes were dark brown and her breath was warm and smelled of goodness. She held me close and her milk was hot and dense and infused me with bliss from those swallows.

When I burped and lolled away, Mother swiped her phone screen and a large amount of money moved from her bank account to Yasmina's. With that, my personal sherpa was sent away.

I was wrapped in a towel and yoga mat and driven home.

In the nursery, my parents hovered around the state-of-the-art bassinet to peer at me. And I peered at them.

Mother, Evelyn, was a young woman of twenty-five. Styled. Coiffed. She was pretty, but clearly a matron-in-training. Requisite pearl necklace and earrings. Dressed via money. She wore a stiff smile hinting at a deeply buried distress.

Father, Philip, stood behind her, tall and imposing with Ostentatious Good Looks. Dimpled chin, strong jaw, one lock of hair carefully out of place. All of him was charismatically handsome but for something cold lurking in his eyes.

Mother shifted her pursed lips from one side to the other. "Do you think—the face—?"

"I'm positive," Father said with his ubiquitous confidence. "The features are still in flux."

"It's been hours."

"Patience, my dear."

Later that night, my parents checked on me again. Shining a phone light, they discovered that time had brought me no closer to the ideal they'd planned for.

One eye was green, the other brown. My scalp had a splotch of pale thin hair, another of dark curls, and a spike of red. On my forehead was a birthmark of white spiderweb lines. My right leg seemed plumper and darker than the left—which was muscular and had a ragged scar around the thigh. One arm was pink, had freckles, and baby rolls at the elbow, the other was tan and weathered and sinewy. I was—

"Not acceptable," Mother whined.

"Perhaps—shall we call Yasmina? See if she wants the child."

"We can't call Yasmina. Remember? That was your brilliant idea. No contact whatsoever."

"She can't have disappeared back to New Orleans already. It's only been half a day."

Mother turned to him, "We can't give this creature to our housekeeper—but maybe—we could do—the A word?"

Father looked at the ceiling, staring at it like he was running through the words that start with A. Apple. Airplane. Adirondack, Aardvark. "What's the A word?"

"Adoption. I could call an agency tomorrow."

"We must do it anonymously. I won't have the Gaston name associated with—"

At this moment I pressed my little lips together, pushed a sound through them, then released the lips. "MMMMM—AAAAA!"

It came out good so I did it again. "MMMMM—AAAAAAA!"

Mother looked at me, surprise widening her features. "Did you hear that? She said Ma-ma!" Mother leaned close. "Yes, you did. You said Ma-ma." She turned to Father. "We're keeping her. She's of our genes. She may not have gotten any of the good ones, but they're our genes, and our ancestors' genes, and we're keeping her."

Thus began my relationship with Evelyn and Philip.

After much Googling, my parents settled on the name that matched the monogram E.G.G: Elizabeth Gillian Gaston.

CHILDHOOD

THROUGHOUT MY CHILDHOOD, I tried to match each year's Vision Books expectations but Mother and Father had decorated the pages with magazine clippings of their expected young boy, young teen, young man—a Hero—never altering the books when they got me.

It was not just the hero's gender that I bore no resemblance to, but every one of those compiled manifestations was beautiful. They were thin with straight blond hair, and all had a look of intellectualism, artistic awareness, and a benign tolerance of whoever was the lesser behind the camera.

My visage *had* changed since infancy. It had gotten worse. I was an amalgam of leftover parts. Oddly stout in places, thin and knobby in others. My skin color varied from limb to limb. My hair continued to be a mess—sections of dark curls, strands of shiny black, tufts of blond, and the one lock of red.

Hair tinting was discussed, as was plastic surgery to meld my mismatched bits, but Mother insisted on patience. "Elizabeth hasn't hit puberty yet. Let's wait to see if ugly ducking becomes a swan." They bought a six-foot plush frog wearing a crown for my bedroom, undoubtedly hoping that if I kissed it often enough, I'd turn into a princess. I kissed it all the time.

After eight years, my parents decided that all the effort and planning they'd put into the perfect child was worth another try. This time they did everything to ensure the correct gender and, suspecting that my visage might be due to contamination from being incubated in the dark, short Yasmina, they opted for a more appropriate vessel. Zoey, a thin, blond NYU student.

Nine months later, Findley arrived. He was on schedule and entirely as anticipated. All the missed years of cooing, cuddling, and coddling rushed in to envelop him. If I was jealous it was well buried, for I saw him clearly as all I was not. There was good reason for this outpouring of love, this focus of care; he was dearly lovable, while I had never been.

BIRTHDAY AND BURNING BOOKS

TODAY, APRIL FOOL'S DAY, is my birthday. As I turn eighteen, I implement my plan. I have my I.D. and have done the vehicle registering and title transfers and insurance, bought several Visa gift credit cards, and squirreled away a nice collection of cash. I've been figuring since The Straw happened and hopefully, everything is in place.

Mother and Father are at the Veuve Clicquot Polo Classic, so I'm charged with watching Findley, now ten. I sit in his room wondering when to make my move as he browses one of his Vision Books.

"Elizabeth," he says with a whisper of wonder. "Check out this one! I'm gonna get it when it's *my* eighteenth birthday."

I look over his shoulder. Pasted into the book is a handsome man in dashing clothes, standing beside an impressive red sports car, a blond model in a bikini lounging across the hood.

"That's me in only eight years," he says, puffing out his little chest.

I bet it is. Findley has the sanctioned good looks. His hair is straight and blond, his eyes blue, and he's got limbs and bones in all the right proportions. He'll be exactly the man in the book, and that's what I'm afraid of.

"I'll give you a ride when I get that car," my brother says.

A jolt thumps my chest. Maybe I mean something to him. "I'll have to get off the hood though," I say, laughing.

"That's not you. She's pretty."

7

Bingo, kid. This makes me sad and mad and I decide to add to my plan.

I go to his bookshelf and the other Vision Books. These are the ones created for me, but as they were of pitiful relation to my ill-suited being, they were passed along to one more appropriate. Pull from the shelf Book One, Two, Three... my arms are full by Book Seventeen and I saunter out of the room. Findley is intrigued but doesn't want to let it show.

Come back for the rest—up to age thirty. That's when a man should be well established and have his own family with their own Vision Books. I disappear again, calling over my shoulder for Findley to join me and bring Book Eighteen.

In the game room, beside the fireplace, I strike the first match and light Book Ten.

The blond boy in the pages smiles as his teeth shimmer with flames and smoke rises.

Findley peeks his head in. "What the—"

"This is the one time it's okay to play with matches. Give it a go."

He moves closer as I light book twenty-eight. Outside a church, a bride and groom look ecstatic as falling ashes cover them. The glossy men and their accessory women squirm and writhe, burning black. Topiaried poodles puddle. Book twenty-nine catches fire. Flames lick a Lichtenstein. Cartier watches crackle. A massive corner office buckles orange. All the coveted images blossom with volcanoes from within.

Finley pulls at my match arm. "Stop! Those are mine! That's my life!"

"These were made for me. They're mine."

"But the hero is ME! He looks like ME!"

"That's back when they thought I was going to be a boy. You don't want these. They're hand-me-downs."

Book thirty. Flames pockmark and consume manicured lawns. Mansions curl and flake and two smiling children smolder by the pool.

"Stop! I hate you! You're burning my whole life!" He falls to the rug, sobbing.

I had no idea he was so attached to these. "Okay, okay. I'm stopping!"

The fireplace crackles as the year dissolves to ash. Bits float up, rising weightless in the swirling currents. Unbound. It's cathartic and metaphorical. This is about to be me. Unbound.

After a while, Findley raises his tear-smeared face. This just might make my plan work better. "I'm sorry, Findley. I'll make it up to you. How about I take you somewhere special? We'll drive there."

"But Alberto's already driving Father and—"

"We're taking my birthday car."

Findley perks up and gives me a gleaming smile. A perfect smile. Experts have coddled his teeth since he started hatching them. I wonder if I can make some of those straight ivories crooked.

I steer Findley into the elevator and we glide down to the first floor. In the foyer, I leave a note on the polished marble table with my credit cards and cell phone. Miroslav, in his crisp grey uniform, opens the door for us and we're gone.

It's my birthday and I'm taking a trip with my little brother.

I suppose in some circles, one could use the vernacular: kidnapping.

AUDI AND METRO VAN

BUT ONCE AGAIN, I'm getting ahead of myself.

Skip back to May the year before. I'm seventeen. I'm standing in the enclosed courtyard of Rothschild's Academy after the graduation ceremony, which my parents were unable to attend due to previously scheduled conflicts. As usual, none of my giddy classmates are yearning for my company. I text Alberto and he pulls up to the gate to shuttle me back to our Central Park West home. Perhaps home is the wrong word. Our building is six floors, not counting the basement with its wine cellar. The roof boasts an infinity pool, topiary trees, and an outdoor kitchen for casual dining. We have a fitness room, sauna, media room, game room, five bedrooms, the massive parlor, the intimate parlor, a formal dining room, a family dining room, father's office, mother's sanctuary, and a library. Staff are sequestered in rooms off the massive kitchen. All entirely for the four Gastons.

As we near this "home," Alberto says to the rearview mirror, "Miss Elizabeth should close her eyes now."

I don't want to, but as it's Alberto making the suggestion, I do.

The car slows and smooths to a stop. Albert's door clicks open, taps shut, his footsteps round the car to my side—and humid air and sounds of the city rush in. "Keep them closed and take my hand."

I reach out and am met by a warm, steady palm. His skin feels rougher than any I've felt before. But then, I don't feel anyone's skin. I squeeze my eyes tighter to keep tears in as a strange sob threatens my throat. I *have* been touched before. This shouldn't cause such an uproar inside me. I have a spurt of memory of a Chinese man taking my hand—then, a flash of blue velvet—

"Vámonos." Alberto gently guides me out of the car and, as I find my footing, Mother's voice intrudes, "I'll take it from here." Alberto's hand releases me and a smooth one takes its place. I'm steered several steps and turned around. "You can look now."

I open my eyes. Parked at the curb is a shining sky-blue car, complete with an oversized bow and oversized *Congratulations, Graduate!* card. Father stands proudly with his hand on the hood.

How'd they keep this parking space? Did Theresa and Consuela take turns guarding it? When did they start? How long were they standing sentry? Was it all night?

"What do you think?" Mother asks.

"It's exactly what I wanted!" I lie.

No one who is anyone drives in New York City. At Rothschild's Academy we had to take Driver's Ed and subsequently got our licenses, but not one of the graduates of my class, all of whom are getting their requisite automobiles today, will drive. One is *driven*. There is no chance I will use this car. Yet, here it is.

"It's the Audi Roadster Convertible," Father says. "Everyone said graduates want SUVs but your mother and I are a little more savvy than everyone. You like it?"

"I do. It's so—me."

"Keys are in the visor. Take it for a spin. But no speeding," he says.

Like I could speed in these streets clogged with taxis, double-parked delivery trucks, buses, and maniacal bicycles.

Father steps to Mother, offers his arm, and Miroslav holds open the door as they sashay into our building.

I look at Alberto. If only I had some reason to hold his hand again. It was so calm and warm and supportive.

"Let me take off the decorations, Miss Elizabeth. More aerodynamic without them." He does this, carefully placing the bow and card in the back seat. "Drive through the park. It's better."

Traffic is slow. People push strollers or jog with packs of dogs leashed around them. None of them looks like my species. At least not the people. I take the car across Central Park, and can't help but think of the memories at the zoo area and the model yacht club boathouse. Tears spill out and I fumble to find the windshield wipers, as if that would help. The clip-clop of horse hooves sends a rush of panic into my chest. I pull a lever and a spray of windshield fluid flies high and wide, sprinkling a couple in a horse-drawn carriage. Curses follow my new car.

After a loop through the park, I return to our street and the parking spot is gone. Alberto rushes from our building, waving for me to stop. I push the brakes too strongly and jerk against the seatbelt, which almost sets me crying again. Alberto opens my door, warm hand extended, and steadies me out. "I'll get it parked, Miss Elizabeth," he says. We switch places and he drives off.

Miroslav holds the front door for me. "Did you have a pleasant drive, Miss?"

"Where's Alberto going to park?"

"Two blocks away, there's a big building only for parking. They have a car elevator. Your family has several spots on the tenth floor. It will be safe there."

Safe or not, I doubt the Audi Roadster will be ever driven again.

I am wrong.

Months pass. Summer boils away. Fall arrives. And a few days after Thanksgiving, what I call The Straw takes place. Because of The Straw, I realize I need to take action. I form a plan. The plan will take a Scheiße-load of preparation, and secrecy is imperative, so I take up an interest in poetry.

A week later, on the first of December, I tell Mother and Father I'm going to an afternoon poetry reading.

"Be sure to tell us all about it when you get back," says Mother, using her phone camera zoomed in to study the progress of the woman doing her pedicure.

"Oh, yes, you must," adds Father, occupied with countless important items on his phone.

"Will you be back for dinner?" Mother asks.

"I reckon so," I say.

"Reckon?" Father laughs. "You sound like a western hayseed. If this is what poetry does to your lexicon, I reckon you should reconsider."

I open my mouth to indicate a guffaw and rush off to my lie.

Miroslav gives me the location of the parking building and I emancipate the Audi Roadster and drive it out to Long Island to the first used car dealership I find. Google told me the value of the car. I decide on a nondescript grey Toyota and am about to trade my car for it and some cash when a flash of chrome winks at me. A rusting monster vehicle lurks in the tall grass beside the garage.

"What's that?" I ask the man, whose name tag reads *Ricardo*.

"A 1959 International Harvester Metro Van."

It looks like it's a delivery truck from the old days. Something the smiling milkman would drive. My right hand rises like it's mesmerized by the Van and points.

"Does it run?"

"It limps."

"Can I see inside?"

Ricardo leads me to the hulking thing and lifts the pitted, chrome-faced hood to reveal a dust-covered engine.

"Inside the inside, not the motor."

He leads me around to the passenger side and pulls the sliding door. It resists. Herculean heaving on the handle opens a gap wide enough to stick my head through. The interior is cavernous and a mess. Vines curl through a broken window in the rear. Decaying leaves cover the floor, which has gaps where the ground is visible. A bird's nest snuggles above the visor. The rotted driver's seat faces a post where the steering wheel should be.

I don't know why, but I want this van more than anything I've ever wanted. It's a complete disaster and I love it.

"How much?"

Ricardo looks at my Audi. I'm sure he knows it's worth over fifty thousand.

"This here's an antique. Not many left."

He's working on naming a price but doesn't want to lowball himself.

I interrupt his thinking. "If you could get this Harvest—"

"1959 International Harvester Metro Van."

"Yes,—get this Metro Van roadworthy and inspection proof, spiff out the back for two people traveling, beds, table, cabinet— fix the driver's seat and add a passenger's—we'll do an even trade."

His eyes do the cha-ching sound with dollar signs popping up. "What's your timetable?"

"It must ready be by the first of April. April Fool's Day. Any later and the deal's off. Okay?"

"Done."

I get a weird tickling thought and add, "Put a spare key in a magnetic container behind the right rear bumper."

Ricardo nods, tapping his nose like I'm smart. I don't even know what I just asked for.

"I'll set up the transfer of the Audi's insurance to this vehicle for April first."

"You'll need the VIN number," Ricardo says.

Seeing my cluelessness, he points to a strip of metal on the dashboard. I step to the passenger door and squeeze through. Leaning close with my phone, I take a picture of the number. The smell of dust and oil and something rotting stings my nose. Something must be dead in here.

HEINRICH — KÖNIGSHARDT, GERMANY — 1944

THE SMELL WAKES ME. *Was ist das?* Smell of dirt and blood and death. Smoke. An ox lies beside me in this ditch, its black bloated belly swarming with flies. Listen—constant barrage of heavy fire. The Luftwaffe is strafing the enemy, but far off. Sounds of marching is close. Is that our side or the Ami swine?

Panic rises immediately. I need to escape.

Something's crushing me. An oozing body. He's headless but so heavy I can't get a good breath. I'm unable to move. My head is tilted and I can see my muddy boot. My left leg. Flies keep landing on the open wound.

Will they lay eggs? Give me maggots?

Marching gets closer. They're speaking English. I can't wave the bugs away because the enemy is so near. If they see I'm alive, I won't be. Flies are a good disguise of death for the living, but watching them mingle with the blood and muscles and torn bone makes me unable to keep still. I have to twitch my thigh to scatter them. Have to twitch my thigh. Twitch my thigh.

My thigh does not twitch.

The soldiers march on the road above this ditch. Dull tired steps. They've had enough of seeing and smelling death as well.

A crow caws. Please don't fly near while the soldiers are passing. The caw comes again and a big black bird lands beside my leg. Don't peck me. I need to be still.

My eyes stay on my leg as I hear a jeep follow the last of the parade and the motor and boot-falls fade.

Still, better to wait. Let the flies nibble or feed or lay eggs. Just don't let that crow eat me.

The crow cocks its head. If I shoo it away, the soldiers may return. Black wings flap and the bird lands on the headless body on top of me.

I jerk and hiss without meaning to. The crow cries an alarm and flaps into the sky, alerting the world. Heart thumping too loudly, I wait.

No consequences.

I get my arm around the dead man's shoulder and push the body off my chest. Finally pull in a deep breath and bile bubbles up in my mouth. Sit up. Must leave and find shelter. I try to stand and the top of my thigh moves, but the leg remains. It isn't mine anymore.

Above my knee is a belt tourniquet. I'm here because of that. How did that happen?

After the blast, someone was leaning over me, speaking in a whisper, pulling his belt tighter, tighter, and—another explosion —the headless savior collapsed on me.

But now I'm free. And in two parts. Heinrich here and Heinrich there. *Nein, nein, nein.*

I pull myself up by the exposed roots of the trees edging the ditch. My leg stares at me, accusing, wondering, pleading. That leg's been with me through everything. From my first steps on the cold tile, to being immobilized in the plaster cast, to peddling down Friedrichstraße on my bike, to kneeling at communion, to the marching on the street with the grown boys, to pushing between Solveig's legs trying to open them, to pulling on these boots and clicking my heels. This leg has scars and muscles and hair and toes, that danced and ran and kicked and fled. This leg can't be left to the flies and crows.

I let go of the roots and fall back into the ditch. My head now facing my body-less foot. I tied these laces this morning. For what?

Scavenging a rifle strap from a body, I tie an end around the detached knee and strap the other end to my belt. My crotch is cold. And wet. I peed myself! Not only is my leg off, but I peed myself! If someone comes to help, they'll see this. A soldier disgraced.

Red with shame and blood, I climb the roots while dragging my leg. The crow in the branches overhead calls out my stupidity. Over and over. I can't help it. This is my body and I'm not leaving it behind. I'm alive and so it's alive. We'll get put back together. We're meant to be one.

Crows laugh as I pull myself and my leg out of the ditch and inch into a stubby field. It's terribly hard with a missing leg. The harvested field is full of thick stalks that poke and scrape me. There is no way I'll make it across this expanse while towing my leg.

I can't leave it here! These toenails were just clipped. There are blisters I got today from marching. It has history, verdammt!

There's a farmhouse across the field. I'll crawl to it and ask for help. I untie my leg and give the calf a soft pat to let it know I'll come back. It looks strange all alone. I inch forward again but there's a figure approaching. He's dressed as a farmer, so he's German. He'll take care of my leg and see that it's nursed back to health.

STRAW

AS FOR FINDLEY'S KIDNAPPING, it was easy to imagine the reaction of Evelyn and Philip, as I'd seen a smaller version play out before.

When I was twelve, a Picasso lithograph, small enough to slip under a winter coat, was stolen during a Christmas party. It wasn't worth much more than twelve thousand and Evelyn didn't particularly care for it as it depicted Don Quixote and she had never been a fan of that character after an unpleasant experience with a Cervantes professor in college. Nevertheless, the theft was an affront to all my parents held dear. They hired private detectives to retrieve it, lawyers to prosecute the guilty, and saw to it that the perpetrator was punished to the "full extent of the law," not only seeing the fellow sentenced to prison, but suing him for pain and suffering which deprived him of his home and assets. Ultimately, they spent much more on recovery and revenge than the value of the stolen art.

With this lesson, I understood that property was sacred and not to be trifled with, so I knew what it meant to abscond with Findley. He is worth much more than a Picasso.

You wonder about my motivation for this kidnapping. Let me tell you of *The Straw*. The Straw that broke this camel's back.

It was a few days after Thanksgiving. Dear brother Findley and I were together as, once again, I was entrusted with minding him. It now occurs to me that this might have been my evolving role—the designated sitter/sister.

Findley insisted he was hungry and, although it was nearly dinner time, I escorted him down to the kitchen. Maria and Alberto were there.

"I need a roast beef on rye," Findley declared.

Maria looked up from her meal preparation.

"Please," Findley added with the tone of a psychologically induced arm twist.

"I'm sorry, Mister Findley, dinner is in thirty minutes and we don't want to spoil your appetite."

Findley repeated his request sans the polite addendum.

Maria repeated her apology and said the dinner was a favorite of his.

My brother straightened his small spine. "You work for me. You serve and obey. You do not talk back."

Maria was taken aback. "I understand, little sir, but—"

"That's enough. Your behavior will not be tolerated. You're fired."

"Come on, Findley," I said. "You can't do that. Maria has been with us for—"

My little brother turned to me. "You are not in charge. I am. I'm the favorite and I'm a boy. I'm more important than you," he turned to Alberto, "—and you," and to Maria, "—and you."

My brother was only ten and already a jerk. Maria laughed un-easily.

"No joke, Maria," Findley said. "Get your ugly ass out of my kitchen."

Crying, Maria hurried out as Findley stepped up to Alberto. "Roast beef on rye."

A swirl of hate rushed over me and my body started twitching and shaking. *Oh no. Not this.* Things had gotten out of hand before (we'll get to that), but with therapy, it had all been fixed. My left leg stomped on the ground and my left arm tried to hold down my right. My throat closed and my entire body went haywire, limbs jerking and spasming. *I thought this was under control! Please!!!*

Findley grimaced at me. "You goin' spazy again? You're so gross. Alberto, forget the sandwich. My sister made me lose my appetite." He sauntered away.

Alberto put a wet cloth on my head and said calming words in Spanish. When I hobbled back to my room, I took one of the muscle relaxants Doctor Sanford (who you'll hear of later) prescribed. Twenty minutes later I joined the others in the family dining room, my limbs soothed but my mind still dazed.

As Alberto brought in the coq-au-vin, Father looked up from his phone, asking if Maria was ill. Before Alberto could answer, Findley explained what he'd done. Father nodded his thanks to Alberto, who bowed.

Mother waited for Alberto to depart, then turned to her son. "Don't be absurd. You can't fire Maria."

"I did," Findley said proudly. "I wanted a sandwich and Maria said no because it would spoil my appetite. She said 'no' to *me*."

Mother exhaled her long-suffering sigh. "It *would* have spoiled your appetite. Elizabeth, weren't you watching him?"

I started to speak, but Findley said, "Elizabeth isn't part of the equation. I do not require watching. I am a GASTON!"

Father chuckled, and Mother turned to him. "Don't encourage him, Philip. We are going to have to apologize to Maria, give her a raise, and—"

"Hold on, dear, let's hear Findley's side of things," Father said. "What were your grounds, son?"

"I asked Maria to do something for me and she refused."

Mother repeated her favorite sigh. "Findley, the staff is obligated, by our admonitions, to refuse you a snack if dinner is nigh."

Father nodded at Mother, smiling with understanding. "But Findley didn't know that, so unaware of these preconditions, he was acting on what he believed were his momentary self-interests." He turned back to Findley. "Employee insubordination —legitimate grounds for termination. But be assured, actions have consequences. Maria has been with us for years and deserves a generous severance package. This will come from your allowance."

Findley screamed, "NOOOOOOO!"

"Philip, please be serious," Mother said. "It's not right, even in jest. Maria is an outstanding cook. No one does coq-au-vin like her. She's indispensable."

Philip put his hand on hers. "Darling, Findley must learn to think before he acts. The stock market, Wall Street, I profit there because early on I learned *Deliberation, Patience, and Timing dictate Action.* Not a momentary whim. We wouldn't be living this lifestyle if it wasn't for my learning that in my youth. It was a severe, terrible lesson, but I got it."

"Deliberation, Patience, and Timing dictate Action. I learned it! From now on, I will always think first," Findley promised.

"Lessons don't work that way, son. You have to feel the consequences. You fired Maria and your decision will stand."

My brother jumped from his chair and hurried to Father's side. "Please, please, please, I'll tell Maria sorry and I take back what I said. Please!"

Father put his hand on Findley's little shoulder. "Sometimes what's done can't be undone. Your own actions can cause *you* pain. This lesson you need to learn."

Findley screamed, "NOOOOOOOOO!" and raced out of the room.

Father shook his head sadly. He almost looked like he was about to cry. "He'll learn," he whispered.

Mother lathered a tense smile on her lips. "Elizabeth, go see to Findley. I'll have your dinners sent up."

I did as I was told. As I ate the coq-au-vin, a muffled argument raged downstairs, and Findley raged beside me. He screamed against the unfairness of his punishment, vowing that not a cent of his allowance would go to "that Maria bitch."

"Don't call her that, Findley, she's—"

"This is your fault! You were supposed to be watching me! *You* pay the money! *You* learn the lesson!"

I watched my brother throw his meal against the wall and somehow saw him acting the same at twenty and at forty. This boy was on his way to becoming a despicable man. I knew that this evening's events, and others far worse, would be repeated over and over unless someone took action.

The only someone I could think of was me.

METRO WITH FINDLEY

YOU KNOW I GRADUATED in May, got the Audi as a gift, and as soon as The Straw happened in November, I crafted my plan. For several weeks I carried shopping bags full of items to store in the Audi. Shoes, undies, pants, shirts, and all the essentials Findley and I might need. Vehicle registration, inspection, insurance, cash, check, check, check, check. Knowing that people are tracked with their mobile phones, I wouldn't take one, ergo no GPS—so, Road Atlas—check.

The plan unfolded on April 1st, my eighteenth birthday. That morning, Theresa, the replacement for Maria, tapped on the door. "Miss Elizabeth, time to wake up."

I groaned my familiar response.

At breakfast, my parents wished me happy birthday and Findley wished me happy fart-day.

Mother adjusted her smile. "As you know, we have an event, but we'll be back in time for dinner. Think about where you want to celebrate."

"Text me and I'll make a reservation," Father said.

Mother sniffed disdainfully. My parents' demeanor had been strained for months, ever since their all-night argument about Maria's firing. Mother hadn't been able to reverse that decision and she was still furious. My plan would undoubtedly add more stress.

We resumed our normal breakfast routine—ate our individually prepared favorites and focused on our phones. Afterwards, I went to my room, pretending to browse the internet, but was really getting nervous. At eleven came the expected tap on the door. I tried to sound bored saying, "It's open." Evelyn entered, dressed in summery finery. She adjusted her hat and said, "We're off to the Veuve Clicquot Polo Classic, Elizabeth. Keep an eye on Findley for us."

"The green one or the brown one," I said, knowing how much she hated my mismatched eyes.

She ignored my quip. "Make sure he doesn't get into too much trouble."

"You want me to see he stays safe and sound to grow up as a good man?"

Mother looked at me as if worn out by my obtuseness. "Yes."

"Then I'll do that."

Father cleared his throat in the hall. "Let's go, pet."

"Bye, Mother, Father. Have a nice day."

Father offered his arm to Mother but she ignored it and they left.

An hour later, I'd burned several Vision Books and Findley was excited to be taking a drive. He had his phone but I figured I'd be able to steal it away from him at some point.

On the first floor, as Miroslav opens the front door for my little brother, I leave the note: *Gone with Findley. You said you wanted him safe and sound. Hoping this will do it. Don't wait up. Elizabeth*

Twenty minutes later, we were in the Audi cruising on the Long Island Expressway. Findley was ecstatic, bopping and hopping in his seat. When I pulled into the used car lot, I turned to him. "I didn't tell you, but there's a surprise here and it's like a game, Findley. We're pretending to be different people. You are from another country and can't speak English."

"I'm from Canada. A spy."

"Perfect. Stay in the car for a sec."

I stepped out, greeted Ricardo and he led me to the Metro Van. It didn't look any different. Still a rusted hulk. He pulled the driver's door. It slid easily, and—WOW! There were two new seats, a steering wheel, updated wiring and gauges, patched floor, and repaired windows. It was so exciting! Ricardo moved to the passenger door and slid it open. The dome lights went on in front and back.

"Only thing I didn't track down is why the lights don't go on when you open the driver's door."

"I like it this way. Lets me sneak around more," I said, hopping in. Everything smelled fresh and new. The large back area was outfitted for traveling *and* living. Like a motor home! Single beds on either side and they had blankets and pillows already! Hangers in the thin closets. In the kitchen area—a built-in table and chairs, and a cabinet with *strapped-in* bowls, plates, and cups! The table drawer had silverware, a can opener, chopping knife, and even a corkscrew! A mirror was mounted over a basin that had toothbrushes! He thought of everything.

I got tears in my eyes. "It's magnificent, Ricardo!"

He shrugged, grinning. "Engine is loud but it purrs."

Ricardo and I had already dealt with the titles and registrations, so everything was done. I waved for Findley to get out of the car and he watched me move the many shopping bags from the Audi trunk to the back of the Metro Van.

"What's all that?" he asked.

"Part of the surprise."

I exchanged the Audi key for the Metro's, pulled myself into the driver's seat, adjusted it so I could reach the pedals, and invited Findley in.

He whined, completely forgetting he was a Canadian spy. "This is a piece of crap. I'm not getting in this heap. Take me home."

"Mother and Father have a big surprise just for you. Don't spoil it."

"What's the surprise? Am I getting stocks of my own?"

"I promised not to tell. Get in and we'll go meet them."

Findley pulled himself up onto the passenger seat. There was a wide gap between us and he looked so small in the massive interior. He kicked the dashboard again and again.

"Stop it, Findley."

"Who cares. This is a dumpy wreck anyway."

Maybe it was time for emergency protocol number one. I fumbled through my backpack for the metal thermos and the prescription bottle. Mother would be quite perturbed to find her Ambien gone.

"Take this vitamin, Findley. I don't want you getting germs from this old van."

He swallowed it eagerly.

I turned the key, and the engine roared and scared me. I'd never driven anything this big. Was I really doing this?

Ricardo adjusted my side mirror, then headed around to the other side.

Maybe we could take the train home and call it a day. Call it a life. I didn't need to do this.

As Ricardo leaned in to move the passenger mirror, Findley recoiled from him. "Stay back, you filthy pig!"

Yes, I needed to do this.

I mouthed apologies to Ricardo, put the Metro Van in drive, and stepped on the gas. We lurched forward careening over dirt and trash—*this has too much power!*—headed for the garage and Findley screamed, "LET ME OUT!" as I swirled the wheel and dodged several parked cars in the lot, barely grazed the *No Parking* sign, dropped over the curb—missing the street light—heading for honking oncoming traffic—*are those frightened faces the last thing I'll see?*—pulled to the right and too far, so left, and suddenly my right hand slapped my left HARD—that hand let go and the right gripped the wheel like it was born to hold it and I was steering and wheels were pointed forward and we drove without hitting anything and Findley stopped screaming.

Follow the signs. Stop at Stop. Yield at Yield. I was terrified but my right hand was doing great. We got on the Cross Bronx Expressway. It was scary to be in something this big. I felt like we were taking up two lanes. Whenever we passed under an overpass, I thought we were going to hit and scrunched low. We left NYC, crossing the George Washington Bridge with thump-thump-thump over the grates and the Hudson River below—*Don't drive over the rail! Stay on the bridge!*. Traffic came to a halt. We paused, and I finally took a breath as the engine rumbled in a loud idle. Was the Metro Van shaking or was that me? Maybe I should check on my brother. I pried my glare away from the car in front to see if Findley was as terrified as I. He was asleep. His head was slumped against the seat and his mouth was open. Time to get his phone. The top edge was visible in his front pants pocket. My right hand gently slid his phone free. Not a flinch from Findley. Removed the SIM card and dropped the phone out the window.

Findley, so sweet and innocent-looking while asleep, was destined to become a horrible man. Could I redeem him or was it too late?

He wouldn't understand why he needed redeeming. He is rich and the rich don't have the same views as others. At least that's what I've experienced. The only reason I'm not like my family is —I came out so unforgivably wrong. I know what it is to be looked down on and despised for not being perfect—or even average. I've never been accepted. Not at home, or at school. I have no friends. The only people I talked with were Alberto, Miroslav, Maria…

I vowed as I watched Findley sleeping. *I will get us to the other side of the tracks. The wrong side. Findley will change with all he experiences. Findley. I need to change that upper-class name. From now on, my brother is Finn.*

And it's time to give up Elizabeth Gillian Gaston. Even if I'm not a brave new me, I can pretend. Maybe that will help create a new me. Izzy will be my moniker. Iz for short. I Iz.

Someone honked, I stepped on the gas, and we headed off into The Great Unknown. My plan was successfully completed and now we were barreling into uncharted territory, on the run, with no agenda except *GO!* But the enormity of what I'd done/ was doing—overwhelmed me. This wasn't me at all. I wasn't brave or calculating or adventurous. I was a worthless, unlovable dumb-fuck rich kid with no experience and no skills and way outta my depth. Someone else should run this idiotic fiasco, not a completely incompetent misfit. Yet, my right hand drove on with confidence. I made an unintentional timid squeak as I decided, at least for now, to let that hand be in charge.

DRAGON LADY — LINCOLN COUNTY FAIRGROUNDS, KENTUCKY — 1962

I BELLOW A FULL-THROATED ROAR, my hand revving the engine of my Indian motorcycle, urging it to pull! The heavy log chained to the bike snakes in the mud, swirls out, back tire spins, spattering the onlooking assholes as they stare in shock that a chick can handle this machine. 'Course, with my short beatnik hair and my cool shades, half of them figure I'm a man. I pull the bike perpendicular to the hilltop and spin sideways, switch-backing up the rise—impossible, but doing it—men cursing to the right and left as their bikes slide backwards down the slick hill. Hitting the apex, I angle just so, and with a blast in first then spinning in reverse, the log slingshots around the end of the bike and slides, ass-first, over the finish line. I raise my fists in triumph and scream out my victory.

The M.C. yells into the mic, "And across the finish line is—" He pauses as Beau crosses the line behind me. "—Beau Tompkins!"

What the hell?

I drop my bike and march to the cluster of cats around the microphone.

"You jivin' me? What part of me crossing the finish line first isn't winning?" I yell.

The guys look sheepish. "You aren't using a regulation chain. Disqualified."

"There ain't no regulation chain! Let me see that in any rules." I raise my fist. "Show me now or you all'll be seeing stars!"

The M.C. shudders with a mock-terrified face. "I'm so scared. Seeing stars."

A crowd has gathered, eager for blood.

"You are a bunch of boys who can't stand to be beaten by a chick!"

Beau pushes me aside as he moves to the trophy stand. "Pardon me, Lady."

"Fuck you, Beau! You stole this race!"

Beau laughs and points at me. "Look at Maxine. She's crazy mad. A Dragon Lady."

The onlookers latch onto the name and chant, "Dragon Lady! Dragon Lady!"

Beau bends to the microphone. "Give Dragon Lady second place. A courtesy cup."

Courtesy cup, my ass!

The engraver's tool hums, etching grooves in a silver cup. He hands the cup to the M.C. who announces, "And in second place for the 1962 Log Race, Dragon Lady!"

And Beau tosses the engraved cup to me. "Second place, Dragon Lady."

I snarl at him. "I'll bury your cock in a shoebox like a dead hamster."

Beau laughs.

Raising the trophy cup, I scream over the crowd. "You suckers ain't never gonna forget me now. I'm Dragon Lady!"

GLAZING PUTTY

MY THROAT IS SORE from vomiting my meds on these little plants. Did you forget about the nuthouse? Lithium, etc? Anyway, turns out I have a green thumb. Or maybe a psychedelic thumb. The veggies are doing very well. So well that I'm thinking this vegetable plan might work, which means I'd better get to figuring out part two—the escape plan.

This greenhouse is large and probably as old as the Institution. The panes of glass are that wavy old-fashioned kind. The distortions make the view of the manicured grounds look

27

like an undulating green sea. Can these panes be removed? They are large enough that, if I could remove one, I could slip through to freedom.

I push on one. It feels very solid.

My brain lights up with possibilities and I squat abruptly. My left hand searches the edges of the lower panes where the rain splatters up. *Good thinking!* Perhaps the harsh Connecticut winters and wet summers have—*YES!* Bits of the wood are rotting and the black stuff holding the glass in place is chipped and cracked. Maybe it's lead or painted glazing putty. I push on the glass and bits of stuff fall on the other side. Push again and more glazing stuff crumbles. This window will come out easily if I scrape at the rotten wood—WHACK! My right hand slaps my left. *Ow!*

The greenhouse door swings open. I dart up from the floor. The janitor/handyman Hazeem backs into the room, pulling a bucket on wheels. He turns, sees me, nods, and looks away. Close call! If I'd gotten the window pane free, Hazeem probably would have noticed and repaired it and any others that were loose. I've got to be careful not to take the pane out before I get a plan for how to keep it looking like it's still in place. Good thing my right hand slapped my left! But of course, that's not unusual.

ALMOST A FIELD TRIP

ONE OF THE FIRST INSTANCES of my limbs acting independently was when I was twelve before puberty-hell hit.

I'm getting ready for a Rothschild's Academy field trip. Our field trips were always to venues for the wealthy. In this case, we'd be looking at the pinnacle of rich-people furniture at the New York Design Center.

I'm about to slip into Mother's favorite outfit for me—the designer light blue dress—but when I try to reach for it, my right arm doesn't move. Am I paralyzed? Am I having a stroke? I look at the dress and look at my arm. My arm's expression: *no.*

Because I think I'm generally messed up and weirdness isn't a surprise, I ask my arm, "What would you like to wear?"

You would be hard-pressed to see an appendage jerk out with more fervor. My arm flies to grab black jeans and a dark blue pajama top.

Of course, seeing me "dressed like a beatnik" Mother puts her foot down and refuses to let me out of the apartment.

I put my foot up and kick the Chippendale hall table. Well, *I* didn't kick, my leg did.

Mother slaps me.

I slap her.

It's such a shock, we both burst into tears and run to our respective rooms.

Slapping my mother is not who I thought I was. How can I be such a horror? Maybe I'm not only ugly, and female, but *mean!*

I cry for a long time, hoping Mother will come in. She doesn't. The stuffed frog with the crown stares at me with disdain. A princess doesn't act so horribly.

When I emerge penitent and in the blue designer dress, Mother informs me that I've forfeited the right to the field trip and that my violent behavior will not be tolerated. I want to ask about her violent behavior but don't.

Back in my room, I vow never to be violent again. A voice in my brain says, *good luck with that.*

PUBERTY

PUBERTY DID ITS WORST. Never has there been a more horrible example of the disasters it brings. At twelve there was hope that the ugly duckling might turn into a swan, but after that, as changes appeared, hope devolved into despair. Perhaps kissing that stuffed frog in my bedroom was turning me into one of his species instead of the intended reverse. Whatever the cause, I was becoming neither swan nor princess but more of a Frankenstein's monster. The melting pot of my gene pool did not melt.

The oddities? Again, my hair. Dark curls with a shock of silky blond, the rope of straight shiny black, and a swirl of red. The weird spiderweb scar on my forehead became more prominent. I took to combing the lock of red so it'd cover the ugly mess.

My mismatched eyes remained as they were, one green, one brown. My arms grew different from one another. The left was wide like a man's with tiny curls of orange fuzz and freckles. The right arm, sinewy, weathered, and muscular like a bad-ass woman's, sprouted a ragged scar on the forearm.

My left leg grew muscular, like an athlete's. The calf became angular. The ankle thick. And the right leg, plump and womanly, had what my mother called "a birthmark." A warm, light-brown, toe-to-crotch, entire-leg birthmark.

But worst were my breasts. They came in at different speeds and sizes and shapes. One started its painful push to the surface in my thirteenth year, inching to a girlish handful. The other lagged a year and then, when I was fourteen, exploded forth like an appendage of Barbie's. Mother insisted I wear a bra that made the two match.

Around this time, I got interested in photography. It was something I could do without engaging with other people. I could pretend I was present, but hide behind the lens. My constantly taking pictures caught the attention of the school's photography teacher and he asked to see the results. Flipping through my phone, Mr. Archibald insisted he could tell native talent and that I was overflowing with it. He suggested I study with him and invited me into the school's darkroom.

Inside, he lit the red *do-not-enter* sign and locked the door. He asked me to peruse the photos drying on the line and stepped behind me as I did. Without warning, he grabbed my Barbie breast, squeezing like a pimple to be popped. I tried to move away but he was much bigger and held me fast. His other hand felt the companion—and found nothing resembling flesh. A laugh barked from him and he pulled the wadded pantyhose from the bra cup, as a magician pulls colored handkerchiefs from a clenched hand.

Giggling, he honked the full breast with a full-throated, "Aaa—OOOOO-Gah!" and the childish one with a high pitched, "meep-meep." Tears flowed from my dark-room invisible eyes. Both my legs started twitching weirdly and my fingers curled into fists. An unfamiliar feeling rose in me that I can only label as RAGE.

The knock on the door sent Mr. Archibald re-stuffing my bra and waving for me to do up my blouse. He whispered, "Nothing is spoken of or you're in serious trouble." The door opened to Mr. Lichner, whose eyebrows rose as his eyes dropped to the area of interest. His glance darted up to Mr. Archibald with a wink. "Aaa-OOO-Gah!" he dittoed.

I didn't bother stopping at the nurses' office to say I was sick. I ran out and hailed a cab, arms tight across my chest. At our curb, as Miroslav opened the taxi door, his face shifted from surprise to anger, but he was well aware of his station and stayed silent. I said nothing, but my salty tears told everything.

KELLY — ATLANTIC OCEAN — 1911

ANOTHER CRASH OF WAVES on the hull sends a salty mist of sea intae me eyes. 'Tis grand to be on this ship, escaping a life of poverty and toil, but I cannae say I enjoy the journey. Still, 'tis a mighty blessin' t'ave a spot for tae move. Potter County, Pennsylvania. Hope it's a bonnie land.

I cling tae the railing and look oot at the grey cold sea. No one else is on deck. Too rough, I imagine. The waves be crashin' and the swells be tossin' and I cannae find a way t' hold me stomach that'll settle it. God knows what the wee bairn 'tis feeling inside.

31

A poor being battered in the waves inside a poor being battered in the waves.

An' there it be, kickin' again. I naer cared much for the lot o' women-kind. 'Tain't nothin' like that o' men. We got the toil and strife as all do, but only we got the birthin' which too oft leads tae dyin'. And we must struggle 'gainst the ne'er endin' unwelcome assaults from lads both young and auld. I dinnae ken one lass that nae be messed wi' inna shop, in school, on the moors—anywhere. It gets right predictable. Ach! Noo I'm gettin' maudlin. 'Tis time tae think on somethin' else.

It'll be a few days yet 'til we'll arrive in the Port of New York City. We'll see that lady of liberty everyone talks aboot with her torch held high. Not sure she'll welcome me in particular as I'm quite a scalawag, shiftless, ne'er-do-well 'cordin' to me mah.

A man in a bowler hat steps on deck and approaches. *Please dinnae talk t' me.* He stands tae the railing as if mesmerized by the waves but keeps glancing o'r me.

"Rough seas, eh?" he says by way of conversatin'.

"Aye."

That seems to give him permission tae move close. He sidles up aside me as if we're kin.

"Scottish, I'm guessing. Darker skinned Scot. You're a pretty one. How about a kiss?"

'E wasted nae time.

"Nae," I say, turning away.

The eejit grabs me arm and pulls me 'round to face 'im.

Alright, then. Me hand moves up tae touch 'is face. He's surprised and pleased. Me fingers slide doon his cheek gentle-like and keep gaen lower, and his eyes light up with the promise, and me hand finds his cockles and takes hold like a wolf at a ewe's neck. Nasty fella dinnae ken I hae brothers.

He's 'boot to strike me when the wolf clamps tighter and he folds. I gee the bits a twist and jerk away—jest as me fella steps up on deck.

Alex comes close with 'is face cloudin' mad.

32

"'Tis all fine, husband," I say. "'Twas jest 'slpainin' t'the fella aboot Scottish courtesy."

The bowler man limps away with his head doon.

"I'm glad yer able t'fend fer yerself, lass, but I'd be happy to be of assistance ney 'n then."

I slip me arm through his and pull 'em to the railing so's to change the subject.

"Bairn's kickin' angry like," I say.

"How's you fairin'?" Alex asks.

"Tollerable horrible," I answers.

"I'm glad y'r trouble tae the likes o' im, lammie, but you's put the babe and yerself into harms way a'times. Ye 'er do a fool t'ing like that 'gain, I'll have t' disown ye."

"I'll think on that proposition," says I.

"Gimme a kiss and we'll gae doon below wher"tis warm," my Alex says.

I give him that kiss and pray the new land we're headin' for will be all we hope i'tis and wi'out sech men as that bowler hat one. Nae likely.

PLASTIC SURGERY

AFTER THE EPISODE with my photography teacher, I had a bit of a meltdown and said I wasn't going back to school. Mother guessed that I might be having trouble with "unwanted innuendos." She suggested that if my breasts were making me uncomfortable, I could alter them. Diminish Barbie.

So at fourteen, I went to the plastic surgeon. Because Father insisted that Mother join him for a luncheon at the Metropolitan Museum of Art honoring donor benefactors, Alberto drove me to the doctor and asked me to text him when I was done. I was ushered into the exam room and told to sit on the papered table. I dutifully climbed up onto the high perch and waited. Goose bumps rose. It was freezing in there. The air conditioning must have been at the lowest setting. When I was nearing hypothermia, the doctor entered with a knock. I assume that he did a lot of work on himself for he looked like a perfectly proportioned mannequin.

"Hello Elizabeth, my tablet says you're fourteen and that you're interested in a reduction of the larger breast to match the smaller."

I nodded.

"Let's take a look."

I didn't move except for the rush of blood to my face.

He waved his hand at my blouse with an "undo this" motion. Although I knew I should, I couldn't move.

The doctor looked impatient. "Don't be silly. If I'm going to operate on them, I have to examine them."

This made sense and something in me released my arms and I opened my blouse and mismatched bra. My nipples hardened in the cold, cold room. The doctor exposed a self-satisfied smile. Undoubtedly the same one he had every time he turned down the air-conditioning. He peered at my chest and "hmmm"ed and "ahh"ed as he shifted position to get alternate views. Then, "My hand may be cold."

It was. He cupped my Barbie breast and jiggled it as if to gauge its weight. "You've got one spectacular beauty here." He looked with disdain at Non-Barbie. "And a less than stellar companion. Sorry to be blunt but, it's clear that you don't have many similarly attractive assets. Don't diminish this wonder to match the inferior specimen. Stick with what's of value. I can make you a second delight that will lure and amaze. You'll go far with the set I'll give you.

His hand stayed on Barbie, continuing to check its weight as his body moved closer. His lab coat brushed against my leg. "I need to examine consistency. Texture. Flexibility. What we call *return to stasis*."

And so he did—his hand squeezing, exploring—he moved even closer, pressing what was behind his lab coat against me. It couldn't be that he was rubbing his crotch against my leg. I was misinterpreti—

My left knee jerked up and rammed the middle of that lab coat, hitting hard flesh hard. The doctor crumpled, folding in on himself.

I jumped down from the table, exclaiming, "I didn't mean it!" while my left hand grabbed his hair, yanking his chin up, and my right fist smashed him in the face. He screamed as blood rushed from his nose.

"That was an accident!" I protested.

The nurse burst in as my two fists punched him in the corresponding eyes and my right foot indented his stomach.

"I'm sorry!" I hollered.

"Help me!" the doctor cried.

"You monster!" the nurse bellowed.

She pulled me away from the floundering man, who no longer looked like a perfect manakin, and shoved me to the door.

The doctor screamed, "Your parents will hear from my lawyer!" as my violent legs marched me out and down to the street and I remembered I was supposed to text Alberto but when I reached the curb the left leg suddenly stopped and my right arm shot up, no doubt propelled by the unanticipated halt, and a cab skidded in front of me thinking I'd hailed it—so, I got in.

By the time the cab reached our building, my parents and their lawyers had already been called. I retreated to my room to await the verdict.

Of course, I was lucky. Mother and Father made amends in such a way as to prevent the matter from going further. I have no idea of the size of the pot of gold but I'm sure it was significant.

On a side note, I did an online search, found a female surgeon, and the operation took place. Barbie shrunk.

ON THE ROAD

THIS IS ALL OUT OF ORDER because my brain is out of order. I'm flashing on things here and there and sorry if it makes no sense.

I drive more than I've ever driven. Drive in bits of New Jersey, Pennsylvania, and a smidgen of Maryland. It's weird to be outside of skyscrapers and gridlock and pedestrians and taxis. There's nothing out here. Just the road and green. I thought Central Park was green but this is really *endlessly* green. And redundant. Around a bend you might see, like, a view. A view of green hills dotted with barns or something. They even have signs that say *VISTA*. Sometimes you can see absurdly far—as if you were up in the Empire State Building and looking out at Brooklyn and Queens and the Statue of Liberty. That kind of far, but we're not even high up. It's weird. And sort of relaxing.

We pass the *Welcome to West Virginia* sign and Findley—I mean Finn—wakes.

"What's this?" he says, looking baffled at the expanse of green edging the road.

"Countryside."

"Why are we in countryside?"

I should have been thinking up some good lies these last few hours.

"We're on the run, Finn."

"Don't call me Finn. Why are we on the run?"

My brain whirrs—*because of the fire, the earthquake, the flood, the invasion, the epidemic, the tsunami, the shooting, the financial meltdown, the hostage crisis, the E. coli disaster, the zombie apocalypse...*

I decide on the latter.

"Can't be," Finn says. "Rich people don't let zombies near. We've got guards and surrogates."

"Surrogates?" I ask, surprised he knows the word.

"To take your place when you don't want to do something."

"I know what it means. Why do rich people have surrogates?"

"Duh. To have babies."

I wonder if he thinks Petri dish fertilization and rented wombs are the normal way to have children.

"And," he continues, "to have the zombies eat the surrogates instead of them."

"Why would any surrogate agree to—"

"Hell-oooow. Monnneeeey."

He's right. The zombie apocalypse will take place in the streets among the poor and middle classes. The mansions and penthouse apartments will be safe. Helicopter pads. Quick flights to Saint Kits or any heavily-protected island.

If Finn's right about the rich being safe from zombies, why are we on the run? "Mother and Father forgot to pay the guards and the surrogates."

"Automatic deposits, dummy."

"We are on a mission. Our very existence is at stake. If we fail, there is no future. Are you with me, Finn?"

"It's Findley!"

"This is part of our incognito plan. You're Finn and I'm Izzy."

"Not playing. Where in countryside are we?!"

I toss him the road atlas.

"What am I supposed to do with this?"

"Find out where we are."

He tosses it back to me. "That doesn't tell you where you *are*, it tells you all the places you *could be* and you have to somehow figure out which one. I'll find us." Finn reaches into his pants—a rush of panic widens his eyes. Every pocket is checked. The floor. His seat. "WHERE'S MY PHONE?!"

"It was taken by the zombies."

"NOOOOOO!!!! YOU CAN'T DO THAT!"

"Sorry, Finn. Your phone isn't part of the plan."

"GIVE ME YOUR PHONE! I'M CALLING DAD!"

"I don't have a phone either."

"WE'LL DIE!"

"We won't die."

"I HATE YOU! YOU ARE STUPID AND UGLY AND—"

"SHUT UP, YOU FUCKIN' BRAT!"

The force and vitriol in my voice shocks both of us. Finn does as he's told and shrinks low in his seat.

I should apologize but my mouth won't let me. It starts humming something I don't know. A waltz.

SIMON — OXFORD, MISSISSIPPI — 1898

THE COTILLION IS COALESCING. The orchestra starts. Of course —a Strauss waltz. Would that it was the latest Scott Joplin rag instead.

My tie is choking me. Dwight Spencer stands beside me looking ravishing in his tux. His hair is shiny with Pomade but the circular whorl at the hairline can't be controlled. That swirl makes me dizzy. I imagine how it smells. I imagine slipping my hand under his cumbersome cummerbund.

Trevon flicks my ear with his finger. Hard. "Eyes on the ladies, Simon."

I turn toward the wide marble staircase and look up with my fellow escorts, awaiting the newcomers to society of 1898. The music sets the cadence for the flowing gowns as the debutants descend the stairs.

Trevon whispers to me. "I wouldn't mind having a go with any one of these."

I smile, trying for enthusiasm. I fail.

Trevon leans close. "Get your head right, Simon. Tonight's the chance to prove you're one of us."

Once all the young ladies have made their descent, we gentlemen know our prescribed actions. We step toward the awaiting ladies as I pray this night will pass without pain or ridicule.

I approach the most downcast and withdrawn of the girls. She accepts my entreaty to dance. We clasp clammy hands and commence the waltz. It's rote by now. Back straight, arms stiff, head turn this way and that.

She doesn't seem to be enjoying this. That gives me hope.

"Are you alright, mademoiselle?"

"Bien sur. One survives. Adapt or die."

"Darwin."

Her eyes flash up to mine—wondering. "Survival of the fittest."

"Or most brutal," I add.

"I'm Irene," she says.

"Pleased to meet you, Miss Irene. I'm Simon."

We dance and talk about the Galapagos Islands and Darwin and move on to the Spanish-American war. We agree on everything. She is clearly no more interested in the ways of this societal stratosphere than I.

Strauss ends and we bow/curtsey each other. I offer to procure her a glass of punch. She accepts and we take our drinks outside. A walk along the veranda. Smells of magnolia blossoms. We remain outside, talking and sharing ideas. She knows poetry —Yeats, Tennyson, Whitman, even Blake!—plays, novels, she's even been to the Smithsonian and traveled its halls.

"Forgive me for saying," she whispers. "You seem like a different species from your fellow gentlemen."

"Yes, it's true. And you, Miss Irene?"

"Guilty as charged."

I don't know exactly what this might mean, but this Irene seems genuine. I nod, as if understanding.

Her breath is hot and close and I know if I were normal it would bring a rise below, but it does not. However, it does bring a rise to my heart.

MR. MARKS IS SO WONDERFUL!

ALMOST SIXTEEN. Junior year at Rothschild's Academy. Favorite class? Science. Well, maybe not the science but the science teacher, Mr. Marks. He's got a really nice smile and curly hair and beautiful eyes and always gives lots of praise. Some of the other students think he's a joke because he isn't mean. Not me. I'd take science class with him all day if I could.

I watch him draw on the board. Even his back is nice to look at. He turns to us again, pointing at the squiggles.

"I can't draw, but this blob is Germany, and this line—is how it was back when Germany was two parts, East and West. There was a very hostile border. East Germany would kill anyone who tried to escape. There was a fence all along the way, some of it electrified. This fence didn't affect only people, it affected animals as well. Deer were either on the East German or the West German side. They couldn't cross. Now guess what happened after the wall came down. Any ideas?"

I don't have a clue and look behind me to see if anyone is guessing. They're not guessing. They're not even pretending to pay attention. It makes me mad and feel sorry for Mr. Marks, so I raise my hand with no idea of what to say.

Mr. Marks smiles and that gets me all fluttery 'cause I know I made him happy that I'm paying attention.

"Um, the deer could cross the border now," I offer.

Mr. Marks points at me triumphantly. "You would think that. It makes sense, but NO! The fascinating thing is, even years, even DECADES after the fencing was removed, the East German deer and the West German deer never went to the other side. NO FENCE, but something was keeping them apart. Ideas?"

I don't even bother turning around. I raise my hand. "Maybe it got passed down in their genes."

"Maybe. Maybe the Deoxyribonucleic Acid, which we know as DNA, actually absorbed this knowledge of the fence, but the study posits that it is more likely that the baby deer, the fawns, followed their mothers, learning their territory, and each subsequent offspring got the same lesson. A fascinating example of information spread over generations."

The bell rings. The class rises, heading as a herd to the door. Mr. Marks holds up a finger to me.

"Stay a moment, Elizabeth."

I freeze and wonder if I said something wrong.

"I value your participation," he says as he closes the classroom door. "Your input is much appreciated."

I feel my cheeks turning red. *Does he know I have a C-R-U-S-H on him?*

"As is your attention." Mr. Marks smiles warmly. "Come sit."

I sit on the teacher-chair he gestures to.

"You're a bright girl. Unique. Not like all the others."

I know I'm not like the others. But that's not a good thing. I look at the floor, turning redder.

He sits on his desk. "You know it's true, right?"

My heart does the talking, booming in my ears. My left leg twitches, then the right.

Mr. Marks smiles warmly. "I can tell you something about being your age. It's hard. There's pressure to fit in and if you don't, you're left on the sidelines. Kids can be very cruel. Very often the most interesting people are the ones that are ignored. I get the feeling that things are hard for you sometimes."

I can't believe he's talking to me like this. How can he know?!

"And now you're wondering how could I know this."

He's reading my mind!

"It's not that I can read minds, it's because when I was your age, I was just like you."

I look up and meet his eyes. I love his eyes. The long brown beautiful lashes. He's so good looking I have to turn away.

His voice continues. "I was a very isolated and insecure kid."

Was he really like me?

"I'm guessing you feel that way sometimes."

I nod.

"Maybe you're doing what I did. Sometimes if we're insecure and sidelined, we gravitate to academic excellence. I gravitated to science. Does science interest you?"

I nod again. *Anything he taught would interest me.*

"I'm very glad for that. Science, nature, biology, all fascinating. So much to learn." A muffled vibration comes from his pants. He reaches into his pocket for the phone and smiles at me. "Thanks for this talk and for sharing your feelings with me. The more we can share who we are deep inside, the better. I just want you to know—I'm your ally. Okay? I'll see you next week."

I hurry to the door and slide out.

"Let's talk again soon!" follows me down the empty hall.

I'm so jittery and jumpy. *Mr. Marks is wonderful!* My heart is beating so fast!

JENNY — PENNSYLVANIA AVENUE, WASHINGTON D.C. — 1916

PROUDLY CONGREGATING outside of the White House, I lift my banner high, and endeavor to calm my over-excited heart. President Wilson cannot pretend he is unaware of our protestations in front of his residence. He must respond!

"Mister President, how long must women wait for liberty!?" I shout as I straighten the ribbon across my chest.

A man approaches me and rends my banner from my grasp, hurls it to the cobblestones, and expectorates in my face. "You witches are going to HELL!"

"If your presence is evidence, I currently reside in said aforementioned locale," I say with a beatific smile.

A woman in a smart hat and frock calls tentatively to the man blustering before me. "Sinclair, hadn't we better press on?"

The man, one must assume is Sinclair, spins toward her and raises his index digit as a warning. She lowers her head submissively.

"The tyranny of the brute," I remark. "Subjugating those whom they are duty-bound to—"

Sinclair punches me in the stomach. I bend into the pain as my compatriots converge around me. Please let this not hurt my child! My husband knows how much our struggle means to me but will he forgive a miscarriage? I un-bow my spine and raise my shoulders, endeavoring to rise against the hurt. The man stomps to his cowed wife, grabbing her arm roughly. I hope she won't suffer because of us, but if so, it's a price we must all pay.

Margaret, our fearless leader, helps retrieve my banner and I shake it sharply. It makes that *thwap* of clean sheets before they're put on the line.

A sharp whistle sends me revolving to see police on horseback galloping toward us. They have batons raised. Last week, Frances got bloodied from a blow to the head. They're getting more aggressive.

We proudly stand our ground. The policemen's countenance is that of rage.

This is what we do. We create rage in men, simply by wanting equality.

The horses clatter on the paving stones, those majestic beasts also bending to the will of their masters, spurred on, kicked, and broken. *Horses, throw the brutes off! Claim your liberty!*

The police infiltrate our line, jostling us with their rearing beasts, sending fear through our ranks from the danger of those hooves. I endeavor to stay firmly rooted but am accosted by the hot flank of a brown stallion. A baton swings and smashes my shoulder, the crack of my collarbone sends me stumbling, reaching for any place of purchase to prevent my fall and the occasion of a trampled death. I grab the boot of the policeman, loosening it from its stirrup. The man yells in alarm and swings his stick across my wrists. Crack. I let go and fall to the street, palms flat against muddy stone. A hoof lands sharply on my left hand. More bones crack. Should I survive, there will be pain in that future, but for now I attend only to the rush of terror for that growing life inside me. Stomping hooves land near. I'm not dead yet but will be at any moment. Panic courses through me as hooves stomp by my head, snagging my hair in that iron shoe, and ripping out a large portion of my brown locks. Someone grabs my shoulder and extricates me from the melee, a savior, and I'm led backwards, hair and blood obfuscating my view, swirls of movement and screams everywhere, a violent yank raises me high and I land abruptly on metal—an enclosure—back of a vehicle—another woman is thrown on top of me. Twelve more women—some unconscious, some flighting, all bloody—are flung into this wagon with no more care than a child has for an unwanted doll.

The door slams. Darkness. The combustion engine starts. We lurch forward amidst the painful exclamations of my fellow passengers. I'm trembling all over. Tears fall and I'm glad for the darkness. We all try so hard to be strong for each other, but this terror is real.

What will they mark as our malfeasance this time? We were not impeding traffic. We were peaceable. Not rioting. What will be their excuse? They don't need one. They make the rules.

There is something hard against my back. A bench? I would like to sit. I turn to feel it—!—wrenching pain. My collarbone, shoulder, hand, and wrists. Are they all broken?

Somehow I get myself up onto the bench.

We are bounced and jostled for a long time. The air reeks of blood, sweat, and urine. Have I relieved myself without knowing it? That thought proves more distressing to me than I care to admit. A voice in the blackness moans. This box is becoming an oven. Will they let us out before we're cooked?

The vehicle slows and comes to a stop. Steps sound around the side and the doors swing open to glaring sunlight. We all wince against the view of a large fortress-like building. Iron bars festoon the windows.

"GET OUT!" a man commands.

The first of our league struggle down. In the back, I watch my brave comrades exit. I want to embrace them all. We are making a mark, if only with our blood and pain. People will care. I have complete assurance they will rise up upon hearing tales of our plight. Victory will be ours.

MR. MARKS

A WEEK BEFORE MY SIXTEENTH BIRTHDAY, as we are seated for dinner, Mother tells me she's had a call from my science teacher, Mr. Marks. Apparently he told her I was really excelling in the class and he thought it would be valuable to discuss some advanced topics via a field trip to the zoo.

As I listen, my heart races and I feel myself turning a deep red.

"He said you have a keen mind and suggested there are many possibilities ahead, so he wants to help you excel." Mother looks at me with unusually worried eyes. "Do you want to go?"

"Go where?" Father says, lifting his head from his phone.

My six-year-old brother scrunches his face in disgust. "Dorky lessons from Teacher. Nerdo!"

Mother strokes her hand in a weird way, like she's trying to keep it from shaking. "She doesn't have to if she doesn't want to."

Father gives me his attention with a benevolent look that never quite works—his eyes always carry something cold and unyielding. "What's the subject?"

"Science," I say.

"Science is good. Lots of new advances. You want to be a scientist?"

I have no expectation of being anything but I know I can't say that, so I say, "Maybe."

"Good choice. I've got a lot in science stock—mainly pharmaceuticals. Spectacular investments. You should accept that teacher's offer."

I nod that I will, as inside I'm screaming, *YAAAAAAY!*

I spend all the rest of the night getting ready. I chose the designer light-blue dress and comfortable but stylish shoes. An hour is spent fighting with my uncooperative hair and trying to figure out a way to make it less bizarre. Nothing works. When it's time for bed, I kiss the massive stuffed frog, trying to do it slow and sexy, like in the movies. The frog doesn't kiss back.

The next morning, Mother catches me at the elevator. "Perhaps jeans would be more appropriate."

"I thought you liked this dress."

"Yes, but—it is—not right for this—for a trip with—for a trip to the zoo. Hurry and change."

I'm too happy to argue, so rush back and slip on my favorite jeans. Mother nods with a "call if you need anything." She never says that but I've got a certain someone taking up my mind, so can't wonder about anything else. School is deathly dull and slow and when it's finally over, Mr. Marks is waiting for me as I exit my last class. I'm so nervous. *Can he tell? Does he know how much I love him?*

He takes off his tie and stuffs it in his jacket pocket as we walk out the gates of Rothschild's Academy. "Free at last, eh?"

I don't know what to say, so I giggle.

Two blocks away, after we've passed all the chauffeurs picking up students, he stops and turns to me. "Elizabeth, I know you might be nervous but you don't need to be. How about we say, instead of teacher and student, we're friends? Are you okay with that?"

I nod, probably way too enthusiastically.

He continues. "Now, you know me as Mr. Marks, but since we're friends—call me Kevin. Okay?" He puts his hand out like I'm supposed to shake.

I shake it just like a grownup. His hand is so warm and strong!

"So, we've got a date with some animals!"

He said date!

We walk to the Central Park Zoo. Me and my friend Kevin. Only I can't think of him as Kevin. He's Mr. Marks.

Mr. Marks buys us zoo tickets and I pretend our date starts.

"So, Elizabeth—or do you prefer Liz? I'll call you Liz. It's more exotic."

I can't believe how wonderful he is!

He leads us to the snow leopard. "It's great to see these animals, but I wish they weren't trapped. It's a shame to take these creatures out of their natural habitat, don't you think?"

"It's sad to see them caged."

All the other people at the cement barrier have their phones up, taking pictures.

Mr. Marks points to the lounging leopard stretched across a fake-rock precipice. "This cat looks bored. He would rather be stalking an antelope than lying around watching tourists take selfies with him."

"Or he'd rather be stalking one of them," I add.

Mr. Marks laughs loudly and puts his arm around me to give me a squeeze. Too bad he takes his arm away so fast, but he leans close. "Look at the leopard's eyes. Did you know that predators have eyes in the front of their head and prey have one eye on each side? Deer, rabbits, horses, chickens, mice, sheep, cows—they all have eyes on the sides so they can keep track of the dangers from several directions at once. Eagles, hawks, lions, bears, wolves—have eyes in the front of their heads so they can focus on what they want to kill. Predators are about attack. Prey about defense."

That is a great bit of information, but part of me is sad. This is going to be a science lesson after all.

"Let's see if we can find some prey."

We walk a bit and come to the petting zoo. Sheep gather around our legs.

"Prey. Eyes on the side of the head. They can see on both sides at once. Looking out for that leopard predator. Let's take a stroll."

Leaving the zoo, we walk casually through the park. At the curve of the lane, he takes my hand. "Liz, is it okay to hold your hand?"

YES! My heart is beating sooooo crazy fast I might pass out. Maybe we could become a couple and we could get married. Men can marry girls much younger than they are.

"I hope you don't mind if I ask something personal," he says, giving my hand a squeeze. "Do you like me?"

I'm so shocked I can't speak and instead, give his hand a return squeeze. He seems to understand because he smiles and nods. "I like you, too."

HE LIKES ME!!!!

We walk hand-in-hand all around the lake and then at a dock he pauses. "I don't know about you, but I could use a rest. Let's stop a while." He points to a small brick building with a green patina roof and steeple. "This is the CPMYC. Central Park Model Yacht Club. They have all sorts of events. Not really anything this time of year, but hey, let's go in."

Loons, standing in the marsh at the dock, turn their long necks and witness me nodding.

The metal door creaks heavily as it's pushed open. The large room is dark and cool, with a few scattered tables and chairs and many historical pictures on the walls. Miniature sailboats are lined up along one counter. A man comes toward us and Mr. Marks walks quickly to meet him. They shake hands like people who are in the same club. Mr. Marks pats the man on the back and the man leaves the building.

"My old pal. Sitting here all alone and bored and trapped in here like a snow leopard in a cage. Told him to take a break. We'd watch the building for a while."

Mr. Marks pulls a thick tarp off of a table. The tarp swirls and spreads open across the wooden floor. I don't know why, but this looks like a move that has been done many times.

Mr. Marks's hair is even curlier from the humidity and his eyes are twinkling and he bows like a prince asking the princess for a dance. Could I really be the princess? I don't know what to do, so I giggle again. His hand gestures for me to sit on the tarp. This makes me nervous 'cause it might lead to just what I dream of and I don't really know how to do anything, regardless of practicing with Mr. Frog.

"Come. Rest a while."

I sit quickly so he won't think I don't like him. The tarp is cold and damp.

Mr. Marks drops next to me and takes my hand again. I hope we can stay like this forever. The minute I think it, he moves close. His face is red and he looks like someone who's holding his breath for a contest. A vein in his forehead swells. An image flashes in my mind—a swinging lantern, snow falling around it.

His hand moves up my arm. It's hot. I don't move. He leans close and I love him so much and maybe I'll finally get to kiss—

I'm jerked away by something inside and both of my hands fly up, pressing his chest to keep him back.

Mr. Marks laughs. "Oh, my gosh. Don't worry. I was just going to give you a kiss. You've been kissed before, haven't you?"

I'm sure every girl my age has been kissed. And a whole lot more. I try to smile like someone sophisticated. It obviously doesn't work because he adds, "Well, there's a first time for everything. I bet you're a natural."

That makes me feel better and Mr. Marks leans close but my hands continue to push him back. "There, there, sweetie, I'm on your side. An ally, remember?" He puts on a pretend sad face. "Come now, Elizabeth. Don't be that way." I don't like being called Elizabeth, I want to be Liz again.

He lifts one of my hands off his chest and presses it to his lips. That's the gesture they always do in romantic movies. It does feel romantic.

"I like you. May I steal a kiss?" he whispers.

He asked! That means he's considerate. Like he respects me. *Yes, please kiss me!!!*

I don't say anything but he moves close, knowing that I gave him permission, and his lips are soft and warm and he backs away in a second, and *that was so wonderful!*

"See, it's easy. And you *are* a natural."

He smiles and leans in again. A pillowy pressing of his lips on mine. The kiss becomes harder and it's lasting a long time and some of his chin is scratchy and then his tongue presses into my mouth. He's doing the French Kissing! I back my tongue out of the way to give him space but there's not much room.

After a long time, he pulls away, lies back on the tarp, and smiles up at me. "That was absolutely lovely."

I guess I *am* a natural!

"Come here," he says, pulling me to lie next to him and his mouth is on me again and that tongue is moving around and his hand is wriggling up my shirt and he's on his knees over me and the other hand fumbles with my jeans zipper. Is this why Mother wanted me to wear jeans? It makes it so much harder for him. I should have worn the light blue dress—

"I'm not going to hurt you," he whispers close to my ear. "You don't need to be afraid."

I am afraid but he's so kind and considerate and—

Don't listen to his jive.

His hand slides over my breast and I'm sure I'm supposed to do something, but I don't know what. It's like I'm not here, but only watching. I've seen women moan in movies. Should I do that?

Mr. Marks screams.

My teeth are clamping his tongue.

I let go. "I'm sorry! I didn't mean it!"

"Fuck! That's fucking too much." His eyes are furious. He takes a big breath. "No, it's okay, honey. No harm. We can still do this." His hand pulls down my jeans a bit and my hand yanks them up.

"Damn it, girl! You said you wanted to."

"I'm sorry, Mr. Marks. I do want to."

"Good. So stay fuckin' still."

Another try with the jeans. He pulls down. My hands pull up.

I'm making him mad. *Please forgive me, Mr. Marks!*

He makes a movement like he is about to caress my face or strike me but my left arm flies out to block him as my right hand punches him in the mouth. Mr. Marks lifts off me a bit and I cry, "It's not me. I want to."

My right leg jerks up, knee slamming toward the ceiling—Mr. Marks's balls get in the way.

PREY

I RUN OUT of the Central Park Model Yacht Club building and keep running until I get back to the zoo.

Standing in front of the snow leopard, I remember what Mr. Marks said. The predators have two eyes in the front. So how come I have two eyes in the front? I'm not a predator.

But—was Mr. Marks being a predator?

Men always be taken what they wants. You're his prey.

No. He was nice. He asked and I let him kiss me. He was just doing the normal birds-and-bees. I would have been loved! I would have been cared for and made into a princess! I'm always messing things up! Why did I hurt him?! I'm terrible! He'll never forgive me!

BREAKUP BEDROOM

I'M SWEATING BY THE TIME I get back to our building after running from the zoo. I tiptoe to my room and quietly shut the door. My heart is pounding. What is happening to me!? I'm a mean, violent person!

I collapse on my bed. The stupid stuffed frog with its stupid crown stares at me. Fuck you.

Once upon a time there was a frog and it was supposed to have a princess kiss it 'cause they said it would turn into a prince but this isn't about that frog, this is the ugly girl-frog that gets everything wrong—

Mother knocks on my door. I don't answer, so of course she opens it.

She looks at me with concern. "What happened?"

"NOTHING HAPPENED!" I scream.

"Elizabeth, you can tell me. I won't judge. Tell me—"

"I PUNCHED HIM AND KICKED HIM AND BIT HIM AND ALL HE WAS DOING WAS BEING NICE!"

"Tell me what he—"

I leap from my bed and must look frightening because Mother backs away quickly and I SLAM my door on whatever she was going to say.

The moment the knob clicks, my left leg starts twitching. Then my right. Both arms stiffen and spasm. I want to scream for help but my mouth is clamped shut, the vocal cords smashed as if someone's choking me.

A flood of images obliterates the real world. My desk becomes a mound of rubble, bricks, and suitcases. My lamp sprouts black wings and *caws* down at me. The overhead fan roars like a motorcycle and spins out of control. Dirt splatters my face and the sounds of screams and bees and bombs and waves bombard my ears as smells of vomit and sweat and alcohol and gasoline make me gag. Adrenaline speeds through me, heart racing, skin prickly, metallic taste in my mouth—and my right leg lunges forward on a mission.

Panic rises as I try to stop the leg's lunge, but it has more power, and more will, than I. It slams into the door and starts kicking, and I'm a bystander in my own body. Frantic, maniacal kicking, and although I'm only a teenage girl, the door isn't a match for this surge of anger. Mother screams behind the splintering wood. As my foot blasts through the door, I fall backwards and leaves and dirt cover my face and someone yells, "Turn to the side!" as I fade into darkness.

JENNY — OCCOQUAN WORKHOUSE, LORTON, VIRGINIA — 1916

THE PRISON OFFICIAL YELLS, "Turn to the side!" The camera clicks and I'm next to be photographed. I feel very inclined to adjust my hair, with the hopes of obfuscating the bare wound that the horse's hoof created. Even at this juncture, I want to look pretty. How deep this indoctrination seeps! In the midst of demonstrating for my equality, I still am caught in the web of my prescribed feminine role. The camera clicks, the man rolls the film forward and barks, "Turn to the side!" I do and a second photograph immortalizes me.

I'm shoved into a crowded room. All my compatriots are undressing, folding their long frocks, helping each other remove tailored jackets, skirts, and corsets. Against all propriety, our subjugators mingle amongst us to distribute shapeless gowns. The material is unbearably coarse and clearly unclean. I endeavor to banish from my mind thoughts of the last woman who wore this.

They put us three-to-a-cell, but provide us with only two hard beds. Surely this is against all decency.

My friend Margaret is my cellmate, along with a young woman I've not seen before. Margaret, being the oldest and who she is, touches the young woman on the arm. "I'm Margaret, matron of the Maryland chapter. Who do I have the pleasure of acquainting?"

"Penelope, I'm—just starting," the woman answers. She presents as not yet astride the age of twenty. It's heartening to witness the youth involved.

I proffer my hand. "I'm Jenny. Provocateur. Suffragette."

Margaret and Penelope are removed from of my cell after each of us endure a sleepless night. I don't know if they have been released or are sequestered in another part of this penitentiary, but for the time being, I'm alone. The guard doesn't speak when he brings me food. I endeavor to impress upon him that mine is an illegal imprisonment, yet I get no response beyond his fist to my head. I'm at once grateful he has spared my womb and so, my child, such harm.

In the daylight hours, I contemplate the green moss articulating the spaces betwixt the stones of my walls. To observe this growth and life balms my soul, yet I wonder how that which grows within my being is affected should my confinement persist. Where is my husband? Surely he knows of my arrest and plight. Why hasn't he facilitated my release? Who is caring for our children?

Time drifts. My long hair is turning white. How can that be? I'm only thirty. Vomiting continues as my belly protrudes. I learn from newly arrested suffragettes, brought in bloody and bruised, that my husband has been trying to secure my release. It warms my heart to know he is advocating for me and I'm sure to have freedom soon.

As the others are moved, I'm once again alone but I continue to articulate my rights. "Illegitimate incarceration! I shall not partake of your manufactured supplication of one gender to the governing patriarchy. Women are people! I demand my rights!" My mouth says all this, but is it my mouth? I wonder at its boldness. It readily expounds righteous diatribes, which are unacceptable to the general populous. Perhaps somehow these thoughts were embedded in me, as if I'd been born male. As if I was worth something. I do not pretend to understand how these notions flourish in my being, but I cannot silence them. If they were said by a man, that figure would be powerful and righteous. From a woman, they're emblematic of the inflammation of the womb. An overabundance of feminine elements. And thusly, I'm labeled a hysteric.

The men secure me in a jacket with sleeves more suited for the appendages of a giant octopus. These are tied to constrict my movements and a cloth is bound over my mouth to constrict my tongue. I'm carried out and driven to a massive complex. The Government Hospital for the Insane.

Inside, I am met by a doctor. He informs me I must relinquish my claim on the matter.

"What matter?" I ask when the gag is removed.

"The impending birth of your child. Sign this paper."

Two guards undo the bonds constricting my arms and hand me a quill. When I insist on reading the contract, the guards force my hand to make an x on the document. "What is this? I demand to know what you have coercively set my mark to."

"Your child will be taken away when it is born."

"I refuse!"

"You are not fit to make that decision."

"You have no right to take my child! My husband will not allow this."

"Your husband is no longer a participant to your circumstances."

The shock must register on my face for he continues. "Your husband has come to understand that he will be seen as mutually culpable, and liable to stiff penalties, if he continues to petition for your release. The State has charged you with sedition, insurrection, child endangerment, and immoral behavior. You have been found guilty in abstentia but because we doctors have determined that you are inhibited by the hysterical humor, we thusly conclude that you are certifiably insane. Remove her."

They drag me to my cell as I scream, "I shall not be forgotten!!!!"

A few hours later, because I resist all attempts to silence me, I'm pulled out of my cell for 'treatment.' They assure me it won't harm the baby. As the white-suited attendants drag me down the long hall, other patients watch.

"STAND UP FOR JUSTICE!" I scream. "I AM NOT INSANE!"

THERAPY

I'M CUCKOO. After several years of escalation—slapping my mother, attacking the plastic surgeon, attacking Mr. Marks, busting the door of my room—it's clear I'm a danger. Psych evaluation and treatment are ordered.

And so, I open the door of Doctor Sanford.

I am immediately confronted with a wall. Below it stands a credenza with magazines across the polished surface. *Gardens and Guns. Sports Illustrated. Comfort Food. Star. Ebony. True Crime. Forbes. Scientific American. Vogue. Wired. Women's Day.* They're spread so that all are visible and none is more important than the next. Undoubtedly a test. I don't touch any.

The waiting room must be beyond this wall. I can probably access it by rounding to the left or right. Another test? I decide to take the right, so as not to look iconoclastic or confrontational. That brings me into the waiting room. The space is a mix of dark corners and light from tall windows. (The view isn't spectacular like our building. Just the facing offices across Columbus Avenue.) Hanging above me is glowing imitation moon with all the grey spots and craters. Scattered about are an assortment of seating choices. Another test. One cushy armchair with vibrant colors. One nondescript wingback of muted grey. One modern black leather lounger. One wooden chair with a stiff back. One neon-red beanbag. There's a couch grouping designed to promote chatting. A quiet corner for two. And a solitary chair facing the only dark corner, its back to the room. I'd sit there but I imagine that would label me as melancholy, so I remain standing, facing the only door. It has a peephole. I don't smile at it. After a moment, the door opens and a tall woman with flying gray hair steps out.

"I'm Doctor Sanford. Elizabeth, I presume."

I nod and she, seeing that I'm not choosing a chair, gestures to the couch. I sit. She pulls the vibrant armchair up closer and asks me to tell her about my life. I tell her the dull facts about my parents, brother, school...

She laughs. "If I had a life the way you describe it, I'd want to punch someone, too."

I decide to cut to the chase. "I'm crazy."

"That's a scary word. What makes you say that?"

"I'm a jumble inside. I probably have split-personality."

Doctor Sanford doesn't laugh. "I see. That would certainly be something to be concerned about. Do you black out and find yourself somewhere and not know how you got there?"

I shake my head.

"Do you have gaps in your memory or lose time?"

Shake again.

"Multiple personality disorder, or dissociative identity disorder, usually contains those symptoms. Separate personalities rarely know about each other and if one personality takes over, the others are clueless as to what happened during that period. We won't preclude any possible future diagnosis, but let's not jump to conclusions. Tell me about the incidents that brought you in. Why do you think you attacked the plastic surgeon and teacher?"

How can I say that I misinterpreted what the doctor was doing? I went to him for breast surgery so of course he was touching my breast. And Mr. Marks, he liked me and I liked him and I wanted to do those things... I shrug.

"No ideas? Did you feel threatened—?

"It wasn't me."

"The doctor and nurse both witnessed you. The teacher reported it. Your mother saw you busting apart a door with unbelievable fury. You did do it."

"My body may have done it, but I wasn't in control."

Doctor Sanford looks at me with what looks like—respect. "That's really astute of you, Elizabeth. I understand. We often want to dissociate from actions or feelings we can't accept in ourselves."

"It really wasn't my choice. *I* wouldn't have fought. I'm a scaredy cat."

"Fear often moves hand in hand with anger. Were you angry? Anger is a very powerful emotion. You've heard of the phrase 'blind with anger.' That happens. The rational mind isn't in control. We all have subconscious influences—slights, old pain—they can cause what you experienced. What do you think might be reasons for anger?"

Part of me feels it might be possible to get help from this woman. "Maybe because—look at me. I'm a mess. I must be the ugliest person alive."

Doctor Sanford smiles sadly. "You have a unique appearance, but you're certainly not ugly."

"I know what I am. When I was being made, no one stirred me. My genes were never blended. The DNA of my left leg isn't mingling with the DNA of my right. One leg is too muscular. Some skin is lighter, some darker. One eye brown, one green. Look at this tuft of blond in the middle of these dark curls and here's the redhead part. My left arm has pink skin with freckles, a wide wrist, and fuzzy hair. My right is all tan and weathered and tough."

"Like a calico cat. You know, the ones with patches of orange, black, and white fur. You don't think they're ugly, do you?"

"No, but—"

"I want you to read about them when you get home. Read about their genetics. I can't say I remember it all, but the fur color gene is on the x chromosomes. Calicos are almost always female, and they have two X chromosomes. For each section of their body, they randomly shut off one or the other X. This causes patches of one color or another. Completely random. Calicos are a mix that isn't mixed and each is unique and all the more interesting because of it"

"I don't want to be interesting!" My right arm rises quickly to dismiss my words. "See, Doctor! I'm not doing that!"

Doctor Sanford leans forward. "I see a young woman in a lot of pain. A young woman who *does* want to be interesting. A young woman who will, in time, be able to act consciously and believe in and respect and love herself."

Hope bubbles up in me and pushes tears out. Doctor Sanford hands me a box of tissues. The gesture gets me sobbing.

"Keep going, Elizabeth. I've plenty more boxes."

I cry for a long time. When I finally raise my head, Doctor Sanford is looking at me tenderly. "How do you feel?"

I check myself inside. It's strange, but I feel good. I'll sound like a real nut if I say that after crying, so I say, "Better."

Doctor Sanford suggests I do homework before the next session. "Make a list of things you're good at, write down any dreams you have, and read about calico cats."

She stands and I stand. We shake hands and I squeeze a little too hard. *Oops.*

"See, I didn't mean to shake your hand like that. It didn't feel like me. My limbs are always twitching and moving on their own. I have that syndrome where you curse or jerk for no reason."

"Tourette's syndrome. Why do you think that?"

"It feels like I'm not in control of parts of myself."

Doctor Sanford puts a gentle hand on my shoulder. She looks at me with such compassion. "It's scary to feel out of control. We're going to get to the bottom of this. But, please, let me do the diagnosis."

I turn to exit and pause, unable to decide which side to take and what it might say about me. That imitation moon shines down laughing.

KELLY — POTTER COUNTY, PENNSYLVANIA — 1911

T'NIGHT'S A FULL MOON. Step oot o' our stone cottage. Alex is snorin' and forgettin' th' troubles o' th' day. Sometimes with that racket an th' bairn kickin' in my belly I cannae stay t'sleepin so I take the air. 'Ere in this glowin' night, th' air's crisp but nae wi' th' smells o' Ayrshire and the sea.

Across the ocean, way back miles away be my auld home. It 'ad poverty and strife and people doin' wrong, but I miss it.

All the same, we's lucky. It's those that come afore that grant us these few acres. Cousin to Alex set us doon in his Last Will and it brought us tae this home. And the acres are bountiful. An orchard of apples, grapes, walnuts, quinces, and pears. Wi' space for a real garden. The babe grows larger inside me and soon I'll be cleanin' nappies as me preoccupation.

A sound ahead startles me. In the pen aside the cottage Ol' Brick gets tae brayin'.

"Hauld yer noise, mule!" I whisper, prayin' the greetin' dinnae wake Alex.

Another scratchin' sound in the orchard. There t'aint be bear in these parts, be there?

A whine is me answer as a wee tangle o' dog hobbles intae the moonlight afore me. His hair be a mess o' tangles an' brambles and the poor fella 'as only three o' the usual four legs. The tail flips a stick caught tae it to-n-fro.

"Hello, Boy-O. Ye look aboot done in. Clearly wi'oot a home, or they's basterdly, eh? Is ye aimin' tae melt me heart?"

The wee tyke, nae bigger than a grand lady's hatbox, yaps 'is answer.

"Cannae sleep, Kelly?" Alex's voice edges oot the cottage.

"Nay. Not me nor the bairn. And this sorry fella is tryin' for a handout."

Alex leans from the door and Boy-O moves aside me an' growls at the man.

"Protectin' the lady already, is ye?" Alex asks the wee brave fellow.

"Dinnae growl at 'im, Boy-O, 'tis the lord o' the castle."

Alex pushes the door wide. "Come ye both in and we'll get a spot o' supper for the cur and I'll play y' a tune to droop y'r eyes."

And so we do and so he does. And after Boy-O laps doon a buttered mash o' tatties and sausage, he curls 'cross me feet as the fiddle sings the slow lilting lullaby Bà Bà mo Leanabh Beag. The tune calms me and my wee growin' bairn and sends us dreamin' of Ayrshire. Can almost hear the waves.

Mornin' brings a wet lick tae me cheek. 'Tis that dirty three-legged dog. After making porridge for Alex, I get the sheers and commence t' cutting oot the burrs and brambles from the black 'n tan coat o' wee Boy-O. He stands for the process but for a mighty tremblin'.

Lad looks like a 'ighland Terrier. At least I aim tae believe so. 'E's got tae have lost 'is front pin long since as it's well 'ealed and 'e's nae the worse for bein' wioot. 'Is ribs are visible and bring tae mind o' so many o' me kin. If I can fatten this wee one, maybe there's hope for them back home.

DOCTOR PIERSON

REMEMBER THE NUTHOUSE in Connecticut and vomiting meds on vegetables? That's still in the works. It's med time.

Nurse Blinky blinks her fake eyelashes. Why she thinks wearing these in a nuthouse will make her love life happier is a conundrum, but perhaps I don't know enough about what fake eyelashes can do. She's wearing hot pink lipstick today and her mouth looks like two worms wriggling against each other as if fulfilling a couples-therapy assignment.

"Good morning, Elizabeth. How are we today?"

I no longer fight the *we* in her speech. I imagine it is the *we* of *me*.

"We're fine, Nurse. Thank you."

"Glad to hear it." She hands me a small cup with four pills and another with water. I nod a thanks, pills on tongue, drink, show, left, right, up.

"Thank you, Elizabeth."

"Can I tell you about the greenhouse? The vegetables are really growing well—"

Nurse Blinky turns on her *wish-I-could* look. "I have other clients and need to greet them. So sorry. Another time?"

I nod. "Please come by if you have a moment, Nurse." Invitations work wonders for ensuring no one will bother us.

As I turn to leave, she holds up a finger. "You got your monthly letter from home." She offers me an envelope. I pocket it in the elastic waistband of my hospital pants.

Shuffling down the hall, I open the letter. The text is the usual. *Elizabeth, Nothing to report. Hope all is well. Here's a little something for necessities and your favorite treat. Best, Mother*

Inside is a twenty-dollar bill. As part of my plan, I lied and told her the nuthouse commissary only took cash. She sends a twenty every month. This bill will bring my stash to $120. I'm sure it's a hassle to procure these, as the Gaston family doesn't use cash and certainly never twenties. There are undoubtedly a few thousand in hundred-dollar bills in Father's safe, but that's only for "the zombie apocalypse." In the envelope, Mother has also included my BlackJack chewing gum. I doubt BlackJack gum is common so it's probably another hassle. I'm grateful to Mother. Sometimes I think she's not any happier living that life than I was.

I stick a piece of gum in my mouth. It's an odd flavor but a perfect color. Each time I remove putty from the lowest window pane under the potting table in the greenhouse, I roll the gum into a floppy string and press it flat against the glass. Looks just like black glazing putty.

I chew and walk down the hall toward the greenhouse to fertilize the plants with my morning bounty. If I am correct, the three-month growing season will come to an apex soon. Full potency should be reached. Unless I'm wrong. What do I know about plants?

I'm about to reach into the greenhouse door when—

"Elizabeth?"

Doctor Pierson waves from far down the hall. He's a short man with a wide shiny face and a wispy black comb-over stuck to his forehead.

I have no choice but to stop for him. "Yes, Doctor?" A gurgle in my stomach reminds me I only have a brief window before the meds dissolve, my plants go hungry, and I get worthless.

He trots the rest of the hall to reach me and arrives shinier and with the comb-over dangling. "How you are feeling?"

"I am inclined to protest my continued presence in this institution. I can assure you my faculties are quite sound."

"It's good to hear you feel that way, but of course, we'll make that assessment. I just want to make sure you're satisfied with us. Your father recently made a very generous donation and we're quite grateful to the Gastons. We want you happy, dear."

Something about this feels scary. Father made a donation beyond the normal fee?

The doctor smiles benignly and his palm gives my shoulder several moist pats. "You are in good hands, Elizabeth. For as long as it takes, we'll care for you."

For as long as it takes?

There's a squirt of bile in my brain. I recognize that from when I first arrived. Scheiße! *Was ist das?!* The drugs are dissolving. *Focus! FOCUS!!!"*

Danke, Herr Doctor," I mumble.

Doctor Pierson chuckles and waves me away. I try to walk as steadily as I can but the hall is growing longer and the tiles are tilting toward me.

Open the greenhouse door and step in. I rush to the plants and my finger tickles my throat. I vomit, but it's more of a colorful mess than solid pills or capsules. The finger tries again. And again. I vomit onto the cauliflower, carrots, celery, beets, radishes, and turnips but they're moving so much it's hard to catch them. I stick my head under the work-sink faucet. The drugs are pulling me under. I can't stop them.

There is a wheelchair in all the rooms, including this one. Now I know why. I drop into it and vanish.

TRAUMA

Oblivion.
I'm not anywhere.

Fuck that!
Damn right.

There's a tug.
And another.
Something inside.
It's awakening to tell me.
Show me.
Peel the blinders off.

I see.

You're the blond boy crawling over glass to escape the belt buckle.
You're the bright college student shattered by the whim of a teacher.
You're the one leaving everything you loved.
You're the one touching moss on the stone walls of your cell.
You're the one face down in the honky-tonk surrounded by a jeering mob.
You're the one staggering barefoot and freezing through the forest.
You're the one shaking as bombs tear the building apart.
You're the one bleeding on horseback in the blizzard.

You're her and him and them and so much has been done to you that you didn't deserve. That no one deserves. *Fuck deserve!* You were glorious and no one was there to help you.

And the trauma endures.

And the trauma continues.

And the trauma carries on and on and on and on...

PHOTO ALBUM

AS ALBERTO DRIVES ME HOME from my session with Doctor Sanford, I start my therapy homework—that list of what I'm good at:

1. Beating people up.
2. Breaking doors.
3. Being ugly.

This gets me mad and I decide *Being mad* is number four. I'm done with this assignment. I'm done with therapy and no, I won't research calico cats!

The car pulls to a stop in front of our building and Miroslav opens my door, but I'm too angry to thank him or Alberto. In the foyer, I PUNCH the elevator button in a very un-ladylike way. Who cares.

When the elevator opens on my floor, mother exits her room with a smile and asks how it went.

She's hoping I'll say that I'm cured!

"Gee, how was my session? It was full of tests. A magazine test, a left-right entrance test, a chair test, and the Doctor thinks I'm a Calico cat and my genes didn't mix. And that's because YOU didn't feel like being pregnant—"

Mother sputters. "That's not—it's—the doctors said—you can't blame *me*."

"Who *can* I blame? Yasmina? YOU decided I should be incubated in her. Yasmina and I must have swapped lots of DNA."

From the twitching of Mother's eye, it's clear that I'm infuriating her. *Good!* I don't let up. "I want to see Yasmina. Let's arrange a meeting. I'm sure she'd like to see the ugly little bun that was in her oven—"

"Stop this nonsense, Elizabeth. Even if we wanted to, which we DON'T, we sent Yasmina back to New Orleans after you were born and severed all contact."

"But she's to blame, isn't she? My right leg is darker than the rest of me. I exchanged blood and genes and pigment when I was in her womb—"

"STOP IT! YOU HAVE ONLY GOOD GENES! ONLY OUR FAMILY GENES!!!"

She grabs my right hand but it jerks out of her grasp. We're both shocked and stare at that hand for a second. My left hand slides in to make amends and takes Mother's rejected one. That makes me madder, but Mother's somewhat mollified and leads me into the media room. She lifts a massive photo album from its shelf, and gestures for me to sit beside her on the cream-suede settee. "You want to know where you came from? I'll show you."

It's startling to be this near her. She smells of flowers. For some reason, I want to lean my head against her shoulder, but that feeling makes me even madder.

"Yeah, show me who gave me my brown eye and who gave me the green one."

Mother ignores me, opens the album midway, and flips to her wedding portrait. She and Father look so young.

"*This* is where you come from. These two people. Philip and Evelyn. Not Yasmina."

"What part of this mess,"—I gesture to take in my entire being—"came from you, and what part came from Father?"

"Elizabeth, you know very well you come from generations of ancestors." She flips back a few pages. "We don't have photographs of everyone." She stops at a color picture of a couple on a palm tree beach waving at the camera. "Your grandparents on Father's side. Grandma Miriam came from German ancestors and Granddad Albert Gaston was—in business."

"How we got filthy rich."

Mother purses her lips angrily. "Your father was born to privilege but made his own way." She turns to another page. An old couple sitting on a couch. "My mother, your Grandma Susie, came from down South—"

"Everyone's looking pretty dang human, so far. Where are the freaks?"

"—and my father, Grandpa Peter Wheeler, was adopted so we don't know his background."

"Oooo! Maybe that's where the skeletons are hidden! Someone's got to have been a disaster like me."

"I've had enough of your attitude."

She slams the album closed but my right hand is fast and darts into the gap. "There's a key," I say, not knowing what I'm talking about.

The book is opened again and my finger lifts the edge of Grandpa Wheeler's picture, flipping it up. A little key is taped to the back of the photo.

"I guess you've been through this album before. That was the only thing my father's birth mother gave her baby. A key. Great gift."

Damn straight.

"What does it unlock?"

Mother closes the photo album and indicates a headache. "Maybe it unlocks all the answers to all your questions."

"Keep going, I want to see the rest of my gene pool."

"The other pictures may go further back but don't have any writing or identification of who they are. Feel free to make up what you want. I'm through."

She leaves and I flip through the pictures. Everyone looks normal. I'm the only disaster.

HEINRICH / SOLVEIG — FRANKFURT, GERMANY — 1945

FRANKFURT IS A DISASTER. Buildings in ruins. Streets blown up. But the war didn't destroy the wild flowers. Solveig likes flowers. I suggest a hike up in the hills to see them. She seems happy with the idea, or pretends to be. As we walk, she talks of old times and tries to make it seem like everything is still the way it was.

We used to come to this hillside. Young, perfect bodies in their prime. Stepping through the blossoms, sending insects swirling. Sunshine off everything. We were the center of the universe and no one could deny our magnificence. Ja. That was how it was. But now ist alles erased. Das Fatherland. Deutschland. Our great people. The Dream. Kaputt. The war is over and we lost. Our cities are rubble. The person who I thought I was, is no more. And my leg is gone. Now there's a contraption of wood and cloth and leather shackled to my stump.

I hate this life.

I'm awkward with my cane and artificial leg. Solveig moves alongside me, her hair the color of the flowers. The color of the bursting wheat. Solveig pretends she's happy. Pretends she isn't glancing at my left pant hiding the dangling prosthesis. She finds me grotesque. She smiles, but her smile lies.

She asks "Do you need to stop and rest?"

Rage envelops me. I don't want Solveig's pity and condescension. I grab her and let myself fall, pulling her to the ground. Her hair mixes with the grass and flowers and I need to show her I'm still a man. I have to do this. She has to know. Someone has to know.

And it's easy to overpower her. How scared she looks. It makes me feel powerful and I reach under her skirt. Solveig cries out, "Bitte, Heinrich, nein!" but I'm not stopping—

—he's not stopping. I cry out, "Bitte, Heinrich, nein!"

I try to push him off me, but he pins my wrists, pressing me into the flowers and dirt. His good leg jams between mine and he shoves it to open my thighs, while the wooden one flops against my shin painfully. Heinrich grabs my neck and he is mad enough with pain and shame that he can kill me. I stop struggling. He undoes himself and fumbles under my dress and pulls down my underwear and presses in. "Nein, Heinrich. Nein..."

He pushes and pushes and each push jangles his false leg hard against my shin and ankle. If I lay still maybe he'll let go of my neck. If I accept, maybe his rage will vanish.

I watch a bee land on a tall flower over our heads. Pollination. *Bitte, nein.*

Heinrich heaves and presses deep and holds, groaning his release in my ear.

Bugs fly over us. The sun is still shining. He's twitching on me and in me. Will he let me go? I must close my eyes when he rises, so he will feel unseen and maybe he'll let me live.

He raises his hips—*Close your eyes*—and pulls out. It rasps my insides. *Don't react.* I feel him pause. He must be looking at me, looking for my reaction. I've got to be still. As if peacefully sleeping.

Heinrich rolls off, slamming his wooden leg against my knee. I swallow the pain.

Listen. There's the buzzing of insects, bird song, some wind, and cloth rustling. There is a sound of leather and something unbuckling. A heavy thud hits the ground and then a hop and a step, tap, a step, tap, a step.... If he is still close, will I be able to run? I wait until I only hear the insects and birds and wind and open my eyes. He is far down the hill, hopping on one leg, using the cane to keep upright. Why is he hopping? His artificial leg lies beside me. The shaking floods me and I can't breathe for the sobs.

SESSION TWO

I TELL MY PARENTS that the therapy isn't helpful, but they insist on me continuing as it's part of the negotiated settlements with various injured parties. The next session I tell Doctor Sanford I forgot to do the good-at list and lie that I researched calico cats.

"What about your dreams?" asks Doctor Sanford. "What are they like?"

I feel myself turning red. "If you thought I was crazy before, my dreams will make you know for sure."

"I don't think you're crazy."

I squirm a bit on the couch. She lets me take my time. "It's like I'm having other people's dreams."

The doctor waits.

"I don't dream about my life, going to school, our building, my family. I dream about people and places I don't know. And I'm not me. Sometimes I'm a boy or a man. Sometimes I'm speaking another language. I'm in strange situations that I know nothing about. Not even this time period. In one, the person seems scared all the time. There's another seen through the eyes of some brave lady. Elizabeth Gaston isn't doing the dream. It's all these other people I don't know. That's why I thought I was split personality."

Doctor Sanford smiles slightly. She's thinking of calling the men in white coats to take me away.

"We humans like to make categories. We like to think in absolutes. Binary thinking. Black and white. Good and bad. Male and female. But life isn't like that. Life is messy and doesn't have fixed borders. Neither do people. We have different aspects of ourselves. Masculine aspects. Feminine aspects. Brave *and* fearful aspects. Serious and silly. Rigid and flexible. This is completely normal. If you were only one way, you wouldn't be human."

"But dreams aren't aspects of me. They're of different people than me."

"Dreams can be manifestations of what we desire and also what we fear. Perhaps there are parts of these dream personalities that you want to integrate into your being, and other parts you want to be rid of. The unconscious is usually pretty brilliant in what it is trying to tell us, even if the message is sometimes too mysterious to fully grasp."

I slump lower on the couch. "I'm not smart enough to figure my unconscious out."

Doctor Sanford taps her head. "Leave that to me. I have an unconventional but exciting idea. There's been a lot of recent studies about treatments that can allow a patient to explore their inner terrain and create new pathways and connections that seem to 're-set' or 're-boot' the brain. It's helped a lot of people. You know those old-fashioned LP records?"

"Vinyl?"

"As we live, we get our needles spinning in the same grooves over and over. It's nearly impossible to get out of our habits of thinking and being. This treatment can hop you out of the old record and give you a new un-grooved record to live in. You make new pathways. New synapses. New ways of thinking. Would you be willing to try?"

"I'll try anything."

"I'll make a tentative appointment at the university hospital where they're doing the study, but I need your parents to sign a consent form. Now bear in mind, they may not give permission considering the kind of treatment it is."

"Why?"

"It's psilocybin. Magic mushrooms. You'll go on a trip. "

RUBY — BODIE, CALIFORNIA— 1877

I TAKE A TRIP WITH SLIM around the floor to the pian'r music but keep notice on Mr. Reddy eyein' me at the bar. Sven pours the man a drink and calls out, "Ruby," in his sing-song voice. I give Slim's shoulder a squeeze and sashay toward the bar as Mr. Reddy downs his drink. Like usual, he slides four coins onto the bartop pretendin' they ain't for me. Like usual, I tap each against the wood. They sound solid. Three go into my brassiere pocket and I toss the fourth to Chan, standing in the shadows under the stairway. He catches it with hardly a movement and nods slowly. He doesn't bow like some of the Chinese. He doesn't act like I'm better because I'm white. I like that.

I push through the squeakin' saloon doors and into the cold. I hear the squeak again as Mr. Reddy follows me. He always worrin' 'bout being seen with the likes of my kind.

It's been snowing for a while and the road has few footprints. We go around the block to Bonanza Street and walk past all the other small shacks of the other ladies. Each door has a lantern glowing red with swirls of snowflakes dancing 'round. Seems magical 'cept when you figure what's going on. But ain't we all jes trying to survive? We get to my crib and I cover a bit of the lantern so folk know I'm occupied.

When Mr. Reddy steps inside, I light the oil lamp and he crosses to the basin and washes them private bits. I do the soap with lots of lye to keep the fellers clean. It bites some, but they don't complain. They got other things on their mind.

I lay on the bed and, jes in case, move my hand 'round the edge of the mattress, reach into the pocket to check all is as it should be. There's the cold edge of my Colt. Dandy. Now get in my pose, let down my hair, and arrange the long red curls to swirl around these breasts.

Mr. Reddy rinses and, although his back's to me, from his gestures I can tell he's already hard. He ain't never had no problem in them parts. Mr. Reddy is ready.

He turns and mounts. Reckon all he's learned of sex is from watching animals. Probably stallions and bulls. He props himself at arm's length on his fists, elbows locked, eyes glaring at my breasts bouncing with each thrust. Wonder if this is how he does it with Mrs. Reddy. Prolly not. She so prim and upstandin' you could use her as a flag pole.

He rides me until he seizes and collapses. No sound but a long exhale. I lay under him and get to countin' t'ward one hundred and, like usual, he heaves off me by twenty. By fifty, he's sneakin' out the door.

I hop up and stick my head outside, put my hands together and blow, making the sound of a dove. Two short and one long, "Cooo-cooo, cooooooooo," out into the night. The return call comes back and I wave to the darkness to say goodnight to Chan.

Close the cold out and squat t'clean my parts. Can't be but a few minutes when there's a sound outside and the door flies open. Hardly can I turn when a bright lantern flies at me and smashes against my shoulder. Flames explode and my shoulder is alight. A fury in black looms over me—gown, bonnet—Mrs. Reddy—screaming, "That's the last time you'll corrupt him!"—I got to smother the flames scorching my flesh—my hair is a rising swirl of red and black—"Burn in hell, you jezebel."

She spits on me and stomps to the door just as Chan bursts in. The woman screams, racing into the darkness as Chan rips the blanket off my bed and whips it over me, pressing out the flames on my shoulder and head.

I smell the sickening stench of burnt hair as I feel water poured over the blanket and hear the crunch of glass under stomping boots. Move the soggy smoking cloth off my head and am in darkness but for my one small window.

Chan's voice, "I find lantern. Wait."

The door opens to cold air and the glow of snow. Chan's silhouette fills the door.

"Keep it open," I whisper.

He does and races off.

Is it time to leave Bodie? That woman can make life harder, but maybe if I no longer lay under her husband we can both exist in this city.

Chan hurries in with another lantern and sets it by my bedside. "Okay, Ruby?"

It jolts me that he uses my given name. He would be beaten if the good people of Bodie heard that.

I try to speak but the words don't come.

Chan straightens his long dark braid. "That lady no like you no kowtow."

I raise my eyebrows, trying to ask the question—*Kowtow?*

"Chinese custom. Bow head on floor to Master, show respect." Chan steps to the door. "I go see she gone. You rest."

I nod my thanks.

He closes the door gently.

As the shaking starts and the tears come, I reckon I'll always be this hated.

TRIPPIN'

GETTING MY PARENTS' CONSENT for the psychedelic trip was as easy as forging their signatures, so here I am. The room is cozy and New Age music plays quietly. All the lighting is indirect, hidden and low. It's like a spa. A couch and a chair and a small table with water in a plastic pitcher and a bowl with several sand-colored capsules.

Doctor Sanford smiles warmly. "You can change your mind. I don't want you to feel forced into anything."

I sit on the couch as my answer. She sits on the chair beside me.

"We've found that a lot of external stimulation can get overwhelming, that's why it's so bare in here. You may not feel anything for a while. Maybe an hour. Then things might shift slowly or dramatically. If you get scared, know I'll be here the whole time."

"Okay," I say. I'm scared, but if this can help not be so nutty, it's worth some fear.

She holds out the bowl of pills and a glass of water.

"How many do I take?" I ask.

"All eight of them."

I am not sure this is a good idea, but my right hand scoops up the pills and my left hand brings the water to my lips. My hands feed me all eight pills. They taste like dirt and I have a flash of picking mushrooms in a forest. Which, of course, I've never done.

"Get comfortable. Close your eyes. If you want to talk, I'm here. If not, that's fine. All you do is breathe and relax. Some people say it is like having your conscious brain step out of control. It's still there, but your subconscious is allowed to roam. You may see things, or hear things that aren't there, but you don't need to be afraid."

I lie back on the couch and close my eyes. I stay like this for a while but feel anxious. What if she left?

I open one eye. Doctor Sanford is sitting nearby. Watching. She smiles again. "I'm here. Close your eyes and think about something nice."

I don't know what is nice that I can think about. What *is* nice? Animals. Only that makes me think of the zoo and beating up Mr. Marks. Maybe I'm supposed to think about why I'm so screwed up attacking grownups. That makes me feel bad, so I try to think about school, but that also makes me feel bad, and I can't seem to find anything to think about that's nice.

I open my eyes. "Nothing's happening, Doctor. Maybe my brain is too in-control for this to work."

"Give it time," she says.

For some reason, she's leaning extremely close. I can see the makeup on her eyebrows, little clumps of mascara on her lashes, and her turquoise earrings match her eyes. Her lipstick is the color of dried blood. Maybe it is blood. Maybe she's a vampire. It would be okay if she was. Is she going to bite me?

She's getting closer. Is she going to bite me or kiss me?

Her face fractures into many pieces. A kaleidoscope view of the Doctor. *Doctor Kaleidoscope! That's so funny!*

"Close your eyes, Elizabeth," she says and I do.

The sounds in the room all are amplified. Sounds of a horse. A motorcycle revving its engine. Isn't the horse scared of the motorcycle?

A high bell rings. The front desk and—there's the bellboy, red hat, brass buttons, golden epaulets. Only he's not a bellboy he's a frog dancing to the hurdy-gurdy. Only he's not dancing, he's quite dignified. He bows and his long-fingered hand reaches out—a gesture of *welcome to participate!* I reach out my right hand to meet his—my hand is covered in mud. Did I forget to wash?

The corners of the room fold in and it doesn't worry me, which is odd. The bellboy frog points to an elevator I don't remember seeing. Bronze doors open and there's another ding. Smells hit me as I float to the elevator—sizzling cowhide, olives in gin, cigar smoke, something dead, bloody cotton, magnolia blossoms, electricity...*how can I know these smells?*

The doors close and the frog is Miroslav in a military uniform, like from the old World War II movies. He taps the side of his nose as he looks at me and pushes a button.

Where are we going? my thoughts ask.

Back, his thoughts answer.

We drop and the elevator vibrates and jerks to a stop. The doors open and there's a muddy road and a ditch and a dead ox and it smells of blood and there's a loud BOOM and clods of dirt fly at me and the frog presses the elevator button and the doors close.

We drop again and the doors open onto a dank prison cell with wet, moss-covered walls and screams of women—and the doors close.

I don't want to go to any more floors, but the frog taps his nose again and we drop and the doors slide open and it's night and stars are up and sparks rise from a campfire as crickets whir and olives are dropped into a martini glass.

The elevator doors shake closed but not all the way. We drop and images whir by in the crack—horses stomping down, a tumbleweed, waves rushing forward, spinning tires, tap of coins on wood…a flood of smells and sights and sounds speed by. The elevator lurches and the doors open. Before me is a dark, fog-filled place.

The frog pushes the elevator button and he and the elevator vanish. I'm surrounded by a haze so dense I can't see but I hear muffled movements. Something is coming closer. Or many somethings. A crowd shuffling forward—mostly obscured by the fog. They step nearer to—greet me?—hurt me?—one passes close and I can make out a leather jacket, motorcycle goggles—another moves by—a young soldier, hopping on one leg. A pregnant woman limps past. A couple waltzes by wearing formal clothes. A woman in a straight-jacket. The swish of a long braid of black hair—and behind them—a shadowy multitude of hundreds, thousands—

A gentle hand strokes my temple. "Don't worry, Miss. You'll be fine." The magnolia blossom scent is heavy on his fingers. *How do I know what magnolia—*

"She ain't paying attention. Now's our chance," a woman behind me says.

Something hits my left leg hard, sending me dropping into the swirling mist.

"NICHT GUT!" a man hollers.

"Ye cannae stop it noo. All we folk be movin'," a voice gurgles as if underwater.

A spider crawls out of my forehead and turns into a woman with flaming red hair. She laughs at me. "Reckon you're plum outta your head."

An electric shock jolts through me, arching my spine. A voice whispers, "She's no more mentally unstable than I, and I am most decidedly not afflicted."

My right hand, leather-gloved, grabs my throat. "You ain't up to this, girlie. Ain't tough for shit."

Swirling through the fog a large silhouette moves toward me. Monstrous eyes gleaming like headlights swerving my way. A deep voice resonates, shaking the ground. "My time will come and I will be rid of you." The being gets closer and I scream—and vomit streams from me—I spit up a huge mass of tendrils, pulsating red. I know what this is. It's pain become visible. Tendrils of pain and horror and shame. The vomiting doesn't stop. My feet and ankles and calves and knees are covered with squirming red. The tangling tentacles wriggle higher, up to my waist, up to my chest, up to my neck. They are obliterating me. I'll die. Maybe it would be good to die. I could leave all this behind. Drift to nothingness.

Sounds come to me from far away.

Go away, I'm drifting.

They are so insistent.

"—eth,—ack.———ear—e?"

I can't shut them out.

"—abeth,—ome back.—you hear me?"

A voice is pulling me out of the void.

"Elizabeth, come back. Can you hear me?"

I open my eyes to Doctor Sanford.

"Elizabeth? Say something."

My tongue doesn't feel like my own. It moves like it's on remote control. "I'm alright, Doctor. Quite an adventure."

Doctor Sanford smiles and pats my hand. I see her do it but don't feel the touch. I must still be tripping.

She tells me to rest and I tell her "I will" but I'm not the teller. I'm a passive observer. I wonder what has just been unleashed in me. Or who.

LIFE RETURNS TO NORMAL

ALBERTO PICKS ME UP from my psychedelic experience. I'm very tired and sleep for two whole days. When I wake up, I feel better. Really better. The magic mushrooms worked!

With my new clarity, I realize that all the foggy personas were aspects of myself and I've been integrated. I finally got 'mixed.' I got new vinyl and my needle is making new grooves! It gives me a huge sense of relief. I continue to see Doctor Sanford and take some very specific psychological tests and as the days, and weeks, and months progress, there is no odd behavior. My limbs don't attack people. My tongue doesn't say things I don't want it to. The Doctor prescribes muscle relaxants to use should the twitching return, but I don't need them. All that violent lashing out must have been a weird byproduct of puberty and is well over. I turn seventeen and everyone is happy with my progress. Doctor Sanford and I have a wrap-up session and I cry 'cause I'll miss her, but it's time to resume my paint-by-numbers life.

Then comes November and the Straw and my eighteenth birthday and kidnapping Finn.

GAS STATION

AND HERE WE ARE. Finn and I have been silent since he discovered I stole his phone and he called me ugly and I called him a fuckin' brat. It's been hours. Stubborn idiots.

"I gotta pee now!" he yells.

Since he broke the silence first, I won, so I ease the Metro Van to the shoulder.

Finn stares at me, then looks out at the green surrounding us. "Bears. Poison Ivy. Snakes. Ticks. Backwoods killers. I'm not peeing out there."

We drive for another few miles until a gas station appears. I swerve in and stop at the pumps. Finn rushes into the shop to find the restroom as I jump down to the pavement. I am stiff and sore! It takes me a while, but I figure out how to pay for gas with a Visa gift card on the machine. As I peer around the van trying to find where the fuel goes, on the other side of the pump a bearded dude with tattoos leans against his huge Prick-up truck and glares at me.

"Drive much?" he asks.

No, I've never driven this much, nor worked these gas pump machines, nor kidnapped anyone. I don't tell him this.

"Nein," I answer. *Why'd I say that?*

The dude blinks. "Nine what?"

"Ich spreche kein Englisch," I say nonchalantly. *What was that gobbledygook?*

The guy steps toward me like I said something insulting. I back away a bit dramatically. He snorts and bends to open a little flap by the van's back wheel. When I don't move, he points for me to insert the gas nozzle. I do, but nothing happens. The man stares at me, shaking his head. He squeezes the handle and the gas starts flowing. He clicks a catch to keep it going, then taps his head like *memorize that* and heads into the station shop.

I watch other people filling their gas tanks. They aren't paying attention to the process and after a moment something makes them take the nozzle from the car. I guess I'll find out when the Metro Van is full—and somehow I do! Now off to pee!

Amble through the shop to the women's room. It's pretty clean and well-lit, but I'm not used to public toilets. I maneuver into the stall trying not to touch any surfaces. Pee. Step to the sink to wash my hands. The familiar face in the mirror stares at me. She makes me want to cry. I'm not up for this. I'm just a scared, ugly girl. Who am I to think I could help Finn become a better person? I'm not capable—

Snap out of it!

The face in the mirror startles me. The eyes—both brown!—stare at me with disgust. What's happening? I don't look like me! I look mean!

Get your ass in gear, buy food, get in that van, and make yourself a plan.

Am I really hearing a voice or am I talking to myself?

ASS. FOOD. VAN. PLAN. GO!

That must be stress talking, but I follow orders. Drinks and food are bought and I carry the bag of snacks to the door.

Pick up that lodging mag. Tell Finn to find a motel. Keep him busy.

Okay, that's a good idea, and just because I didn't think it consciously, doesn't mean I didn't think it. It's just me talking to myself. Nothing to worry about.

I carry the lodging magazine and snacks back to the Metro Van and hop inside. Finn isn't in his seat. Rear? No one. Shit.

Back into the gas station. No sign of Finn in the aisles, so I enter the men's room. The bearded dude from the Prick-up truck stands at the urinal. "HEY!"

I ignore him and peer under the stalls. A pair of expensive sneakers in the far corner. My left foot SLAMS against the lock and WHAM! the door flies open. That was impressive. I guess they don't make these locks that secure. Finn stares with wide eyes. I grab him by the arm and drag him out.

"LET ME GO! HELP!"

The Prick-up dude cranes his neck but keeps peeing. "What's going on?"

Finn pulls at my arm. "My stupid sister says we're escaping ZOMBIES! She's lying!"

The dude turns back to his business. "Whatever."

I drag Finn out and, amazingly, lift him into the van. He's furious.

Slip up into the driver's seat and turn the key. "Get your seatbelt on."

Finn puts it on as we rumble out of the station. "I have no phone and no money to buy one and I don't have a pen to write on the bathroom wall to help me escape and I have nothing to scratch with—"

"Why do you want to escape?"

"I want to go home! I hate this! Everything everywhere is gross!"

"Why didn't you ask that man in the bathroom to save you?"

"Did you see him? I wouldn't get near someone like that!"

Finn's nature is my blessing.

OUT IN NATURE. Flying down the two-lane. No one is cruising in the wilds of Maine after midnight, so we're free! Curves galore in both hands. One on the wheel and the other on her tit. She's hot and horny and eager to please when I unzip and release my rocket.

Speedometer says we're at 80 and I'm guessing that's right 'cause the headlights can't even keep up with the rushing view.

The girl's lipstick is a bright red. I think. Let's say it is. She's doing it slathered up and down on me and god damn this shit is the life! I have it all! Those lips dip deep and—

—an animal darts into the road. A rat-like thing. Possum? I swerve, aiming for it—skid, over-correct, and we're flying, end-over-end, WHAM!, scoot low to crouch, WHAM!, the roof flattens, WHAM! these are my last thoughts and WHAM! we slide and jar to a chilling stop. Am I alive?

Settle with smoke and hiss and the devastating knowledge of what my destruction has cost.

The hiss becomes crickets.

I turn to look. The girl's no longer in one piece.

Seatbelt clicks open. Pull myself out. Pain. Something might be broken.

The car sighs. I collapse beside the twisted wreckage. Thank god no one can see me sob.

WHAT AM I DOING?

"I'M HUNGRY!" Finn yells.

I pull off the highway at the next exit. It's a country road with no houses or shops. Just a field of cows munching their cud.

"We'll eat here," I say.

"Do I look like I eat GRASS!" Finn screams.

I grab the bag of snacks from the gas station and step to the back of the van. Spread two ginger ales, a plastic container of cheesy nachos, and two hotdogs on the built-in table. Finn hops from his seat and joins me. He stares at the meal.

"You're kidding," Finn says, pushing a finger into the orange goo on top of the nachos. "What is this? It's not cheese."

"It's close. It looks like cheese. Really orange cheese."

"I won't eat it."

"This cheese is part of our disguise. Remember, we're incognito. We need to fit in among the populous."

"What populous? The cows? Anyway, I don't mingle with the populous. They're dirty, ignorant plebeians."

"Where do you get these words, Finn?"

"It's Findley!"

"Remember, our game? You call me Izzy and I call you Finn."

"Fuck you, E-LIZ-A-BETH."

I realize this is not the time to modify his mind so I take a bite of the hotdog hoping to demonstrate that we're moving on. It's not even warm. Was it ever? I'll die from salmonella.

"Didn't they sell anything edible?" Finn says, sounding a little more plaintive than he probably intended.

Poor kid. He might not be a hopeless cause.

I swallow the tepid bite. "I'm doing this for you."

"Doing what?"

"Never mind. Eat and we'll get on the road."

"You eat. I have scruples." He stomps back to his seat.

I dump the food in the bag, return to my spot behind the wheel, and toss him the lodging magazine. "Young sir, do me the kindness of perusing this journal to look for accommodations."

Finn looks excited to have a mission. Only pretty soon he finds out we can't use the lodging mag, because we have no idea where we are. And we can't use the atlas to find out where we are, because we have no idea where we are.

It's getting dark and we check the signs at each exit for a place to stay. Finally pull off the highway to the pink neon vacancy sign of a Motel. As we park by the office, Finn screams. "I WANT TO GO HOME!"

He's cranky because he's hungry and tired and I should cut him some slack and—

I grab his wrist and shake it roughly. "Listen good, little shit. Your ass is kidnapped and we ain't going home 'til the ransom comes in. I ain't jiving you."

Finn is truly stunned. His little mouth opens in a silent impersonation of someone singing "oooooooo."

"I've got jokers with me here, there, and everywhere. You can't escape. Don't even think of callin' the fuzz. Every fucker we come in contact with is in on the lowdown. You think it's a fluke we pulled off here? Think again, sucker. This entire trip was planned out the wazoo. I'm gonna get us our pad for the night. Check it out, it'll blow your mind."

Everything I say startles me. We drop down out of the van and Finn is much smaller than usual.

The office bell jangles as we enter. A wide man steps to the counter from the back room. "Can I help you?"

"'Evenin', friend. Looking for a room. One on the end, if that's available. Two beds, me and my brother."

"I can do that. Credit card?"

"Greenbacks."

Getting out the cash, I glance at Finn. He is watching intently, wondering whether this man is an accomplice.

"Looks like it might rain," I say, using the only code dialogue I remember from movies.

"Might at that. Chance of a storm," the man says.

"And with lightning comes—"

"Thunder," he says with a grin.

I put up my fist and he bumps his on mine.

That was clearly a programmed, coded exchange and I see that belief in Finn's wide eyes.

We drive down to the room at the end of the row. In the back of the van, I paw through the shopping bags full of the items I'd stashed in the Audi for the last few months.

Finn stares at all the clothes he never noticed were missing. "That's my pajama and my shirt and my favorite jeans! You're a kidnapper AND a thief!"

"If you don't shut your fuckin' trap, I'll be a murderer as well. Get in the room." *When did I turn so mean?*

Inside, I set out his night clothes and toothbrush as Finn stands staring at the orange patchwork bedspreads, matching drapes, brown and yellow shag carpet, and painting of a hunter shooting a deer.

"Is this real? It looks like a movie set."

I know his brain is working on the bedbugs, germs, mold, and unknown fluids circulating everywhere. He's going to insist on finding, at minimum, a Hilton if he thinks this is real.

"It's not real, but it's not for a movie. It's part of the kidnapping plan."

This seems to ease Finn's mind. He nods, impressed. "How much money are you asking for?"

"You don't need to know."

"I want to know what I'm worth."

"You be a person. Ain't no person that's 'posed to be sold."

"But you are selling me, right? Back to Mother and Father?"

"Reckon so."

"And if they don't pay?"

"I expect they'll endeavor to proffer the requested sums."

"If they don't pay, you'll kill me. That's what kidnappers do," Finn offers a bit tentatively.

There's a horrible feeling in me, like when you're about the throw up, but the building force isn't in my stomach, it's all over my body. My mouth twists and—"They will pay! *Sie sind der* golden child! *Das* perfect hero—and I'm sorry, young sir, your genteel countenance—piss-ant cheating chip off the ol' mother-fuckin' blockhead—the quintessential manifestation of Anglo-

Saxon patriarchal dominance—and I dinnea care a shillin' for your lot in their big fancy house—where I reckon you're the apple of their—motherfuckin' rich-ass eye."

Finn stares at me. I want to step to the mirror to see if all those voices changed how I look but when my brother's mouth sputters—"I—I—," I turn and my right fist grabs little Finn by his collar and lifts him off the ground so he's dangling in his shirt. *What am I doing?* The muscles in my arm bulge absurdly. *I don't have muscles. How can I do this?* Finn's eyes grow brims of white seeing my weightlifter veins rise.

"You better shut that trap or I'll bury your cock in a shoebox like a dead hamster," my mouth says.

Finn whimpers. My fist opens and he drops to the shag carpet where my left foot slams him in the chest, pinning him flat. *I would never do this!* I try to lift my foot but it won't move. Finn looks panicked. Tears streak from his eyes. I want to apologize, but my body spins from him and steps toward the door. Shit! I *am* crazy! Doctor Sanford missed it! It's the multiple-personality disorder! I need to warn Finn, tell him to call the police. I try to turn around to suggest this, but I'm stuck in place, facing the door. *Help me, Finn! Can't you tell something's wrong?*

Behind me are sounds of Finn sliding into bed and pulling up the covers. The bedside light goes out.

When I can move, I'll call 911.

Reckon that'd be a wrong choice.

No Fuzz. You get your ass in bed, girlie.

Aye, sleep, lass. Cannae do naught t'night.

It's not me doing it, but I slide the chain lock on the door and get in bed.

I'm so scared.

There, there. My left hand strokes my temple lightly. *You don't need to be afraid, Miss. It's just us, your fellow travelers.*

Someone, deep in me, sings a lullaby—Bà Bà mo Leanabh Beag. I cannae understand a word.

KELLY — POTTER COUNTY, PENNSYLVANIA — 1911

THE BAYLESS PAPER PULP AND PAPER COMPANY is lookin' for men. Since they built the dam a few years afore we came, they're busy as cats at kippers. The town is thrivin' and everyone 'as a full larder.

Alex's got a mind to join the paper factory. I dinnae have a good feelin' for him workin' near toxic stuffs, but I cannae rightly object on feelin's.

"Pray, let's stroll up tae the place so I's can get a look. If y'r tae work there, I want tae have the view in me mind."

"Y're not one for strollin' with the load you carryin', lammie."

"I'll be seein' the place or be puttin' a foot doon aboot ye workin' there."

And he dinnae argue.

Cannae bring Boy-O wi us as the wee fella's become quite the protector o' me and we cannae ken who 'e'll take on. Poor lad's nae happy tae be shut inside the cottage and makes it well known.

Alex 'elps me ontae Ol' Brick and we lumber up Cochron Hollow and the river valley of Freeman Run toward the mill. It's a long way up with a slow ornery mule carryin' my heavy load but we feel our approach via mechanical sounds, and thrummin' air, and growin' smell of sulphur, and finally make the top where the massive assortment of concrete buildings rests. Smoke billows oot of several tall towers and from multiple sections o' the plant. 'Tis true there's a stench of something not quite right to breathe.

A blustery type fellow who may be a foreman comes stompin' oot o' a building lookin' to ask what we're up tae. Afore we can explain, the honk and rumbling of an automobile gets Ol' Brick brayin' and backin' off and rearin' and Alex leaps to grab the lead and I'm tippin' and me man takes my waist t'keep me seated as the car skids tae a stop.

This vehicle 'tis a sight tae behold. Long and polished tae a luxurious sheen. The driver hops oot tae open the door for the back passenger.

A well dressed gent emerges and heads in our direction as the foreman whips his cap docile-like from his head. This fancy fellow with his fastidious hair, clipped mustache joining up aside his ears, gold pince-nez spectacles, and tailored suit steps up tae us directly and puts a hand oot tae me fella.

"Terribly sorry to frighten your beast. I'm Mr. George Bayless. To whom do I have the pleasure?"

Alex responds with the handshake and "Alex MacLellan."

Just as I'm wonderin' how a person's skin can be so clean, the man turns tae me, his hand oot and upturned like I'm supposed tae drop a penny in it. "Ma'am, my sincere apologies. Are you alright?"

I'm sure not droppin' a penny in those cupped fingers so I offer me 'and instead. He takes it and gives the back a light kiss. I never in all me bornd days 'ad somethin' sae odd take place. He returns me 'and 'n' bows.

"Mister Bayless," I say. "Yer factory 'tis quite an impressive conglomeration."

"Let me show you the most magnificent wonder I've built. If you'll join me in my automobile, I'll take you up to view it."

Alex quickly hands Ol' Brick's lead to the foreman fella and we slide into the vehicle. It smells of rich people air. The seats are soft and smooth and in a moment we're rumbling up a side road behind the paper mill.

"Half a mile to go," Mr. Bayless says.

And after another few moments of luxury, we pull over and the driver opens our door.

Beside the road 'tis a monstrous wall of concrete.

Mr. Bayless tells us about it. "It's a wonder of modern engineering. This dam is fifty-feet high, five-hundred and forty feet long. Made of thick reinforced concrete."

I know I should be impressed but I've seen the White Cliffs of Dover and this cannae compare. Besides, I'd rather sit in the automobile and pretend I'm a lady.

Mr. Bayless continues. "Behind this impenetrable wall is all the water we need for the mill. 200 million gallons. A never ending supply. Come."

He leads us down a set of stairs to a grassy bank aside this huge dam. My feet sink into the soggy wet ground.

"Oh, nae, Mister Bayless," I say as I step backwards.

"Have no fear. It's just a little normal seepage. This damn is unbreakable."

"I innae worried for the dam, but, let's nae ge farther—we'll track mud intae yer beautiful car."

FINN DRIVING

A CAR DOOR SLAM wakes me. I open my eyes to the painting of the deer getting shot. The rumble of a motor starting up, crunching on gravel, and disappearing. Where am I? The motel and hurting Finn rushes back into my mind. What was that slam? Him getting into a stranger's car? Was that motor him leaving? Has he found someone to take him home?

After what I did last night, that would probably be best. I can't change him. He's a too-fully-formed entitled jerk. And I'm crazy. I'll hurt him instead of helping. Please be gone, Finn.

I turn in the wrinkled sheets.

Finn is sitting at the edge of his bed, staring at the carpet.

I want to say good morning, but nothing comes out, so I get up and pack our things.

Finn won't look at me. I don't blame him. I've got to figure out how to deal with my craziness.

We get in the Metro Van and he doesn't even put up a fight or complain or anything. As we drive along the country road, I glance at him. He's staring at his shoes.

It makes me sad to see him so cowed. I guess I scared both of us.

I wish there was something—

My mouth takes over. "You're a fine fellow, Mister Findley. I would appreciate your assistance."

"Why are you talking like that?"

"Quite an observant gent, I dare say. Come join me on this bench. My companion wearies of commandeering this carriage."

Finn gives me the finger. "You're nuts!"

And although I agree with him, my mouth says, "Get your scrawny ass over here and take the wheel."

Finn's eyes widen. "Really?"

My right hand lets go of the wheel. *Oh FUCK! Did I do that?*

No, girlie, you didn't. I did. Right arm—Dragon Lady.

Wait a minute. My right arm, that has always been tough and sinewy and weathered, is from a different person?

Damn straight.

I'm definitely crazy.

Finn unbuckles his seatbelt and rushes to scrunch beside me, carefully taking the wheel and staring at the road intently. My left hand tousles my brother's hair. Finn jerks his head away.

I didn't do that. My left hand did it on its own. Don't tell me this left arm, the one with the mannish wrist, freckles on pink skin, and curly fluffy hairs—is someone else?

That'd be me, Miss Elizabeth. Simon. Pleased to make your acquaintance.

I'm having a mushroom trip relapse! I've got the multiple-personality disorder! I need to get to a phone and call Doctor Sanford. I should retake the wheel but my arms don't move. FUCK!

I think loudly—*I know you don't exist and I don't want you here, Simon, Dragon Lady. You need to leave!*

Nein.

WHAT? Who's speaking German!?

That's Heinrich, Elizabeth, allow me to endeavor an—

I think louder—*LEAVE!!!!*

'taint possible.

We your kin.

Ancestors.

You're stuck with us, 'cause we're stuck in your genes.

"Young man, keep the wheel steady. You're doing splendidly," my mouth says.

Finn grins as he steers.

My KIN? Fuck!!! Not only did my DNA not get stirred, but that DNA still has ancestral personalities attached? Right Arm—Dragon Lady. Left Arm—Simon. How many more are in here?!

My right leg, the plump one darker than the rest of me, presses up and down on the gas. *'Tis me 'ere, lass. Kelly's the name.*

My left leg, the one that's so muscular, twitches. *Ich bin Heinrich.*

My forehead with the spiderweb scars furrows. *Reckon you wonder 'bout me. I'm Ruby.*

A thump in my chest—my heart?—*Ich bin Solveig, Fräulein.*

I'm a complete mess! I've always been a mess on the outside but I never knew I was such a mess on the inside! Not only do I have ancestors in me but they're female and male and Germans and who knows what else! I could be filled with horrible people! Tears run down my cheeks—or someone's cheeks—I'm pretty sure they're my tears—and drip off my chin onto my brother's neck.

"Are you spitting on me?" Finn asks, gripping the wheel tightly.

Somehow I get my mouth back to answer. "I just feel kinda teary right now, Finn."

"It's Findley! Go cry on someone else. I'm driving."

A flood of despair and hopelessness overwhelms me. This can't be real. It has to be that I'm crazy.

My left hand strokes my temple. That's—what's his name?—Simon?

It is, Miss. I don't think you met Jenny yet. Ma'am?

My tongue rolls across my teeth. *I'm Jenny. Suffragette. Dear girl, it's the indoctrination of the feminine that conditions you to question your sanity should aberrations arise. But I wasn't crazy, and neither are you.*

PARTY TIME

LET ME TAKE A GUESS. You forgot what today is. My big day at the nuthouse. My make-or-break day. My let's-see-if-vomiting-meds-on-growing-vegetables-does-indeed-imbue-them-with-drugs day.

The crudités are cut. The celery, radishes, peppers, carrots, and cauliflower, are all arranged beautifully. The kitchen roasted my beets, turnips, parsnips, and potatoes and these are spread artistically over several trays. I've stashed my cash in my shoes and hope I've not forgotten anything. Doctor Pierson granted me access to a CD player, so I put on a mix of inoffensive light jazz.

It's Friday, so there should be several of the staff very ready to PARTY!

The sun lowers, shining through the wavy panes as Nurse Blinky arrives. "Good evening, Elizabeth. How are we feeling?"

"Wonderful, Nurse. And you?"

"All copacetic. Look at this spread! You've outdone yourself. This is quite an extravaganza."

The nurses and orderlies and Hazeem the janitor/handyman and Doctor Pierson all arrive. The greenhouse gets crowded. I didn't even know there were this many people working here. Everyone is munching and crunching the freshly grown vegetables. Doctor Pierson disappears and returns with a bottle of wine. This opens the floodgates of permission and everyone seems to have a flask or bottle to share.

I have no idea what effect the meds in the veggies will create, if anything, but adding alcohol can't help but bolster my goal.

Everyone looks normal so far. A lively party, but not at all heading for drug-induced mania. Maybe my plan won't work.

Nurse Blinky undoes the top button of her uniform.

I change the music.

The rave mix. This gets the group moving to the beat and one after another gets in the groove and they dance! The panes of the greenhouse shudder under the thumping feet.

Doctor Pierson catches the rhythm wildly. His comb-over sticks to his forehead in an upside-down question mark as he bounces on an invisible pogo stick.

How can I possibly get under the table, push out the glass held in with the gum, and skip off across the grounds without being noticed? It's a long expanse of grass before the forest edge. The sun has gone below the distant trees, but anyone looking will see me.

Heinrich tenses when Dragon Lady orders *GET MOVING* in my head.

I can't do this, I think.

You must endeavor to escape, prods Jenny.

I can't!

Ja. You can. Du musst, Solveig insists.

I'm sure you can, Miss.

Och, lass, jes geeit a try.

Ruby takes over, making my hips move in a slow grinding circle, a dance of lust. All eyes are on me—the opposite of what I need right now.

I feel a jolt as Ruby usurps my tongue and yells, "Nurse!"

Nurse Blinky turns, looking blurrily at me.

"Get your body over here," Ruby orders.

Everyone freezes and tennis-courts their eyes back and forth between the nurse and me. Nurse Blinky takes a waltz step, a rumba step, a samba step, and we're face to face. Her breath hits my face, warm and moist.

Ruby rides my hand over Nurse Blinky, not touching, but very close. Rides it across that landscape. Hips, waist, breasts, neck...

Everyone watches.

Ruby nods for Doctor Pierson to join in. Doctor Pierson happily hurries over. Now I'm sandwiched between him and Nurse Blinky. Not exactly the escape I had planned. Ruby spins the doctor so all three of us are facing the same way, crotch to butt, crotch to butt. We're gyrating against each other and Ruby shimmies up and down and does a pirouette to face Nurse Blinky and spins her and now Nurse's pressing against Doctor Pierson's butt and they get the rhythm and Ruby yells, "EVERYONE" and it works. Everyone joins in, moving together, body to body.

Orderlies gyrate with eyes closed. Nurses wave their hands in front of their faces, mesmerized by what they see. Shirts are removed. Shoes kicked off. Uninhibited ecstasy shines on every face. They're all tripping.

I dance toward the potting table, drop to my knees, slide under, and pause. No one comes down to check on me. I inch off the lowest pane that's held in with the black gum and as I set it outside, Nurse Blinky drops to the floor. SHIT! She sees me and blinks. I'm so screwed. Simon (left arm) waves to greet her. Nurse Blinky waves back and laughs. She points to the lower halves of dancing bodies we can see from under the table. "Everyone's wanting more."

"Vegetables?" I ask.

"Life."

I nod and she shifts closer to me, almost leaning against where the glass is gone. If she blocks it or falls out, my escape plan is kaputt.

Nurse Blinky whispers, "Lots going on. Too much color," and she closes her eyes. As the bass thuds and the floor bounces with many feet, Nurse Blinky's face drops all tension and becomes that of a beatific angel. Her mouth hinges open and her breathing slows. Snoring starts.

Leave now.

94

I carefully squiggle out the window, tuck myself close to the greenhouse wall, and press the glass back against the black chewing gum. Nurse Blinky shifts, tilting, leaning, until she drops gently across the floor, covering the window.

Heinrich (left leg) raises me to my feet and we all race into the wide yard. *Please don't let anyone notice—*

WHAP! Cold sharp bits hit my leg and gunfire and mortar shells erupt. I dive to the ground in terror, but it's only the sprinkler's spray and rhythmic *whap*. All other sounds are in my head—I mean, Heinrich's leg.

My right hand (Dragon Lady) grabs my face roughly, slaps me, and sets out a finger, pointing to the forest as in—*FINISH LINE!*

I don't know why I get slapped when it is Heinrich's fault, I think as I scramble to my feet.

My right hand punches my left leg. *Better?*

I do feel better yet should be careful not to start an internal war.

Heinrich and Kelly get both legs working, but at different speeds and not exactly in similar directions. When we finally make it to the trees, I look back. The greenhouse is glowing in the darkness. The pounding bass throbs. Everyone is having so much fun. It makes me sad that no one even notices I'm gone.

With Heinrich and Kelly commanding their legs, I hobble through the forest. They can't get coordinated.

Up ahead are lights. Maybe a place of refuge.

I try to set a rhythm by humming a song, but Heinrich doesn't like the pace and won't join in. Kelly stomps on his foot and he kicks her ankle. Dragon Lady punches Heinrich's leg.

"Stop! I'm the one gonna have bruises!" I whisper.

I feel all their eyes on me. Can that be? Do they even have eyes?

For a moment nothing happens, then Kelly and Heinrich walk in sync toward the lights. It's a Quick Stop. No cars around. We step closer, nearing the gas pumps out front.

Suddenly Ruby pulls my nuthouse shirt over my head, undoes my bra, and tosses them in the trash bin. My somewhat-symmetrical breasts object to the cold air and I'm not likin' whatever this plan is, but Heinrich propels me forward. Kelly objects and jams my shoe against the gas pump. There must be a discussion far from my consciousness because Kelly relents and we move forward. Whatever is happening, I'm not doing it. I've no choice but to follow.

Breasts bare and nipples at attention, we push open the door to the Quick Stop. The ringing bell raises the bored cashier's head from his phone. His eyes move low on me. He doesn't see the hospital pants, the hospital wrist-bracelet, or the hospital shoes. He sees my breasts. End of story.

"Help me, please," my voice says, quivering. "My boyfriend's gone crazy. Can you drive me to the police?"

The fellow grimaces at my chest. "I can't leave. I'll call the police."

"He'll be here before they can get here. He's got a gun. He'll kill you and me both."

The guy looks around the store as if others are waiting to provide their input. No one's there. He looks back at me.

My two arms move to hug each other, ostensibly because I'm cold, but deliberately pressing my breasts into a tight package of interest. Deliberately not covering my nipples.

Heinrich spins me to face the door. Solveig turns my head back, terrified. "PLEASE!" comes from her like she's on that wildflower-covered hillside overlooking Frankfurt.

The boy makes several motions behind the counter and the gas pump lights go out, the sign goes out, the store lights go out. He hurries toward the storefront, passing me with his eyes you-know-where, assuming I won't notice in the dark, and flicks the front door lock.

"Come on. Out back."

We follow him through the storeroom and exit the rear door. It slams and we all jump 'cause it sounds like mortars, or jail cell doors, or buildings shattering, or …

"I'm Pete, you're…?"

"Shit, I hear his truck!" one of us yells and we all race to follow Pete into his rusted yellow Kia. He starts it up and curls it out from behind the building with a puttering whir. Not the stuff of drama. That boyfriend would have caught us.

Pete breathes heavily for about three minutes. He keeps his eyes on the road except to check if my breasts are okay.

"Do you, Pete, have maybe an extra shirt or jacket or something?"

Pete shrinks like I found him out and he looks around the back seat while driving. "No. Uh, no. Sorry, uh I don't have anything…"

Chivalry is dead.

Some itch in his brain must tell him to keep searching for a solution and finally he gets an idea and, driving with one hand and then the other, pulls off his t-shirt and hands it to me.

He looks more awkward being shirtless than I. Probably imagines I'm judging his thin shoulders, sunken chest, and hairless pecs. I am, but he doesn't need to know that.

"You've a nice chest," my voice says. I don't know who is talking but it's a stupid thing to say. "I've always liked a man's chest like yours."

Pete looks up to the ceiling of the car, as if he'll meet his erection there. "Th-th-thanks. I like yours."

My hand moves to his thigh. Not everyone thinks this is a good idea. It's heading in a bad direction. Images flood me. A campfire, a relentless man pounding away in the bed, the Central Park Model Yacht …

"Have you ever had a lady in one of these coaches, Pete?" *Who is that talking?*

Pete blinks several times. "In a car? Sure, I mean, one time, but only once—"

My voice curls seductively in my throat. "Looks like you have a roomy chaise in the back of this wagon. Find us a secluded spot." *That's gotta be Ruby.*

Pete doesn't need prompting. He zooms the car off the next exit, takes the first road leading to no-lights, and pulls to the shoulder. Corn stalks surround us.

Pete hops out of the car and opens the back door.

We call out the window, "Take your pants off before you get in. It's easier to do than when we're lying there. Don't want to slow things down wrestling with those."

Pete dives into the project at hand. Zipper—pull pants low—oh, first the boots—unlace, hopping—

A twinge of sympathy and we slide to the driver's side.

Pete falls backwards, pulling at his other boot.

Key turns. Engine putters. Glance in the side mirror. On the ground, pants around his ankles, Pete looks confused. Simon waves an apologetic goodbye out the window, as Kelly steps on the gas and Dragon Lady steers us onto the road and toward some future.

DRAGON LADY — WHITLEY COUNTY, KENTUCKY — 1962

OF COURSE, THE CAMPING TRIP with Beau was scheduled before the jerk stole my first-place position in the Log Race. If I cancelled now, he'd say I was scared to face him, so here we are, about to spend the weekend with the asshole. Unless I can lose the car behind me.

I press the pedal to the metal and bounce over the dirt road.

Jack grabs the dashboard and shouts, "Slow down, Maxine! We're not in a race."

"Don't gimme that jive. You don't know shit, Jack. Everything's a race."

Hubby grumbles, "All I'm sayin' is, take it easy."

"I aim to do like ol' Woody Guthrie says—take it easy, *but take it!*"

The road rises steeply and I jam my cigarette in my mouth to maneuver the wheel with both hands, swirl the station wagon around the curve, and spin it like I'm driving my Indian motorcycle. Don't have to look to know Jack's gripping the armrest. Reach the peak of the hill and the world drops out below—a steep slope—Jack yells!—I SLAM us to a skid, RAM the column shift to *Park*, STOMP the emergency brake flat—and we rock to a stop.

Below us, idyllically secluded in the trees, is a campsite with a fire pit and picnic table. Stretching beyond is a lake surrounded by fall-painted leaves. Mountains behind that. Looks perfect, like in a hardware store calendar.

I step out, dragging my fingers through my spiky leather-black hair. The mannish haircut Jack hates. Spit on the glow-end of my cigarette and flick it to the ground.

Jack lets go a curse of relief that we didn't careen off the hill. Times like these he probably wonders why we got married. A head-shrinker might offer that I chose him because I want to prove I'm as good as a man and so picked a weak one, but who gives a shit about what a shrink thinks.

"Head's up, Cracker Jack," I yell. "Get the tent. I'll tend to libations," and I fast-ball him the keys. They zing his chest before he can raise a hand. Ouch!

Carrying the picnic basket and metal cooler, I trot down the slope as Jack does what he's told.

Up above, Beau's blue Rambler skids to a stop beside our wagon.

I stick two fingers in my mouth and send a shrill whistle up. The sound carries across the lake and back.

Beau yells from above, "You didn't lose me. Try as you might."

"You came in second, like you always do," I shout.

As the guys carry down the tent and sleeping bags, I lay out the accoutrements on the picnic table. Three bottles of Gilbey's gin, bottle of vermouth, two olive jars, plastic sword swizzle sticks, four martini glasses (an extra in case one breaks), and a jigger. I wait until Jack and Beau plop onto the bench facing me before I get the show goin'.

Now that I've got an audience, I sing the melody to "The Stripper" hit to slowly tease my Second Place Log Race trophy from the picnic basket. Beau gives a Bronx Cheer. I ignore him, breathing on the shiny surface and buffing the silver with my sleeve. Scoop a handful of ice into it, add four jiggers of gin and one for the pot, a dash of vermouth, a splash of olive brine, place my hand over the top, and SHAKE.

Beau and Jack watch. I smile at them, showing teeth. The ice is painfully cold against my hand but they'll never guess that. Fuck em. They probably think I'm highlighting a sore-spot, shaking my second-place trophy. I am. I won the fuckin' race. I'll shake it in their faces.

Only, they aren't looking at my trophy. They're looking at my tits. Watching them jiggle with each jerk of the sauce. I'll give you something to ogle! I put my arms over my head and shake the trophy vigorously. Take that, you motherfuckers!

Shit, my hand is cold. I pour the drinks, straining the ice between my fingers. There is a perfect amount of shard-floe on top. Skewer olives with a sword for each drink, keeping eye contact with each guy during the spearing.

Beau grins at me as I hand him the drink. "Thank you, sweetheart. You've got talent at one thing, at least."

Asshole.

I take a hit from the icy liquid. It burns nicely. "Smoke 'em if you got 'em," I growl, and snatch the Lucky Strike pack from my shirt pocket, give it a jerk to make one pop up, and grab the cig with my teeth. Open a matchbook, but I'm out. Beau tosses me his bronze lighter. It's got B.T. engraved on the side. I set the flame to my cigarette and pocket the lighter in my jeans. Let's see him try to get it back.

BEINGS AND NOBODY

WHEN WE REACH A TOWN, Finn declares, "Too many people and trucks. You drive!" He hops over to his seat and I grab the wheel, or someone does. Am I in control of my body again? Have I ever been?

They said they were ancestors in my genes. Finn and I have the same ancestors, these same genes.

"Finn, do you ever feel like you have—I don't know, relatives, ancestors, grandma or grandpa or great-grandparents in your head?"

"Are you nuts?"

He got stirred, I didn't.

I should experiment. That'd be the scientific thing to do. I let go of the wheel. Finn glances over—"I said I was tired!"—and turns to stare out the passenger window.

No one is taking the wheel. Does that mean this Dragon Lady doesn't exist and I'm certifiably crazy? We're drifting a bit. Moving slightly to the right. Will we hit the parking meters? Pedestrians?

I won't steer, I think to them inside. *Not joking. We'll crash…*

My left hand takes the wheel. If I remember, that's Simon. His grip isn't very confident.

Astute observation, Miss. I heard of horseless carriages but never saw one and haven't commandeered one before. But no cause to fret, I observed young Mister Findley.

Just what I need, a novice ancestor in charge.

We're heading for a car parked by the curb—*Hello, you're too far right*—Simon's hand turns the wheel to avoid it, sending us into the oncoming lane and a monster truck headed straight for us! HONK! The terrified look on the approaching driver's face. "AHHHHH!" The terrified yell from Finn. "WATCH OUT!" The terrified scream from me. "NOOOO!" HONK!!! Dragon Lady grabs the wheel and circular tug-o-war takes place between my left and right hands—HONK! HONK! HOOONNNNKKKK!!!!—until

101

someone bends my head to bite Simon's wrist, he lets go, we swerve back into our lane, and the truck roars—HOOOONnnn~~kkk~~—past.

"Are you trying to kill us?!" yells Finn, shaking with adrenaline and fury.

"Not that I know of!"

"Well, don't!"

I have to calm down. Get all of me—do I call myself us?—to calm down. Simon has his arm tucked behind my back. Is he hurt and pouting? Who bit him? Dragon Lady has the wheel. She holds it like a pro.

I am a pro.

This isn't happening. None of this is real.

Elizabeth, endeavor to breathe in slowly and exhale—

I don't know which one you are, but can I have a fuckin' minute to NOT have someone talking in my head?

Silence. Good. I stare out the windshield watching the road lines fly below the Metro Van as the so-called Dragon Lady drives.

After I calm down, I get to thinking. Not that I believe any of this, but Simon said he'd heard of horseless carriages. So if this was really true, he's from a long time ago. Might as well go along with this charade for a bit. I ask in my head if the others know about cars or how to drive.

Heinrich answers *Ja.*

Solveig whispers, *Ich know das auto but don't know how to drive—I'm only 16.*

Sixteen! Being ancestors, I thought they'd be grandparent ages. *How old are you all?*

The others answer. Heinrich is 22, Kelly is 18, Simon 21, Ruby 24, Dragon Lady, 28, Jenny is the oldest at 30, and—*anyone else?*

No answer. So, ostensibly, I have seven people inside and most aren't much older than me.

I'm so fucked.

Maybe Izzy isn't really a person but an amalgam of people. Maybe Izzy doesn't even exist. I always knew I was a nobody, but what if I really am *nobody*?

That hurts. I'm not even somebody. I'm people. A crowd.

My left arm inches out from behind my back. *Pardon the intrusion, Miss.*

Is that Simon?

Yes.

You're the polite one.

I do my best, but one doesn't always succeed. At any rate, perhaps you've heard of the writer Walt Whitman. I'm an admirer of his poetry. He wrote, "I contain multitudes." Perhaps you and he are similar.

Somehow this doesn't make me feel better.

Ever since I can remember I've had not only dreams but visions of lives that weren't mine. One minute I'm walking down the hall at Rothschild's Academy and the next I'm dragged down a long shiny hall to a terrifying room. One minute I'm in my slippers and the next I'm in muddy combat boots. A caw of the crow or the clip-clop of horses' hooves or sounds of rushing water floods me with fear. This makes me think all of this stuff about ancestors inside me really could be true. And what about my body doing things I had no control over? The reasons I went to Doctor Sanford...

You all have been hiding for a while, I think to them, *but you were pretty active back when I beat up people. I didn't do that. You did. That plastic surgeon and my poor teacher Mr. Marks.*

Girlie, you're nutzo to feel sorry for that pecker-ass. He was hell-bent on gettin' into your panties. 'Predator-eyes' bullshit. You was prey. (Okay, I'm guessing that's Dragon Lady. She's the curser.)

I explain to her. *I loved Mr. Marks. He was an ally and even asked to kiss—*

I cannae believe you're as daft as all that. Yer a bonnie lass an' it's aboot time y'ken that e'ry lad'll try t' get in yr knickers. (Kelly's got the British accent.) *Nae! T'aint ne'er o'that lot. I'm a Scot and proud t'be.*

I had to fight those men disrespecting you, Miss. I wasn't going to let that happen to you. (Simon with his Miss and Mister.)

Reckon that teacher got what was coming to him. (Ruby always says reckon with a western accent.)

Patriarchal dominance makes you doubt your experience. (Jenny sounds so formal.)

Ich wurde raped.

What was that?! *Solveig, you were raped?* I ask.

Ja.

Reckon given my occupation it's a mite strange but, me as well. The pecker-ass bastard knocked me out to do it.

Images flood me. A hill of flowers, juke-joint backroom, a shack, a broken mirror, the swing of a flaming branch. Glimpses of these rapes.

In my left arm, Simon trembles. *I did that crime, Miss.*

Und, Solveig adds, *Heinrich did das to mir.*

My right leg shakes in anger. *Das ist eine lie!*

I can't believe this! I'm a total horror! I have rape victims and rapists in me! How can that happen!? Did *all* my ancestors get raped or rape others?

Izzy, you got seven folk: Solveig, Dragon Lady, Simon, Heinrich, Kelly, Jenny, and me—Ruby. Seven with traumas that got seared into our beings like red-hot branding irons, but they ain't all rapes. Way I figure, it's the trauma that makes us be stuck to you. Seems like you reckon we're an awfully high percentage of ancestors with trauma, but I reckon you're thinkin' wrong. Doing the countin', you got two parents, four grandparents, eight great-grandparents, sixteen great-great, and the numbers double each generation back. Hundreds and hundreds of ancestors ain't got no trauma seared into them, so they aren't in here with you. Thousands of folks related to Izzy ain't got some kind of hell. Reckon they might 'ave had cozy, comfy lives. Happy even!

Okay, okay, I think loudly, *but you were all hidden and gone since my therapy. I can see why you showed up when you thought I was in trouble, but why show up now?*

Girlie, you don't know shit, Dragon Lady thinks with palpable anger. *You can't defend yourself. You can't drive. You can't fuel up the van. Can't shop for food. Can't communicate with normal people. Can't make a plan. You're a dumb-fuck, rich kid with no experience and no skills and you're way outta your depth. We had to intervene to save your ass— 'cause your ass, is our ass.*

DRAGON LADY — WHITLEY COUNTY, KENTUCKY — 1962

THE MARTINI GLASSES broke hours ago. Jack commented on "the incongruity of martini glasses and swizzle sticks in this rustic setting," so I threw them into the fire, shattering all, and sending up blue flames of gin.

I shake booze in the Log Race trophy and slosh this round into a thermos lid, an olive jar, and a used Chock Full o' Nuts coffee cup Jack scrounged from the floor of our Rambler. As I hand a drink to Beau he asks, "Dragon Lady, I'm curious about something. How'd you get to be such a bitch?"

"I'm curious, asshole. What makes a person a bitch?" I ask.

Jack clicks on the transistor radio. "Let's see if we can pick up any music in these here parts—"

"A bitch is a woman who thinks she is equal to a man." Beau smiles, showing Kennedy teeth.

Jack tunes in a station. Elvis, of course.

"You think I'm not equal to you?" I ask Beau.

"I know you're not."

"You're right. I'm not equal. I'm better. Better racer, better—"

Jack turns up the volume as far as it can go and joins Elvis yelling, "DON'T YOU STEP ON MY BLUE SUEDE SHOES!" He's drunk, as we all are.

"Anyone hungry?" I grab the steaks from the ice chest. "Jack, set up the grill up so we can get these beauties scorching. Beau, tell me what you think JFK is doing wrong."

VAN DINNER

WE DRIVE ALL DAY and Finn takes a turn whenever the traffic is light. He's getting good at it and I tell him so. Since I still have my foot on the gas (or Kelly does), he has to scrunch next to me on the driver's seat to steer. I look at him tucked in close. His little arms grabbing at ten-and-two. The back of his neck, thin and pale. A vibration comes from his body—a pent-up energy— simmering against my torso. This is the closest we've ever been. I don't remember the two of us ever touching before. No one touches in our family. Father shook hands and slapped backs. Mother did air kisses. Finn'd never say, but I think we both like this.

As for my private Trauma Group, they seem to have retreated into some hinterland. I'm glad. I need a break from that crowd.

Every once in a while Finn comments on the strange world speeding by. "Look at that shack," or "Those people have chickens!" or "I don't want to see another tree for the rest of my life!" But mostly he repeats, "Where are we going? When are we going to get there? When can we stop? How much is the ransom? Do you have a real plan, or is this all fake?" I remind him I'm a badass with accomplices all over, but I'm not sure he's buying that anymore.

The sun is low and it's getting darker, so when we stop to refuel, I suggest we go into the market next door to buy dinner. "Maybe they have something ready-made. Fried chicken. Salads. Cold cuts. Or sandwiches, if you like."

"I know what dinner is," he says impatiently. "Give me money. I'll get it. You stay here."

He's going to escape if I let him go alone. "I'll go with you."

"NOOOOO! I want to pick food out and have it be a surprise!"

I explain that I'll stay far away from his shopping cart and let him buy whatever without me seeing, but I'm not letting him go in alone. And I do just that.

At the checkout, he glances back to see me watching and Dragon Lady raises my fist, so he slumps and doesn't look at the cashier and shrugs to whatever she's saying.

When we return to the van, he dumps the plastic bags of groceries at his feet and points to a motel across the street. "Let's sleep there."

I'm scared of what I did in the motel last night, so drive past the motel. I won't stop for lodging until I can confer with my inner horde and insist that they behave.

"My butt is sore and I want OUT!" Finn screams.

"Got a place lined up just a little farther."

"NOOOOOOOOOO!!!!!"

Finn grabs the plastic bags and stomps past me to the back of the van.

"Come back here! You need your seatbelt on!"

"I'M SETTING OUT DINNER!"

"GET BACK HERE BEFORE YOU SMASH YOUR HEAD ON SOMETHING!"

Finn stumbles back with the empty plastic bags. He makes a big show of clicking his seatbelt, then rolls down the window and tosses out the bags.

I jam on the brakes, glad he's wearing that seatbelt. "What the hell, Finn! Go get those bags!"

"It's garbage. Someone will pick them up."

"The world isn't full of your personal housekeepers! Get them!"

"No!"

I undo my seatbelt and slide my door open, march down the darkening road to retrieve the bags, and march back.

"See, I told you someone would pick them up," Finn says when I return.

"You know about recycling and pollution, but what you don't know is—plastic bags come in handy!"

Finn snorts. "Name one thing!"

I put the van in drive and get to thinking. I'm going to figure out how to use these bags for something really important.

"Ha, ha, can't think of anything—"

My right arm spins the van abruptly and we leave the highway to go careening down a dirt road. *Dragon Lady?!*

We race through the forest, swishing past trees and bouncing over holes, splashing mud, our stomachs leaping with the jolts.

Dragon Lady, where are we—

"Where are we going?!" Finn screams.

"Takin' your skinny ass into the woods. If you want to sleep in a motel, you can hike back in the dark."

"You're mean!" he says.

"You're a soft, whiney little pecker. I'm gonna toughen you up or kill you tryin'."

Both Finn and I believe her.

Someone jams on the brakes, the van skids to a stop, and Finn jumps out.

He grabs a fallen branch and bashes other trees with it until it shatters. He hurls rocks. He stomps away just far enough to worry himself and stomps back. Figuring he's too scared to escape in the dark, I carefully fold the retrieved plastic bags and carry them to the back of the van.

On the table is the dinner Finn bought at the market. Twinkies, Red Vines, Cheez Whiz, spray Cool Whip, Slim Jims, and Yoo-hoo. Neither of us has ever tasted any of these. I doubt we even know what food groups they belong to.

After placing the folded plastic bags conspicuously at the back edge of the table, I light a candle so I can search the kitchen as it gets darker. Ricardo thought of everything. I set the table with placemats and paper towel napkins, add old-timey enamel plates and not-silver silverware, light more candles for ambiance, and although I know Finn is angry and might smash them, I give us both wine glasses. I open the food and lay out the Twinkies, intersperse Slim Jims and Red Vines among them, and then, like in the finest restaurants, I squirt squiggles of Cheez Whiz and dollops of Cool Whip around the plate-edges. It looks like modern art.

Finn clomps into the van and stops short, staring at the arrangement of his junk food.

Sitting, I spray a line of Cheez Whiz along the length of a Slim Jim, cut off a bite, dip it into a Cool Whip dollop, and eat. Finn watches for a reaction.

"Darling," I say. "This is the apex of fine dining. You simply MUST acquaint yourself with the chef's culinary masterpiece."

Finn straightens up and pinches his lips tight and low, doing his version of an aristocrat. "I do declare, fine dining is my only salvation."

He sits and tucks a paper towel into his collar and holds his silverware with both pinkies out. He serves himself a Twinkie, slices it open longways, lays in several red-vines, and sprays Cool Whip across the top. Takes a bite. "Astonishing. I shall write a five-star review."

I pour Yoo-hoo into the wine glasses and raise mine to him. "To your health, dear fellow."

Finn raises his drink and clinks it with mine. "Jolly good."

The meal digresses. Cheez Whiz and Cool Whip become mustaches and eyebrows and beards, while we smoke Slim Jim stogies. I've never heard Finn laugh so much.

But we both get stomach aches. And we're sticky. It's dark and kinda scary outside when we step out to wash the goo off using a gallon of water. Then we pee on opposite sides of the van and hurry back in. I lock the doors, blow out the candles, and we slide into our bunks. There are a lot of sounds outside. Things we never heard in our building on Central Park West. A dim glow comes through the back door windows. Across the interior of the van, I can see the glint of this light in Finn's wide eyes. He's probably looking for zombies.

I want to say so many things. I want to tell him how much fun I had with his food. How I'm hoping to change him. How I might love him—but I don't say anything.

Outside, wind tickles the van. Crickets or frogs or zombies chirp. Finn whimpers softly. I hop out of my bed and hurry to his bunk.

My left hand reaches for his shoulder and pats gently. His body shakes with silent sobs. Simon's hand moves to my brother's head and strokes his temple.

Finn takes a deep breath and asks, "Why hasn't Father paid the ransom?"

Shit! He's hurt because he thinks Father doesn't love him enough to pay a ransom! Poor kid!

"Finn, I did kidnap you, but I haven't asked Father for money. See, I wanted to give you a look at life outside of those Vision Books. I didn't want you to live out all the planned pages and have a life that wasn't one *you* chose."

Finn jerks his head away from Simon's hand. "But I *want* all those things in the Vision Books. It's who I *want* to be. I hate being here in the dirty countryside. I hate this filthy old van. Eating weird food. Having no phone and NOTHING to do. I want to go HOME and live the life I'm supposed to!"

"We need to give it time—"

"Get off my bed!" he screams.

I slink back to my bunk. I planned the logistics but never imagined what this trip would actually be like. I thought of myself as saving him, but didn't realize he might not want to be saved.

RUBY — BODIE, CALIFORNIA — 1877

THE KNOCK ON THE DOOR wakes me. I glance at the window. It's dark and ain't no sound out yonder but snow hittin' glass.

Slide my Colt from under the mattress and point it at the door. The shakes come to me. Is it Mrs. Reddy again?

"Got a peacemaker pointed at your heart. Come in if'n y' dare."

The door opens on Chan's familiar silhouette. My gun lowers.

He stomps and shakes to knock the snow from him and steps inside, setting his lantern on my bedside table. "Old Chinatown mother make paste for burns."

I thank him and pat the bed. He doesn't hesitate and sits beside me.

Reckon this is what I like about Chan. Like me, he knows he's living in an unequal world, but although he knows the rules, 'taint going to bend to them.

He opens a leather pouch and a strong, sheepy smell rises. Wool grease and herbs. He offers the ointment to me.

I don't move.

Chan nods for me to take it.

I shake my head. "You do it."

The lantern flickers with what just happened. Chan knows and I know. He smiles and slides his hand into the pouch. Fingers covered with shining slime emerge and move toward my shoulder. I open my nightgown and turn my head aside to give him access. He rubs the lotion in—slow and gentle and smooth. His fingers aren't afraid of me.

I turn to face him and it's clear this next notion is the same on both our sides.

"You must have burns, too, Chan. Putting out the flames."

He smiles slightly and looks at his hands.

I scoop out a bit of the ointment and rub it over the back of his hand. It rises to press into my palm, turns to press palm against palm, sliding with the thick grease. It gets my heart racing. Like riding at full gallop across a plain after a storm. A heat rises in my core that isn't there with my clients. I want this man. It's a new feeling.

"No other burns?" I ask, my voice trembling in a way it never does. It makes me want to back away, but—

Chan's moving. Unfastening his shirt. Pushing aside the long braid of black hair. "Burns all over."

I can't help but smile and he can't help but join me. And we're kissing and pointing out more burns and laughing and there is nothing about it that's my profession. T'aint nothing in me I separate from. I lie with the man who has been my paid protector and we relish each other.

TEE PEE MOTEL

WE'RE TWO HOURS from the nuthouse escape party and that cornfield where we left poor Pete with his pants down and stole his Kia. Some of us are fuming.

Solveig shifts angrily inside. "Was ist das, Ruby? Nicht gutte."

"Reckon I don't speak German, Solveig."

Jenny twirls my tongue. "To use the exploitative strategies of the oppressor is to defeat the intention of the cause."

"Reckon I don't speak highfalutin neither!"

Simon waves my left hand to calm things. "Miss Ruby, I believe that what these ladies are trying to express is they don't want you using this body in a sexual manner to—"

"Reckon you don't have no right to say nothing 'bout a woman's body, Mister."

Kelly presses down on the gas pedal. "I dinnae come this far to be showin' men my lassie parts so's they gets to wantin'. They gets tae wantin' and they gets tae takin'."

"I get what y'r saying, but iffn you recollect, we're on the run escapin' the nuthouse and what I did got us this carriage, so don't go whinin'."

"Listen," I say, "we're all exhausted. Let's find a place to sleep and we can make a plan in the morning." I look in the rearview mirror as if I'll see a car full of people, forgetting they're all inside. Simon reaches across Dragon Lady's grip on the wheel and adjusts the mirror so I can see my eyes. I get a jolt. They don't look like my eyes at all. They're hard and cold and—

"Who are you?" I ask.

The eyes morph back into mine. Fuck. I'm not cut out for this.

"Was that any of you? Kelly? Heinrich? Anyone?"

Everyone says it wasn't them.

Do I have another silent *other* along for the ride? That terrifies me.

Rain plunks against the windshield. Intermittent tapping like it's a coded message I'm supposed to understand. Maybe Heinrich knows Morse code.

"Nein," he says.

The rain becomes a much more frantic message.

I pull the wiper knob and the blades swing caught leaves back and forth. A blur of road with every wipe. A streaky light appears and as Dragon Lady drives closer it becomes a green neon VACANCY below the red TEE-PEE MOTEL sign. There is a large ragged tee-pee in the front of an otherwise normal retro motel. We pull into the space nearest OFFICE. I'm about to dart out when Jenny reminds us to get cash from my shoe so I won't have to do it inside. Cash in hand, I dart from the car, hunching against the rain, trying not to get Pete's t-shirt wet and clingy. The door jangles as I enter. I stand patiently, hair dripping. Goose pimples sprout on different parts of my body. Some inside me are feeling ill at ease. Are we being watched? Is it a predator?

He comes out with a smile. White. Thirties. Puffy, like he never leaves his computer monitor.

"Good evening. Just one?"

I'm not about to tell him it's me, plus seven and counting. I nod.

"Name?"

I can't use mine, so I borrow one. "Kelly MacLellan."

"Kelly. I like it. I'm Bradley."

Someone in me gives him a smile in such a way as to look unwelcoming.

"$39.95 for one. You sure it's just one, right?"

I nod, give him cash, and keep nodding until I get the key. Hustle back to Pete's Kia, drive it to the end of the row, and race through the torrent to number 12.

The room smells like cigarettes and chemicals but I don't care. I drop onto the bed and pray to silence my crowded brain.

There is a tap at the door.

No.

It comes again. Slow and insistent.

I'll take care of this motherfucker. I'll bury his—

I open the door to Bradley. Ruby gives him an inquisitive look as Kelly gets ready to kick and Heinrich tenses. Solveig wonders if we can scoot past him and Jenny thinks the bathroom window is too small to crawl out of. Simon holds down Dragon Lady's arm—

"Sorry to bother, Miss MacLellan. You left your headlights on. Might have no juice in the morning if you don't switch 'em off."

Oh.

"Thanks," I say and grab Pete's keys. As I unlock the Kia and push the lights off, I wonder—maybe we should stop assuming every man is a creep.

KELLY — POTTER COUNTY, PENNSYLVANIA — 1911

THE BAIRN IS KICKIN' so I cannae stand it. I cannae sleep or eat or even step outside as the ne'er ending deluge of rain has me penned in. The leak in the roof pings in the catchin' pot and the noise has me ready to scream. E'en wee Boy-O is at the end o' 'is teather. He gi's a whine as if 'tis all my doin'.

"Ach, Boy-O, I ken yer frustration. E'en angry, I'm glad yer 'ere. Who else will listen tae me squalkin' 'boot me troubles? Wi' Alex a' work, 'taint none but ye tae keep me comp'ne."

Write t'yr mah, I imagine Alex would say. *Tell her y'r troubles an' joys and prayers for the babe. After all, we have a treasure of paper for t' do letters noo 'at I'm workin' at the mill.*

I don't want to write to me mah. It'll sound like a rotten life if I put pen t' paper noo.

Boy-O cocks 'is head, lookin' at me odd-like.

"What 'tis it, lad?"

'E raises his nose and sniffs the air, steppin' closer tae me.

A powerful jab stabs me insides.

Boy-O's eyes widen as his nose quivers.

Another jab sends me grabbing the table. *Please not now. Not with Alex at the mill.*

Boy-O steps close, his nose risin' betwixt me legs.

The wee lad ken what's happenin'

I hobble wide-legged tae the door and look oot. Boy-O looks wi' me. The rain 'as stopped. If I can make it across the orchard and doon the slope to Granny Miller's, she could summon Alex and get me help. There's no way t' get myself up onta Ol' Brick withoot fear o' breakin' me neck, so I wrap the oilcloth around me and step oot intae the wet. Another jab pain has me doubled for several breaths, then off I gae wi' Boy-O aside me.

Boy-O barks down the hill tae make Granny look. She sees me huggin' atween the apple trees an' rushes up. "It's time, yes?"

"Aye, 'tis. Ye find a soul t' hurry up tae the paper mill t' fetch Alex an' I'll pull meself back t'home and wait f'r yea 'ere."

"I'll send that Schuler boy. He's got a pony and will get to the mill quickest. You settle in and I'll be there right swift."

Boy-O and I start back, me prayin' the Schuler child will bring Alex t'me afore the babe arrives.

Inside, I lay doon and count atween the pains. Boy-O stands a' the ready for whate're comes next.

ESCAPE

SOMETHING WAKES ME. It's my right hand pinching my nose.

What the hell!?

Wake up, Girlie!

I raise my head and squint at the morning glare blasting in through the front windshield. Eyes blink and my next sight is the table smeared with leftover Cheez Whiz and Cool Whip. It's disgusting. Why is it still like this? Guess I'm also used to someone picking up after me.

Dragon Lady's hand turns my head—Finn's bed is empty.

Shit.

I hurry outside and search around the Metro Van, looking under it and into the thick forest. I can't imagine Finn would have gone into this wilderness. Did he go back on the dirt road?

My right leg leads the way, stepping along the muddy tire ruts. Kelly's foot points to a print on the ground. "Aye, there 'tis. He's taken the road."

Start the van and back between two trees to turn around.

He can't have gotten far. He isn't a hiker.

Three minutes and I'm anxious. What if a bear got him? Five minutes and I'm terrified. What if he didn't go this way and he got lost? Six minutes and his little hunched figure comes into view, trudging down the middle of the road.

We slow the van and follow a few feet behind him. After a while he stops and steps to the passenger door, slides it open, and pulls himself in, not looking at me. I drive on like nothing happened.

It's a silent ride back to the highway. As I turn onto it, my stomach rumbles for breakfast. I'm sure Finn is hungry. Next exit gives us Denny's and a McDonald's. I head for Denny's but—*This little-pecker will make a move if we're around people*—and my right hand steers us to the drive-thru of McDonald's. Smart.

I've never eaten at McDonald's and I doubt Finn has. Even if we had, they don't have drive-thru in Manhattan. We watch the car ahead yelling an order to the menu display. I hope we can do this right.

"What is your preferred repast, Mister Findley?"

"Shut up with your stupid fake talking."

Dragon Lady leans my face close to Finn. "Listen well, little prick. You say anything except what you want to eat and you'll be seeing stars." My right hand makes a fist and shakes it in my brother's face.

At the menu display a loud voice says, "Welcome to McDonald's. Can I take your order?" It takes us a while to figure out what we want and we annoy the girlish voice on the other end of the microphone quite a bit. When told the price, seeing no other place to put it, we try to slip cash into the microphone slots. The cars behind us honk and the girl of the girlish-voice leans out of a little window to yell for us to drive to her to pay. Simon apologizes amazingly well but the cashier clearly thinks we're idiots. After way too much aggravation, we finally get a big brown bag and Dragon Lady steers us to the small deserted parking lot of a boarded-up building.

Finn takes off his seatbelt.

"Keep that on," I say. "We'll eat in our seats 'cause you left a mess in the back."

"YOU'RE the mess." Finn unwraps his McMuffin, poking at the orange cheese drooping from the edge. "You're nutty and ugly and mismatched and talk weird and have no idea what to do with your life—"

Dragon Lady turns to my brother. "If that little prick mouth of yours doesn't shut the fuck up, it'll meet a knuckle sandwich."

"Knuckle sandwich?"

Dragon Lady lifts her fist.

Finn lowers his eyes and focuses on his McMuffin.

MISS IRENE AND I can't stop talking about art and poetry and music and she knows Matisse and Edvard Munch! We talk of Freud and Einstein and Claude Debussy and I've never encountered a woman—a person—as like-minded and curious and eager for new ideas! I'm thrilled we've met and I'm sure this is destined to be a glorious friendship.

A sharp pain on my ear again. Trevon.

"Having fun, old chap? Bunch of us are absconding to the dark side of town. You and Miss—"

"Irene."

"—Miss Irene, must come. No excuses. We'll know. Let's hook it!"

Trevon drags us both to the waiting buggy. It is already overloaded with drunken men and frightened girls.

"We'll catch up," I suggest.

"Nonsense, old chap." Trevor roughly pushes me into the rear backboard seat and I offer my hand to Irene. She hesitates, taking in the traveling companions, then places her hand in mine. Oh, would that this might give me a tingle! It does not.

We clip-clop to dark town as screams and hollers and singing grow close. A raggedy barn turned barrelhouse juke-joint. Inside, Negros eye us warily and move to the edges of the vast space. They don't want us here any more than I want to be here.

Things get wild. Liquor flows. Applejack, moonshine, sourmash. It all burns going down and may make us blind, but I don't care. Neither does Irene nor anyone else. A singer wails, the banjo is ringing, and boogie-woogie's hot on the piano. We drink and dance and the music is on fire and we all lose our inhibitions. Bodies press and lurch, shimmy and grind.

Dwight is across the room downing drinks and ramming his hips against the piano. Would that I was that piano. He is closer. Am I moving? He is in front of me—not seeing me. I need him to see me. I slide under his arm and am face to face—he's startled—

and my lips leap to his, oh so soft—he pulls back, and—SLAM of his fist to my jaw and CHIME of piano strings.

"Fuck off, abomination!"

That snaps the liquor from me and captures everyone's attention. I stammer about "kidding" and "a dare" as Trevor and Dwight and all the other men gather 'round and I'm lifted by rough hands and hauled into a back room. Behind us, all the debutants wobbling on drunken legs look frightened, not daring to intervene.

As the door closes, another fist hits my face and I fall against the circling bodies. They toss and punch and slam me from one person to the next. Something smashes my left arm—a crack sends pain over my body and I cry out and everyone is jeering—"Sissy" and "Girly-boy." Another fist hits my eye and I drop—but they won't let me fall. I'm hauled up to meet another barrage. This mob means to kill me. Blink the blood away and—

"Leave him alone!" yells a female voice. Irene pushes her way into the circle of torment. She sees my face and I must look terrible because her eyes widen in fear and shock. "Here to save the sissy?" someone yells.

Irene takes my hand saying, "He's my date. Let him go."

And someone shoves her into me. "Do it!"

"Do it and we'll let him go!"

I lean my face against hers and whisper, "Go, please. They'll hurt you,"—and step back. Her cheek is smeared with my blood.

"Prove you're not a sissy! Do it!"

"I WON'T!" I scream.

Someone grabs the front of Irene's dress and rips it. Her eyes are spinning with fear.

"LET HER GO!" I yell as she is yanked to the ground.

And several hold my arms and someone pulls my pants low and there's a hand on me—a person making me hard—*what are they doing!?*—another punch to my head and Irene's gown is gone and her corset exposed. Her eyes meet mine. They are deep gold and say *save me*. I'm shoved over her—I scream as my shoulder bursts into flames. My left arm dangles limply.

"Do it, Sissy!"

"If he ain't want her, I'll do it!" some voice calls out.

Irene lifts her head close to mine, whispering, "If you don't, it's everyone."

"I can't do this to you," I say.

"You must."

Dwight squats beside Irene's head and looks into my eyes. He smiles with those white perfect teeth. "You do it or we'll cut it off."

Irene reaches down and takes hold of me and guides me in and I look up at Dwight, hating him, hating his chin and his brown eyes and long eyelashes and his spiral hairline whorl and his wisps of fur hiding below his collar and his lips and his lips his lips—lips—lips.

"I'm sorry. I'm sorry." I keep repeating to the ear against my face as I thrust into Irene.

Noises creep in. Someone yelling, "Back off!"

A gunshot blast silences everyone and with a moan, I end and shudder still and something hits my head—

STOP THE CONTINUATION

I CAN'T TAKE ANY MORE of this horror. Another terrifying vision. This time Simon raping a woman!

"You froze up," Finn says, picking at his hash-brown wafer.

"Just thinking."

"You were like a statue, except your eyes were moving. Like someone in a virtual reality game but without the VR goggles."

"I hope it didn't scare you."

"Nope. Next time I'll know and—outta here!"

"Eat," I say.

Finn goes back to testing what's edible in his breakfast, but I can't. I'm too shook up about Simon doing that. Maybe it was forced on him, but—how terrible! There must be something I can do so I don't have to live through these horrific traumas! Why haven't they ended long ago in some earlier generation? Maybe it's like Ruby said, these events are scorched into the genes. A branding iron imprinting the trauma forever in the DNA. I can't have all these ancestors torturing generation after generation! This will continue if I don't do something. There's got to be an end for me and all those *in* me. But how?

It's obvious, now that I ask the question.

I have to kill myself.

Girlie, shut y'r jive-ass mouth.

Miss Dragon Lady, you have to understand that this is an impossible situation for Miss Elizabeth. No one should have to contend with what we're putting her through.

Shut up, Simon. You're a pansy and—

Reckon you better not be talking' to him that way, Dragon Lady.

Aye, dinnae be insultin'—

See! I yell in my head. *How can a person live with this crazy bunch fighting inside!? I am going to kill myself and get us all some peace.*

You ain't got the balls to do that shit, girlie.

Dragon Lady, you're the one who said it, I say. *I can't drive. Can't defend myself. Can't even find the gas tank. I'm a 'dumb-fuck, rich kid with no experience and no skills and I'm way outta my depth.'*

Ain't no reason to snuff yourself.

How about this reason—I've got seven traumatized ancestors torturing me! If I kill myself, that'll put you all to rest.

Beside me is a quiet click. I turn and Finn slides the door open, drops to the ground, and is OFF!

Damn it, I have to kill myself and all he can think about is escape! I spill my breakfast getting out of the van and my legs aren't working in sync but they're fast and strong and taking me across the parking lot and Finn looks back to see me gaining on him.

"HELP!" he yells.

And a kid riding a bike skids to a stop a few yards in front of him.

"Gimme your bike!" Finn demands as he runs toward the boy.

The kid stares at Finn, baffled.

Finn reaches the boy and pushes hard. The kid and bike fall, one crying, and my brother yanks at everything, trying to disengage the little legs from the spokes and pedals, screaming, "I'm kidnapped. I need this bike!"

And we're there and Dragon Lady has Finn by the arm and Simon has him by the waist and he's up on Ruby's hip and Heinrich and Kelly are pounding us back to the van and inside and the door slams and the motor starts and Simon pulls a bill from my pocket as we slow along side of the crying boy and tosses the hundred-dollars to the kid—and I know I shouldn't use money to solve things but I can't stick around to apologize right now—and we speed away.

When we're far from town and people, I turn to my brother. "Why can't you enjoy this? We're having an adventure! Why do you want to leave?!"

"You're DEPRIVING me of my DESIGNATED life. My perfect life!"

"I should have burned all those stupid books."

"First thing I'm going to do when I ESCAPE and get home is have someone recreate the Vision Books you burnt. Book Ten. That's what I'm meant to be living NOW. Book Twenty-eight. That's when I get married and move into a fantastic mansion. Book Twenty-nine, I make tons of money and have a corner-window office. Book Thirty, my two smiling children play in the swimming pool!"

Oh fuck.

"You can't have children," I tell my brother.

Finn glares at me. "Of course, I'll have children. It's in the book. A boy and a girl. The boy first."

"We have bad genes. We can't pass them along."

"We have the best genes and I'm going to have the best kids! They're in the Vision Book and they'll have Vision Books of their own and we'll have perfect lives!"

I have to kill Finn.

Miss Elizabeth, you're not thinking right.

I'll kill Finn and kill myself.

I dinnae think so, lass. Cannae let ye.

The generations of abusers and abused will die.

Nein.

By killing Finn I'll say *fuck you* to the rapists in our genes. I'll say *rest in peace* to the victims in our genes.

Girlie, you can't pull off a kidnapping, let alone a murder.

Watch me.

Finn is still talking. Reciting his paint-by-numbers life. That life'll be over soon.

How should I kill him? I can't poison him or chop his head off. I could drown him. Can't do it in a tub or swimming pool. I need to find a lake. I'll find a secluded lake and do it tomorrow.

"Finn, I'm sorry about all this. I know you want to have this all end. Let's have one more day together."

My brother looks at me with real surprise. "Really? You'll let me go?"

"Let's make this last day special. You want to go camping?" Neither one of us has been camping, but I've seen it in movies and maybe one of the ancestors will help.

"Like with a tent?"

"Yep. Flashlights and fireflies and stars and peeing in the dark on leaves."

"What if I need to go number two?"

"We buy a shovel so we can bury it."

"A campfire?"

"Wieners and marshmallows on sticks."

Finn looks at me like he's scrolling through all the options and isn't quite sure.

"We'll buy a tent and supplies. It's an adventure! We'll go by a Target..."

He scrunches his face at the mention of Target. I'm losing him. "Finn, wasn't there a picture of a tent and a boy beside it in Vision Book Ten?"

"I think there was! Camping boys make whistle sticks. Get me a knife and I'll go."

I think he means *whittle*, but as I've never done it, I'm not going to correct him. "We'll get you a pocket knife that folds."

Finn looks suddenly like a little boy. A grin on his face and sparkling eyes. It's going to be hard to kill him.

TARGET

IN TARGET, on the way to Sports-Fitness-Outdoors, we pass through the Electronics department. Finn screams, "A PHONE!"

I hurry beside him, "No phone."

"We need it to find out where we are!"

"You're right." I grab a small GPS device and pop it in the cart. Finn fumes.

We move through the store and load the cart with a tent and sleeping bags and a shovel and a cooler and ice and firewood and matches and wieners and buns and marshmallows and Fritos and I don't know if we'll get to it but I buy a fishing rod setup just in case and when we get to the canned goods I stare and stare and *Schweinefleisch* pops into my head and I don't know what that means except I'm focused on the cans of potted meat and it seems like a good idea so I get SPAM and move on to collect bug spray and flashlights and soda and while Finn is deciding on the pocket knife, I slip a bottle of wine into each sleeping bag. I can't show I.D. 'cause I'm not old enough. If they catch me, shoplifting's better than kidnapping. Isn't it?

Finn holds up his choice. "Swiss Army knife!"

My left leg twitches angrily in response. Does Heinrich have something against the Swiss?

We get to the checkout and my stomach tightens. Is it better to have the sleeping bags scan through first or at the end? What do I say if they find the wine? Could I say I didn't put it in there? Do they have videos all over the store and to catch me in the lie?

"We're going camping," Finn yells at the cashier.

"It looks that way," the man says as he slides the wieners over the scanner. "Where are you going to camp?"

Finn looks at me. I shrug and pass the first sleeping bag onto the conveyor belt.

It beeps through as the cashier suggests, "KOA are always good. They got the amenities with facilities and showers and spray the grounds and you feel safer."

I want to keep him talking, so I pick up on the last word. "Safer? What's dangerous about camping besides burning your fingers on marshmallows?"

The man looks at me like I'm daft. "Bears. Coyotes. Wolves. Bats with Rabies. Lyme disease ticks. Not to mention sickos looking for a girl-like-you to mess with if you camp in the middle of nowhere."

"They won't mess with my sister. I've got my SWISS ARMY KNIFE!" Finn screams.

The cashier rolls the next sleeping bag over the scanner. The tip of the wine bottle peeks out. The scanner doesn't beep. He rolls it again and the bottle peeks out more. No beep. Roll again and it beeps and I help move it to the massive bag, pushing the wine back in.

"You take care of your sister then, Little Man."

Finn's face curdles into Father's favorite expression. "Little man? Are you being condescending to me?!"

Oh no. Not now. "Finn, this man's being friendly. Sorry, sir."

Finn goes on. "You wouldn't treat me that way if you knew who I am."

"Yeah, who are you?" the cashier asks.

Dragon Lady's hand drops heavily onto Finn's shoulder and squeezes. My brother's little body tenses and his head drops in submission.

"He's a little, spoiled jerk," I answer. "Sorry about his behavior."

The register shows the charge—$423.67. I hand over five hundreds, accept the change, and push the cart full of the bags toward the door. As Finn and I cross the threshold and the automatic door opens, a loud alarm sounds and a gruff voice calls, "Hold up there, Little Miss."

Now I know why Finn got so mad at Little Man.

I turn to see a muscle-bound security guard stomping toward me. His hand is on the gun at his waist.

All my parts spring to attention and anticipation. Each has a different idea of what to do next.

The automatic door closes against the shopping cart and reopens.

"Yes, sir?"

"You plannin' on payin' for all you got?"

"Sir, I—" I wonder if it might be better to admit I stole and—

Finn starts crying. "I didn't mean to. I got excited and forgot." Finn tearfully pulls from his pocket the Swiss Army knife, still in its package.

"I could haul you to jail," the guard snarls at my brother.

I realize the store's anti-theft alarm may have gone off because of the wine, but maybe we'll get away because Finn didn't pay for the knife.

In my relief, I feign being upset the best I can. "You, Little Man, can march right back to that cashier and pay for the knife." I hand my brother a fifty-dollar bill and shake my head at the security guard. "Please accept my apologies. I will make sure this never happens again. If you would be so good as to escort this ne'er-do-well, I'd be most grateful."

The guard grabs Finn by the back of his neck and leads him to the cashier.

The automatic door closes on the cart again and reopens. I push the cart outside and watch Finn at the register. *Here's your chance, little brother. Tell them you're kidnapped. Point me out to the security guard. He'll call Mother and Father and you'll go home. You'll live a long and privileged life. Do it now. Tell them. Please. Tell them.*

Finn, looking very contrite, pays for the knife.

In a moment, my brother hurries out and together we cross the parking lot, open the van, stuff in all the purchases, and climb in.

Driving off, Finn squirms as volcanic bubbles of rage and fear and shame rumble through him. I'm about to ask him why he didn't try to escape when he kicks the dashboard. "He was going to send me to jail! That would have been worse than being kidnapped and on this stupid trip with you! Why did you leave? You should have protected me! You should have come with me! I had to face them all alone and it WASN'T FUN!"

I keep forgetting you're a little kid who's been coddled his whole life. But that life is almost over.

When we've both settled down from the drama, I pull over, get the GPS hooked in the cigarette lighter and find out we're in North Carolina. Search for a secluded lake. Find one and punch in for directions.

We're led from our highway to smaller and smaller roads, walled in by tall pines.

When the GPS lady says "Turn right." I slow. Where? There's only the alley of pines.

Finn points. "There's something up ahead."

I pull down to a very narrow, overgrown dirt road. Two deep ruts for tires and a grassy middle. We bounce forward, rocking over the uneven ground.

Finn looks excited, leaning forward in his seat.

The road curves and I realize it's so narrow and surrounded by trees that we can't turn around.

"Watch out!" Finn yells.

There's a thick branch from a leaning tree encroaching into the road on Finn's side. Heinrich jams on the brake and I put us in reverse gear.

"We have to go back, Finn."

My right hand disagrees, puts the van in first, grips the wheel, Kelly steps on the gas, and we lurch forward.

No-no-no.

Dragon Lady has control and—BAM! The branch hits the corner of the windshield and Finn crouches and Kelly gives us more gas and there's a creaking and I hope the window will hold and the tires spin but Dragon Lady knows her shit and the branch groans against the glass and it rises and slides onto the roof and SCRAAAAAAAPPPPPPPEEEEEEESSSSSS down the length of the top, and there's a WHAP as it snaps back in place behind us.

As I breathe out slowly, Finn screams with triumph.

Dragon Lady punches his arm. "Kid, always remember—Take it easy, but take it."

Finn repeats the advice with unusual enthusiasm. He looks more excited than I've ever seen him. I can't kill us just because we have traumatized genes. My plan is horrible.

UNKNOWN — SYRACUSE, NEW YORK — 1998

HIS CRAMPED OFFICE smells like old books. Probably because there are shelves of them obliterating nearly all signs of the brick walls. Above us, the bare florescent tubes flatten the room unkindly. A fly buzzes somewhere, looking for a way out. Is there a way out?

The professor moves close and smells of damp wool. His eyebrows arch and curl their heads down, like bulls about the clash.

Why did I speak? "I'm sorry I spoke—"

He slams me against the file cabinet.

Should I scream? Will anyone hear in the hallway?

His hand is up my skirt, ripping down my panties. This can't be happening.

"Professor, please don't."

His other hand moves to my neck and squeezes with enough force to scare me. If I struggle, will he kill me? What would he do with my body? How would he get it off campus?

He jabs into me. This is happening. I stare at the framed art print on the wall as he slams my tailbone against the handle of the cabinet with each thrust. Please, please, stop...

CAMPING

"PLEASE, PLEASE, stop."

"We can't stop in the middle of the road!" says Finn. "There's no place to camp!"

I must have drifted away again with that vision. Another rape! My ancestors deserve to have this trauma end. I've got to stick to the plan. No more second-guessing. Finn and I will die tomorrow.

"Okay, Finn. I'm not stopping."

Dragon Lady handles the wheel like the pro she is and steers us toward the shimmering glittering sparkles peeking through the trees at the end of the road.

Finn leaps from the Metro Van as Dragon Lady puts it in *Park*. All my beings get out, stretching their distinct parts. They seem to have either forgotten that I'm going to kill Finn and myself tomorrow, or they're in agreement to that plan now.

"We can put the tent here!" my brother screams, pointing to a spot by the edge of the large lake.

I'm about to say okay when my right hand points to a clearing farther off. "Reckon yonder suits me. Higher ground in case of rain, less trees in case of winds or thunderstorms. Away from the water so we don't startle drinking critters and maybe get caught in a ruckus."

Finn stares at me. I don't blame him. I don't know any of that, nor do I use the word ruckus. I smile as if I'm fine with Ruby's lingo.

Finn seems placated by the smile and opens the back of the van to unload the haul from Target. He very pointedly folds each plastic bag and adds them carefully to my pile on the still-filthy table.

I unload the sleeping bags, removing the hidden wine for later.

Finn unpacks the tent but the fold-out directions in seven languages are very complicated, so I suggest we get a fire going first.

With Kelly's help, we set up sticks and wood in a tee-pee shape. Finn tries to light it but it isn't taking.

"I'll look for some paper," I say, heading into the van where I'm sure if I rip out the Alaska page of the road atlas, it won't be missed.

When I return, the fire is well underway.

"Good work, Finn! You want to tackle the tent now?"

Finn doesn't look too sure.

"We'll do it together. Hand me the directions and we'll figure it out."

Finn points to the fire. "I needed paper."

Oh.

With campers more experienced than the two of us, we get the tent set up except for one long section of rope and some plastic things with holes that we don't know how to use. I dig a pit for number-two and leave the shovel ready. Doused with bug spray, we skewer the wieners and sit twirling them in the flames, watching sparks dance into the sky.

A little frog hops by my right foot. Instantly, my hand swooshes out to grab it gently.

"This be a leopard frog. They's friend a mine."

"Kiss it," Finn orders. "Maybe you'll turn into a beautiful princess. NOT!"

Thanks, brother. Keep reminding me of my mission.

Finn sticks out his little hand. "Gimme that."

"Nae, ye cannae 'ave 'im," Kelly says.

I carry the frog to the lake and let it go. The air's cold away from the fire. What was Finn going to do with this frog? Throw it in the fire? Skewer it with a stick? I'm definitely doing the world a favor, ending this lineage. I close my eyes and think about my plan for tomorrow. How long will it take to get Finn drunk? Will he struggle underwater? Is it easy to drown someone? How will I drown myself after I kill him? The lake is large enough that if I swam to the middle, I'd probably be tired and unable to come back. But what if I could? I should wear a lot of clothes and have them weigh me down. Put stones in my pockets.

Finn yells at me, "You like marshmallows flaming or blackened ooze?"

After too many marshmallows and lots of burnt fingers, it's time to get ready for bed.

I pick up the bags of marshmallows and wieners. "See if anything dropped. We don't want to attract wild animals."

"Huh?"

"We're supposed to keep food inaccessible to bears or whatever. Don't want it in the tent or van where they might try to break in to get it."

Finn listens wide-eyed.

"So, we take a PLASTIC BAG—which we HAPPEN to have—and put the food in it and hang it from a branch away from the tent."

I make Finn fill the plastic bag and tie the leftover-tent-rope around it and after twelve throws, he manages to fling the rope over a branch and we tie the bag up high. See, Finn, plastic bags do have a purpose!

We sit on a log by the lake's edge. The sun is down but the glowing sky is reflected in the still surface. Something leaps and plops, sending circular waves echoing out. A long-necked white bird flies over the water, dives, and rises with a struggling fish in its sword-beak. There are hooting sounds and as the sky darkens, flapping things swirl overhead. Finn shivers and slides next to me on the log, pulling my arm over him. It's so unlike the brother I know, but here he is, under my arm. Makes me wonder again if I'm planning the right thing.

"Hey, Finn. It's pretty, huh?"

"Hmmm," he answers, and his head drops against my armpit.

All the different bits of me, including me, seem to say—there's no way killing him is justifiable.

Finn yawns and I stand us both, pointing him toward our campsite. Passing under the hanging food bag Finn says, "If animals come for the food they won't get it, but if illegal aliens come they might cut the rope and steal everything."

"Illegal aliens?"

"They sneak into the country, taking jobs, committing crimes, and using our society for free. They're a plague."

I'll kill us both tomorrow.

DOING THE DEED

I OPEN MY EYES and stare at the tent top. There's a dim glow on the thin fabric. Dawn?

Glance left. Finn's gone. Maybe illegal aliens came and took him to save me the trouble of my mission. I try to sit up but— something's very wrong. Arms lie dormant. Legs as logs. Tongue asleep. All of me is lifeless.

Wake up, I say to my parts.

No one moves. Have they left? What if they left? I'd be empty. Am I anything without them?

WAKE UP! I scream in my head.

And no one does. There must have been a meeting and I didn't get the memo. They must have gathered while I slept and conspired against me.

I have to use my body with no help from anyone. It takes a lot more concentration than I'm used to. I slowly wiggle out of the sleeping bag and squiggle to the door and make my left arm rise and grip the zipper tab. Pull. It's a Herculean task! I finally get the flap open and peer out.

In the dim light of the slowly waking sky, Finn is hunched over the lake-side log. I concentrate on each muscle and crawl out of the tent, pull myself upright clinging to a trunk, and stumble from tree to tree toward Finn. I feel like a paralyzed person controlling a robot with their mind. I feel like my body is made of lead or I've been reintroduced to gravity after years away. Nearer my brother, I see he's stabbing a frog on the log.

"Bye-bye, Prince Charming," he brags.

"LEAVE THAT ALONE, YOU SICK FUCK!" I yell. Me, not one of the others.

We're both surprised. Finn backs away from the bloody frog and I take a step and carefully bend without falling and close my fingers around a stick. I can control my own body, damn it! With the stick, I lift the remains of the frog and carry it to the water's edge. I try to fling the frog far but it only flips two feet into the lake. The mangled frog floats on the surface of the water, pale and splayed. Something grabs the frog from below and WHOOSH— it's gone. That'll be Finn soon, and then me.

I've got to concentrate. Left leg out, lean forward, start to fall, and place the foot to stop the fall. Now right leg. Falling forward motion, they call walking. It's slow going but I step myself back to the Metro Van and force my fingers to clamp tight around a bottle of wine and glasses.

As I return to Finn, the sun is just peeking over the trees, shooting orange across everything.

"Whoa," Finn says.

"Have you seen dawn before?"

"No."

"Then, here's to your first dawn. Let's toast."

It takes a lot of concentrating but I pour glasses of wine for both of us.

"I'm not old enough," my ten-year-old brother says.

"I won't tell."

Finn sniffs the glass of dark red liquid and takes a sip. "Bitter."

"Add ginger ale," I suggest and Finn rushes to the Metro Van, returns with a bottle, adds it to the wine, and takes another sip—"Yummy." He drinks it down like his favorite rich-person sparkling water.

I pour him another.

As the sun rises higher and shines over the lake, I keep my brother's glass full. Finn falls off the log and finds that hilarious. He's blurry and loopy and pliant. Perfect. Now I just have to figure out how to get him in the water.

Finn yells, "I want marshmallows again!"

"Maybe later."

"I'm going to make another fire. The biggest fire ever!"

"Not a good idea. Do you want to die in a forest fire?" I ask Finn.

"Duh, we can always jump in the lake."

Thanks for the segue, Finn. "We could. Show me how you would do that."

"It's cold."

"Not when you get in the water. Pretend the fire is all around us. Ahh, Help! Fire!"

"Don't want to."

"We can do splashing."

I hate when Finn splashes me. I never go in our rooftop infinity pool with him because he's always splashing me.

"Yeah!" Finn rises and falls. "I'm drunk! Look at me! I'm drunk! It's like virtual reality skydiving!"

"It's even more fun to be drunk in the water."

I can't believe I'm saying this. But this is the right thing to do. We can't keep the trauma going. It has to end with us.

Finn gets up and starts to take off his pants.

"Let's keep our clothes on. We'll be warmer." Finn grins like it's a grand idea and I take his hand. It's small. He's just a kid. How can I do this to him?

Cattails wave in the orange light. A bird sings. A dragonfly lands on a leaf. Brother, take in these moments. They're the last you'll see.

I lift one leg and then the next and slowly walk to the lake's edge and into the water. Finn's right. It's cold.

"When we get out a ways, you splash me," I say.

That gets him moving and we push through weedy things and the water clears and it's up to his thighs, his waist, his chest. He splashes me, both hands working, screaming with glee. I hate it. I drop underwater to escape the bombardment. His legs are dark stumps in the murky water. I push off hard on the mud bottom and, staying underwater, swim farther from the shore. My lead legs feel even heavier in wet clothes. They weigh me down. What if I drown before him? Muffled shouts from Finn. "ELIZABETH! COME UP! ELIZABETH!"

I feel a glow of revenge in scaring him, but something else jolts in me—a well of panic. Kick and kick and rise, gasping for air. Finn is wide-eyed, head spinning, looking for me.

"Bet you can't get me now, Finn."

He slogs through the water and at neck deep, starts swimming. It's kind of a dog-paddle-breast-stroke. He wriggles and kicks, moving closer.

"Everything's spinning!" he yells, clearly struggling.

When he reaches me, I know I have to act now or lose my purpose. "Let's see who can hold their breath underwater the longest. Ready? One, two, three—"

We both inhale deeply and Finn drops under. I put my hands on his head and push. He understands immediately and struggles to rise, but I keep a hold of him and push lower, sending him under my body so it blocks his escape. Kicks and scratches and my right leg convulses—*I cannae breathe!*—there's a piercing jab to my shoulder—*Dinnae drown me!*—a board snaps my leg—*T'ain't any air!*—my right leg kicks madly and I'm flooded by its being. My left arm pulls Finn's face out of the water as my right arm punches my head. Finn isn't moving. I'm flipped onto my back and Finn is tucked under my left arm, his head high. Legs kick furiously, right arm stroking us backwards toward land.

At the shallows, Finn is gathered up in these arms, and these legs march through the weeds and carry him to shore. Not me, but everyone else.

They set Finn on the carpet of leaves. Head back, chin up, hold the nose, and blow into his lungs. Again. Again. No response. Again. Again.

Turn him to the side and whack his back. Nothing. Breathe in his mouth again. Nothing.

Grab his feet and everyone's lifting him high, upside down, jerking him like a ketchup bottle.

Water and wine spew from him. He coughs terribly as they set him down and turn him on his side. My left hand strokes his temple. Parts are checking his vitals, parts thinking ahead. I'm watching. Not allowed to do anything. I'm a passenger now.

AFTER DROWNING

FINN SHIVERS. Several in me hang back, not sure what to do. Jenny and Kelly take over. They strip Finn and find dry clothes and dress him and put him in his sleeping bag alongside the fire pit. They gather wood and get the fire crackling and all the while, everyone talks inside me.

Reckon the boy'll remember this?

He's imbibed enough to have impaired recollections.

We'll tell the little pecker he was drowndin' and we saved his ass. He'll believe that jive.

'Twas I that saved 'im. 'Twas me went underwater and I couldnae let it happen to this lad.

We know, Miss Kelly.

Ja, das ist true.

I can hear them and feel them and I try to say *I'm sorry* but they've me pushed down so far I'm unable to make a peep or move a finger. Is this my life from now on? A prisoner in my own body?

Finn groans.

They all seem to stumble and bump into each other, pushing and shoving to get upfront.

Finn coughs.

Ruby steps forward and becomes the designated driver. "How you doin', young fella?"

Call him by his name, Miss Ruby. Call him Findley. Miss Elizabeth calls him Finn, but he doesn't like that.

"How you feelin' there, Findley?"

"What happened?"

"You got y'rself half drowned. We got you out in time."

"We?"

"Me, myself, and I."

"I feel sick."

"Ain't no wonder. All the libation you partook of."

"What?"

"You sip this water and see if that don't settle you some."

Finn drinks and stares at the fire. "You pushed me down underwater."

"Ain't so. You got pulled under by them wet garments. I 'bout drown tryin' t' pull you up. You bucked like a foal first saddled."

"I thought I was going to die."

"You were on the way to it, if—we—I—hadn't pulled you up."

"You saved me?" Finn asks, looking like he wants to believe.

"Damn right."

Finn looks directly at me. "Thank you. You're a good big sister, Elizabe—Izzy."

AHHH! He used my new name and it's not because of me! It's because of all them. *They're* Izzy. I am, and always will be, nobody. Down in the depths of my being, I feel the horror of what I did. I want to cry but I don't own my eyes anymore, let alone my tears.

After Finn is asleep and warm by the fire, everyone walks my body to sit by the lake.

What we fixin' to do 'bout her? Reckon she fancies t'send us t' hell.

Aye, she cannae be in charge. 'Tis clear she's t'be stopped.

Ja. Elizabeth ist gefährlich. Dangerous.

We shall communicate our demands and she will see the justice in our cause.

Nein. Wir regieren sie. We rule her.

Damn straight. We've got hands on the wheel now. This is our fuckin' party and we're gonna get wild!

It doesn't seem fair to make Miss Elizabeth do things she doesn't want to.

Reckon it wasn't fair for you, Simon, but you seen what she tried with Finn. She's more dangerous than a rattler in the privy.

Alright. How do we do this? Do we vote?

I try to speak but I'm closed down.

There is a chorus of responses. *Her life is ours!*

It's unanimous, since I don't get a say.

NAHRUNGSSUCHE

FINN IS HUNGOVER AND HUNGRY and he tries to untie the hanging bag of food but the owners of my being aren't willing to have hotdogs and marshmallows again. "Get y'r ass in the van. We'll get some grub," Dragon Lady says.

"Where are we going?"

"Nahrungssuche," answers Solveig.

Dragon Lady backs the Metro Van all the way out of the forest and, with Solveig scouring the landscape, she steers past a farmhouse and cornfield and down to the great wide meadow at the edge of what looks like an old homestead. The remains of a chimney and an overgrown fruit tree orchard jut above the wildflowers. Butterflies, bees, and hummingbirds zoom about.

In the back of the van, Solveig pulls the pillowcase off my pillow, grabs a plastic bowl from the kitchen area, and hops us out into the orchard.

Kelly spins us around, taking in the trees twisted with age. *'Tis a sight t' get me happy and frightened a' the same time. Cannae say more but it be a strong memory f'r me.*

Some trees are blooming, some have tiny starts of fruit. Birds scatter from a tree as we approach. "Der bird show das ripe food," Solveig whispers.

That tree is full of purple berries. I've never picked berries but I thought they grew on bushes. They don't say raspberry *tree.*

"Das sind Maulbeeren," says Solveig.

"Mulberry!" Finn guesses as he reaches high. He's not tall enough so Simon bends me low and has him climb onto my shoulders. I can't believe my body's strong enough to hold Finn like this, but I guess there's a lot of them doing it. Finn kicks my side like I'm a horse. "Giddyap!"

Ruby corrects him. "Tip your heels low when you spur the hide. Y'ain't fixin' to hurt the critter, just let 'er know who's boss. And click your tongue to set 'er movin.'"

Finn gives me a gentle heel tap and clicks his tongue. If I was part of this, I'd be able to laugh, but I'm stuck behind everyone. Finn's little fingers stain purple as he picks. When we have the bowl full, Ruby says, "Reckon best give the beast a rest. Get ready to dismount."

Simon bends low and Finn flips his leg over my back like he's hopping off a horse.

"Well done, young fella. You're a right natural!" declares Ruby.

Finn beams and trots around like he's the horse.

They move me to another tree with fuzzy orange fruit.

"Are these baby peaches?" Finn asks.

Good for you, Finn. I think. *That'd be my guess, too.* No one notices me.

"Nae, laddie, apricots," says Kelly.

Simon picks several and puts them in the pillowcase.

Another tree has small droopy yellow-brown sacks hanging off it.

"What are these little water balloons?" Finn asks.

"Reckon they look like prairie oysters, t'me," Ruby says.

"Prairie oysters?"

"Testicles."

Finn groans.

"Das ist figs," Solveig explains.

I've heard of Fig Newtons but never had one.

Simon plucks handfuls of figs and puts them in the pillowcase. They move to the meadow where Solveig collects all sorts of things that look like weeds. She mumbles words in my head as they pick. *Sorrel—Sauerampfer. Yarrow—Schafgarbe. Dandelion—Löwenzahn. Chickweed—Vogelmiere. Wild onions— wilde zwiebeln.* In the woods behind the orchard she find mushrooms of many kinds that she promises will not kill us. Everything goes into the pillowcase or the bowl that Finn carries.

When Solveig thinks there is enough, Dragon Lady drives us back to our campsite. There, Kelly teaches Finn how to dig up worms for bait and how to catch fish and gut and clean them with his new pocket knife. Simon shows him how to snag crawdads, making them snap their claws onto a dangled piece of red cloth. With the ancestors all working together, they have him put wild chives and mushrooms and other plants inside the fish and surround it with crawdads, coat the body in thick muddy clay, and set this on burning embers. As the meal cooks, they even figure out a way to make a competitive game of cleaning up the Cheez Whiz and Cool Whip crusted on the van's table. Maybe if my ancestors rule me forever, Finn will become a much better person.

Simon sets the table and arranges the food on the plates in such an artistic manner we're all awed.

"It's like in a magazine!" Finn says.

"Thank you, young sir. And I venture it'll taste as good as it looks," replies Simon.

Finn stares at me. "I'm not eating weeds and things from the woods!"

"Das ist Nahrungssuche," Solveig reminds him. "Collect wild food."

"I like tame food—"

Kelly steps forward. "Ye cannae ken what 'tis like when 'ere nae be food. Try livin' wee a lack o' coin."

Solveig joins her. "Or der war bombardiert die city und stores und cafés are kaputt. Du starve if du kein findest food."

Finn stares at the spread. "Mother did this last year! She had Alberto drive her and her friends to a farm near Princeton and they paid *big* bucks to do this—I think she called it foraging."

With that, Simon has Finn crack open the mud-clay covering on the fish. Steam rises with a delicious aroma. Everyone relishes the flavors, delicious crunches, and squeaks of the foraged food. I can't interact but I can taste and savor everything. I never knew there could be so many different flavors from plants. And fruit! Mulberries are tangy and sweet at the same time. Figs are like pockets of melty candy. Apricots taste like sunshine. The flavors pop with razzmatazz!

Finn sits back, pats his belly and says with a familiar western accent, "I reckon I'm plumb full!"

Ruby, of course, responds. "Yep. Reckon so. Dang fine vittles."

"Dang fine vittles," Finn repeats, giggling. "Ve go Nah-rung-ssss-suche again, ja?"

OH MY GOD! My brother has learned German!

"Natürlich, liebling," Solveig answers.

"I dinnae ken when I've eaten sae well," my brother says with with an amazing Scottish accent.

"Och! Haud yer tongue, ye scalawag," counters Kelly.

Finn cracks up. It makes me glad to see him laughing but achingly lonely that it has nothing to do with me. I'm a horror as a sister. Kidnapper, killer... It's probably for the best they've taken over. Only, I wish I didn't have to watch.

"Pardon me, Miss Elizabeth," Finn says. "Perhaps we can give the staff the night off and share the dish washing?" Now he's doing Simon!

Simon agrees. "I think that's a splendid notion, young sir."

Finn is way too rambunctious washing dishes in the lake and splashing me, but everyone, except me, seems to think is just fine.

"You're different, Izzy," Finn says. "More fun."

This breaks my heart to hear.

Jenny takes Finn by the hand. "We should all endeavor to have more fun, young man. It is an essential aspect of the human condition, yet at this moment, I need an interval of repose. Let's retire by the fireside."

They get comfy near the flames.

"I'm glad you saved me from drowning, Izzy."

Everything my brother says makes me feel worse.

"And I'm glad you kidnapped me," Finn whispers.

Ruby knows someone better answer, so she jumps in. "Me, too."

"Maybe, we don't have to go home right away," my brother adds. "Let's pretend there was a ransom and Father didn't pay."

I'm stunned.

As the fire dies down and dark comes, we all lie back to stare at the stars.

"I heard of the Big Dipper. Where is that?" Finn asks.

Jenny points it out. "It's that pot with the handle."

"Nae, that be the Plough," says Kelly.

"Nein, das ist der Großer Wagen—Great Wagon," corrects Heinrich.

"You're so nutty, Izzy. Do you know any other star shapes?" Finn asks.

"Reckon that shape up yonder looks like a fish," says Ruby. "It's the fish constellation—that one you caught."

"You made that up."

"How do you reckon folk got constellations? They looked up and said, 'That looks like my horse or my pianr.' Folk made them up."

A look of wonder spreads across Finn's face. He scans the sky. "I know that one over there. It's got the shape and see the tires? It's the van."

The Metro Van is a constellation! A flurry of tears hits me, but I'm not near my eyes. Simon points at another group. "What about that one? It looks like a frog."

"I shouldn'ta killed that frog. I wish I hadn't."

They all remember a sister trying to drown a brother. Jenny whispers, "I suspect we all have things we regret."

Finn points. "That bunch of stars over there—see the top and the sides—it's the tent!"

My brother comes up with all new constellations. The Van. The Tent. The Slim Jim. The Weiner. The Flaming Marshmallow...

Finn slides his head close to touch my shoulder. "I'm tired, but I have one more. See up there? It's a big group—like so, so many. That's you. You have all these different people in you and they all combine into being my sister. I'll call it The Izzy People."

The shiver hits every part of me—all those that make me who I am—only, I'm no longer part of that constellation.

REVENGE

ONCE MY BROTHER is asleep, the others move to the fire pit to confer.

Forgive me for asking the obvious, but what is our plan for Miss Elizabeth's life?

I'm of a mind to advocate avenues of justice and reparations.

Was ist das?

Restitutions. Restorative actions to balance the scales.

Can you translate your jive-ass bull shit?

I reckon Jenny's talkin' of revenge. Give those what done things their due.

Aye, that 'tis the plan f'r me.

'bout time folks got their comeuppance.

Ja. Rache!

What that is, Heinrich? "Rache."

Das ist REVENGE!

Revenge!

Excited, they all scramble to say who they want revenge on.

Ruby wants revenge on a violent client.

Simon wants revenge on the cotillion gang of boys who forced him to have sex with Irene.

Kelly knows she wants revenge but she's hazy on who.

Heinrich wants revenge on the soldiers who blew his leg off.

Jenny wants revenge on the doctors who had her institutionalized.

Dragon Lady wants revenge on Beau and Jack.

Solveig wants revenge on Heinrich.

This takes everyone by surprise.

How you reckon to get revenge on Heinrich, Solveig? Ruby asks.

Cut das leg off, she answers.

Oh shit.

Heinrich jerks in protest but Kelly kicks him in the ankle. Jenny asks for calm inside. *Solveig, your wish is very understandable, but you must understand that if we remove Heinrich from our midst, we'll be forced to complete the rest of the revenge plans inconvenienced by a missing limb and that will hamper us considerably. Would you mind delaying your restitution until after the others can have their day of reckoning?*

Solveig agrees to wait.

So who shall be first? Jenny asks.

They get to figuring and thinking and in a few minutes of doing the math, it's pretty clear revenge is easier said than done. The soldiers of WWII are dead. The whore-house client is dead. The boys of the cotillion are dead. The doctors institutionalizing the suffragette is dead. And whoever Kelly wants revenge on is sure to be dead.

Could be my fuckin' asshole perpetrators are alive, says Dragon Lady.

This sends a buzz of excitement through them all. *Alive perpetrators! Let's get 'em!*

Dragon Lady gestures with my right hand. *They wanted me dead but I don't die easy. Fuck me if I don't bury their cocks in shoeboxes like dead hamsters!*

Her words rally us all, even me. She has a way of putting things that makes you want to take action.

My husband and his friend did it. Jack Fredricks and Beau Tompkins. Let's find those pecker-assholes and get revenge!

DRAGON LADY — WHITLEY COUNTY, KENTUCKY — 1962

I'M SO COLD! How long have I been cold? As my consciousness grows, so does the pain. Where am I? I'm face down on my stomach. My head feels like it's been dismantled and reassembled with axle pins. I'm not sure if I should even try to move. The organs may be all in the wrong spots and will spill out if I shift.

I crack open my eyes, but they're full of grit. Can't see. Only black. I need to clear them, but my arms won't move. What happened to me?

It's hard to breathe. I shift my head and the pain floods me—open my mouth to scream—pain flames over my face—my jaw must be broken. Breathe. Pull in air—and dirt—coughing, spit mud. I jerk away and feel the weight on my back. *What is that?* A massive weight pinning me down. All over my body. Dirt and weight and—am I buried?

A jolt of fear. I jerk to the side.

Don't turn, the dirt will fall and cover your face and suffocate you.

Another jolt of fear.

Get a grip. You are alive. Figure out what to do next.

Shifting just slightly, I feel sharpness against my skin—everywhere. I must be naked. My left arm is under my chest. *Move it.* It won't move. *Move it.* It's asleep, no blood. *MOVE IT NOW!* I pull with all the combinations of muscles that work and slide my arm out and press the elbow up—wriggling it through heavy dirt, muffled crackling of leaves and sticks, grains trickling down to fill in the void—*Please don't cover my face!*—stop with my elbow skyward and my palm flat beside my shoulder.

Get working, Lady. You moved your arm, so that means the dirt isn't deep or it's not compact. Maybe 'cause it's Fall there are lots of sticks and leaves, so it's lightweight. Who cares why. Get your other arm up and get the fuck out of here!

I pull to move my right arm. It does nothing. I'm not even sure it is part of me. It might be dead. How could my arm be dead? *What happened to me?*

If my other arm can't work, I've got to get my back into this. Got to get my knees up so I can push. I squirm and squiggle and wriggle and the pain is unbearable. My stomach has been pummeled. My crotch sears me. *What happened!?*

You're the Dragon Lady. Buck the fuck up!

146

Knees rise and the trickling dirt fills in the space. Chunks roll past my chin, covering my mouth. I don't want to die like this!

I finally get my knees below me. It's impossible to breathe. My nose is clogged with dirt. Won't suck in anything but dirt with my mouth.

I put everything into my back and PUUUUUSSSSSSSSHHHHH! A crumbling, tumbling, cracking mountain rises with me and— LIGHT AND COLD AIR! Grab the edge with my left arm and PULLLLLL to look out of my grave.

The sun is beautiful as it hangs low, backlighting the mountains. Heavy mist over the lake. I breathe through the pain and turn to look at the campground. Tent gone. Up the hill— station wagon gone. Rambler gone.

Fuckers messed with the wrong Dragon Lady.

SEARCHING FOR JACK AND BEAU

NEXT MORNING, after Finn makes fig, mulberry, apricot "stew," we break camp, making sure to collect the hanging bag of rotting hotdogs. Driving out, Ruby turns us to Finn. "I 'spect you're an expert at divining the whereabouts of those we've lost contact with."

"What?"

"Reckon if you got your hands on a 'puter contrivance, you'd find anything."

Finn giggles and with his Ruby-western-accent says, "Reckon if you're talkin' about a COMputer, you'd reckon right."

In the first large town, we find a library and book an hour on a public computer. As they sit me next to my brother I wonder, if he was to leave would they let me be part of my body again? How could I get him to leave? He doesn't want to escape anymore. I'm FUN now—now that I'm not me. If I concentrate, maybe I can spell *GO* on Finn's back with my finger. Should I write it forwards or backwards for his point of view?

Och, lass, yer wastin' a lot of brain power. Everyone's ken t' y'r thinkin'.

As Finn searches Facebook and Geneology.com and Google, he asks, "Who are these Jack and Beau people I'm trying to find?"

The librarian scolds, "Keep your voice down."

Jenny jumps in whispering, "Jack was the husband and Beau was an acquaintance of Maxine—one of our relatives."

"Are they rich?"

Everyone in me has the same reaction I would. Simon steps forward. "Surely, young sir, you don't believe that only the rich are worth interacting with."

"Duh."

All of them lean me close to Finn's face. Dragon Lady grabs the little smooth chin and roughly turns him to meet our eyes. She hisses, "You little prick, your sister kidnapped you not for money, but to get you out of that fucked up life. To have you see something other than those idiotic Vision Books, so you might not end up a complete asshole. So far, her plan ain't working."

"SHHHH," from the librarian.

Finn's eyes fill with tears.

You're hurting him, Dragon Lady! Let go of my brother! I yell inside.

She continues. "'Cept for a robber-barron pecker-head, your genes come from regular people—poor people even—and they're *all* worth more than your shitty snobby rich ass."

A tear trickles down Finn's pink cheek.

Let go of him!

The librarian "SHHHH"s at us. Simon has us smile contritely at the woman as Dragon Lady lets go of Finn's chin.

Finn turns back to the computer screen. A tear hits the keyboard.

I watch from deep inside, feeling terrible for my brother. He diligently searches the internet for Jack and Beau but can't find anything and I'm sure he is too scared to say. We may just sit here until the hour is up.

Reckon you heard Kelly afore, Izzy. We know what you're thinkin'.

"Mister Findley, you have a wonderful facility with this contraption," Simon whispers. "You use it with impressive skill."

Dragon Lady hops back in my mouth. "'Bout time we got barkin' up a different tree. My sister—I mean our great aunt—is Luella Meakim. She was in Carlisle, Kentucky last I knew. Look her up."

Finn gets searching. In seconds, he points at the address on the screen.

"Hot Damn!" Dragon Lady yells. "Let's fire up the beast and blow this pop-stand!"

The librarian glares as we race out, Dragon Lady dragging Finn by the wrist.

On the road, Simon asks Finn to find out how to get to Carlisle in the road atlas. Finn speaks timidly. "Can I use the GPS?"

"Of course, Mister Findley."

Finn sets the course and whispers, "Six hours and fifty-three minutes," then turns away, staring out the passenger window.

I think loudly. *My brother's hurt and scared. Don't leave him this way. Please. I beg you.*

After a moment, Ruby says, "Finn, reckon you feel a mite miffed, and with good cause. I plum forgot my manners. Fact is, I'm a reckless ne're-do-well shootin' off my mouth like a six-gun. I'm one sorry cuss."

Finn doesn't move.

Jenny slips in with, "Sometimes, because I'm an amalgam of too many ideas at once, I don't always take the most judicious action. You have my apologies."

Heinrich mumbles, "Ich bin ein dummkopf."

"Ja, dummkopf," Solveig agrees.

Finn hunches slightly. "I didn't mean to say all people who aren't rich are worthless."

Dragon Lady barges in, "Listen, bub, you got a lot of jive-ass shit dumped in your head from day-one but you ain't all bad. As for me, I'm a hothead and a fuckin' asshole. Like they say in Rome, mea culpa."

Simon pushes past her. "All you really need to know is—no matter how she talks, your sister loves you very much."

Kelly whispers, "Aye, 'n' that cannae ever change."

Shit. They're much better at being me than I am.

Finn turns to us with a smile. "You're loony."

VISITING LUELLA

SEVEN HOURS LATER, the Metro Van pulls up to a small one-story house. Scalloped aluminum awnings jut out over the windows like buck teeth. Pastel-colored sculptures of children and gnomes dot the tidy yard. The mailbox is pink with artificial flowers vining up the post.

Dragon Lady nods my head. *We found her place alright.*

"Is this for real?" Finn asks, staring at the house. "Someone lives here?"

"My—your relative's sister lives here. Let's pop in."

Finn shakes his head. "I'll stay here. That place looks weird."

Dragon Lady growls, "We talked about this. You're coming. Maxine's your relative, too."

"No."

I feel my right arm twitch. Dragon Lady's about to grab my brother. Ruby pushes that arm down. "Finn, I recollect you had your eyes glued to one of them picture shows in the box. A fella solving crimes? Weren't there a house like this?"

It never occurred to me that these ancestors were watching all the stuff we saw on TV. I would have been more discerning.

Finn's eyes widen. "The detective's partner lived like this!" and he slides open his door and hops down.

As we walk to the house, everyone starts talking in my head with plans and ideas. Jenny suggests that Solveig, Heinrich, and Kelly stay quiet so as not to confuse things with German words or Scottish accents.

Dragon Lady rings the bell. After a moment, shuffling sounds approach. A timid voice asks, "Who is it?"

"It's Dragon—" There's a scuffle inside me and Simon takes over. "Pardon us, Ma'am. I'm Elizabeth and this young gentleman is my brother, Findley. We've come to see Luella."

The door opens a crack. A wrinkled, dried-apple face peers out. Dragon Lady jolts back. *She's so damn old!*

"I'm Luella," the woman says.

Do I look that old!? We were one year apart! She's ancient!

Hush now, Dragon Lady! "Could we talk with you about your sister?"

"My sister?"

"Maxine."

Finn straightens up. "We're like that detective on TV and we're investigating our ancestors. Maxine is related to us."

Luella smiles at my brother and opens the door. She's dressed in a floral muumuu and wears an auburn wig that doesn't completely cover her white hair. "Come on in, Mister Detective."

The house smells of talcum powder.

Dragon Lady is having a conniption in me. *Oh, shit! It is the same as it was in the sixties! Luella never changes! Look at this place!*

It does look like no one's redecorated in over half a century. The wallpaper is pink and silver. The thick carpet is wall to wall and there's foamy stuff on the ceiling. A pink couch faces matching chairs. It's very retro grandmother style but well cared for.

"Set a spell. Make yourself t'home," Luella says.

They sit me on the pink couch and Finn wanders, looking at figurines, needlework, a collection of bells—staring at everything like it's from an alien civilization.

"He is quite the detective, isn't he?" Luella says, taking a chair.

Dragon Lady turns and freezes, staring at a framed paint-by-number of swans. "You always had a thing for paint-by-numbers, Luella."

The old woman looks at us strangely. "What makes you say that?"

Someone in me tries to cover Dragon Lady's tracks. "We're—uh—I'm impressed with the art is all."

"Some wouldn't call it art, but I enjoyed them. All you had to do was follow the numbers and you got something perfect. You didn't need talent, just follow the rules."

"Opposite of me," blurts out Dragon Lady.

"I suppose it's a very conventional way of being. You don't look conventional."

Ruby takes control of our tongue. "Reckon it takes all kinds. I'd be much obliged to hear of Maxine. Like my brother said, your sister is related to us."

"Can't be *too* related."

"Why not?"

"Maxine never had children."

"Are you sure?" Dragon Lady asks a bit belligerently.

"Quite sure. My sister died tragically before she ever had a chance to be a mother. She went camping and a bear pulled her away during the night."

"Bear, my ass."

"Excuse me?" Luella says.

Everyone in me holds Dragon Lady back as Simon steps forward. "Pardon me, ma'am. You say a bear? And her body wasn't discovered?"

"Not a scrap of cloth."

I want revenge! Dragon Lady screams in me. *Where's Jack!? Where's Beau?!*

Patience. We shall endeavor to find answers to your queries.

"Maxine's husband, Jack—is he around?"

"Jack took up the drink after Maxine's death and crashed into a Sycamore tree."

Hope he suffered!

"And that fella, Beau, on the camping trip?"

Luella looks at me quizzically. "How do you know so much about this?"

Finn turns from a rack of souvenir spoons to squint at Luella. "I'm a detective. It's my job."

Luella laughs.

Jenny adds to Finn's answer. "My mother told me when she was explaining the family tree. Is Beau still alive?"

"He is. Should be here soon. He usually comes by about four to check on me."

Dragon Lady's so startled her hand clamps down on Kelly's thigh. Kelly jerks and kicks the coffee table. Simon dives forward and catches the candy dish about to tip. "What time it is now, ma'am?"

"Nearly three. You're welcome to stay. Beau might be able to help with information about Maxine." Luella grins and leans closer. "Those two fought, but I think Maxine had a crush on him."

It takes all of them to keep Dragon Lady pinned inside me. The struggle must make me look like a kook. Ruby responds, "We'd love to stay. Much obliged."

Jenny lectures in my mind. *It is of the utmost importance that you calm yourself, Dragon Lady. There is a time for revolt and a time for patience. Be patient and quiet now or you'll never get the revenge you desire.*

I'll cool my jets, but can't guarantee shit once that pecker Beau arrives.

Finn plops beside me on the couch and reaches for the dish of colorful candies on the coffee table.

Simon taps Finn's hand. "Findley, a gentleman never takes without asking."

Finn stares at me, then turns to Luella. "May I please have a candy?"

I am stunned that he would even know these words! My brother, being polite! Good for Simon!

Luella stands. "You just help yourself. Since you can stay, I'll set us a spread." And she shuffles out of the room.

When that fucker Beau arrives, I'll kill him, Dragon Lady says.

Nay, ye cannae do that. No in front o' the laddie.

Reckon we could send the boy t' sleepin' with that vitamin Izzy gave when we first got the van.

We shall endeavor to get the child to swallow the pill, but, Dragon Lady, you must refrain from any brutal actions until he is verifiably asleep. Jenny gets us up. "I shall return promptly, Finn. Don't partake of all the sweets."

They pull me out to the van, get one of Mother's Ambien and we return as Luella brings out a tray with glasses of root beer and round crackers with some sort of potted meat and American Cheese on them. "This will get you started. I've got pigs-in-a-blanket in the oven that'll be ready in a jiffy."

She disappears again and Ruby hands Finn the Ambien. "So you don't git tooth-rot, take this here tablet."

He downs the pill.

Piping hot, the pigs-in-a-blanket hit the spot for Finn. Heinrich and Solveig love the potted meat, but insist that Ruby eat off the orange *künstlicher Käse* topping it. Ruby happily obliges eating the American cheese and the Germans eat the *Schweinefleisch*. I don't know if they can really taste individually, but I taste it all.

Luella brings out a photo album and sits on the other side of me and shows pictures of Maxine as a child (looking cute but challenging in a little white dress), at her wedding (looking dubious and challenging in a long white dress), a pre-motorcycle race photo (looking dangerous and challenging), and a post-motorcycle race photo where she's covered with mud and wears a shit-eating grin.

"Tough through and through," Dragon Lady says with pride.

"She wasn't like most ladies. She thought anything a man could do, she could do."

"Damn right," Dragon Lady says.

Luella looks at me sharply. "I prefer you keep that language out of this home."

Dragon Lady squirms, about to make things worse. Simon pushes past her. "I'm so sorry, ma'am. Please forgive my manners."

Luella leans close and pats Kelly's knee. "Never you mind. You almost made me laugh, sounding as rough as Maxine. She had a sailor's vocabulary."

Finn lies back on the couch. The Ambien is taking effect.

Luella and the ancestors chat until, at four, there's a friendly knock and the front door opens. Dragon Lady flinches.

Jenny whispers inside. *Remember, he won't recognize you, Dragon Lady. He'll see Elizabeth—an eighteen-year-old girl.*

"And this is my Beau." Luella beams as Beau enters the room.

Beau looks nothing like the handsome, rough man I've seen in Dragon Lady's visions. This man has got to be over eighty, walks with a cane, and is bent low, like he's reaching for something and forgot what he's reaching for and won't straighten up until he remembers.

Dragon Lady snarls. *Damn! He's got one foot in the grave already! Who's the big shot now?*

He stops when he sees me and Finn. "You've got company, Luella. I'll come back later."

"They're kin. Connection with Maxine somehow. They want to meet you."

Beau straightens his neck enough to squint at me and Finn. "Kin with Maxine. Don't know how that could work. Poor woman died before she could have children."

My right arm shakes. Simon holds it down so it looks like I'm just a tense person holding myself.

Beau doesn't seem to notice. "Tragedy about Maxine. I was with her and her husband, Jack, that weekend. We were camping. A bear took her. Real shame."

"Can we ask you some questions about that night?"

Beau sighs. "I'm afraid it was so long ago. I don't remember much. We got woken up by growling noises but we didn't know Maxine was out of her tent. When we couldn't find her in the morning, we drove to the nearest payphone and called the police to report her disappearance, telling them we'd heard the bear. They searched and found nothing. That's the whole story."

Dragon Lady shudders with rage. Everyone tries to calm her as I twitch and jerk from the brawl inside.

I need to kill him!

Endeavor to calm yourself. We will pursue a plan if you behave.

I came for revenge!

We ain't fixin' to let no killin' take place here. Don't want Luella tangled up in this.

Luella's my sister. I'll decide what she gets tangled in.

Jenny gives her orders. *Simon, you will say our goodbyes to Luella and inquire if Beau might assist us fixing a shelf in the vehicle. Once we have him enter the interior, Dragon Lady, you may take over.*

They jostle and bump but seem to agree to act like one slightly-sane human. Simon does as Jenny suggests. Luella is clearly disappointed that we're leaving so soon. "We'll keep in touch, Miss Luella. It's good to meet our kin."

Luella gives me a hug. Dragon Lady's arm pulls her close and holds her longer than I would. Kelly wakes Finn and tells him, "Up nae, Laddie." He stands groggily.

Simon turns to Beau. "Sir, could you give us a hand? There's a shelf we need help with in the van."

Beau smiles, looking glad to be needed. "Happy to, miss."

Dragon Lady is stopped from punching him and we all step out—Finn, Beau, and the conglomerate that controls me.

They open the back doors of the van and Finn crawls up and drops onto his bed—asleep the moment his head hits the pillow. They step me in and Beau pulls himself up and as he enters, Heinrich trips him, Ruby shoves him deep into the van, Kelly drops her knee into his chest, and Dragon Lady growls, "Now I've got you, cocksucker!"

"What the hell!" Beau screams.

STOP! I scream inside. *You can't do this! It's my body and I'll be the one in trouble!*

Shut the fuck up, or I'll wake your little pecker brother so he can watch! Dragon Lady threatens.

I shut the fuck up.

Ruby swirls rope from our tent-kit around Beau's wrists, yanks his hands low, and swirls the rest around his ankles. A quick, impressive knot and he's immobile. It's clear she's an expert. All inside me do a question mark expression.

Grew up ropin' on Pappy's claim in the Western Territory. Steers are harder. I can brand and snip him too, if y'r asking.

"Let me go!" Beau screams.

Ruby pulls the pillowslip off my pillow, grabs it in my teeth, and rrrrrrrrrriiiiippp.

OUCH! That hurts! I have weak teeth.

I have strong teeth! Ruby says in my head.

Ruby puts the ripped cloth around Beau's face and suggests he "open wide" to accept the gag. Beau doesn't. Dragon Lady punches him in the jaw. He opens wide.

Finn looks up groggily from his bunk. "What's going on?"

"Another kidnapping," Dragon Lady says.

"He's not a kid."

"Oldmannapping."

That seems to satisfy Finn. He drops his head and goes back to sleep.

Dragon Lady starts the van and we drive off.

I'm terrified. Dragon Lady's revenge will destroy my life.

Someone in me says, *Your life was never yours. Not back in New York with those Vision Books and not with us. We own you. Get used to it.*

DRAGON LADY — WHITLEY COUNTY, KENTUCKY — 1962

WE'VE ARGUED ABOUT JFK and burnt the steaks and had countless martinis and the sun is long gone and there's just a big ol' moon shining down on us three. Beau sits at the picnic table and Jack stands wobbling over the fire—"tending" it. All he's doing is poking it with a long branch. He should add a log, but I ain't talkin'. There's silence enough to hear the crickets and crackling flames but this kinda quiet ain't good. It gets people stewing. I turn on the transistor radio and pour another round, spilling half on the table.

"One for the road, then I'm hitting the hay."

Push a drink across to Beau and stumble to the fire to bring Jack his replenished soggy Chock Full o' Nuts cup.

Olive jar drink in one hand, Lucky Strike in the other, I stand swaying, singing along to Elvis's "Return to Sender."

There's a twig snap nearby. Jack raises his fire-poking branch defensively, its tip flaming, and peers into the dark woods around us. He looks like he's probably seeing double. "Are there bears out here?"

Beau chuckles. "Beavers." He grins, fire gleaming off his teeth. "One beaver."

I raise my middle finger to him.

Jack sneers, his face lit from the fire's glow. "One beaver is right." He takes a slug from his paper cup and spits the drink into the flames. "Why are we drinking martinis? I don't even like martinis. Where's the Schlitz, Maxine!"

"Dragon Lady," Beau corrects.

"I'm going to bed." I click off the transistor and down the dregs in my jar.

"I autta slug her," Jack mumbles.

"You and what army?" I shout back.

Jack turns his head to face me, wobbling. "I want to know. Why are we always doing what you want, Dragon Lady?"

"You don't like it, step up and make a decision. Be in charge for once."

Jack screams. "You won't let me!"

"Someone's got to wear the fucking pants in our house," I yell.

You will get yourself in trouble a voice in my head says. Men hate me because I don't kowtow to them. *Kowtow.* A flash of something flits into my mind. A Chinese man with a long braid of black hair says, "He no like you no kowtow." The vision startles me—*why am I thinking this?*

Jack stabs the fire with his branch, making the flames rage.

"Jack, you should take your fucking pants back," Beau slurs.

I snap at him, "Stay out of this or I'll bury your cock in a shoebox—"

"—like a dead hamster. Think of something new, Dragon Lady."

I turn to them both. "You cocksuckers don't know me. I always been top of the heap. I drag that log uphill, bike roaring, mud flying like a shit house in a tornado and cross the line FIRST —and you give me second place! I was first, assholes! Engraver was shaking when he carved *second* on the trophy. He knew who won. But you fragile boys can't handle it. You can't stand a chic being better than you!"

Beau laughs. "Dragon Lady, guess what? You're *always* gonna be second place—"

"Fuck you. Stop poking the fire, Jack!"

"—because you may wear the pants, but you got a beaver under them and that makes you second place forever."

"Fuck you! I'm better than any—"

"I want my god-damn pants back!" Jack screams, and there's a swishing sound and I turn to see the flaming tree branch as it SLAMS my head. I drop to my knees and SLAM—I crumple and—

Flash—someone's choking me in a lantern-lit room—

Flash—two men run beside a rice-paddy carrying the rich master in a litter—

Flash—a tiger leaps—

—and I'm flipped onto my back. I reach to claw Jack's face and CRACK—the branch shatters my wrist—my arm drops and Jack stomps, CRACK, pinning it broken to the ground—and Beau's over me like a beast—pulling off my pants, ripping my underwear, tearing into me—ramming into me—

Past his head, past the trees, the stars jolt back and forth with each jab. They've seen this so many times.

Beau snarls with a hard thrust and jerks and jerks and jerks, lifts his fist—

BEAU'S COMEUPPANCE

WE DRIVE FOR A WHILE and end up bouncing down a dirt road. After a bit, we hit a rise and curve and Dragon Lady slams us to a skid and rams gears to *Park*. We rock to a stop on the steep hill overlooking a lake. The trees are much taller, but from the visions of Dragon Lady's ordeal, I recognize the same campground and the lake and mountains. We've arrived at the scene of the crime.

Dragon Lady reverses and does a three-point turn and backs us to the edge of the sloping drop. She turns off the motor and stomps on the parking brake. All of them hang back while Dragon Lady drags Beau to the rear of the van, opens the wide doors, and KICKS. He tumbles down the hill, punctuated with grunts of pain.

When he stops, Dragon Lady grabs the shovel and trots us down to the campground. She peers intently at the tree branches, roots, view of the lake. She takes a few steps to the left and scrapes Kelly's heel across the ground.

"Here's the spot," she says. "Here's your grave, Beau."

Beau squirms in the ropes, protesting behind the gag.

The digging commences. They take turns, but since it's all the same body, it gets wearing. Of course, I wouldn't participate even if I was allowed to.

Reckon that's plenty deep.

I agree. As this is not a sanctioned entombment, there are no precise standards we must adhere to.

'Tis certain plenty 't cover t'ol' numpty.

Gotta be deeper, Dragon Lady insists. *Deep enough that this cocksucker won't be crawling out like I did.*

She keeps everyone digging. Finally, when it's wide enough and deep enough to cover him with two feet of dirt, Dragon Lady drops the shovel and steps up to Beau. She grabs the rope around his ankles. Eyes wide with fear or anger, he yells something unclear.

Seems like the fella wants claim on his last words, Ruby says.

They remove the gag.

Beau coughs an old man cough. "You can't treat me like this!"

"Like what? Like you treated Dragon Lady?"

Beau stares at me. It's clear he sees an 18-year-old girl—Elizabeth—and not everyone else inside. "Who are you?"

"I'm kin of Dragon Lady."

"Dragon La—Maxine had no children, she was killed by a bear—"

Someone gives him the WRONG ANSWER BUZZER sound. "She was raped, broken arm, smashed head, and buried alive."

Enough yammerin'. Dragon Lady gives Beau a shove.

He drops into the pit, landing on his back. "No, no, no!"

She scoops up a shovelful of dirt and flings it—hits his tied feet. Probably on purpose, so the torture will last.

Beau thrashes his legs to knock off the flying earth. He puts on a *have mercy* face. "We'd been drinking. She was provoking me and Jack. We reacted. It was a stupid mistake."

"BEATING and RAPING and BURYING ALIVE is a MISTAKE?!!
You wanted to kill me!!"

"You?—what?—"

More dirt flies in. Shoes get covered.

"Please!" he screams.

Earth over his calves and bent knees.

Beau sobs. "I went back the next day!"

Clods fly from the shovel and smack his thighs, his groin.

Please stop! I yell inside. *He is scared, and that's enough. I don't want to be a murderer!*

No one pays attention to me.

Dirt pounds his stomach. Tears and snot and spittle spill over his chin, darkening his collar. "The hole was empty. She got out. She lived!"

Dragon Lady keeps shoveling. "Yeah, asshole, I know she lived. You know how I know? Because she's my an-fuckin'-cester! She *did* have a baby. She got pregnant when you raped her!"

He's got old man white skin, but Beau's face turns paler. "Pregnant?"

"I got your piece-of-shit DNA in me, and the memories of what you did to Dragon Lady. It was traumatic to her but I'm sure it wasn't traumatic to YOU!"

Beau shakes his head back and forth. "It was! I was petrified! I kept waiting for the police to arrest me. Everyday I expected them." Dirt covers his chest. He spits as clods hit his face. "Why didn't she go to the police?!"

They pause Dragon Lady's shoveling.

Surely you went to the law, Dragon Lady?

Das ist normal, Solveig thinks. *Ich tell nicht person. Tell ist dangerous. Und no one believes.*

Much as the establishment may eschew such things, it is imperative to report these abuses in the fight for justice. Knowing Dragon Lady, she did just that. She's not afraid to stand up for herself.

Reckon that's so, but why didn't the police come for Beau? With all that was done to her, there weren't no shortage of evidence. Beau wouldda spent years in jail.

Aye, 'tis true. Canye 'splain t'us why ye didnae tell, Dragon Lady?

None of your fuckin' business!

It is! We are your fuckin' business! What aren't you telling us!?

DRAGON LADY — WHITLEY COUNTY, KENTUCKY — 1962

WITH MY ONE-WORKING ARM, I search the pit I'm standing in. Paw through leaves and sticks and dirt. If I was meant to die here, they would have buried my clothes as well. All I feel are sharp twigs and wet earth. I'm freezing. Sun's almost gone. I'll die of the cold if I can't find—*ah!*—there's cloth. Pull out my jeans—*keep looking!*—and my shirt—put it on to stop the shakes—*keep looking!*—my hand is bleeding from all the scratches. That's all I can find. No socks. No shoes. Did they keep them as souvenirs?

I haul myself out of the pit and struggle into the jeans. My right arm is useless and limp at my side. Undo the middle button of my shirt and gently guide the arm in as a sling.

Get moving. It's a long walk out.

Stumbling to the campsite, I look up. The hill seems so high now. I try walking but my balance is crap and so I crawl. A three-legged beast. Stones jab my feet and knees and the one palm.

At the top—there are the tire prints of where I skidded to a stop and that snuffed-out cigarette butt in the leaves. I put it in my mouth and reach into my jeans pocket—pull out Beau's bronze lighter. Flick left-handed and get a flame. Smoke the stub down to the filter.

If I can make it out, I'll go straight to the police. Those assholes think they got away with it. They will pay.

Time to walk.

I take a step and stumble over a root, falling forward, face in the dirt. Stunning pain stabs my right arm. It's got to be broken and maybe dislocated. There's no way I can go on.

You've had your face in the dirt before and loved it. Get up. Show 'em what you can do!

This is different.

You sliced your arm in the second lap wreck in '61. That hurt like hell, but it didn't stop you. Came in third.

I get up slowly, trying to keep my arm from being jostled in the shirt-sling. Let the pain move through. Step. Stones pierce my bare feet. Step again. My right hand's numb. I try to wriggle the fingers but nothing happens. God damn it! I better not lose this arm. I better be able to race again.

How far is it to the paved road? I can't remember how long we drove on this dirt road coming in. Jack droned on about fly-fishing when we left the highway. Seemed like he talked for at least fifteen minutes but was that because I was bored? We were going bout twenty miles an hour, so maybe it's five miles to get out?

I stumble again but stay upright through the searing agony in my arm.

Keep your eyes on the ground. Watch the track!

Looking down, watching for rocks and roots. A shiver comes over me. It's getting dark and really cold. I can't walk far in my condition. Five miles might be too much.

Touch my head. The blood is dried and caked over my face and short-cropped hair.

A greenish blob lies in the ditch beside the road, half covered in dead leaves. A tarp. Must have blown off the back of a truck. I pull it from the ground and—the pain of my arm is terrible, but got to keep warm, so—wrap it over myself.

I slog on, jiving myself that I'm on my bike, trying to hear the motor roar and whine, making each foot move as if it's a wheel spinning, hurtling me forward.

My brain fogs, is jolted by pain, and clears. Fog, pain, clear. This must last for hours.

Where am I? I'm not in a race? What happened?

There's a hiss of tires. I lift my head and a car zooms by at the end of the road. The blacktop!

Pull the tarp closer around me and stumble out onto the two-lane. Forest road in both directions. It's night-time dark. How long have I been walking? Damn, it's cold! If no one comes, I'll freeze to death.

Headlights in the distance. Approaching.

Get in the road. Make sure they see you.

I step into the middle and the pickup slows and pulls beside me. A hunter type. Cap and camo. His eyes widen when he sees me close. "Hell! You alright? You need a ride?"

My voice doesn't work. I nod.

"Get in."

I open the door with my left, slide in, and pull it shut, trying not to move my right arm.

"You're all busted up. I'll get you to a doc, buddy."

Buddy. No one's ever called me that.

It feels good.

Really good.

BEAU'S BURIAL

EVERYONE IN ME wonders what that means.

WHAP! Dirt hits Beau's face. He scrunches his eyes and mouth against the impact, then gasps for air. The weight of it on his chest must be making breathing difficult.

He pants. "I'm sorry! I shouldn't have done what I did. It was horrible. Criminal. But she got what she wanted."

"What the fuck did you say?" Dragon Lady asks.

"Maxine got what she wanted."

"Being raped!? Buried alive?!"

Another shovelful hits the old man's face. He spits, sobbing, "She got to start again. To be who she wanted to be!"

They stop Dragon Lady from shoveling again. "What're ye' goin' on a'boot?"

"Maxine must have realized that if everyone thought she was dead, she could have a new life. The one she'd always wanted."

"And what life was that?"

Beau spits out a glob of mud. "Back in the day, I used to be champion racer—"

"FUCK YOU," Dragon Lady yells, struggling with everyone for the shovel. They hold it tightly.

"Go on, Mr. Tompkins," Simon urges.

"I read an article about a racer out in Los Angeles, California. Max Dragon. I researched him. Pictures always showed him with a helmet on. Sometimes goggles. But it looked to me like— Maxine became Max."

Dragon Lady drops inside us, making Heinrich and Kelly's knees buckle, and we all sink to the ground.

I don't remember becoming Max.

Reckon that's 'cause we only know what was passed on in the baby's genes. Your awareness stopped the moment the baby was born, Dragon Lady.

Your transformation from Maxine to Max must have been after the child.

Beau coughs.

'Ave yea got a notion what t' do we'im?

My left hand rises. Simon. *Two wrongs don't make a right.*

My left leg twitches. Heinrich. *We scared him mit das—he would die. Dragon Lady lived through das bury und rape. Nicht really as bad as—*

Kelly kicks my left foot. Dragon Lady punches my left thigh. Simon pounds that leg, Jenny bends and bites, Ruby and Solveig slam Heinrich on the inside. I would join in if I could.

"YOU WILL NEVER EVER EVER CONSIDER RAPE AS ANYTHING LESS THAN TRAUMA!" they all scream at Heinrich.

Beau sputters. "Yes. Never. Ever. Ever. Rape is trauma."

As we endeavor for justice, I propose that we take a vote to decide on our next course of action.

Damn it, Jenny, no voting! This is my fuckin' revenge and I'm fuckin' doin' it. Dragon Lady rises us up, grabs the shovel, scoops up a load of dirt and—WHAM! Right in Beau's face. He screams.

She'll kill him and I'll go to jail! I yell. But no one hears me.

Dragon Lady whips another shovelful into Beau's face. Simon grabs the shovel and they struggle. I feel several in me coalescing behind Simon.

Ruby ambles into our mind. *Reckon you're doing somethin' that's gonna get us all in trouble, Dragon Lady. You fixin' to send your kin to jail? Your sister Luella saw Izzy and she's gonna be wonderin' 'bout her Beau. You gonna go back and kill that witness? And the other one—Finn. Have to do him in as well.*

I feel Dragon Lady slump and they wrench the shovel from my right hand and fling it to the ground.

"Mr. Beau?" Simon leans us over the cowering man in the grave. "My suggestion is for you to spend the rest of your life helping ladies in distress. Anything they need, housing, money, food, kindness—you give it. You're going to make amends. Is that clear?"

Beau sobs his agreement.

They untie the old man and help him up to the van. I'm grateful to find Finn is still asleep in his bunk. Back in Luella's neighborhood they drop Beau at a gas station and drive away, none looking back. Everyone thinks it's best to sleep in the van tonight, so they return down that dirt road to that same spot—the scene of the crimes.

They undress my body in silence, slip me into my t-shirt, and crawl me into the bed across from my brother.

'Twas the only man alive from th'olden times. Donnae hae nae more t' find.

Reckon that's right, Kelly. Our revenging days are o'er.

Solveig murmurs in my head. *Nein. Heinrich ist next.*

Heinrich twitches angrily, *How you know Ich nicht come back und marry you und take care of you, Solveig? We don't know alles moments of our lives. Just das trauma burned in at conception. You don't know!*

"Gute nacht, Schätzchen," she whispers.

SOLVEIG — FRANKFURT, GERMANY — 1945

MY BACK ACHES. Heinrich disappeared after that day on the hill, but what he left behind is growing. I can hardly care for myself and my sister, so I doubt this baby will survive.

I nod to my sister and we wait for one of the American jeeps to zoom by and then cross to the other side of Friedrichstraße. We climb up to the top of a pile of rubble and move bricks, looking for anything. One day we found a pair of shoes. Another, a can of beans. Several months ago, I found a blue ribbon. I'm saving it to give Miriam for her twelfth birthday in November. If we make it those four months. Turn over another brick. Give us something. Anything. Another brick. Nothing. Another. Nothing. The rags covering my fingers are disintegrating. My hands are raw. Another brick. Nothing.

Miriam inhales sharply. I turn to her and she looks around the street, wary of the other scavengers. There are many figures scattered about, pecking like crows at the ruins of this city, but none are looking at us. My little sister widens her eyes for me to join her. I move as if disheartened so as not to draw attention. By her battered shoe is the tip of a leather handle. Please let it be more than a handle! We sit, feigning exhaustion. She kicks the dust angrily as if she's a sullen child, not the elderly soul she's become. Behind her, I slide bricks to the side. The handle is attached to more. A small leather suitcase! I have a coughing fit and click the clasps open behind my rasping. Miriam feels me tense. She doesn't miss a beat of her childish boredom kicking.

Inside are three man's shirts, two pairs of socks, nice shoes, a toiletry kit, soap (!), and a flattened hat. An unbelievable treasure. We can't take it from this rubble now or others will steal it from us. Need to wait until dark. Shaking with excitement, I close the case and cover it with bricks and dust. How can I mark this place?

"Miriam, touch my back, pretending you're concerned."

I put my filthy bloody fingers down my throat and press that deep spot. I haven't eaten anything except the bit of rotten apple we found under the tree by the river and the few snails. Please let there be something left of it in my stomach.

My stomach wrenches and spasms. A squirt of brown bile spatters up.

Fingers again.

Another spurt and, with it, chunks of half-digested food. The smell is retched. Hopefully, that will keep the others away.

The miraculously undamaged clock tower chimes twelve. I sleep but keep an ear open. Chimes again at one. Two. At three, I slip out from under the blanket. Most of the drunken G.I.s should be off the streets and with them, the scavengers, thieves, wild children, and women trying to survive any way they can. Miriam sleeps as I tuck the blanket around her thin form. She won't survive if we don't find food.

Leave the tiny room, a surviving closet beneath the stairway of what once was our apartment building. The cold air hits. I close my eyes and imagine the way it was. The marble floor intact, the walls rising up to the glowing lamps. The stairway to our floor with all those memories. All that is left is the stairway, leading to nothing, with our little room underneath. I pull the nub of chalk from my pocket and re-mark the words on the door —*Typhus hier*. Hopefully, that will dissuade anyone from entering.

Pass the rubble of the kinder school. Miriam was still going there a year ago. Cross the playground and the twisted metal that once was a swing set. Cross Friedrichstraße. There are no lights in the city and the moon is obscured by clouds. I hope I can find the treasure. A cobblestone or piece of ruin trips me. Knees and palms meet wet stone. Scrape upon scab. Move to the shattered building. Slowly climb the mountain of bricks. Sniff. Hope to smell my vomit. Nothing. The clouds part and two eyes shine up ahead. They stare, blink, and go back to their purpose. I hope that is the spot—a raccoon foraging my last lost meal. I get near and hiss. The eyes glare and scamper.

Bile smell is faint but evident. Dig. Searing pain in my fingertips. I can't do this much longer. Feel only brick and dust and stone. This has to be the place! Throw a brick aside. *Someone will hear!* There's the handle. Flood of relief and joy and pull it up. Running, tripping, stumbling, falling, and into the building that's no longer here, and across the pock-marked marble, and open the door under the stairs, and slide in. Miriam feels so warm coming in from the cold. Breathe. Tomorrow we can trade our bounty and eat.

Papa and Mama sing at the piano. The candles flicker, sending dancing shimmers on our wallpaper. Miriam spins the metal top across the floor. Papa smiles and hands me a present. The rosy and plump twins, Daniel and Hannah, crawl on the carpet squealing. Our little dog, Spätzle, barks at all the merriment. Mama leans close to kiss me, "Solveig, liebeshien." She smells of her Paris perfume.

Sweeping sounds intrude. I don't want to leave this dream. Please let me stay with Mama and Papa. Let them still be alive. Let our rooms be standing. Let me see Daniel and Hannah grow. Papa smiles. The top wobbles and tips as the sweeping gets louder. I wake and everything is the way it is now, instead of the way it was then. I hate it.

Miriam is still asleep. I don't want to take care of her. I want someone to take care of me!

All my upbringing tells me to get up and start the day. Do my best. Perform my duties. Be the older sister. But I don't want to!

Miriam whimpers. She's also lost her mother and father and the little twins and home and country and everything else. All she has is me.

I will do my best. I promise, Miriam.

I stroke the strand of hair from her cheek. Her skin is hot.

But she's not feverish. I'm sure. She's a child. They run hot.

Get up and step out of the closet. Frau Muller's sweeping the step of her shop across the road. The front window is boarded up, but she has three of four walls. A mix of tarps and metal and wood covers the missing back wall. Frau Muller nods to me as if nothing's changed. "Guten tag, Solveig."

Guten Tag? Did I miss the morning? The clock tower answers with two chimes. I slept most of the day!

"Guten tag, Frau Muller."

"How is your sister Miriam?"

"Fine. But children, they run hot, right?"

Alarm crosses the stern woman's face. "She has the fever?"

"No, no, not that kind of hot."

Frau Muller gets back to sweeping.

Should I ask her? I have no choice. "Frau Muller, I wonder if I might trade some items for food."

Frau Muller skips a beat with her sweeping. "You think I have food?"

"Perhaps you know where I can trade."

"What do you have?"

"Shirts, shoes, toiletries,—"

"Soap?"

I nod.

Frau Muller stops sweeping. She peers at me. "You come inside."

In her shop, the shelves are bare. Maybe she has nothing but now she knows I have something. Will she steal from me?!

A sound in the corner turns me. A girl of Miriam's age sits on a stool, pistol in her hand. I remember her singing in the choir beside my sister. Gretchen was her name. I smile, but she just stares at me.

Frau Muller nods to a worn tarp covering something. The girl pulls off the tattered cloth, startling the pigeon in its stick cage. Wings flap in terror. "You can have."

"I can't cook, you know that. Any smell of food on a fire and the wild children will swarm us. What do you have like cans, bread, crackers,..."

"Schweinefleisch."

My mouth springs saliva I didn't know was even possible anymore. But I need more than potted meat. "That's a beginning."

"Two turnips."

"Yes, and?

"You have soap. Tooth powder?"

"Almost a full container. And the brush."

"Fish oil. And a lemon."

I know she's a businesswoman, but hope she's still a mother. "And for Miriam?"

Frau Muller flashes a look of anger. She reaches into her apron pocket, pulls out a key, unlocks a drawer, and lifts out a chocolate bar—U.S.-made. A soft cry of "mama" comes from Gretchen. She tenses, her small hands shifting on the pistol. Is this her chocolate I'd be taking? Frau Muller hisses to her daughter and turns to me. "We have deal?"

"Okay," I say. "I'll bring the items."

Miriam is awake when I step in.

"I thought you'd left forever."

"I will never leave you, Miriam. And I have a great surprise for you. Come with me."

We cross the street with the suitcase wrapped in our blanket. Miriam feels hotter than ever under my arm.

Frau Muller hurries us inside and locks the door.

Miriam immediately rushes to the corner. "Gretchen! How are you!?"

Gretchen melts from guard into girl. "Miri, I missed you!"

As I trade the suitcase for food, the two classmates chatter about what scared them, who's dead and who isn't, what they miss of school, and what they'll do after it's all back to normal. Hearing my sister laugh drops me into deep sorrow and joy at the same time.

"We'd better go, Miriam," I say. Miriam reluctantly leaves Gretchen's side as Frau Muller loads the food and finally the chocolate onto the blanket.

"Einen moment bitte," my little sister says. She opens the Hershey bar, cracks off pieces, and passes out squares between the four of us. My heart aches with the pain of what I've lost and what Miriam hasn't yet lost.

Frau Muller puts a square in her mouth and closes her eyes. Maybe she's seeing a different time or maybe she's seeing right now and how good this can be. I put the square in my mouth and all of me melts with the sweetness.

Miriam waves to Gretchen and we step out.

Checking that we're not watched, we cross the street and go back into our closet below the stairs. We open the can of Schweinefleisch and the smell makes both our stomachs growl. We eat the entire can and it floods us with joy and energy. Miriam looks happy. She has two sips of fish oil, smells the turnips, and lies down rubbing the lemon against her cheek. "I stole this lemon from Mama, who's making her lemon cake for dessert. She's yelling and laughing, pretending to be mad. You and me are hiding in this closet and Mama and Papa and Daniel and Hannah are all upstairs and they're going to search for us and Spätzle wants to sniff for us but the lemon smell will trick him and they'll look and look and when they finally find us, we'll all celebrate."

"I hear Mama yelling, 'Who stole my lemon! I need it to make my Zitronenkuchen!' She's stomping on the floor and Papa's stomping on the floor. They're acting like they're mad, but we know they aren't mad."

I push my fingernail into the lemon rind to spark the scent. The juice stings my wounds but I ignore the pain.

Miriam gives me a kiss. Her lips are scalding. She's very feverish.

Miriam whispers. "Let's not give up until Mama and Papa find us. You know they're looking. They'll open the door wide and say 'There you are!' Then we'll all eat Mama's Zitronenkuchen."

I agree, but I don't think she's pretending anymore. The fever has her mind. I should leave to find a doctor. But where do I look for a doctor? And if I find one, will he come if I've no money? Will he take two turnips? What if Miriam gets worse and I'm not here? Will she try to find me in the dark streets? Will I lose her forever?

"Solveig, come close. I'm cold."

I lie beside her and hold her tight.

Miriam shakes, in and out of sleep. She mumbles and groans, calling for Mama and scolding little Spätzle for barking. I try to think of where a doctor might be but keep waking up to find I've been sleeping. When the clock strikes midnight she asks for Zitronenkuchen. I give her three spoonfuls of fish oil and try to tempt her with a turnip. She falls asleep again. Moments later, the clock tower strikes six. I wake and Miriam is no longer feverish. She is no longer warm. She's cold and stiff. This can't be. I put my head to her empty chest. There are no sounds but sobs.

Why didn't I look for a doctor? I could have saved her. She's dead because I wasn't smart enough or brave enough to do that simple thing. Why couldn't it be me?!

I'm all alone now. I hate Miriam for leaving me alone. Hate my whole family for leaving me alone. I've no one to care for but myself and I'm not worth saving.

She doesn't look like herself with nothing inside making her smile or cry or laugh or be mad at me. This form is not her. Still, I should do something. I tie the blue ribbon I was saving for her birthday around a bit of her dirty hair and pretend she's happy.

Am I supposed to do something with her? Burn her or bury her? I don't know how to do this. Maybe I don't have to. I'll stay here and have her fever take me. I'll soon become cold and empty like my sister. Someone else can deal with us.

A gunshot BOOMS close by, giving me a jolt. My heart and body raise me quickly, acting on their own, apart from my will. They want to go. I don't. Something or someone in me takes over and decides—*Time to leave Frankfurt. NOW!*

MOVE THE ROCK

I DON'T LIKE WAKING UP to something already in progress. I'm on the ground, lying in front of the Metro Van at the edge of the hill over the campsite. There's a rock wedged to keep the right tire from rolling and my left leg lies stretched out before that tire. If the rock is moved, the van will roll downhill and—

Whoa! I think loudly. *Don't move that rock or Heinrich's leg will be crushed!*

Das ist der plan, says Solveig.

Two heavy branches are under that twitching leg, no doubt to ensure that bones crack instead of getting pressed into the dense leaves. Kelly's leg is crooked up, out of danger.

If Heinrich's leg is crushed, my leg is crushed!

Pull the rock, Simon, Solveig orders.

Simon reaches for the rock, murmuring, *We are both guilty of terrible things, Heinrich. I'm horrified at what I did to Irene. We deserve punishment. I'm afraid you do as well, Miss Elizabeth.*

Heinrich screams. *Nein! Nicht want to do das, aber Ich was hurt. Nein! Bitte!*

I push and pull and do anything to control my left hand but Simon isn't letting me in. He slips his fingers around the rock and tugs. It wiggles but doesn't move. The weight of the Metro Van has wedged it in.

Pardon me, Miss Dragon Lady, can you assist me?

The others twist my torso and Dragon Lady leans—and puts her hand around the rock.

No, no. Don't do this! I plead. *Please, Solveig, none of you will be able to do much without this leg.*

Izzy, you were going to kill Finn und yourself. Ich only taking this leg.

She nods my head for Simon and Dragon Lady to pull.

Solveig, I'm sorry! Heinrich twitches violently. *Das was an unforgivable act. Ich am so very sorry. Bitte, forgive me.*

Ruby answers. *Reckon you'd propose to a rattler if you thought it'd keep you from bein' bit.*

Nein. Ich mean it.

I try to close my eyes, try to bite my hands, try to kick someone out of any of my limbs, but nothing works. They've locked me away from this body.

Please endeavor to settle yourself, Izzy, Jenny thinks. *One must accept consequences.*

Heinrich and I both plead.

Solveig shakes my head. *Nicht gut enough. Du bist kaputt. PULL!*

Simon and Dragon Lady pull together and the rock SQUEAKKKKKS out from under the rubber. There is a quiet stillness in the next moment. Then—a little crunch as the tire inches forward and cracks over a twig. It's not on a real roll yet, but will be in a second. FUCK!

I try to get Heinrich's leg out of the way, but everyone in me is holding him down. They think I deserve this, too! The van tire cracks another twig and my leg is next. The horror of what is about to happen muscles me to my own mouth and I scream, "I'm sorry about Finn! But Finn's alive!"

"No, I'm dead!" a faraway voice yells.

We all turn. Down the hill, Finn lies waving in the grave we dug for Beau. Down the hill—directly below the Metro Van.

"FUCK!" we all yell, and my leg is whipped back as the tire SNAPS the thick branches beneath where it was.

"FINN, GET OUT OF THERE!" I yell as everyone gets me up and we're pushing on the front bumper, feet sliding backwards as the van moves forward, nearing the steep drop, and Heinrich kicks the rock to get it back in place, but it doesn't go far enough, and Kelly wedges her tender foot against the tire and as everyone enters the small space of her eighteen-year-old toes, that foot swells, and we all scream, "PUSH!"

And the van stops.

Finn trudges slowly up the slope. "What are you yelling about?"

I can't speak so Jenny steps in. "Finn, put that rock under the tire and kick it hard."

When the rock is in place and has been checked by everyone, Dragon Lady backs the van away from the edge and sets the parking brake.

I'm shaking with adrenaline and anger. *You idiots just about killed me and my brother. You're not any better than I am! You all have your agendas and plans, but I am part of this body, so I get a say!*

For some reason, they agree.

As I sit in the driver's seat, overwhelmed by what could have happened, Finn asks, "What about the old man you kidnapped?"

Shit. He remembers. I sputter, trying to think of an answer. I'm finally able to talk and I don't know what to say!

"I'm the detective," Finn says. "I found the rope you tied that man with and the gag. But no sign of blood. And he wasn't in the grave. You buried him and he escaped, or you lost your nerve and let him go."

I nod.

"If he escaped, he'll come back with the police. And if you let him go, he'll come back with the police."

A spasm of fear runs over us all. Can we trust Beau?

Dragon Lady thinks loudly *NO.*

I scan the forest from all the van windows. No sign of anyone. But they could be out there. Beau told the police. They're surrounding us. Any minute the helicopter will appear over the lake and sirens will wail and SWAT teams will descend from the trees. Everyone in me is hyper-attentive. "Time to go, Finn. Don't want to be here if the police arrive."

"I'm ready," he says, hopping into his seat and looking like a child about to embark on an adventure.

"Seatbelt?"

"Check."

"Nose?"

"Check."

"Bravery?"

"What will we be doing?"

"Bravery!?"

"Check."

And we slide into reverse, three-point-turn around, and roar back up the dirt road. Please don't let us meet the police coming in.

We get to the highway without getting caught. "You're a smart detective, Finn," I say.

"The private detectives after us are probably smarter."

Luckily Dragon Lady has the wheel, 'cause I jolt with fear. "Private detectives after us?"

"Father uses them all the time. For everything. He told me that's what we Gastons do. We don't want to ever get our hands dirty." Finn looks down at his filthy hands—"OOPS!" and laughs. "He took me into the study to give me instructions on how to be a Gaston."

I don't need to guess why I never got instructions about how to be a Gaston. "What did Father tell you?"

"Never involve the police or media or anything that will bring notice from the populous. We should be unthought of and so far above that we don't exist to them. So there's no way he'd have a nationwide search with alerts and pictures of me all over the country. He'd keep it quiet."

"And hire a detective."

"Probably a team of detectives."

I feel sick. What will happen if they find us? Finn will go back to the Vision Book life and I'll be thrown in jail. My plan—making Finn a better person—will be over. But so far, I'm not doing a very good job of that anyway. So far, I've kidnapped him and almost drowned him and gave him his first hangover and kidnapped an old man and almost buried him and almost crushed my own leg with the van and almost had the van run over Finn. I'm not a good enough person to teach Finn anything, but maybe those inside me are.

Reckon he should study on how you gotta work if you hanker for something, Ruby says.

Lad's got tae ken 'bout scratin' f'oats an' bein' poor, says Kelly.

Expose him to different kinds of people, says Simon.

Quite correct. The foundation of civility and respect comes from interaction with the other, adds Jenny.

Dragon Lady grumbles, *Little Pecker won't learn shit. Tiger can't change its stripes.*

Heinrich suggests Finn needs a *good Prügelstrafe*.

No beating, Heinrich! snaps Solveig.

Finn keeps scanning the van mirrors. He's on the lookout. "The detectives Father hired will hear of the old-man-napping if he tells. I think we need to get somewhere safe and stop driving," Finn suggests. "Maybe there's someone we can stay with. Someone they would never think of."

The kid is smart.

"I'm afraid I don't know anyone. I didn't have friends and the only person who was really nice—she only saw me for a short time."

"Who was that?"

"Yasmina. My—the lady that—incubated—"

"The surrogate. We should visit her."

"I don't know her last name. She was our housekeeper, but I only know she was from New Orleans."

"Hello-o. If she was a housekeeper, she got paid. We get on a computer and get into Mother's bank account."

"Isn't there a password?"

Finn looks at me like I'm clueless. "My birthday."

"I'm glad I have a detective with me, Finn." I hope he knows it's me saying this and no one else.

RUBY — CLEARWATER CREEK, CALIFORNIA — 1877

CHAN BORROWS TWO HORSES and we head out for a ride 'fore the dawn even thinks of wakin'. No one is gonna cotton to us being together. We need a safe place to be us.

We ride as the light changes and head down past where the treeline starts and the snow ends. It's warmer and it's dang glorious to see leaves and plants and even flowers! I been up in Bodie, that wasteland of a town so long I plumb near git bawlin' at the sight of greenery.

Chan points at the road runner standing in the middle of the trail. We pull back on the reins to watch. The bird flits its long tail, tilts its head, eye on us. It's a magic moment and then the fella races off.

We trot on to where the river drops from the mountains. Aspen and cottonwoods surround the waterfalls, their leaves spinning and shivering in the breeze. We spread a blanket and lie with each other again.

The sage smells strong, scrumbled by the blanket beneath us. The horses nibble fresh shoots of grass and drink from the river. Two quail call each other. Everyone's happy. I relish the smooth skin of the man beside me. So good to feel safe and loved.

"Grow back good." Chan touches where my hair was burned. He kisses my shoulder. "Xǐyuè wǒ de," Chan whispers.

"What does that mean?"

"Joy of mine."

I try to pronounce it. "See-you wodder."

"Xǐyuè wǒ de."

I try several times but can't get the right sounds. "Sorry, Chan, I'll call you See You Water and you'll know I mean Joy of mine."

NOLA

FINN AND I FIND A LIBRARY and fifteen minutes later we're logging off the computer and on the road heading for New Orleans.

I'd love to tell you all about the trip. How Finn and I bonded more and how we fought and how we made up and bonded again and who in me started being a real prick about disciplining Finn (Heinrich) and who in me connected with him (everyone else), what we ate, the places we camped, the new constellations we named, but I've got oodles more to get through so—sorry.

It's raining as we drive onto a bridge that will take us to New Orleans. We can't see much beyond the car in front of us. The rain makes the road slick, and a low guardrail is all that separates us from dropping into the water. Heavy drops clatter against the Metro Van—a percussion class gone wild after the teacher has left the room.

A minute goes by. Finn wonders, "I don't like being so close to falling. Why isn't this bridge ending?"

"I don't know. Check the GPS and program in Yasmina's house in New Orleans."

He does and the female GPS robot says, "Keep straight on Lake Pontchartrain Causeway Bridge for twenty-three miles."

"The bridge is twenty-three miles!?" Finn screams. "Turn around!"

"We can't turn around, Finn. This is one way."

181

"This van is big and that fence won't stop it. We'll fall. I'll drown!"

I did this to him. I tried to kill him and now he's terrified of water.

'Tis me as well, Kelly whispers in our head.

"Izzy, hold the steering wheel tight!!!" yells Finn.

Dragon Lady has her wrist casually draped over the top of the steering wheel.

Dragon Lady, Simon, can you hold the wheel with both hands? I ask inside myself.

Simon puts his hand on the wheel, but Dragon Lady keeps her wrist draped over the top.

Please.

It's a straight fuckin' road. I don't need to steer.

Please.

Dragon Lady sighs loudly (which makes me worry Finn will think it's me), and reluctantly grips the wheel. I don't care if she thinks we're scaredy-cats. We all feel better.

I try to offer topics to engage Finn, but nothing takes his attention from the fear of falling and the bridge goes on and on. Half an hour of terror later, we exit the bridge and drive onto solid ground. The rain lessens to a slow finger-drum on the rooftop and finally sunlight blasts the windshield as the clouds part. Everything is sparkling with the glare—cars, pavement, stoplights, buildings—all covered with the millions of stars that escaped the sky.

The GPS voice has us drive and turn and take a fork and bear right and take the next left... and we pass through areas of two-story buildings with wrought-iron balconies, neighborhoods of brightly colored cartoon-looking bungalows, streets with everyone sitting on their steps chatting, turn left, turn right...

"You have reached your destination."

The block is weird. There are several lots with front steps, but no houses. There are houses with boarded-up windows. We check the address number for Yasmina. It's a small suburban home with a raggedy yard and beat-up car in the driveway.

"How's it look to you, Finn? If you don't like the idea, we can take it easy somewhere—"

"Take it easy but TAKE IT!"

"Yeah!" Dragon Lady reaches out her hand to him.

Finn grins and slaps it. "Let's go see this lady."

I'm so proud of him.

We step out and walk to the front door. Ring the bell. All of a sudden, the flood of memory comes surging back. The warmth. Her breast. The cooing. Songs in Spanish while I sloshed in the womb. I'm afraid. She will never live up to this miracle of a person.

But no one comes to the door. Nothing happens. As I pull back tears, Finn rings again. Nothing happens again. I turn away, feeling a rejection in all my cells.

Finn kicks the door. "Hey, open up! It's your baby."

A slight sound from inside.

Finn kicks again. "It's your baby from your tummy!"

The click of locks turning. The door opens a crack. Darkness inside. No face there. "What you wakin' me up for?" A man's voice. Challenging and belligerent.

What else is new? They're all assholes, thinks Dragon Lady.

Not so, says Simon.

Finn continues, "We're here to see Yasmina. We know her. Well, I don't, but my sister does."

"I don't know no Yasmina. Get yourselves lost."

The door closes with enough force to rattle the windows across the front.

I head back to the van with a depressed slouch. Finn must notice 'cause he touches my elbow as we walk down the path. "She probably moved," says Finn. "We'll find her."

Slide the Metro door open and someone's calling, "Espera! Espera!" A woman, round and squat, with dark hair pulled up in a bun, trots toward us. "Yo soy Yasmina. Y ustedes?"

The words come up from somewhere and tumble off my tongue. "Yo soy Elizabeth. Tu hija de los Gastons."

Yasmina rushes forward and grabs me, kissing my face and hands, and murmuring and cooing, and I slip into her embrace like returning to her womb.

"Quien es este?" she asks, looking past my arm to Finn.

"Mi hermano Finn."

Finn is hugged and welcomed like one of her family. He happily melts in Yasmina's embrace like I did. I've never seen him accept a hug like this. We both have been slowly touching more, but a stranger? And someone poor and not white? This trip *is* changing him. I've done good.

"What are you doing here?" Yasmina asks, holding both of our hands proudly.

"We're traveling. Thought we'd say hello," I say, not knowing how to ask to stay with her.

"We're on a road trip, Miss Yasmina," Finn adds, undoubtedly channeling Simon. "We hoped we might impose on your generosity and stay for a while."

Yasmina laughs at his politeness. "Of course, Mijo. Bienvenidos." And she leads us inside.

The house is small but filled with cozy elements. Lace curtains soften the windows. Fanning out from a hanging tambourine and maracas behind a yellow-blue-and-red flag are pictures of relatives or ancestors filling the space with smiles. Paper flowers and South American tapestries add color everywhere. Cacti and succulent plants line the window sills. The furniture is probably second-hand but it's well kept and the place exudes the feeling of care. And in the middle of the open-plan living/dining/kitchen area is a man sitting in front of a big flat-screen TV. "Bruce, this is Elizabeth and Finn. They're children of —a previous employer."

Bruce is a big white dude with a shaved head, tattoos on his calves, and a brown chin beard that shouldn't have been attempted. He stands slowly and walks close.

Yasmina puts her arms around us—a bit protectively—making me wonder about this Bruce guy. "They're on a road trip and will stay with us for a while."

"Is that so?" Bruce asks Yasmina dubiously. His eyes scroll my body.

"Sí," Yasmina says definitively and leads us to a short hallway. "Bathroom, and this room has a fold-out sofa you can both sleep on."

The room is small and very cluttered but in an organized way. A desk holds a large sewing machine in front of a pegboard with scissors, tape measures, ribbon rolls, thread spools, etc. Surrounding it are bolts of fabric and a dressmaker's dummy. A serious workspace.

"We don't want to get in your way—"

"Don't think of it. Ahora, a road trip means no showers or baths? And you need laundry done, si?"

While Finn showers, I go to the van to gather our laundry. As I'm collecting everything, Bruce opens the back doors and steps in. The Van tilts with his weight. He crooks his head and shoulders to the side in the low-ceiling.

"On the road, eh? Where from?"

"Up north."

"Where exactly?"

"New England area."

Bruce moves closer, making the axle springs creak.

"I asked where exactly?"

"Connecticut."

Bruce smiles. "Mind if I look around? Never been in one of these before."

Simon lifts his arm in a "welcome" gesture, making me mad. I back against my bed as the man moves forward. He lingers just a moment too long as he's moving past me, taking time to scrutinize my form. He steps to the front and opens the glove compartment. Lifts a paper.

"Registration says Elizabeth Gaston, New York City. Why did you lie to me?"

Finn hops into the back of the van wearing only a towel. He's pink and shining and looks to be glowing inside. "That was the best shower ever!"

I hurry to him, pulling the bundle of laundry off the bed and hustling him outside, "Let's get you some clothes and I'll shower next." We leave Bruce in the Metro Van. I can't stand the idea of him in our space, but need to escape further questions and looks.

In the pink bathroom, I adjust the water temperature, worrying about my conversation with Bruce, but the minute I slip into the hot deluge, all thoughts disappear. When was the last shower? Who cares, this is bliss. I wash and wash and stand under the warmth until it shifts to cold. I've heard about this, but never experienced it in our Central Park West apartment. The rich never run out of hot water.

Yasmina gives me a robe to wear while our clothes are washing. She serves us huevos with beans and cheese and tortillas. Finn and I eat until we can't anymore. Thankfully, Bruce stays in his spot in front of the TV, absorbed with his phone.

When our clothes are clean and dry, we dress and Yasmina hugs us again. "You make me so happy that you came back, Querida. Bruce—take a picture."

Bruce lumbers to us and Finn starts away, but Yasmina grabs his arm and pulls him close. "I want both of you, my babies, in the photo."

Bruce takes a few photos with his phone and steps back to the TV as Yasmina tells us to get ready for a great tour of "The Big Easy."

It's hot outside and the air is heavy with humidity. I expect Finn to complain but he looks really happy. Yasmina drives us a short way to another neighborhood, we park and walk to a group of people standing by some tracks. Within a minute an old-timey streetcar comes squeaking up and we hop on. It's all wooden seats inside and so retro. Finn and I love it. We go past old mansions and trees dripping with green cobweb-like hair and cemeteries and we get out and walk to the French Quarter where we eat and listen to music and eat and go to the Mississippi River and eat hole-less donuts that are square and everywhere are musicians in the street and tap dancers and it's like a city of fun and the day passes in a blur of love. When we can't walk anymore, Yasmina gets us back on the streetcar, back to her car, takes us to her home, and even though it's only seven-thirty, we both go to bed.

As we lie together on the folded-out sofa, Finn turns to me. "Izzy, when you were in the shower, that man asked if we ran away from home."

A spasm of fear goes into me. "What did you say?"

"I said no."

"Did he ask you anything else?"

"No. I don't like that man."

I put an arm around him. "If you want to leave, we can."

"Let's leave. I like Yasmina, but that man is scary. And, I don't like the way he looks at you."

"We'll leave first thing in the morning."

We lie in silence until Finn says, "'Member that cashier who said we shouldn't camp where sickos could mess with a girl-like-you?"

"I do."

Finn sighs. "That happens a lot, doesn't it? Men messin' with girls."

All of me wants to cry. Ruby, Solveig, and Dragon Lady were raped. Simon was forced to rape. Heinrich raped. Who knows if there are others inside I'm not aware of. And with all I'm learning, I think Mr Marks wasn't really on my side. I think rape almost happened to me.

I don't want to say all this to my little brother and I don't want him to feel guilty for being male—after all, it isn't every male—but he's asking, so I need to answer. "Yes, it happens a lot, Finn."

Finn sighs. "Sorry."

There is a knock on the door. Yasmina comes in and makes sure we're cozy and warm and safe and sings the lullaby and tells us everything is all right.

I sleep like never before. I sleep like all the parts of me are peaceful—before their traumas happened. I sleep like I imagine a child would sleep when they feel loved. I dream of things I don't know. Strudel with cream. The road runner standing in the middle of the trail. The dawn illuminating women gathered in front of the White House. Walking through an orchard with a man playing fiddle. Brushing the long hair of a young sister. Wiping grease into the ball bearings and smelling that deep, pleasurable scent. Mama and Papa playing piano and singing in the parlor. And touching blue cloth. And gazing at the new constellations of stars. Gazing at the stars...

KIDNAPPED

THE BANG WAKES ME. I'm pulled from the bed and slammed to the rug, knee in my back, loud yelling from all directions. Finn screams as Dragon Lady and Simon's wrists are cinched together with plastic zip ties.

Pink dawn hovers in the room as Finn is whisked into the arms of a huge man dressed completely in black. Even his face is covered. The man races out as I'm hauled up by two similarly dressed men, one on each arm. A flash of white-coated orderlies dragging me down a long hallway interrupts my sight for a moment and is gone.

Yasmina screams in Spanish as Bruce holds her tight, keeping her from interfering.

I'm dragged out the door and across the ragged lawn toward a black SUV. Beside it is a limousine. My mother rises from inside that long car as Finn is deposited in her arms. She sobs and hugs and touches and clutches, hungry and desperate to make him

188

hers again. Her eyes dart to me for a moment—the look is unreadable: disgust, pity, concern, anguish? I don't know—but she turns back to hold her darling one.

Finn cranes his head to look at me. His throat does a little bobble of a swallow. He looks about to speak but the men press my head down, lift me into the SUV, barrel in beside me, and SLAM the door! Smells of blood, sweat, manure, and urine rush in and overwhelm me. Flashes of billy clubs and horses' hooves outside of the White House.

I look out the tinted window to see Yasmina sobbing and pounding on Bruce—who looks very satisfied. Finn is pulled into the limo and his (now) shaggy hair is my last glimpse before that door closes.

I wonder if I'll ever see Finn again. I love you, brother. I never got around to saying that.

A seatbelt is clicked over me and a hypodermic jabs my arm. The two men move to the front of the vehicle and that's the last I know.

CAUGHT UP

NOW YOU'RE pretty much caught up. So, onward!

We wake before dawn and peek out of the Tee Pee Motel room. I'm happy to see Pete's car still there and no sign of the police. Dragon Lady starts the engine and we race away.

Time to think. By now, Nurse Blinky and Doctor Pierson will have woken, hungover, and perhaps in the same bed, to report a missing patient. By now Pete will have walked, cold and shirtless, to report a stolen car.

Mother and Father will be told and they'll hire a private detective to search for me. It probably won't be the massive search as it was when I kidnapped Finn. Maybe Mother and Father are hoping I *don't* get found. Maybe I won't even be missed. Pete's car however, *will* be missed.

"We're gonna have to get another vehicle," Dragon Lady says in the gravel monotone of someone who doesn't give a shit.

This starts a loud argument in my head with lots of shouting and interrupting and I can't make out a thing.

Dragon Lady swerves the car onto a highway.

"Where are we going, Miss?" Simon asks.

"South. I don't like driving this flimsy piece of shit. I want the Metro Van."

"NEW ORLEANS!??" we all scream.

"It's too far away and not a viable option," Jenny says.

Ruby adds, "Ain't safe neither."

Kelly taps her foot on the gas. "Tinkin' what's safe is'nae always the way t' go."

"Ja, das ist true," Solveig says quietly.

"I think you're forgetting that those hosts in New Orleans told on us. They will do so again," says Simon.

"Not Yasmina," I say. "She was furious—she didn't know. It was Bruce. He was asking questions. I'm sure he called Mother and got a huge reward."

Heinrich shakes my head. "Ja, Bruce ist ein traitor. Ist nicht good."

Kelly continues, "Nae persons gonnae guess thad we'd gae back. Ye dinnae suspect people t'return tae their truble spots,"

Ruby chimes in, "Kelly's right. They won't suspect we'd be that feeble-minded."

"We have no reason to presume that the vehicle will still be residing on the property. It's a reckless notion," says Jenny.

Dragon Lady snaps her fingers. "Listen, motherfuckers, we're goin' down to New Orleans. I'm gettin' my hands on that Metro Van. It has room and board and ain't stolen. Anyone not with me can get out now."

I figure by the twitching and squirming of my limbs and innards that there's no chance of anyone getting out even if they wanted to. We're stitched together.

"New Orleans it is," I say. I hope the Metro Van is still parked in front of Yasmina's house.

HEADING FOR NEW ORLEANS

THE CASH FROM MOTHER'S LETTERS is gone. I panhandle to get gas money. I eat and sleep at a homeless shelter in Virginia. In North Carolina I pull Pete's Kia into an Exxon station. The fuel light has been on for miles but I've no money. I scan the people filling their tanks. A beefy trucker wearing a tractor cap is staring at me. I turn away and step toward a woman gassing up her SUV.

"Do you think I could borrow—or have—a dollar for gas?"

She grimaces at me and edges back like I have cooties. I spin to look for another possibility and Beefy Trucker is right behind me.

"I heard what you said and 'spected as much. I'll fill up your tank."

Oh, no. He's going to want sex or—

"You're about my daughter's age," he says, swiping his card in the gas pump and putting the nozzle into Pete's car. "She's off to college and I swear it gives me the heebie-jeebies to think of her out alone in this world."

When the Kia is full, he returns the nozzle. "Last time you ate?"

I can't remember.

He hands me a twenty-dollar bill and looks at me hard beneath his cap—"You stay safe, sweetie."—and lumbers back to his truck. Another good man example.

I buy a sandwich in the station cafe and save the rest for the next time I need gas. (Okay, I also buy Cheez Whiz to remind me of Finn.) South Carolina brings rain and sleeping in the car. More driving. I'm hungry and so we pull off the highway and drive into the countryside. Solveig forages berries, dandelion leaves, and mushrooms. That makes me miss Finn and our camping adventures and I eat all the Cheez Whiz and feel sick in his honor.

We lay on the hood of the car and watch the world. The tall grasses are sparkling, backlit by the setting sun. The air buzzes with shining insects. Cicadas whine. Birds dart about catching dinner. It's magical and beautiful and makes me wonder about those in me. "Did you remember happy times? Good memories? Moments like this?"

Solveig nods. "I was in the parlor with Miriam, my sister, and we'd just opened presents from our Grandparents. Chocolates. I was teaching Miriam how you could make things last and last if you had discipline. She tried it, eating minute little nibbles, and then looked at me and we both devoured all the chocolate."

Jenny laughs. "That brings to mind my children. Benny was four and Agnes was three when I last saw them before I was arrested. I loved their pudgy legs and their smell when they were babies. I can't describe that smell other than it was unique and intensely calming and compelling."

Heinrich chimes in, "Der smells are big in memory. Papa smelled of wet wolle and tabak. Mama of brot und Reichsmark notes she hid in her bluse. Ve vere on der trolley und Papa küsste Mama."

"Dirt," Dragon Lady says. "Not the kind from being buried, but dirt with grease and gasoline. Taking that muddy machine roaring to the finish line. I loved every moment."

"It was a shinin' day like this, we rode the borrowed horses and watched a road runner," says Ruby. "At the waterfall, I'm tucked in the crook of Chan's arm. Smellin' the musky residue of smoke in his hair. Reckon that's mine."

"Och, so many times," Kelly says. "As a lass in Ayrshire I'd spy out t' window tha tall man walkin' the moor tae court me. Could see 'is bonnie form from miles away. If the wind were from t'sea it'd bring those smells and the growin' lilt o' his fiddling. The joy of that approach be e'er wi' me."

"Simon?"

Simon answers, "There was a moment. I was shoppin' with Mama in Tupelo. We were in a millinery and I drifted away to a bolt of blue satin. There was a boy—his eyes seemed to say yes. He came next to me to look at the cloth and his hand reached under the smooth fabric and found mine. It was electrifying. It made the world seem full of possibilities. Then his mother came in and told him to wait outside, that this was no place for a boy. I bought a yard of that blue satin and kept it for years."

"What about you, Izzy?"

"Maybe I only am getting started. Being with Finn, making those crazy meals. That was good. Having him give me, us, a constellation. I loved that."

We watch the sun go down, all of us wrapped in our memories.

Next day, we take side roads to skirt Atlanta. We pass plantations with the white columns and signs saying *Have Your Wedding in Ol' Dixieland*. Who would want to be married with the echoes of brutality and horror screaming around them?

We keep heading south. Down past juke-joints and folks waving from their porches like any vehicle going by must be a neighbor. Past dead dogs on the side of the road, plucked at by buzzards. Past Confederate flags and Black Lives Matter signs. Past buildings taken over by kudzu vines. And the cicadas sing throughout it all.

We putter into New Orleans at ten pm. Pull to the curb a block away from Yasmina's. Parked in the back is my Metro Van. Bruce has probably decked it out with beer cans and porno.

I slip out of Pete's car and walk like I'm taking a stroll, down the block, past the dark house, turn around like I've forgotten something, tie my shoe while looking at the Metro Van—and walk toward it. Please don't let anyone see me.

Dragon Lady taps my nose and reaches behind the rear right bumper, feeling for the magnetic box holding the key—that one she told Ricardo to place before I knew she existed. It's there.

I slide the door and am so grateful this light never worked. Slip up into the seat. It feels so good. Like home. Smells of all my travels with Finn. Only with something added to the mix. Unknown sweat? Cigarette smoke?

Key in the slot and turn. The engine coughs but doesn't catch. Try again. Another cough. Again. BOOM! I duck—was that a backfire or a gunshot?

Turn the key, the engine catches, Dragon Lady reaches for the gear—the door slides wide—and a shotgun jams under our chin.

REMI

YOU NEVER KNOW HOW MUCH LIFE MEANS until you have a shotgun under your chin.

A man's voice says, "Out, motherfucker," and I comply. It's too dark for either one of us to see the other. Should I run? He pokes my back with the dangerous end of the gun. I decide not to.

"On the ground, face down. Hands back of your head."

Shit. This guy sounds like a cop. Again I comply. The ground smells of moldy dirt and leaked oil, which Dragon Lady probably likes. The man over me jams the gun barrel between my shoulder blades. As the shotgun presses me down I hear the Metro Van engine cut off, the key slide out, the door slide shut. Still pinning me, the man moves a hand to Kelly's hip, down the thigh, around her ankle, and up the inside. Down Heinrich's hip, thigh, around the ankle, and up the inside, stopping to feel.

"Fuck. You a girl?"

"Mnnn," I answer, not wanting to commit as I'm made of so many.

"Turn over."

I do and he orders me to keep my hands up.

"You got any weapons on you?"

I shake my head. But he gestures to my pockets. I turn them inside out to show they're empty.

194

"Get the fuck up and go inside. Any sudden moves and you're splattered."

Kelly and Heinrich get us on our feet and we step across the garbage-strewn yard to the house. I hope Yasmina is awake.

I step inside as he flicks on a light. The place has changed since I was here with Finn. It's got all the same furniture, lacy curtains, South American tapestries, except there are beer bottles, fast food cartons, dirty t-shirts, and engine parts on top of everything. Yasmina must have given up.

The man shoves me into the nearest chair. If he's a cop, he's undercover. He looks like a wasted meth addict. Stringy long hair. Tattoos covering his bare arms. Bad patchy stubble.

"You stealing my van, babe?"

"It's actually my van. Is Yasmina awake? She can explain."

"Yasmina and my cousin moved. Got them a new fancy pad with the reward money. Bruce gemme this place, seeing as I's family an' all."

"Could you call Yasmina? She'll tell you it's my van."

"It's my van. Came with the house."

I don't feel like I'm in much of a place to argue. Maybe I can buy it back from him. "I could pay you for it."

"You forget. I seen your pockets."

He's right. I don't even have an I.D., license, or anything. Didn't find time to pack on my way out of the loony bin—ha, ha.

"I can get money."

"How 'bout—you figure a money plan and I figure what I'm gonna do with you. Whoever comes up with a solution first, wins." He grins like that's real funny. Yellow teeth with several missing or rotting black.

I don't know what to do. *Help me, someone. Simon? Ruby? Anyone?* They've all shrunk back into their compartments, silent and still.

"Let me introduce myself, I'm—"

Everyone in me jolts.

Keep your real name private, Jenny warns.

I continue. "I'm Jenny. You're—?"

The man smiles. "You can call me Remi."

"As in Rémy Martin?"

"Who?"

"The cognac?"

He pats the side of his gun barrel. "As in Remington, the shotgun."

"Okay, Remi, the truth is, I escaped from somewhere recently and didn't bring all my identification or phone or bank cards, but if you let me make a call—"

"Where'd you escape from?"

Maybe this guy *is* an undercover cop. If I say the nuthouse, he'll turn me in.

Remi bangs the Formica table top with Remington. "I asked where did you escape from?"

Answers flood my brain. *Battlefield! Poverty! Prostitution! Society! Buried alive! Insane Asylum! Frankfurt ruins!...*

Remi squints at me. "My guess is you don't want to tell 'cause you think I might call someone to take you back."

I nod. That seems safe.

"I got my guess, but we'll see if I'm right later. You were sayin' you want to make a call?"

"I'll have a thousand dollars sent to your bank account."

"Ain't got no bank account."

"Then, another place, a check cashing place. Whatever you like."

"I like cash and a thousand ain't shit. If you can get one, you can get five."

Fuck. This is not going to end well. If I can get five, he'll ask for more. Ruby steps in. "Remi, it's true I can get more than one thousand, but five ain't in the cards. I'm a working girl and—"

"I knew it. You escaped a pimp, di'n you?"

Ruby balks. She won't even entertain a lie about having a pimp. Simon pushes past her to my mouth. "Mister Remi, I'm sorry to say he violated me most egregiously—," Dragon Lady

196

jumps in, "Fucker beat, raped, an' buried me. Two thousand is all you're lookin' at."

Remi squints. "You know that van is worth more than that. It's an old piece of shit but got beds and all, so I could rent it out as an apartment. Three thousand."

"Let me see if I can get that. Phone?"

THE PHONE CALL

THE PHONE RINGS and rings.

I look at Remi and shrug. Ringing continues. A little voice comes through, "H—Hello?"

I yell, "Finn! Finn, It's me! Iz-Jenny!"

"Izzy! Where are you? You know what I did?"

Remi reaches across and pushes the speaker on the phone.

"Finn, I need a serious favor."

"I made our meal for Mama. I call her Mama now and she likes it," Finn says in his groggy, little boy voice. It breaks my heart to hear him. "The Cool Whip and Cheez Whiz and—"

Remi raises his fist at me.

"Finn, that is so cool, but I need your help."

"They've got a detective looking for you," Finn says.

"I figured. Listen, I've got to get money right now."

No sound from the phone.

Remi looks at me like I'm tricking him and lifts his gun in a *get-the-fucking-money* gesture.

"Finn? Did you hear?"

"What do you want me to do?"

"Go to the safe and get three thousand in cash and put it in a box and have Alberto take it to an all-night shipping place. Have them overnight it."

"Father'll kill me."

"Tell him you had a dream about the horses and lost it on a bet. He'll laugh. But seriously, must be *Overnighted Priority Fedex*."

"Where do I send it?"

Remi passes me an electric bill. His name is Arthur Penzil. I read Finn the address. He repeats it as he takes it down. A shudder goes over me. Fuck. Maybe he'll tell Mother and Father where I am and the detective and men with nets will come to collect me and haul me to the nuthouse. I can't do that again.

"Finn, don't tell—"

"I had fun on our trip," Finn says. "It was the most fun I've ever had. I wish—"

Remi grabs the phone and hangs up.

I could kill him for cutting off whatever Finn was going to say. Maybe my eyes show that 'cause he growls. "Enough. Time for sleep. Tomorrow will come soon enough."

Remi points down the hall. I step down toward the sewing room I slept in before. "Nu-uh, this one," he says, shoving me into another room.

He turns on the light. A large, unmade bed fills most of the room. The rest is a flat-screen TV, beer bottles, filled ashtrays, and an incongruous pink floral lamp on the cigarette-burn-scarred side table. The air smells of sweat and something else. *Sex*, several in me offer. I guess I wouldn't know, having only gotten close that time with Mr. Marks.

"You lie down there."

I do as he orders. He looks around the room, yanks a cord from the wall socket, whips an intimidating hunting knife from the leather holder on his belt, and slices the cord, freeing it from a pink floral lamp. A step toward me.

"Don't tie me," I whimper.

He ties the chord around Simon's wrist and—surprise!—ties the other end around his own wrist.

"So you don't sneak off." He gives it a tug and lies beside me. The man smells of beer and cigarettes and rancid clothes.

I'll wait. Be still. As soon as I hear him snoring, I'll carefully untie Simon's wrist, slide out of bed, slink down the hall—

"Shit. I can hear what you thinkin'. C'on." Remi pulls me up and drags me down the hall. There's a motorcycle in the middle of the living room. Parts strewn about. He paws through a plastic crate on Yasmina's coffee table and pulls out a length of braided metal cable.

"This little metal do-hickey is called a ferrule. I slide the cable through one of the holes, cable goes 'round your wrist—you ever notice this wrist is thick, like a dude's? Fucking weird. The cable then goes in the second hole of the ferrule and we take this—" Remi grabs a monster tool, clamps it down on the little piece of metal, and HEAVES. The ferrule is crushed around the cable. "Try to get out of that!"

He repeats the process on his wrist and drags me back to the bedroom.

SLEEPING WITH REMI

I LIE NEXT TO REMI on the bed, tied to him with the cable. He stares at me.

"You have one brown eye and one green eye."

"I know."

"That thick wrist. The eyes. This patch of straight blond hair in your curly mess. And this red streak. You're like Frankenstein."

He thinks he's saying something unique.

"What other weird parts do you have?"

"Nothing else."

Remi laughs like he knows a thing or two about lying. "It's like you got pieced together from different people. What about the titties? One big, one small? What's that pussy like? Bet you're missing the action down there since runnin' from your pimp."

I stare at the ceiling fan. It clicks as it swirls unevenly.

Remi's breath is sticky near my shoulder. He grins. "How 'bout a freebie? We're stuck together, might as well enjoy it."

"Not tonight, mister," says Ruby.

His stubbly face moves closer. "Come on, babe. It's no skin off your back."

"I said no," Jenny says.

Remi moves his cabled hand to my breast and Dragon Lady moves it off. Remi slams Dragon Lady's hand down and pins it. "I hear that *no* means *no*, but that's someone else's book. *No* means you like it rough. That right?"

Dragon Lady pops into my mouth. "ASSHOLE, I'M NOT FUCKING INTERESTED!"

Remi lies back.

Wow. Maybe I should have said something like that when the photography teacher did his 'Aaa-OOOOO-Gah!' Or maybe with the plastic surgeon. Or maybe Mr. Marks.

With a swift spin, Remi covers me with his body. One arm pins Dragon Lady as the other pulls on my jeans zipper.

Everyone in me rises. Furious.

Kelly slams her knee between Remi's legs. Dragon Lady digs her nails into his arm. Ruby slams my forehead to smash his nose. Solveig jams her pelvic bone up to pin him. Heinrich repeatedly kicks Remi's ankles with his heel. Jenny bites down on the man's ear. Simon spins the cable over Remi's head to circle his neck and pulls tight. Remi struggles and thrashes against the attack from the mob.

"Ahh! Stop! Stop!"

Dragon Lady snarls, "*Stop* means *stop* to some, but I think that means you like it rough."

Ruby slams Remi's bleeding nose again. Kelly twists her leg over his hip and jams her foot between Remi's legs and works in unison with Solveig to vice his balls. BAM! BAM!

Dragon Lady bends his finger back and he screams. Heinrich pounds Remi's ankle tendon with his heel creating a sound almost like a rubber band breaking. Simon pulls the cable tighter.

"Stop! I give up. You win."

If my ancestors didn't control my body, I'd be lying terrified and trembling under Remi as he had his way. I'm so lucky to have them all.

Remi coughs, his face turning red. The cable presses into his neck deeply.

"I think an apology would be appropriate," says Simon.

"S—s—sorry." Remi spits, drooling blood.

Simon lets the cable slacken just a bit.

"What the fuck did you say, fucker? We can't hear you?" The man's finger bends under Dragon Lady's pressure.

"I'm sorry. Please. I'm sorry."

Ruby moves into our mouth. "Reckon we jes gettin' started."

"Take the van! It's yours! Just stop, please."

Dragon Lady swings the twisted hand behind the sobbing man's back and pulls it up to meet the protruding shoulder blades.

Jenny slides out front. "Let me endeavor to explain what's next. You now find yourself in a submissive position with this cable around your neck and your arm strategically high behind your back. After your legs are unpinned, and after you are directed to, you will rise slowly with us. Any abrupt movements and you'll contend with our force again. Is that sufficiently understood?"

Remi sobs what sounds like a yes, then asks, "Who is 'us'?"

Dragon Lady takes over my mouth. "Us are the MULTITUDES, motherfucker. Us are all those who lived through what you tried to do here. And us are FUCKING DONE WITH ASSHOLES!"

Remi quivers his acknowledgment.

"Simon, keep that cable tight on this fucker. Heinrich, Kelly, let go of his legs."

They both move my legs away. Remi starts to get up.

Ruby interrupts. "Hold on, pard. Not so fast. Where's your ol' side-by-side?"

"What?"

"The Remington."

"Bedside floor."

"When you're on your feet, you'll kick that side-by-side under the bed. Alright? Nice an' slow. Get yer ass vertical."

Remi slowly stands and kicks the shotgun so it slides deep under the bed. Everyone stays behind him as he walks into the living room. I certainly have no courage or skills to add, so hover in the background.

Jenny asks, "Would I be correct in assuming there is a method for severing this cable?"

Remi nods to a cluttered table. "Bolt-cutter. Red handles."

"Simon will reach for it, but as he makes this maneuver, the process will result in the cable becoming tighter, so you may have to contend with a reduction of breath."

We back up to the table and Simon reaches, pulling the cable, Remi gasps, and the bolt cutters are retrieved. They're about to cut when I think loudly, *Uh, just a sec. If you do that, he'll be free and he should cable himself before you release him.*

There is a pause. Even Remi must wonder what's going on.

Good thinkin', girlie. You tell him, but don't do it sweet. You've been messed with, too.

No, you're the experts. I'm just—

You can do it, Miss Elizabeth.

I can't. I don't know how to be tough.

Reckon you do.

Aye, 'tis yer time tae get angry.

Ja. Du bist wild. Fierce.

I feel them all waiting for me. Take a deep breath...

"Remi!" I start.

It isn't very tough.

"Jerk!" I add.

That was inadequate. And stupid.

Feeling inadequate and stupid makes me flash on all the times I've been inadequate and stupid and scared and weak and ignored and used and abused and...

"ASSHOLE! We have a fucking HIVE MIND and can think of everything! Don't assume we're idiots! Cable yourself to that chair NOW, FUCKER!!"

I did it!

Inside, everyone cheers.

Five minutes later, Remi has secured his ankles to the chair legs and sent a second cable through the previous cable loop on his wrist and attached that to the rungs.

"I think we're ready, Simon?"

Simon puts the bolt cutter around the cable and, with the handles between his arm and Remi's back, presses. Clink. We're free!

Now what? It's still hours until dawn. There's a check-in and discussion. We could drive the Metro Van away, but everyone hates the idea of Remi getting that money after what he tried. Besides, the mob is exhausted. We decide we'll be okay to sleep on the lounge chair if we can be sure Remi can't move.

Solveig steps in. *Auf dem deutschen land die cows wear glocken. Bells.*

What could we use for bells? We scan the room. On the wall, hanging in front of the yellow-blue-and-red flag, are Yasmina's tambourine and maracas.

Dragon Lady punches through the drum of the tambourine and slides it over Remi's head. Simon gives the maracas a shake, rattling all the whatevers inside, and sticks them down the front of Remi's shirt.

We lie back on the lounge chair and close our eyes.

Solveig remains alert. *Ich listen, you sleep.*

Heinrich moves by her gently and whispers, *Ich—do watch. You schlafen.*

After experiencing this night, maybe he feels bad for what he did to Solveig in the field of flowers so long ago in Germany.

FED EX AND GOOD—BYE

THE FEDEX TRUCK PULLS UP at ten-thirty delivering a small flat package addressed to me. I pull the tab and there's a tied bundle made from torn pages from Architectural Digest magazine. I open it and inside are lots of hundred-dollar bills and a post-it note:

Izzy. When can we go camping again? It was fun. Take it easy, BUT TAKE IT! Finn

Damn. I can't believe I was going to kill him.

What about Remi? Are we going to kill him? several in me ask.

I tuck the package of money in my jeans and Heinrich turns us around and leads us to the bedroom. He kneels and Simon reaches under the bed for the Remington. We head back to Remi. Simon points the barrel at the tied man's chest. Dragon Lady lays a finger beside the trigger.

"No, please. I'll be good. Take the van. Take the money."

"We intend to, but there's some debate as to whether to kill you or not. Why should we let a wannabe rapist live?"

"I swear I'll never do that again."

"We could see to it you don't." The barrel lowers, pointing at Remi's crotch.

"No, no, no. Please." A puddle of yellow spreads onto the linoleum floor below Remi. He groans.

Solveig hisses, "Ve came für den Metro Van. Ve go now."

"Listen to her. She's right," Remi says. "Key's in my pocket."

He's tied and none of us want to go into his jeans' pocket. Heinrich finally volunteers. He slides into Dragon Lady's arm and reaches into the pocket. It's hot and wet but the key is retrieved.

"Second key?" Dragon Lady asks.

Remi nods to the tabletop. In possession of both the keys, we all feel relief.

Kelly steps to the workbench. We put the end of the rifle barrel in the dining-room-table-mounted vice and Heinrich, Dragon Lady, and Simon push against the stock. Kelly, Jenny, and Ruby join in, but there is no progress. Solveig adds her weight.

The barrel remains straight. "IZZY, get your ass in here and PUSH!" I don't know how to move between them all, but I try. I push. The barrel starts to bend. Kelly yells, "PUSH! EVERYONE!" We leannnnnnn... and the barrel curls farther and farther. We ROAR with our power.

That's a bizarre sound. Echoey. Like multiple voices yelling at once. But that's not possible with just my vocal cords. I must have heard it like that 'cause they yelled in my head, while I yelled in reality.

We turn to Remi. He's shaking. Simon puts the bolt cutter in one of his tied hands. "Try not to drop it."

We step to the front door and Ruby says, "Don't forget us."

RACING THROUGH NEW ORLEANS

AS WE TURN THE KEY in the Metro Van there's a feeling of euphoria in us. We fought back and won. The motor spins but doesn't catch. Try again, inhaling deeply. I'd like to get rid of that unknown sweat and cigarette smell, but that'll have to wait. The motor says *I'm trying, I'm trying*. Turn the key again and it catches—

BAM! A gunshot pierces the side of the van by us. Dragon Lady throws the gear in reverse as BAM! another pops a hole in the door and just misses Heinrich! He'd feel real bad to lose his leg again! BAM! We tear out of the yard and into the street, with Dragon Lady steering in reverse and Kelly jamming the gas pedal to the floor. Remi stands in the driveway in pee-soaked jeans, firing a pistol. BAM! None of us screams in pain so I guess we're all still here as we zoom down the block in reverse.

Dragon Lady has most of our eye focus, staring at the mirrors as she drives backwards, but Solveig notices Remi getting into a rusted white car.

"Trans Am—Muscle car." Dragon Lady mumbles, then orders, "Kelly OFF. Heinrich, NOW!" and Heinrich steps hard on the brake and Dragon Lady shifts out of Reverse while jerking the wheel and we're skidding, spinning, about-facing and "Heinrich, OFF! Kelly, GO!" and the two switch motions and we're in Drive and roaring down the street—in the right direction. Side-view mirror shows the white Trans Am speeding behind us. We're on a narrow street with cars parked on both sides. No way for Remi to pass us, but we certainly can't outrun him.

"Anybody know the city?" Dragon Lady asks. No one does. "Okay, we get lucky or we don't."

She spins the wheel at the corner and we hit a torn-up street. Potholes and cracks everywhere. We zoom by the houses, some boarded up, some newer ones suspended on stilts, overgrown vacant lots where houses once stood. Remi roars behind us. He's got one of those mufflers that proves how tough he is.

We spin around another corner and knock a garbage can into a yard, spilling crap across the grass. I feel bad but I get over it.

I wish all these people in me were separate. Someone could look up where we are on the map while Dragon Lady, Heinrich, and Kelly drive. "Do it!" Dragon Lady says. "I can chew gum and fart at the same time." Simon reaches across Ruby's lap to grab the road atlas. He flips through to Louisiana and finds New Orleans. But where the hell are we?

WHAM! Remi rams the back of the van with his bumper. I'm sure he's not happy putting a dent in his muscle car. He must be getting impatient to kill us. "Simon, drop it. I need everyone here." Simon drops the atlas and Dragon Lady spins left, careening us down a larger street. Shit. Remi sees his opening. He roars up, moving alongside us. BAM! BAM! Two bullets pierce the van right behind my head!

"He's out of bullets for his six-shooter," Ruby says.

"Counting nicht work. Pistols carry more now. Das Luger has eight in das magazine," Heinrich answers.

I don't tell him that's old news as well.

The neighborhood changes and the street narrows again. Small colorful houses, brightly painted, jammed together. Well-cared-for lawns. WHAM! Remi rams us again. We swerve, but Dragon Lady knows how to react to everything. A dog trots along the roadside and then turns to cross. Simon HONKS and the mutt freezes in our path. Fuck! Dragon Lady yells "Heinrich!" and he brakes and we skidddddddd—the dog darts off—and a screeching behind us—WHAM!!! The Trans Am slams hard into our rear—We hear Remi scream in fury. He fires again BAM-BAM!

"Reckon that ain't a six-shooter," Ruby says.

Dragon Lady spins us and she's got us heading for a canal on our left, Remi must see because he RAMS us, pushing hard. Dragon Lady yells "Heinrich" and he jams the brakes as she jolts the wheel right. We fishtail as Remi pushes, and slip away—as he zooms past, flies over the little berm, and splashes into the canal.

"Kelly!" And we're off again the way we came, eyes to the rear-view mirror as Remi pulls himself from the mostly submerged car and points the gun and—nothing happens—as we disappear around the corner.

MAGNOLIA MOTEL

WE DRIVE THE METRO VAN away from danger and speed on and on.

"Keep your eyes open for a road that crosses the river," Dragon Lady says. "We cross and we'll be in a different state. If that pecker called the fuzz we'll be safe."

"Good idea," I say. "In TV shows they always have the bad guys cross state lines. We can find a place to get food and rest."

We look for a road to cross, and after just a few miles of driving North a sign leads the way and we cross that wide river and soon read *Welcome to Mississippi*. We're safe. No one feels like camping or roughing it and we all want to wash Remi off us, so when we see a neon vacancy sign, we pull into the lot of the Magnolia Motel. There's a restaurant attached, so FOOD.

"One room for the night." I don't tell the clerk how many people are joining me.

Minutes later, we're in a small room. It's clean and quiet and perfect for tired, emotionally exhausted travelers. A long shower washes all the strange horrors away. There's a menu for the restaurant by the television set and none of us want to be around people, so we order over the phone and they offer to "trot across the parking lot to deliver it." I pull a hundred-dollar bill from the package Finn sent and wait by the window. In a bit, a young man comes trotting, and I open the door, collect our meal, and give him the bill with "Keep the change." He's quite happy.

I unload the fried chicken with the side of collard greens and mac-n-cheese and to-go bottle of Muscadine wine. I don't know what muscadine wine is but that was their only choice. Whatever it is, we all need it. Somehow today held fighting off Remi in bed, tying him up, getting the FedEx package, racing through New Orleans, getting shot at, and escaping across state lines. No wonder we're tired!

We eat the chicken—which Ruby, Simon, Kelly, Dragon Lady, and I love, but Heinrich, Jenny, and Solveig think is too greasy— and the collards—which only Simon likes—and the mac-n-cheese—which pleases everyone—and taste the wine—which no one likes but me. We lie on the bed with our legs stretched out. Beyond Heinrich's pale, knobby man-foot and Kelly's plump, darker, womanly-foot is a crappy credenza and a big mirror. I raise my plastic cup of sweet Muscadine wine to the reflection and try to toast everyone, but all I see is the usual mismatched ugly me.

WHAT ABOUT ME?

SIMON WAKES ME with a pat to my temple. "I was thinking, Miss Elizabeth, now that we're in Mississippi, why not visit where I'm from. It's not far. I could see what happened to me."

A jolt goes through us. Thoughts pass over me quickly—fragments—*possibly find my grave—did I get out?—what did I become?—was I a good person?—did I live past this age?—what about me!?*

The flood of questions overwhelms me to the point I yell, "Please! One at a time!"

Everyone stops. That worked for once. "I'm going to get dressed and order breakfast and then we can slowly—one at a time—go over everyone's questions.

Maybe they're all hungry too because they stay silent. I order waffles for Heinrich and Solveig, eggs for Ruby, coffee for Simon, tea for Jenny, muffins for Kelly, and bacon for Dragon Lady. Everyone enjoys their portion and I enjoy the peace.

After I clear off the table, I sit down with all the paper I can find. The receipts for the meals, the *Sanitized for Your Protection* toilet seat band, covers for the plastic cups, the *Thank You for Staying with Us* tip envelope signed by Jianna, and two messy napkins. It's embarrassing that I don't own paper.

And no pen.

A squeaking sound moves by the motel door and a shadow crosses the window. The maid pushing her cart. I hop up with the tip envelope and stick my head out. "Excuse me—Jianna?"

She turns wearily—undoubtedly expecting a problem she's supposed to solve.

"Could I borrow—or buy—the pen you used to write this?"

She pulls the pen from her thick black hair and hands it to me. It's hot.

"Do you have a pad of paper, by any chance?"

"Only them envelopes."

"Could I have a few more?"

She reaches into her cart and holds out a stack. "Welcome to as many as you want. They don't ever get used nohow."

I take eight. Seven for everyone in me and one for Jianna. "Thanks. I'll make sure to fill one for you."

She nods like she doesn't believe me.

Back inside, I put the name of each ancestor on an envelope. "Okay, Simon, you first. You mentioned you were near here."

"Oxford, Mississippi."

"How old were you and what was the year?"

I write his answer on his envelope. *Simon Devery, 21 year old in Oxford Mississippi in 1898.* "Did you stay there?"

"I don't know, Miss. I don't have many memories like some of you. Mine stop in the midst of being—uh—in poor Irene."

Jenny perks up. "That's interesting. When do your memories stop, Heinrich?"

"Alzo same. Ich was—was—raping Solveig."

Solveig uses Dragon Lady's arm to punch Heinrich's leg.

"And Solveig, your memories, when do they end?"

"Ich habe das baby und name her Ursula. Zlata mit de scissors cut cord—und das ist alles."

"My memories also stop at that moment," Jenny says. "All interaction between mother and child ceases once the umbilical cord is severed."

I join in. "It's the last time when the DNA could be imprinted with any traumas. Anything experienced after that, wasn't passed on. So Simon and Heinrich only passed on moments up to the point they ejaculated. That sperm was on its way, carrying its traumatic, *but finite,* memory."

"Das ist why Ich bin twenty-two forever," says Heinrich.

"If Simon has no more elucidation of his specifics, I'll be the subsequent personage," says Jenny.

She summarizes her particulars and I write them down. *Jenny Carswell, 30 years old, suffragette in the National Women's Party. Arrested for protesting in front of the White House in 1916, sent to jail, committed to Washington D.C.'s Government Hospital for the Insane.*

Kelly MacLellan, 18, from Ayrshire, Scotland. Moved to Austin in Potter County, Pennsylvania in 1911. Married to fiddle player Alex who worked at the Bayless Pulp and Paper Company.

Ruby Pollard, 24, lived in the booming gold rush town of Bodie, California in 1877 and worked as a prostitute. Chan was her bodyguard after leaving the railroads. He lived in the Chinese section of Bodie.

Dragon Lady, 28, motorcycle racer. WON the Log Race in 1962. Staggered from her rape and burial and hitched a ride. Beau said Maxine, aka Dragon Lady, may have become Max Dragon, a racer in Los Angeles, California.

Solveig, 16, left Frankfurt after her sister died and wandered starving in post-war Germany. She met Zlata Rosenbaum and had the baby named Ursula.

Heinrich Neuffer, 22, German soldier from Frankfurt. Lost his leg at age 21 in battle in 1944.

"Und rape me in 1945," Solveig adds.

"Nein! Das ist MY facts, nicht YOURS!" protests Heinrich.

"Enough! These are only facts to find you all. Not whole biographies!" I yell. "Simon is the closest, so we'll go there first."

I gather the notes, put a hundred-dollar bill in the envelope for Jianna, and step out to the Metro Van. We start it up and open the atlas for Simon's last known place.

OXFORD, MISSISSIPPI

IT'S AFTERNOON when we get to Oxford, Mississippi and we drive slowly around the main square. In the center is the Lafayette County courthouse. Simon recognizes it, as he does many of the buildings surrounding it.

Where to begin? There's a bookstore on the corner so we go in and ask about how to find out about a person who lived here years ago. They direct us to the historical and genealogical society in the courthouse. One clue leads to another and, hopeful, we drive to a large old house on the south side of town. There's a sculpture in the yard—a twisted mix of heavy machine gears, hubcaps, bicycle chains, and chrome automobile bumpers. It's really cool. As we park and get out, the wind catches the sculpture and it spins, creating several tones—like blowing into bottles.

There's a sign on the front door: The Werks. A knock brings a young man around my age. He's got yellow-tan skin with dark freckles and tight coils of reddish hair—all of which makes me think he's a mutt like me. I introduce myself as Izzy and tell him I'm looking for information about Simon Devery.

"Came to the right place," he says, leaning out to look beyond me. "Cool ride you got."

I thank him and he opens the door wide.

"I'm Micias," says Micias, leading me into the cool darkness of the foyer and then into a large room filled with paintings and sculptures. "Here is where we have the rotating exhibitions. It's the biggest room, so we can fit the public during openings. Sometimes shows spill over to other rooms. The artists live and work here for year-long stints. We've got six artists staying now. Most stay upstairs and sleep in their studios. I'm what you might call the latest caretaker. It's room and board but the foundation can't afford to give stipends. Do you want to fill out an application?"

"Uh,—I—I'm not an artist."

"Oh. With the cool van and your—unconventional look—I thought you had to be."

This makes me happy. *He doesn't think I'm a freak. He thinks I'm an artist! Maybe I am! Maybe I could be if*—Simon pinches my side. *Oh. Sorry.* I get back to the issue at hand. "Do you have any information about Simon Devery?"

"Of course. This was both home and the art school. It became a foundation after their death."

"Their?"

"Mr. and Mrs. Devery."

Simon's arm spasms.

"I just want to make sure we're talking about the same Simon Devery. He was born in 1877."

"Yep, sounds about right. They bought the house in 1901."

Simon shakes my head. *I would not have gotten married.*

"Who was Simon's wife?"

"Irene."

Simon makes us light-headed and we tip—

Micias grabs Dragon Lady's forearm. "Whoa, you okay? Sit down, I'll get you some water."

Micias pushes a pile of books from a chair, helps us sit, then hurries out.

"I married Irene," Simon whispers, stunned. "How—why—what could have made her take me after—what I did?"

"There is the possibility that she was similarly inclined and it was a practical solution amenable for you both," Jenny suggests.

"Similarly inclined?" Simon asks.

Ruby chuckles, "We all know you're a cock that fancies roosters."

Simon stutters, "I've *never* done such a thing!"

"Maybe no in yer time, but ye dinnae ken o' the later years," says Kelly.

"You think—I was—*with* a man?" Simon asks.

"We can hope so," I say.

Simon spreads a shy grin across my face. "Imagine!"

Micias enters, "Excuse me?"

I take the water he offers, saying, "Just talking to myself."

"I do that all the time."

Micias leads me through the house and into a bright, wide room that must have once been a porch. Non-stop windows and the back door frame the space. Light bounces off everything. And there's a lot of everything. Shelves and cabinets overflow with parts of machines, bits of wood, doorknobs, postcards, pictures and magazine clippings, doll legs, tools, paints, and clutter of every kind. I've never seen anything like it. It looks like a thrift store and antique shop and hoarder house all in one.

"My laboratory," Micias says. "Ever hear that line Thomas Edison said? To invent, you need imagination and a big pile of junk. At least I have the latter. Now, somewhere..."

Micias rummages through shelves, moving bird nests, lifting hubcaps, and finally hands me a thin paperback. "It's about Simon and Irene Devery. The book caused quite a scandal in town. Pretty tame now."

On the cover is a picture of Simon and Irene standing together, holding hands, but to either of their sides, they are also holding hands with others that are out-of-frame. *Love Outside of Love* by Lorraine Devery.

"Lorraine Devery?"

"Their daughter."

Simon can't hold the book, he's shaking so much. Micias notices. "Are you okay?"

"We're—I'm—kind of emotional 'cause this is a relative of mine and I'm only just learning about him, them."

Micias opens the backdoor leading to a shady grouping of mismatched chairs. He points to the rocking chair. "Sit and read. I'll be working for a bit. Since it's my turn to make dinner, I'll fire up the grill later. You're welcome to join us or I'll tell everyone to stay out of your hair if you want. They're artists so they get it when people want to be alone. Okay?"

"Thank you."

I sit in the shade and open the book. Simon's arm shakes and his tears overflow my eyes. I blink and blink until I can read the words.

"Mom and Dad loved each other, but theirs was not a typical marriage. In their day, their predilection was defined as "Sexually-inverted" and it was not only against the law, but could foment dire consequences if discovered. But they hid with each other as allies. For a long while, I was not sure how I came into being at all. I guessed that perhaps they were both trying so hard to pass for "normal" that they somehow managed to have sex with each other. When I learned the horrible truth, I came to love them all the more. I couldn't have wished for better parents. Although Simon and Irene lived together as man and wife as far as the world was concerned, their passions lay outside of the home. In fact, next door. There, Clark and Willa Beecham pretended to have their own "normal" marriage. I would learn much later that the shared driveway was not the only thing these neighbors shared."

I don't know when I've been so happy.

AJAX DINER

I SPEND THE DAY READING as Micias works on his sculptures. I read about Lorraine's childhood, the constant flow of artists, the intense love and support, the founding of the art school, the enthusiastic students, the difficulties with suspecting townsfolk, the powerful commitments, the secret marriages, the fears, the joys...

As the sun sets, Micias gets the BBQ grill going. The smell of the food is wonderful but I'm so in the world of Irene and Simon and Lorraine and Clark and Willa, I don't want to break away. When the welded iron bell is struck to call everyone for dinner, I don't move and lower my head into the book. Micias understands and keeps the household of artists from me. As they eat and drink and chat with each other, he plugs in several hanging strands of colorful lights, brings me a plate of ribs, beans, cornbread, and a beer, then leaves me alone. I read of the decision to create the art foundation, and the death of Simon at seventy. I read of the talk Irene had with Lorraine about that night at the cotillion. How Simon came to her home afterward in shame and horror and how they held each other and cried and how when she learned she was pregnant, they both were overjoyed at the thought of raising this child together.

Simon is crying so hard I can't see the words on the page. When we finally can see, I read of the death of Irene and how they're both buried in the Oxford Memorial Cemetery. After I close the book, I sit watching Micias work on a sculpture. He's got nice arms.

Nice arms, girlie? Dragon Lady mumbles in my head.

They are nice arms, says Simon.

Micias glances up and catches me looking. He smiles warmly. *Shit!*

I stand and stretch. I've been sitting forever!

Micias yells to me, "You look like you could use a walk. Interested?"

"Yes!"

I set the book in his laboratory and we step out the front door. We walk in the middle of the street in the cooling night air. Sounds of cicadas or frogs and crickets. There are very few street lights and it feels eerie but also nice.

"Powerful book, don't you think?" Micias says.

"Simon and Irene were heroes," we say.

"They were. To each other and their daughter and all the people they taught. Several students became well-known artists. And their legacy continues with the foundation. And continues with you—since you're kin."

The moon is large and bright and I hope he can't see my cheeks reddening.

After a few blocks we come to a cemetery, the gravestones and obelisks and statues glowing in the darkness.

"This is the Oxford Memorial Cemetery, where they're buried. You want to go in?"

I don't want to go in with him in case Simon gets emotional. "Another time."

"A few more blocks is the square. There's a cool place there. Ajax Diner. Can I buy you a drink?"

Blood rushes to my face. *Does that mean he likes me? Should I say yes?*

*NO—no—yes—abstain—yes—no—YES—*are the answers inside. I'm the deciding vote. "We say yes."

"We?"

"Me. Just me. I've got so many characters living inside me sometimes I say us or we when I mean me."

"I hear ya. I mean, I hear *all y'all.*"

We get to the town square. There are more people out now that it's cooler. Lots of student types. Micias opens the door to the bustling diner and we get a booth. He suggests the Ajax Bloody Mary. I agree but when the waiter takes the order, I'm carded. Since I don't have ID, nor am I twenty-one, I shrug. "Ice tea—unsweet."

The waiter leaves and Micias apologizes. "Sorry, they can be sticklers."

A shattering of glass and a deep voice yells, "Scram, you fuckin' dykes!"

Micias and I both look to the commotion. Two guys in Ol'Miss t-shirts stand over a booth where two women sit together. "Take your lesbo girlfriend and git. We don't want to see your kind."

There's not a moment of hesitation. All in me rise and march to the table. I slide between the guys and the booth and stare up at the idiotic faces. The one with the crew-cut leans low to breathe in my face. At the peak of his hairline, there's a swirl. A spiraling hair whorl.

"You're Dwight," Simon has me say.

"I don't know you, freak."

"Well, I knew your great-grandfather, Dwight Spencer. You're just like him."

There's a moment of confusion in the guy's face that lets Simon know he's right, but it's quickly squashed, with the scintillating observation, "So?"

"I want you to leave."

"You gonna make us?" the fourth generation Dwight asks.

"We all are going to make you. Me and us and all *my* great-grandfathers and great-grandmothers."

Dwight snickers to his buddy.

Simon's arm shoots out like a striking cobra, its mouth chomping down on the guy's balls.

"Ahhh! Let go!"

The other dude reaches for Simon's hand, but Heinrich is faster, his foot connecting with the asshole's groin. The guy staggers back, bent in pain.

All of us roar together, "GET THE HELL OUT OF HERE BEFORE YOU REALLY GET FUCKED UP!" Our voices are high and low and guttural and furious and reverberate across the entire diner. The guys stumble away, terrified, like they've seen a Hydra. Do I have many heads instead of one? Did all those voices really come out together? I know that's not possible.

Micias stands a few feet away, staring at me. The two women huddle together in their booth, mouths open.

"Sorry for the disturbance," Simon says.

"It's okay—thanks for—helping," the short-haired woman whispers.

I need to get out. Everyone is watching. I give the women a little wave and head toward the door. The mass of patrons edge back as I pass. Micias hesitantly follows me.

Outside, everything feels off—like I just did something terrible and everyone saw. I'm scared. I'll never not be a freak.

Micias clears his throat.

"I can't talk right now, Micias. Could you just walk me back?"

Micias walks beside me through the dark streets in silence. All of me is overwhelmed.

When we get back to The Werks house, I stop at the Metro Van—my refuge.

Micias puts out his hand. "I know you don't want to talk. I'll just say goodnight."

I put our hand in his. He's warm and maybe if I wasn't so bombarded with feelings, I'd enjoy the tingling going on between us, but I just let go with a nod and slide into the van.

SIMON'S GRAVE

I WAKE UP DRIVING. It's dark out and no one's on the road. Wherever we are. Someone is holding the wheel, someone has a foot on the gas, someone is looking out the windshield, but it's not me. This isn't cool.

"What the hell? You have to wake me if—"

"We figured to let you sleep," Ruby explains.

"That's not right. It's *my* body!" I yell.

"Which part 'tis thee?" Kelly asks.

Luckily I'm sitting, 'cause this 'bout knocks me down. She's right. They all have parts, and there's no part that's me. I shouldn't even be here. I don't belong.

"Hush now, Miss Elisabeth. You belong. Relax and enjoy the ride. Look at the moon glow."

I try to forget not having a part in this body and look at the moon. It's full and heavy. Is it coming or going? There are strange points of light throughout the van. I can't understand these. One is near my head. *What is that?*

Reckon y'ain't seen a bullet hole afore, Ruby answers.

Moonlight streams through all these holes. I had no idea we were hit so many times.

Some came and went, I 'spec, Ruby adds. *Still, coulda been worse.*

She uses Dragon Lady's arm to point at the passenger seat. There's a hole right where Finn's head would have been. I'm horrified.

Dragon Lady steers us to the curb, Heinrich brakes, and Simon pushes out the headlights.

We get out, walk under the glowing moon into the Oxford Memorial Cemetery, and let instinct lead us toward the right grave. Simon's arm begins shaking. A few more steps and we stop. A mossy stone with DEVERY across the top and two names below—Simon 1877-1947 and Irene 1878-1955. Between their names are the words: Best Friends.

We kneel and Simon moves his fingers across his name and Irene's feeling the soft moss inside of each letter.

Dragon Lady taps Simon's wrist and points. The grave beside Simon and Irene reads Clark and Willa Beecham. They're neighbors even in death. That makes us all feel good.

"Take dirt," Simon says.

He puts his hand on the wet earth and presses his fingers into the ground, past insects and seeds, deep among the roots. The ground feels as it is throbbing. Vibrating. He lifts the red soil. It has a dense smell of the clay some say humans were formed from. Ancestor clay. Simon and Dragon Lady dig their hands into the vibrating dirt, pulling up fistfulls of the clumpy ground. It goes in my pockets. We tuck in my shirt and pour earth down to fill my waist. I bet you could bake a brick with this dirt. Form a clay vessel. Maybe someday we'll do that.

A dog barks somewhere nearby. Ruby sighs. "Best skedaddle now."

We stand and Simon lingers.

Solveig whispers, "Liebling, ve need leave."

"I believe I'll be staying."

This surprises us all. Can he do that? "Can you do that?" I ask.

"Don't know, but I want to try. I want to reside here where I'm buried, where my loves and friends are. I'm so happy to find out what happened to me. I was forgiven by Irene. Had a life that had love. And it seems like I was surrounded by people I cherished. Just like now with you all."

I get teary fast, or me and several others. "Don't you want to stay and find out if your daughter Lorraine is alive? She must have had kids and so you could meet your grandchildren and see how your kin turned out."

Simon strokes my cheek. "I know how my kin turned out. I couldn't be prouder of you."

No one's ever been proud of me before. I get so choked up I can't speak.

Simon pats different parts of me, Dragon Lady's arm, Jenny's throat, Ruby's forehead, Solveig's heart, Heinrich's leg, Kelly's leg, and he caresses my temple like he did so long ago when I first became aware of my fellow travelers.

And then, without warning, he pulls. It's not just his arm, although that's the bulk of him—he pulls from all over, a gentle tugging and stretching and—something snaps and he's out. There before us is a blurry figure of a young man wearing a tuxedo. His face is soft and boyish. Simon smiles. Wispy clouds of fog or mist coagulate and spiral and become other figures. A woman in a cotillion gown. A tall lanky man with a devilish grin. Another woman in a wide garden hat. Simon floats to them and turns to blow us a kiss. The breeze swirls and combines the figures into a dance and there's far-off laughter and—the fog disappears.

I get back to the Metro Van and in some time-lapse kind of sequence, we're back in front of The Werks house and I ask everyone left to promise not to drive any more tonight. They agree and we clear Simon's dirt from my pockets and inside my shirt and collect it into one of the neatly folded plastic bags (See that, Finn!?) and crawl into bed. As I stare at the streams of moonlight coming through the bullet holes in the van's walls, I feel so much smaller. So empty without Simon.

COFFEE OR TEA?

I'M UP WITH THE BIRDS and the first glow of light hitting the windshield. I turn in the bed and something's uncomfortable. Dragon Lady slides her hand across the sheet under me. It's full of crumbs. Did I eat in bed last night?

Sit up. There's red clay residue all over the sheets and across my belly, breasts, and back. Oh. Simon's grave. I raise my left arm slowly. It takes effort and doesn't feel natural. It feels weak. Visually, it's different. It's lost its pink tone, the width in the wrist and hand, and Simon's freckles and fuzzy hair are gone. This is disturbing and scary. This can't happen again. The others want to find out what became of them, but I don't have to allow that. I can keep them in me forever and be safe.

Reckon that ain't a solution, Izzy.

Aye, ye ken we can drive while you be asleep. Ye cannae stop this road trip.

Jah, und ich drive next! Ich take over Simon arm!

Nein, Heinrich. Can nicht take over territory, Solveig insists.

I peek out the window at The Werks house. The pink of dawn has inched across the lawn and up to the porch where Micias sits cupping a mug. He waves. I wave back. He holds up the mug, pointing to it as a question.

Gonnae no do that, lass.

Reckon best to not linger here.

Ja! Ve go!

Gotta burn rubber. Find out what happened to my ass!

I ignore them all and using my newly acquired left hand, I slide open the passenger door, step down, but my left leg doesn't follow. Heinrich isn't budging. I pull at him with my left arm but Dragon Lady wrestles in to fight me off.

Micias hurries from the porch. "You okay?"

We freeze in this weird position and I turn to Micias. "Listen, just to let you know, I was in a nuthouse and I escaped. I'm not a danger to you, or myself—or at least *most* of myself—and I don't think I'm nuts, but I do have a unique situation that can present itself to others as psychosis or a serious personality disorder."

Micias smiles just a bit, and when I don't return it, becomes serious. "Can I ask you a question, Izzy?"

"Yes."

"Coffee or tea?"

It seems to occur to everyone that fighting over coffee or tea is better than fighting to stay or leave, so Dragon Lady lets my left arm go, I release Heinrich, and he steps us down from the van.

Micias stays a bit out of reach as we walk to the house. I don't blame him.

The cupboard has a lot of choices. I want the smoky Lapsang Souchong tea but Ruby wants black coffee. Solveig wants English Breakfast with milk. Kelly doesn't want English Breakfast but, as there isn't any Scottish Breakfast, she'll settle for Irish. Jenny wants Camomile with lemon. Heinrich wants coffee with cream and sugar, and Dragon Lady wants a gin martini. I intervene before they can place their orders. "Micias, please give me whatever you're having."

I sit at the paint-stained kitchen table and when I'm blowing on the tea, Micias asks, "Are people after you since you ran away from—the—?"

"My brother Finn said there was a detective hired to find me and return me to the loony bin."

"Why were you in the loony bin?"

"I kidnapped that same ten-year-old brother. I did it to save him from becoming what he was becoming."

"What was that?"

"An entitled rich white asshole."

Micias laughs in a way that spreads across his whole face. "Yeah, we don't need more of those. You think the detective will find you?"

"I doubt anyone could guess where I'm headed since I don't know that myself. I'm trying to find out what happened to my ancestors. Like here with Simon."

"And you know where the other ancestors ended up?"

"I've got some research to do since I only have the clues they give me."

"*They* give you."

I really want to tell someone. Could that be Micias? Everyone in me screams *NOOOOOOOOO!!!!* I ignore them. "These ancestors are in me and are distinct beings and even control different parts of my body—hence the awkwardness you saw getting out of the van. Heinrich—in my left leg—didn't want to move, so I used what used to be Simon's—the ancestor who built this house with Irene—his arm to pull Heinrich's leg, but Dragon Lady—my right arm—wouldn't let me."

Micias stares at me over his cup.

"And of course, this is in no way meaning to ignore Solveig, Ruby, Kelly, and Jenny, who are also in the mix."

You really screwed up now, girlie.

Reckon y'better leave before he calls the police.

Raus hier!

"No wonder the nuthouse," Micias says quietly.

I nod. This was a mistake. "I've got to go. Thanks for everything."

I set my mug in the sink and head for the door, trotting down the drive, the tears overflowing. It's so hard being me and having no one know or understa—

"Izzy! Hold up."

I turn and Micias is walking toward me. "I don't know if you are crazy but I know that you did some weird shit at Ajax Diner last night with the fighting and—your voice was—well, it sounded like a crowd. So, let's just say, whether or not there is a more logical or normal explanation, I accept what you say."

I get all wobbly, tipping sideways, and Micias grabs me. "Come back inside," he says, leading me with an arm around my waist. It feels so nice.

He takes me back to his cluttered studio and clears a chair. "You don't have to tell me anything else. I just want to help. What can I do?"

"Could I borrow your computer to research where to go next?"

"I'll set you up in incognito mode so whatever you look at, I can't know, just to be on the safe side. You should call your brother and find out what's going on with the detective. You shouldn't use a phone that can be traced. There's an electronic shop that sells cheap pre-paid cell phones. You'd make a call and get rid of the phone. If you want, I can get you one, or a few, while you research."

There is the distinct possibility that this young man is saying this as a ruse, Jenny warns. *One should expect him to return with the authorities and I, for one, do not relish re-incarceration.*

Solveig, Heinrich, and Dragon Lady agree. Ruby and Kelly doesn't. *Reckon this fella done right by us so far.*

Aye, the lad's a goodun.

Micias looks at me strangely. Maybe this argument is playing out on my face. He nods. "Or, I stay. I don't want you to worry that I'll rush off and tell on you. I can sit here, give you my phone, so you know I'm not secretly texting—"

"I'd love to just take a minute. I've never told anyone this before and there is a lot of chaos inside me now."

"Then let's not think about it. How about I make you a genuine Southern breakfast? My mama was a great cook and she insisted her sons learn."

I get all teary and he gives me a hug. "You want to take a shower?"

I'm not sure what he's suggesting.

He reaches out and gently lifts a bit of red clay off my neck.

Oh.

After a wonderful hot shower that sends lots of Simon's grave dirt swirling down the drain, I spend the next hour watching Micias make biscuits, and grits, and fried okra, and sausage gravy, and eggs. The other artists come downstairs talking of the smell and saying things like "Ooo, Micias is trying to impress someone!" and he dismisses the kidding but smiles at me and it feels good.

RESEARCHING THE ROAD TRIP

AFTER THE MOST PERFECT BREAKFAST, Micias sets me up to do incognito browsing and leaves to get the cell phones. From the van, I grab the atlas and Jianna's maid-tip envelopes with everyone's info and commence my online research.

Jenny was taken to the Government Hospital for the Insane in Washington D.C. We find it's now Saint Elizabeth's Hospital. Still in business. I scribble down the address. Put a circle on the USA map.

Ruby is easy. The town of Bodie in California. Circle the town on the map.

Kelly is easy as well. Austin in Potter County, Pennsylvania. We find it and circle the map.

Dragon Lady. We find articles about a Max Dragon who was a motorcycle racer operating out of Los Angeles. Won a lot of awards. There's an M. Dragon in the city. I write down the address. Circle.

Solveig isn't so easy. We'll go to Find-a-Grave, Genealogy sites, German war sites, but don't find a Solveig Von Engel that has anything to do with our Solveig. Solveig suggests we look for Zlata Rosenbaum. We find one in Levittown on Long Island, New York and an old newspaper article about this Zlata's daughter, Ursula. Solveig's sure we have a match and I write down the address. Circle on the map.

Now Heinrich. Looking through the site of records of German military during WWII we find a Heinrich Neuffer who emigrated from Germany in 1951 and moved to Salina, Kansas. Local paper has an obituary stating he was a baker and died in 1990, survived by a wife, three children, and four grandchildren. There's a Heinrich Neuffer III and a Heinrich Neuffer IV. This pleases Heinrich. "Das ist gut. Tradition kept. Der Familienname. Ich bin Heinrich Neuffer II."

I write down the address of a Heinrich Neuffer III in Salina. Add a circle in the middle of the country.

I draw a route. "We're in Mississippi, so first we'll go north to Kelly in Pennsylvania, then across to Jenny in Washington DC, then Solveig in Long Island—"

"Nein. Wir gehen Salina, Kansas," Heinrich says.

"That doesn't make sense," I say. "Kansas is on the way to California for Ruby and Dragon Lady."

"Ich bin next! Ich war—"

Ruby chimes in. "Listen, fella, I reckon you been with us long enough to learn the lingo, so get y'r tongue waggin' in English!"

"Jah, jah. So ich was somebody! Ich—I—did something—a baker, a family. I provided!"

"Okay, but 'taint no reason f'us t' wander off the trail—"

"I want Solveig to see was became of me. If we go she first, she stay like Simon and never know I be good man."

Solveig barges into my mouth. "Du hast—You *raped* me und want me to see you as good man?"

"JAH! Das was mistake! Ich was twenty-two, gebrochen—broken—by war, shamed Deutchland lost, half a man, and—and —IN LOVE WITH YOU!"

"Und you ran away. Das ist nicht what love does," Solveig says quietly.

Jenny suggests a vote and it's six-to-one against Kansas being next. My left leg won't stop twitching. Heinrich's furious.

THEO S.B. FORR

MICIAS ARRIVES with three disposable phones. "I've put my cell phone number in each one—in case you ever need to call."

"Thanks. What do I do when I use a phone so it can't be traced?"

Micias holds up a hammer as his answer. "I'll leave you alone so you can call whoever."

He leaves and I dial my brother's cell number. Finn picks up quickly and sounds terrified to hear from me. "You shouldn't call! They'll get your phone number and find you!"

I tell him about the disposable phones and the tension drops from his voice. "I'm so sorry, Izzy. I lied all I could but the detective found your call on my phone and also got the address I sent the money to in New Orleans. I heard the detective telling Mother that you're driving a Metro Van. The guy in New Orleans gave him a picture. You gotta get rid of it."

I promise him I'll think about it, but I know the answer. I don't need to vote. No way.

He tells me of foraging in Central Park and how he's learning to tell mushrooms apart and that he made a special meal for Mother from fruit and weeds and berries and that she loved it but Father wouldn't even try. Finn sounds excited and funny and smart and I'm so proud of who he's becoming.

"I'd better go, Finn. You take it easy."

"Take it easy, but take it! Bye, Izzy."

I hang up and smash the phone with Micias' hammer. It's quite fun.

When I tell Micias of the call, he suggests I change the van.

"No. I stick with my Metro. It suits my personality—or personalities," I say.

"I'm not saying to ditch it, I'm saying change it. Give it a paint job. Put a mural on the sides. I've got a house full of artists and paint."

This is a very good idea. "I don't want a van that looks like it's from a hippie commune. No paisleys or psychedelic art. Have it be like an old delivery truck. A real business."

"I'll get the paint and crew together. You think of your business title."

I like this guy. He handles things. I wonder if I could ever do that.

Since I have several people thinking in me, we get a cool idea pretty fast. I do a sketch and hand it to the woman Micias says will orchestrate the project. We walk around the van and she asks me questions about font and color and serifs and if I want to have the bullet holes repaired. An hour later, the van is in the backyard, we've got music going, pizzas, wine, and beer, and the artists doing their thing. They patch the bullet holes and work on turning my bad drawing into super-professional-lettering on the sides and back of the van.

THEO S. B. FORR CONGLOMERATED

"Who is Theo?" Micias asks, sitting next to me on the picnic table.

"It's Those Before, Conglomerated. My ancestors."

Micias squints at the sign. "I wonder if we all have what you have, only we don't pay attention. Sometimes I feel taken over by someone who isn't me. Mostly it's when I feel rage. One more dis after a day of disses and a year of disses and a lifetime… I feel this accumulation of anger that seems bottomless, like it goes way back. Way, way back. Like generations."

I can't do anything but nod.

The painting goes fast with so many people working on it. And they are all good! When there is nothing left to do, one painter suggests that I break a wine bottle (empty!) on the bumper to launch the new van. So we don't get glass shards in the driveway, they wrap the bottle in several bags. I lift the bottle, aim at the bumper, and swing!—it doesn't break. Try again. No. One more time—not a chance. Dragon Lady takes the bottle from my left hand and swings—SMASH!—and everyone cheers. Micias looks at me with wonder, aware of what's happened.

As it gets dark, Micias plugs in the hanging strings of lights and the world feels like a party-land. Glowing in the middle is the Metro Van. It looks amazing. It's a deep forest green with the words spelled out in a yellow, old-fashioned font edged with red and black. Stunning!

As the artists drift inside, Micias sits to my right on the picnic table bench and hands me a beer.

"Thank you, Micias. The van looks beautiful!"

He clinks his bottle to mine, looking into my different colored eyes. "*You* look beautiful."

A jolt of many things goes through me. Joy is first. Escape is second. I'm not sure which is from me, or one of the others, or all of the others. He's not like so many of the men I've encountered. *We've* encountered. There are good men. Is he one? Am I prey to him?

"Thank you," I try. Maybe that will end it and I won't have to deal with wonder or worry. But I do like him. He's only been nice to me.

Men say nice things, but that won't stop them doing bad, Dragon Lady snarls in my head.

Micias slides a bit closer on the bench. "I know it's hot and muggy but—do you mind if I hold your hand?"

Where he's sitting, he'd be taking Dragon Lady's hand. I quickly hop up and move to his other side and offer my left hand —Simon's, but without Simon. *My* hand.

Micias's palm is warm. He gently strokes his thumb across my skin. My heart is jumping and everyone in me is yammering their opinions and advice and I scream as loud as I can in my head— *SHUT THE FUCK UP!!! THIS IS MY LIFE AND I'M GOING TO HOLD HIS HAND! YOU ALL CAN GO TO YOUR ROOMS AND STAY THERE!!!*

There is a lot of scurrying and grumbling, but it seems to have worked. I feel at least my left arm and right leg and mind are under my control.

"Something happened," Micias says.

"Yes, I told everyone inside to fuck off and they did."

"So we're alone now?"

I nod and he leans in, his face nearing mine. I stop myself from jerking away in fear. My heart is thumping so loud and wild I expect he can hear it. He leans even closer but stops. "I'd like to kiss you. Would that be okay?"

"You paid attention in Consent Class."

He laughs. "Yes, I did."

"I've kinda had only bad experiences."

He lets go of my hand. "I'm sorry."

I take his hand again. "I haven't always been able to know what I want or don't want, and most of the time I can't stop what I don't want, even if I know."

Micias chuckles. "That surprises me after seeing what you did in the bar against those assholes."

"*I've* never been good at defending myself. It's just the ancestors that step in. Like breaking that bottle on the Metro Van."

"You underestimate your power. I think you can defend yourself."

He doesn't know. If all my ancestors leave, I'll be helpless.

Micias squeezes my hand. "I expect you'll be off on your road trip tomorrow."

I nod.

"So, how about this? Since you haven't had good experiences, let me be one. I'll ask if I can kiss you. *If* you say yes,—and you don't have to—I kiss you and then escort you to your van and bid you good night."

"Okay."

So he asks again and I say, "Yes, please." He leans close and gently kisses my lips. Not a peck and not a movie kiss. It feels warm and his lips are pillowy and make mine pillowy in a tingly way. It makes me all flibbity and weak-kneed and gets my heart whirling but anxiety peeks in, and just then, Micias pulls back and smiles.

He stands and offers his elbow. I've seen enough old-timey-movies to know what to do. I take Micias's arm and he escorts me to the van, slides the door open, and bows. It makes me feel like that princess for the first time in my life.

"I really enjoyed meeting you, Izzy. I'm glad your ancestor Simon brought you here. Send me a postcard or give me a call during your travels. I'd like to keep in touch. And feel free to come back anytime."

I give Micias a smile, step up into my newly painted van, and lean out to give him a kiss. The kiss feels even nicer with me being part of it and not so scared. It really does feel nice. I could get used to it. Given time and patience.

"Goodnight," Micias says and heads back to the house.

He is a good man.

POTTER COUNTY, PENNSYLVANIA

RUBY WAKES ME. It's still dark. "Time to make tracks. Any later and that fella will be up and we reckon you two don't need t'be sayin' more goodbyes."

Jenny lifts the atlas. "Potter County, Pennsylvania is north and east."

As she plans the route with Ruby and Solveig, Kelly keeps her foot on the gas, Dragon Lady takes the wheel, Heinrich pouts, and I drift off thinking about kissing Micias. I wonder if I'll ever go back. At least I can keep in touch with postcards. That's a nice idea.

We drive until we're tired and park outside of Bowling Green, Kentucky in the parking lot of an all-night grocery store. Lying here, I know I've been lucky. Lucky to have these ancestors in me. Lucky for their bravery and strength and skills. I miss Simon terribly and don't want to keep losing people or I'll end up an empty worthless shell.

Gute nacht, Izzy. Schlaf. Solveig whispers in my head.

Reckon you c'n be Simon f' y'own self, Ruby suggests. *Folks ain't gone if'n we take up their do'ins.*

I move my left hand to my head and stroke my temple imagining it's Simon. It makes me miss him all the more. I'll never get to sleep.

The next thing I know, it's day and everyone's anxious to get moving. We hop into the grocery store to pee and check out the bakery area for breakfast. Heinrich insists on a cherry strudel and Solveig insists on apple, so we get both.

Drive and drive and sleep and drive and finally make it to Potter County, Pennsylvania.

Kelly is keen to find her old house. We drive here-and-there in the town of Austin but she can't seem to find the landmarks or even streets or buildings she knew.

"Are you sure you lived in Potter County?"

"Aye, 'twas ne'er an eejit. I ken were I lived. We had an orchard and a wee stone house and Alex worked at the Bayless Pulp and Paper Company up the hill."

We all look. There is a hill.

A young hipster type walks by with his coffee mug.

"Excuse me, sir. Do you know where the Bayless—"

"—Papermill. Yeah. Everyone wants to see it. Take 872 north a few miles and you'll find it on the left."

Kelly puts her foot to the gas before we can thank him. "I ken it was a big deal back in my time, but cannae understand why everyone would want to see it ney."

We travel up and find the forest-rimmed road and in a little while there is a turnoff at the left overlooking a massive complex of decayed buildings. Pulling over, Kelly rushes us out to the historic marker sign.

> In 1900 on this lot, George C. Bayless of Binghamton, NY. began construction of a large pulp and paper mill. Originally constructed for a daily capacity of 50-ton, in later years it had at times, an output of 70-ton of paper per day. By 1910 the mill had a monthly payroll of $35,000.00 and Austin's population had grown to nearly 3000. The mill survived the breaking of the Austin Dam on September 30, 1911 as well as the flood of 1942. However, a major fire in 1944 caused the mill to close forever. Few remains are left.

Kelly is shaking so much we can hardly stand. "The dam." And she turns and starts us running farther up the road. In just a few bends in the route we see a massive cracked structure stretching the width of the valley—huge segments of torn and twisted concrete splayed like cracked teeth in a mouth.

Kelly collapses and we all fall.

KELLY — POTTER COUNTY, PENNSYLVANIA — 1911

BOY-O COCKS 'IS HEAD and gives a slow growl. Maybe that's Granny comin'. I rise and clutch me massive belly tae open the door. Nae soul 'tis aboot.

"'Tis nae Granny yet, Boy-O."

The wee terrier stands stiffly alert in the threshold, nose quivering and body tremblin'.

"What 'tis it, love?"

Boy-O gives a wild YELP and races off, three-legs a blur o' speed up the hillside and 'es gone!

And jest as I'm set tae call 'im, I see the birds. All aboot they're fluttering, screaming, fleeing in panic. What's happenin'?

And noo—silence. Except nae silence. Someone is shoutin'. A distant woman's voice yellin' "free" or "me" or "flee."

Step ootside and see horror approachin'. See a monster approachin'. See a mountain barrelin' doon the valley t'ward me. Someone yells "find 'ire groun'" and the yell stops.

Boy-O sensed this and ran. I hope he'll make it t' safety.

A never-endin' thunder grows louder. Darkness descends. Is this the apocalypse foretold?

Why is Alex nae here? I sent for 'im—

Hurry tae the orchard. 'Een the trees look afeared.

Screams in the distance under a roar of monstrous dimensions.

The cold hits me first. A rush of cold wind. I turn tae face it. Thirty feet or more, black and angry, the wall of water pretends to be a mountain and rolls toward me.

Too late to run. Can I climb the tallest apple tree?—I'm doing it. Stomach gets in the way but if I can hold on, maybe—if the rush passes—maybe—if the branch holds—maybe—

The Miller's house is blasted tae kindlin'. The Schuler's turned tae matchsticks. All these bits whip intae the wave and— the full force of an angry God hits me—shockin' and cold and unforgivin'. Water engulfs me. Me dress rips off. Debris spears and pummels me. Something large smashes intae me leg and the bone snappin' high tells me—*am I tae live, I'll naer walk ageen.* Turn wi' me back tae the deluge to protect the bairn inside. Turn and know all 'tis lost. The flood overhead is far too high and the current is far too strong and I cannae rise or fight it. I'm dead.

TRY, a voice in me yells.

I let go o' the apple tree and let the surge take me, while pulling up, pushing up, bombarded by objects, me back tae the painful deluge tae keep that child safe, A huge thing hits me flat and wide like someone's front door. The thing smashes me shoulder but I grab hold and let it carry and cover me. A flash of sunlight above. It'll be a miracle if I rise. SLAM! Into something unmoving. A building? Pull at it. Pull and the splittin' of the currant around this immovable thing pushes me higher—higher into AIR! Cling tae this place, legs sliced with each passing piece of someone's life—surrounded by ungodly noise and I find I'm clingin' tae the kirk steeple, the only thing above water for miles. Please let me hold on. Please—

Something is at me face, wet an' frenzied. My bloody swollen eye opens and finds Boy-O, and behind 'im, Alex, t'one I love. Where am I? On wet ground. How'd I get doon from the kirk steeple? I dinnae remember naught.

Alex 'tis sobbin' and pullin' at my insides. I feel all sorts of me spillin' oot. A miraculous cry breaks o'er everything. Me man lifts the wee wailer from me. Our babe!—and I dissolve—

POTTER COUNTY, PENNSYLVANIA

"ALEX FOUND ME. Somehow he found me. But did I live? Did the baby live?" Kelly asks.

"We know the baby did because you're here in me," I say. "Maybe we can find out what happened to you."

Kelly leads us down from the road to the ruins of the dam. There's a memorial with the names of the many dead and her name is there.

"I stood near this ground and the earth was soggy. A right soppin' bog. That man called it normal seepage. He diddnae care. That's who I want my revenge on. I didnae know afore. I want tae find that Mr. George C. Bayless and kill him."

We all nod in commiseration but know that's not possible.

We return to the van and drive into town. Now that we're not looking for specific landmarks from the past, Kelly finds their ancient orchard. The trees are bent and twisted, some have clearly been snapped at their trunks, but new branches sprouted up and it has grown into a gnarled place of beauty and bounty. A pile of stones is all that's left of what must have been their cottage. We gather apples and perfumey quinces and sit on the remaining stones to take in the beauty and sorrow.

"Kelly, I reckon you survived 'cause this place was up the side of the valley aways. When it hit, you were not so deep in the wave," Ruby suggests.

"But I didnae survive."

"Your babe did and that's why our Izzy is here."

"Aye, and of that I'm eternally grateful."

This gets me choked up and the fruit trees get blurry, as does the figure approaching from below the orchard.

With me blinking, the figure turns into an old woman. She pauses before me. "You're trespassing. This is private property."

Dragon Lady wants to smack her but I push past with what I think Simon would say. "I'm so sorry, ma'am. I was just visiting this orchard because my great-great-great grandparents lived here and she died in the dam break."

"Oh, no, I'm sorry. Stay as long as you like."

The woman turns to head back down the hill.

"Pardon me, ma'am, would you know where all those that died in the flood were buried?"

"Well, miss, I don't drive anymore or I'd take you there. I can't rightly make a map cause I only know it by feel."

"Excuse me for not introducing myself," I say, proud to be remembering Simon's politeness. "I'm Elizabeth and my ancestors were Kelly and Alex MacLellan originally from Ayrshire, Scotland."

"Glad to meet you, Elizabeth. I'm Caddie."

"Caddie, if you have the time, I've got a vehicle and I could drive us to where folks are buried."

And so we help Caddie into the Metro Van, which she is very impressed with, and she navigates us through several backroads to a wide meadow. There are a few headstones but not as many as the number that died. She explains that so many were lost it wasn't possible to identify them all with their kin lost as well.

The meadow is a beautiful place. Overgrown with wildflowers of all kinds. Surrounded with butterflies and bees and flitting birds.

We sit awhile with Caddie and she tells of her relatives that died that day. She tells of the mill owner George Bayless and how, to save money, he cut corners in the building of the dam and ignored anyone who suggested it wouldn't hold. She tells how after the disaster, when the town wanted to make him pay, he promised to keep the mill operating and hire everyone, and somehow was never held accountable. We sit eating apples from Kelly and Alex's orchard, watching the sun move low behind the gleaming grasses and flowers, and feeling all the anger and sorrow left here. As it grows dark, we drive back into town and Caddie insists we eat dinner with her in her small house. It's nice to spend time with someone who isn't inside me, and also nice that she's not someone that gets me all flibbity-jibbity inside like Micias did. When we leave, she gives us a kiss on the cheek and it makes me wish I had a relative alive like her.

MOONLIGHT MEADOW

YOU GUESSED IT, I wake up driving, already approaching that wide meadow.

A mist hovers over the ground. We step down from the van and Kelly slowly weaves us between wildflowers deep into the meadow. As we move through the mist, we create a swirling wake behind us. Kelly runs our hands over the tips of dew-covered grasses. There are a few mossy gravestones but she ignores them. She pauses as if listening or feeling for the right spot, takes a few more steps, then lowers us to the ground. It's cool and wet and a deep smell rises from it. She lays us down upon this earth. Sounds of frogs. Crickets. Owls. Whispers.

Whispers and soft moaning. Is that us? Tears slide down the sides of our face and mingle with the dirt.

All around, there is a shifting. The ground feels like it's throbbing. Things moving underground. Converging below us. I get a feeling like when I was on the psychedelic mushrooms, deep in that fog and there were so many—so many—moving down there. Kelly sobs silently, her leg shaking against the earth, and the earth shaking with her. She exhales and the moans and wails of the lost ones ring out across the meadow.

As we lie there, the sobs and moans subside. The moon glows brighter and Kelly sits us up.

"Take dirt," she says.

We presses our hands into the dirt, collecting great handfuls.

"'Tis here I'll be stayin'," Kelly says.

"Reckoned you were fixin' to."

"'Twas a joy knowin' all ye, my kin. Particularly you, Izzy. I'll be watchin' from afar, if 'tis possible."

She gets us up to our feet and there is a leaning inside. A pulling and stretching and un-binding and the pressure grows and it feels as if my leg is expanding and the leaning becomes falling and I stumble backwards to stay upright and she pulls away—separates—There's Kelly in front of us!——A glowing specter, plump and strong, in a simple dress. She has dark hair and rich ochre skin and a beautiful wide face with glimmering eyes.

She laughs heartily seeing herself and the sound is like sheep bells over a moor. And in the field, lit by the moon, arising around the blossoms and mist, are figures. They hover and wander and meld into each other. Babies and children and men and women all shimmer, tangled among the wildflowers. The figures gather and grow into multitudes. Townsfolk who drowned in the disaster all move to greet Kelly. And distant sound approaches. A lilting melody played on a fiddle. The tall figure of the fiddler appears and Kelly covers her mouth at the sight and then turns back to us.

"Dinnae forget me," she whispers in a voice like wind through leaves.

"We will never forget you," I say.

She waves once and turns to her husband and Alex curls his bow arm around her and a breeze swirls the figures together and the shadows under the moon scatter and there's nothing but mist and shivering flowers.

We slowly walk back to the van and Kelly's dirt is emptied from my pockets and shirt into another plastic bag, and everyone goes to sleep except me. My right leg feels so different. It's empty. I miss Kelly.

WASHINGTON D.C.

THE NEXT MORNING, before dressing, I rinse off the dirt from Kelly's meadow. As I send a damp washcloth down my right leg, it feels and looks different. Kelly's darker skin and plumpness have vanished. *I don't want to be without Kelly! She was part of me!*

"Reckon she still is, Izzy. She jes got mixed in. Stirred," says Ruby.

I'm becoming homogenized and I don't like it!

Jenny is impatient to find out about herself so she forces us to get moving. We drive another long way to Washington DC and find Saint Elizabeth's Hospital grounds. It is a vast complex of buildings the size of a large campus. Cars and people are coming and going. Jenny directs Dragon Lady and we leave the bustle. The buildings become more ancient and rundown.

"There it is," Jenny says.

We pull beside a massive wreck of a building. Cracks snake up the ancient bricks. The roof has large dark gaps where the red tiles have fallen. Overgrown trees loom in the weedy yard. A bent and sagging chain-link fence surrounds the decaying site.

We park and I get out. Hopefully, no one will notice us.

The chain-link fence is no barrier. It has been pulled down so many times there are gaps everywhere. As I step toward the wide porch, Jenny gives us a shudder. "I don't think I can go in."

"We don't have to."

"But I want to know what happened."

"Can you close yourself off? Hum or sing something?"

In a moment, her quivering soprano voice sings, "In the shade of the old apple tree..."

Jenny continues, I feel her turning inwards, and a memory slides into our mind. A wealthy-looking parlor. Two children giggle on the ornate rug. A Victrola with its big amplifying horn plays a thick record as a dapper man dances Jenny around the room. She looks happy. Seeing this, I realize how much she sacrificed by going on that suffragette march.

As she's lost in the memory, we step around discarded stainless steel cabinets piled on the ragged porch. The door has a padlocked latch. I guess that means we won't be going in.

Heinrich raises his leg and delivers a mighty kick just below the latch—BAM!—the door flies open, latch screws ripping from the old wood. Jenny doesn't miss a beat of her tune. She must be very deep in us.

We step inside the lobby. The yellow and green tile floor is scattered with leaves and petrified bird shit below hidden perches. The air smells of an ancient chemical. We shouldn't touch anything or even breathe.

I don't know what we're looking for and Jenny isn't helping. We walk through the lobby and down a long hall. Rooms on either side. What looks like an exam room. A cafeteria or dining room. Furniture overturned. Graffiti sprayed on the walls—not a lot—I bet kids who come here to vandalize things end up leaving quickly. Not a place to hang out.

Another corridor. Metal doors with covered slots. I want to see inside but don't want to touch anything.

Dragon Lady scoffs at me and slides open the little door covering the slot. Inside is a small room. Barred window. Thin bed. Is this the kind of room Jenny was locked in?

We head farther down the hall. At the end, there's an open door. A padded table with leather straps. A machine with dials and wires leading to two paddles.

Jenny stops singing.

JENNY — GOVERNMENT HOSPITAL FOR THE INSANE, WASHINGTON, D.C. 1917

I RECOGNIZE THE EYES when they peek in the slot. It's the ogre. The keys jangle, the lock clicks back, and he enters smiling. It's a sadist's smile. "You and me going for a little walk."

I know what is next. The hydrotherapy room. I'll be wrapped for hours in the wet blanket, trapped, unable to move, my face covered, unable to see. It's unbelievably, profoundly horrible. Especially now that the baby is so close to being born. "I refuse to acquiesce to your demands. I will not participate in, nor accept, any abuse to my person. I have the inalienable right to defend myself, my body, my intellect--"

The ogre grabs my legs and pulls me off the bed. I land hard, painfully, and worry for the baby inside.

He drags me by my ankles out of the room and down the hall. My hospital dress rides up to my posterior and my bloomers are visible to all in the corridor. I will not scream and act untoward. "This treatment is unethical and demeaning and criminal. I vehemently protest my illegal incarceration and refuse all treatments. I am not insane."

We reach the junction to the hydrotherapy room and don't turn left. The ogre pulls me toward the end of the hall. This can't be happening. They can't do that now—not with the baby so far along. It would be criminal!

The ogre hauls me past two nurses. I hold my massive stomach, screaming, "Stop this man! You see how pregnant I am. The child cannot be subjected to this!"

The nurses turn away.

"Think of the baby!" I scream as I'm pulled into the room. The ogre bends and easily lifts me onto the padded table.

I sob to him, pleading, "My child is due any day. Don't subject it to this!"

He straps my arms down and moves on to my ankles. "Going to turn your brain into an Edison lightbulb."

"You don't know how this might hurt the baby. Please."

The ogre puts the conductive lotion on my temples. I can't believe he's doing this. My seventh time. It terrifies me. I'm not the same afterward and fear they will slowly electrocute my intellect from me. But what will it do to the baby?

"Please. Don't do this."

"I like when you say please," he says as he sets the paddles against my head.

"Please. My child can't—"

ZZZZZZZZZZZZZZZZZZZZZZZZZZZZ!!!!!!!!!!!!!!!!!!!!!!!!!

LIGHT and PAIN as the world CRACKS.

I'm torqued and torn and twisted, arcing-inside, fire-lit. Something squirts from me, crying. I'm a void as the baby wails in the distance.

AFTER ELECTROSHOCK

I'M ON THE FLOOR. Jenny is sobbing. "I couldn't help it. They did it and it forced the baby out."

We all do our best to hug her.

"Could my baby survive that electrical charge? Did it die a horrible death?"

Ruby murmurs gently, "Jenny, reckon 'bout time you recollect who you're talkin' to. You know that babe survived 'cause you is in Izzy."

Dragon Lady pulls us up from the floor. "Let's see if we can find records of your time here, Jenny. Maybe find out when you left, where you went."

Wandering the rest of the decaying building, we find a room with file cabinets, but everything is empty.

"Perhaps they disposed of the records," Jenny says. "It was a long time ago."

We step back out into the sunshine. A security car is by the Metro van.

I'll do the talking, says Jenny.

No, you're too close to it. I'll do the talking, I say, and step up to the guard.

"Is this your vehicle?" he asks.

"Yes, I'm sorry. I didn't know exactly where to park."

"Not here."

"My great-great-great-grandmother was a patient here. I was told about her and want to find out what records there might be. Can you point me in the right direction?"

"That building—the one that looks almost from our present era. And they have a parking lot."

I thank him and we drive to the more-modern building and park in the lot like we're supposed to.

Searching the cool halls, we come to a RECORDS door. I enter and step up to the counter. Several people work feeding faded papers into what must be scanning machines. They look very bored. One looks up, a young Black woman with pierced eyebrows. "You another 'volunteer'?"

It occurs to me that this might be a way to get the information, but I try another tact. "No, I'm hoping to find a record of a patient from a long time ago."

"Mrs. Rudinsky is on lunch."

"Can you look something up for me?"

The young woman steps over to the counter, seeming relieved to move from her station at the scanner.

Another person hisses, "Mrs. Rudinsky don't allow us doing searches, Jax."

Jax shrugs at the comment and sits at the computer. "You got a name and dates?"

"Jenny Carswell. She was brought in in 1916, I think."

Jax types in the information. "Yep. 1916 admitted. Last entry —1973—died age 88."

We all take a quick breath. "She died—here?"

"Uh-huh. Says she had electroshock 468 times. Says never stopped insisting on her rights."

Jenny's shaking. Ruby tries to calm her while I swallow in order to talk. "She had a child."

More computer tapping. Heinrich locks his knee and Dragon Lady grips the edge of the counter to keep us upright.

"No information about a child."

A volunteer with dyed purple hair and tattoos on her arms pipes up. "They had lots of pregnancies here. Seems like that happens anytime when you lock women up and have men guardin' them. All them babies got given all away and they didn't keep no records on what baby went to who, 'cause nobody wants to know their mother was a nut-case."

Jenny blurts out. "Where is my body?"

Every one of the volunteers looks up at me.

"I mean my relative's body?"

The purple-haired one answers. "She's in the field over behind the running track. That's where they put them that got nobody. But you won't find her. No marker. No stone. They just plow aside the dirt and dump 'em in."

A stout woman comes through the door and Jax immediately hops away from the computer, saying to me, "I'm sorry, Miss, I'm not allowed to look that up."

I nod and we walk Jenny out.

It doesn't take long to find the running track. Behind it is an un-mowed field of mounds and sunken areas spread over a large area. We walk into it. Bees and butterflies swirl over clover and buttercups.

Jenny drops us to the ground. "I never got out. I never saw that child or had a life with it or anyone. I was hidden away and forgotten. I didn't become anything. I didn't contribute."

"You made me, Jenny. You—all of you—made *me*."

Jenny sighs. "I'm glad at least I never stopped fighting," she says. "Don't you ever stop."

I nod.

We sit there for a long time, taking in the trees at the edge of the field, the haphazard movement of the insects, the plaintive calling of the birds. After a while, Jenny has Dragon Lady pull up a clump of clover and dig a hole in the soil. The dirt feels brittle and somehow unwell. It smells harsh and unwelcoming but Jenny says, "Scoop some into your pockets. Take a bit with you." Dragon Lady and I pull up dirt and fill each of our breast pockets. The stench rises from the ground and I have to turn away.

We stand and get prepared for what happens next. It makes all of us sad.

"It's a dang shame that you were trapped here, Jenny," Ruby says.

"So sorry," says Solveig.

Jenny slowly pulls and we're all stretched and then the stretch slinks back.

"Was ist wrong?" Heinrich asks.

"Kelly and Simon had individuals that cared about them at their final resting places. I don't," Jenny says. "I spent my life confined in this institution and I will not spend my death here. Let's go."

We take a step, but Jenny stops us. "And empty that blouse and discard every last infinitesimal granule of this earth. I refuse to carry an iota of it with us."

Ruby unbuttons my shirt as Solveig looks around for anyone watching. We shake and turn the pockets and shake some more until Jenny is satisfied. She spits on the ground. "Now let's leave this God-forsaken place."

We hurry back to the van and Heinrich and Dragon Lady drive us out the gates.

The van takes this-road-and-that and suddenly there's a pedestrian sign for The White House. We can't drive closer but Jenny shakes her fist. "Woodrow, you couldn't stop us! I won! Izzy can vote because of me!"

We all cheer her and turn north to find Solveig's place.

SOLVEIG — ESCHWEGE, GERMANY — 1945

I HIDE EVERY TIME the victorious occupation patrols pass by. In this quadrant, they're all American Yanks. Perhaps they would help me, but I fear them. At least I'm not farther east in the Russian zone.

I survive by Nahrungssuche. I eat onion grass. Wild garlic. Safe mushrooms I can find. Berries. Often I find a berry bush stripped of all but its thorns. I'm not the only one starving. My competitors may be beasts or others like me. Whatever I forage to eat, it's never enough.

How long will this go on? Why am I walking? Where am I headed? To death, no doubt.

How many months has it been since Heinrich pressed me down in the field of flowers? It seems like years, but it can't be. This belly is still growing. The life in it kicks at me. Why does it live, manifesting the horrible memory of Heinrich on me, when my sweet sister Miriam doesn't?

Across the field is a farmhouse. Farms draw me in as there is at least some possibility of stealing an egg, milk, fallen fruit, or a cabbage. I need food and rest and stagger toward it. Something moves in the bushes. I jolt back but I have no strength to fight anything. A wild boar would find a good meal in me.

The creature whimpers. A dog? They are as hungry as we are.

"Bitte. Come out. Come."

The leaves rustle and a little dirty hand emerges, then another, a tangle of hair. A child. A ragged thread of a girl. Maybe nine. She crawls toward me barefoot. She could be Miriam.

"Can you help?" she asks in a raspy voice.

I nod and hold out my hands, suddenly stronger for having a mission. "We will go to the farm and find food and rest. Come. I'm Solveig. What's your name?"

"Zlata," she whispers. "Zlata Rosenbaum." She hunches a bit as if this name will cause me to turn against her.

I take her hands and help her stand. She's tall for a child—
"How old are you?"

"Fourteen."

I'm shocked. How could such a thin child be fourteen? Unless
—"Where did you come from?"

"The camp. The soldiers came and we were freed and
everyone left. I got lost."

"You're found now."

We sneak past the farmhouse and into the barn. The coo of
chickens sends us searching. Hidden in the stacks of hay,
chickens nest and warm their eggs. We search and find, just like
the Ostereiersuche. Zlata had heard of the Easter Egg Hunt but
never participated. I did with Miriam when we were living with
Doctor Von Engel and his wife. With eight found, we huddle
together, cover ourselves with hay, and suck out the nourishment
from the eggs. The joy in Zlata's face is wonderful.

Zlata asks if I will take care of her.

I am so glad to have her to take care of. It makes me feel less
of a failure for not saving Miriam. I whisper to her, holding her
thin body close. "We can be sisters. I had a sister, Miriam, but she
died."

She hugs me and puts her bony hand on my swollen belly.
"When is the baby coming?"

"I've lost track of the months. It kicks but I can't imagine it
will live. It's had so little nourishment."

"It will live. We'll make sure of it."

A kick to my foot wakes me. I look up from my bed in the hay to
an American officer standing over me. I must jerk because Zlata
wakes suddenly and screams. The American says something and
another man appears behind him and speaks to us in German,
asking questions. I tell him we're sisters. Zlata rushes in with the
camp she was held in. The translator speaks to the American and
we're told to get up.

They help us get into their jeep and we drive off. The wind rushes over us. I hold Zlata tight and try to keep her thin frame warm.

We arrive at a gate with a sign reading Eschwege Displaced Persons Camp. The jeep pulls to a stop in front of a brick building and the German translator escorts us inside. He speaks for us. Zlata and Solveig Rosenbaum. Jewish sisters.

The woman types our names on a form. "Because you are Jewish displaced persons, you will be allowed to live here. You'll have food and there will be a place found for you later."

We're shown to our beds and given fresh clothes and have a miracle of a bath. It's so wonderful. I can't imagine how I lived without bathing for so many months.

The days pass and it's a better life, less fear, but still not enough food. Because of my baby inside, I can't move fast and Zlata and I are always near the last in a line for bread. As the server hands me a small roll, a plane roars overhead. The woman spins to look at it and her sleeve catches another roll, tipping it to the ground. Zlata and I see it fall. We can't do anything to get it without everyone knowing.

Zlata points at the plane screaming, "Sie werden uns töten! They will kill us!" As she is surrounded, she glances at me and I know. I bend and grab the roll. We're a good team. Just like sisters.

After, we sneak to the back of our dormitory and share the illicit roll. It's better than all the rest.

Over the days and weeks, Zlata tells me about her family and I tell her about mine.

It's in the food hall when I get the first surge of pain. I scream and Zlata holds me as someone calls for a doctor. I'm floating, carried by several arms to a bed. Someone listens to my belly with a scope and another tells Zlata to leave. Zlata insists on staying, gripping my hand as I squeeze hers in terror and pain.

"How far along is she?"

Zlata answers that we don't remember. Time vanished in the camp.

I feel myself ripping apart. I can't get a breath and pain consumes me.

Noises come and go and I can only tell I'm conscious by the unendurable scorching of my being.

A push and there's a pulling from me and a baby wails. Could this child be alive?

"It's a girl!"

And I tell Zlata, "We'll name her for my mother. She'll be Ursula Rosenbaum."

And scissors move to the cord that ties me to my baby—

LEVITTOWN, LONG ISLAND

I REFUSE TO DRIVE THE METRO VAN anywhere near Manhattan. Everyone thinks I'm crazy to worry about running into Mother or Father but I insist so vehemently that they relent and we drive across Staten Island to get to Long Island and Solveig's relatives.

It's evening as we cruise along the Southern State Parkway. The two-lane road has a wide swath of grass flanking it and, beyond that, a thick line of trees obscuring suburbia. This avenue of green must be the Park in Parkway. All along the way many furry creatures nibble a grassy dinner in the cooling air.

The sun edges lower, stretching the shadows, as we exit the parkway onto Wantagh Avenue. Levittown is not far. I've seen pictures from the old days of this famous suburb with all the houses looking the same. It's not like that now. Everyone must have remodeled. There are even McMansions on some lots. Only a few houses appear to be the original models.

I go to the address we found for Zlata Rosenbaum. It's still the old Levittown style. I pull to the curb and stare at it.

The front door opens and a man of about sixty hurries down the driveway toward me.

I slide open my door. "I don't mean to bother you but I believe I'm related to someone who used to live here. Zlata Rosenbaum?"

He puts a hand out like Alberto did, and I use that steady palm to drop from the van.

"Zlata's my mother. Come, come, the sun will be setting."

I hurry to follow his trot up to the house.

He touches a tiny box mounted on the door jamb and steps through the vestibule to a small kitchen. As he moves into the light, I see he's wearing a Yarmulka over a large bald spot.

"Mom, get decent, we have company," he says as we round the brick fireplace wall separating the kitchen from the dining room. At the table sits an ancient woman in a wheelchair.

Solveig makes us all feel dizzy. She sputters, "Bist du Zlata? Erinnerst du dich an Solveig?"

The old woman blinks. "What are you saying?"

"Sit, dear," the man says to me, "Shabbat." He removes newspapers from a chair at the table and I sit. I'm about to ask what that means—but Solveig shuts me up and has us all get still.

The old woman strikes a match and lights two candles on an antique sideboard. She waves her wrinkled hands by them three times as if pulling in the scent and light, covers her eyes, and says a Hebrew prayer. On the old woman's parchment-thin arm is the ancient tattoo. Her numbers from the camp.

As the prayer finishes, the man turns to me. "I'm Alan. This is my mother, Zlata. And who is blessing our table?"

I'm guessing he's referring to me. "I'm Izzy. My great-great-grandmother was Solveig. She and Zlata were together in Germany after the war. Solveig had a baby—"

Zlata nods. "Ursula."

Solveig leans us forward, hopeful. She thinks her question and I ask the old woman, "What happened to Solveig after she gave birth to Ursula?"

Zlata sigh. "She died, my dear. She gave birth and died."

Solveig slumps, causing me to slump. Alan waves a hand at Zlata. "Enough with the talk. This girl needs to eat."

He rushes to the kitchen as Zlata shakes her head. "I'll tell you, in those horrible days, *everyone* needed to eat. When I met Solveig, we were both starving. In Eschwege Displaced Persons Camp there was enough food to keep us breathing but still so little. That's no way to be pregnant. Solveig had no strength left after giving it all to the baby. She made me promise to raise Ursula as my own and died soon after giving birth. I was only fourteen but I did the best I could. I kept that baby alive. Brought her to America, raised her..."

Solveig and Heinrich usurp my arms and reach across the table, each grasping one of the old woman's wrinkled hands. Heinrich says something clearly grateful in German and Solveig adds more German praise and thanks.

Alan returns carrying a tray laden with food and I quickly pull my hands from holding Zlata's. He notices and I feel him staring.

"I heard you as I came in, Izzy. Where'd you learn to speak German so well?"

"Uh,—school."

"Do you know you switched registers in your voice for each sentence?"

Heinrich and Solveig, no more talking! I smile at Alan. "No, I didn't notice that."

"Make me a plate, Alan. You know what I like," says Zlata. She turns to me. "I'm rusty with my native tongue. You said something about stars in heaven for saving your baby?"

"Jah."

"You mean Solveig's baby."

"Right. Solveig's baby."

Alan keeps glancing at me as he makes a plate for Zlata. He seems to be inventorying all my mismatched parts. It makes me nervous.

"This looks delicious," I say to distract him.

He smiles. "Don't tell anyone—we do the Shabbat candles but —the food isn't strictly kosher. Mom and me call it a Jewish smorgasbord of all the things we like."

Alan points it all out. "Knishes with mustard. Kippered herrings in sour cream and onions. Black olives. Ptcha jellied with chicken and garlic rather than calves' feet. Hard-boiled eggs in green herb sauce."

I want to eat but Heinrich and Solveig insist I ask—"What happened to Solveig's daughter Ursula?"

Zlata laughs. "Oy, what happens to anyone? Ursula grew up here, met a boy, Benny, in high school, they marry, move to Belmore—only a town away, even so, I don't know why they couldn't be closer—meantime, I get married, have Alan, things sour—I divorce—Benny and Urs have a girl, Miriam—"

"My grandmother."

"—and everyone lives their lives and we do holidays and birthdays and phone calls and their Miriam grows up and leaves for the big city—she was a go-getter—and after that Ursula got a lump and that was the end. She'd never been well. Probably from starving as a baby. She died at only forty-four."

Alan passes me the hard-boiled eggs with the green herbs. "She's buried in Belmore. It's close. If you want, I'll take you in the morning."

I take a bite of the egg with the sauce and Heinrich pushes me to my feet, yelling in a deep voice, "Ja! Das ist Frankfurt grie soß!"

Alan wiggles a finger at me. "See, that's what I'm talking about. You spoke in a much deeper register than your other voice."

I nod, as if fascinated, while kicking Heinrich's ankle. We drop back to the chair.

Zlata lifts the glasses hanging from her chest and squints through them, peering at me as if she can see the people inside. "You're Solveig's great-great-granddaughter, but also that soldier's."

Heinrich's leg trembles. "Yes," I answer. "A German soldier. Heinrich Neuffer."

Zlata nods. "Solveig told me. Heinrich was the one who raped her on the hill."

Alan groans as he pours me a glass of wine. "Oy, Mom, Shabbat dinner—"

Zlata dismisses him with a wave. "Solveig thought they were friends. She loved him, but he ran off and she never saw him again. She said if he had stayed, they could have raised the baby together. Had a family life."

My lip quivers and tears overflow from Heinrich's crying.

Alan looks at me curiously, "You alright?"

I leap up. "Bathroom?"

Alan points down the hall and I dart to the room. Inside, I cover my mouth with a towel until Heinrich stops sobbing. Then he yells at Solveig in my head. *You should habben told me! Ich could have stayed and raised little Ursula mit you!*

Solveig snarls, *Zlata is old und got her memory wrong. Ich nicht love you.*

You did! Ich—

Stop it! I yell inside. *We have to go back out there. Everyone, let me do the talking. That man's noticing our different voices. He may think I'm nuts with a split personality and call the police.*

They agree and we return to continue dinner. It's pleasant and there're no more outbursts from any ancestors. Alan and Zlata ask about my relations and where I'm from, and I tell half-truths and obfuscations without giving away too much. As the meal goes on I realize I was wrong that Alan suspects something. He's a perfectly fine host and a step-relative as well. I imagined things from tiredness.

It's nine-thirty when Zlata rolls back her wheelchair. Alan stands. "That's my cue. This is way past Mom's bedtime. Back in a sec with bedding for the couch. It's a foldout and real comfy. You'll stay."

At first, I don't like that he tells me I'm staying rather than asking, but then he adds, "We've got space and you're family."

That makes me feel good. It feels like what *family* would do.

"Come, bubbeleh, let me kiss you goodnight," Zlata says.

I bend to her wrinkled face and she squeezes my arm with a claw-like hand and puts a loud smacking "mmmmmmm-AHH!" kiss on my cheek. It shocks me how alien and wonderful that feels. Mother and Father never kissed me or said goodnight.

BELMORE CEMETERY

NEXT MORNING AFTER BAGELS and cream cheese, blueberries, and more hard-boiled eggs in green sauce for Heinrich, we leave Zlata to her TV shows and step out. Alan squints at the painted letters on the Metro Van, cocking his head.

"Theo S. B. Forr. Those Before."

"It's that obvious?"

"No, I just have a mind that sees things like that. Good at puzzles. Sudoku. Crosswords. Wordle. 'Those Before.' You're way into this ancestor thing, eh?"

"Completely—occupied."

Alan squints at me again, like he's trying to read the puzzle of me.

"Show the way," I say to make him think of something else.

Alan squats, looking at the ground. He picks up two small rocks, puts them in his jacket pocket, then pulls himself into the van passenger seat. As I climb in, he touches the glove compartment door. "What's this?"

I can't see what he's pointing to, so I shrug. He opens the compartment, reaches in, and pulls out a small object. He turns and fingers the hole in the back of his seat. "Looks like you had some adventures." He holds the object out to me. A flattened bullet.

Seeing it, fear rushes over me and Ruby takes over. "Reckon weren't nothin' we couldn' handle. You can toss that fella back where y'found it."

Alan puts the bullet back and Dragon Lady peels us out, screeching tires and roaring engine. I feel Alan's eyes on me and Ruby tries to calm me. *Don't you fret so. Yonder fella ain't gonna figure out nothin' 'cause the dern truth ain't possible to imagine.*

Jenny wriggles in my mouth. *That may be correct, Ruby, however, as Izzy implied last night, the gentleman might suspect insanity by virtue of separate internal personalities. That isn't what we need.*

Alan navigates us past shopping centers with the same chain stores and fast-food restaurants we've seen in every other part of the country. In a bit, we enter the Belmore Jewish Cemetery, park, and follow Alan to a simple gravestone.

URSULA ROSENBAUM
1945-1988
BELOVED SISTER AND MOTHER
DAUGHTER OF SOLVEIG

"They wrote daughter of *me!*" Solveig says.

Alan smiles slightly and hands me a rock from his pocket. I don't know what this is for. He places his small rock on the top of the gravestone with the others scattered there. I do the same. Heinrich and Solveig drop us to our knees and I'm glad because it makes Alan step away to give us privacy.

Solveig cries as Ruby, Jenny, and Dragon Lady comfort her. Heinrich kicks the earth with his foot grumbling, *Nicht ist good mit Rosenbaum name. Should be Neuffer or Von Engel. Nicht Jude name.*

Solveig moves into Dragon Lady's arm and slaps Heinrich's leg. *Our daughter was Jude. I'm Jude.*

Heinrich zooms from his leg into my left arm and he grabs Dragon Lady's arm. *Nicht Jude.*

Solveig struggles with Heinrich. *Jah. Ich bin. My parents were Isaac and Sarah Mermelstein. Before the war, they are frightened by all news and want us safe. Sent Miriam and me to live with Papa's colleague Doctor Dietrich Von Engel. He pretend we his nieces und das made us gentiles. Ja, Heinrich. Ich bin Jude.*

Furious, Heinrich squeezes Dragon Lady's arm hard. Solveig tries to pull the arm from his grip and my shirt sleeve rips—"Stop it!" I yell.

And the words are echoed behind me. "Stop it!" Alan yells.

We turn to see him pulling at a young man kneeling by a gravestone. The young guy spins and sprays Alan in the face with red paint. Alan stumbles backwards, wiping his eyes, and three other young men rise, revealing swastika desecrated gravestones, and move toward Alan.

"Stay away from him!" I shout as we race for them.

The four dudes, all in grey sweatshirts, look at me and laugh.

"More the merrier, Jew," one says. He looks like he'd be on the wrestling team in high school. Thick neck, Supercuts hair.

Alan straightens and blinks the paint from his eyes. "Go home, boys. You're done here."

One guy mimics Alan's words and I'm leaping, Heinrich's leg outstretched, and WHAM!—that heel hits Supercuts in the sternum and there is an audible CRACK. The guy falls back screaming. Dudes Two, Three, and Four look perplexed.

"KILL THAT LITTLE BITCH!" Supercuts yells in agony.

The others charge at me and, while I panic, Dragon Lady punches Two's neck. He falls, clutching his throat. Number Three reaches for my arm but Ruby head-butts him on the nose and he drops screaming. Solveig slides into Kelly's leg and kicks Four in the balls. He folds in on himself.

"YOU ARE OUTNUMBERED, ASSHOLES," we all roar in our multiple voices. Dude Four clutches his groin and hobbles backwards. The others shrink as we near them. Supercuts flings the red spray paint bottle at my head but Dragon Lady swats it aside. "GET GONE!"

As the jerks hobble away, Heinrich groans, looking at the several graves sprayed with red swastikas. "Dumkopfts."

Alan nods to my shirt as I help him in the Metro Van. "You tore your clothing. Good. Kriah—Jewish grieving custom."

ALAN WANTS TO STUDY

AS DRAGON LADY DRIVES, Alan sits in the passenger seat scrubbing his face with my dish soap and sponge. It looks like it hurts and by the time we pull up to the Levittown house, he's still got patches of red—especially around the eyes.

As we park he says, "I need you to explain, you fought four guys—"

"Took judo classes once—"

"I heard multiple voices at the same time."

"Sometimes when I yell loud—"

"The Germans high and low register, there a western-country accent, you've got different hair sections, one green eye, one brown eye, the mismatched arms. From what I've observed, you have multiple unmixed strands of DNA operating inside. How many?"

"You're nuts."

"Listen. This is incredibly important. I wrote my PhD on this phenomenon. The 'Collective Unconscious,' as Jung called it, or the 'Spiritus Mundi,' as Yeats put it. I believe in Genetic Memory. Epigenetics. We are not blank slates coming into the world. But people like you are rare. You are not only multiple consciousnesses, you are multiple physicalities."

"I've got to be going. Say goodbye to Zlata for me."

Alan leans his red face across the van. "I recognized you immediately because of your great-grandmother-Ursula. She had one blue eye and one brown. She had limbs that were as if she was pieced together from disparate people. She was like you and she sparked my entire life's work!"

"I'm going," I say.

He grabs my wrist.

Why does anyone think that's okay?

"Let go now or—"

"—she'll put yer pecker in a box and bury it with the prairie dogs."

Alan lets go. He smiles. "Understood, Ma'am. To whom do I have the pleasure of speaking?"

"Reckon you think you know shit, but you don't know diddly. We're fixin' to skedaddle and you know we ain't gonna be stopped by the likes of you."

Alan's grin gets wider. "And who do we have here? The western gal."

Dragon Lady's hand shoots out and grabs Alan by the shirt collar. "Get out of this van on your own two feet or you'll get out on your ass."

Alan holds up his hands in surrender. "I'd like to appeal to the Germans in you. Heinrich and Solveig. You know my mother Zlata sacrificed so much to raise your baby Ursula. Izzy wouldn't be here and none of you would be in Izzy if she had failed. For all her caring of your baby, I'm begging, let me ask you some questions. Nothing more."

Heinrich and Solveig override all our objections. Dragon Lady drops Alan's collar and we all step outside.

As we walk to the door, Alan turns to me and whispers, "Don't tell Zlata about the cemetery mishigas. She is too old to revisit stuff like this."

Luckily, Zlata is not visible when we enter. Alan peeks in her bedroom, puts a finger to his lips, and waves for me to join him in the dining room.

He asks me to sit at the head of the table and hurries out of the room. In a moment, a strong chemical smell drifts in, followed by Alan with a bottle of paint thinner and a rag.

"Can you help? Mother doesn't have good eyes, but this is still too visible."

He sits before me and I daub the solvent on the paint sprayed across his skin. It's weird touching an older man's face, (or any face), and having him stare at me. I feel like a specimen under a microscope.

"Fascinating. Not only are the eyes different colors but the lids seem of different races. Do you have Asian in you?"

I put down the rag. "I'm not getting it all. Maybe you could use a mirror."

"Of course. I'll be back in a moment."

He returns with a cleaner face and video camera on a tripod.

I wave against Alan's camera. "I don't want to be filmed."

"This is just for me. For my memory."

"I'll do it with audio, no video."

"Heinrich, Solveig, please. This is my life's work! I beg you."

Again, my Germans agree and Alan sets up the camera. Two desk lamps are put on the table to shine at me. The cliché interrogation set.

Alan cables the camera to the television and I see myself on the screen. I look so bizarre on the TV. No one on TV has ever looked like me. They are all beautiful and I'm nothing like that.

Alan turns on the camera. A red light shines. Some of us are nervous, some are excited.

"Can you introduce yourself?"

"I'm Izzy."

"Last name?"

"No."

"When did you know you have these entities in you?"

"They aren't entities, they are ancestors who experienced traumas that got seared into my DNA and stuck."

"How far back do they go?"

"Can't remember the dates of everyone. Simon was from 1898—"

"Unbelievable! The Academy is going to be stunned by this."

Everyone in me jolts. *If he exhibits this moving picture we could be discovered and institutionalized forever,* Jenny warns in my head. *He can't expose us!*

"What Academy?" I ask.

"I won't disseminate to the general public, just the scientific community. Tell me about Simon. Can I talk to him?"

"No. He left."

Jenny swirls in me. *I will not spend another minute in an institution!*

Alan blinks his red-lashed eyes. "How does DNA leave?"

"I don't know. You can't show this to anyone."

"Don't worry, I know what I'm doing. Who else is in you?"

Dragon Lady's hand curls into a fist and Ruby's forehead crinkles with anger. *This asshole's like all the rest. He just wants what he wants and he'll take it from us.* "Seriously, this can't be seen by anyone."

"Sure, of course. Who else is in you?"

He's lying. Ruby says. *He's gonna tell. Even if we flee, he'll expose us.*

There is a squeaking in the kitchen. "Hello," Zlata calls out.

"Shit." Alan pushes *pause* on the camera. "We're busy, Mom!"

"I need my juice!" the old woman yells.

"Just a minute!" He glowers in frustration. "She needs her orange juice the minute she gets up—"

I hop up. "I'll get her the juice. I want to say hi, anyway. "

Alan nods his thanks.

I hurry to the kitchen and greet Zlata while all of us wonder *How can we get away?!* As I find a glass, Solveig gets an idea. I bring Zlata the juice and Solveig leans close. "Zlata, Ich brauche deine hilfe. Denken sie daran, das brot fiel und—"

"What are you saying, dear?" the old woman asks. "I can't understand you."

Solveig thinks real hard so I can know what she wants to say. I whisper close to Zlata's ear. "Zlata, I need your help. Remember the bread roll fell and no one saw but us—"

"You want bread?"

"The bread fell. Remember the plane over the Displaced Persons Camp? You yelled and everyone—"

Zlata shakes her head. "I don't remember—"

"Let's go, Izzy!" Alan calls from the next room. I leave Zlata and go to him.

"Sit."

I do as I'm told. What else can I do? Dragon Lady suggests violence.

The camera's red light goes on again. "How about you introduce me to the entities—"

"Ancestors."

"Sorry, ancestors inside. Who wants to go first?"

There is a cough in the kitchen.

Alan holds up a finger for me to pause. "Mom, we're recording. No sound please." He waves for me to answer.

Another cough. And another.

"Mom, please."

We wait. No more coughing. He waves at me again.

"Uh, well," I say. "You know Heinrich and Solveig—"

There is a heavy thump in the kitchen and jerky tapping.

Alan stands, trying to control his temper. He stomps to the kitchen and—"Oh, my god! Mom! Are you alright?"

I hop up to see. Zlata is on the linoleum floor, lying flat, twitching all over. Drool oozes from her mouth as she shakes and jerks, eyes rolling back in her head.

"Oh, my god, oh my god. Are you in pain, Mom?" Alan asks, kneeling by her.

Zlata moves a trembling hand to her chest. "Heart."

Alan dials his phone. He gives the address and tells them a few essentials.

I've never seen anyone have a heart attack before. It's terrible. Maybe this is my fault for coming here and reminding her of the horrors of the past. "They say aspirin can help. Do you have any?"

"Medicine cabinet."

I rush to find it and return with two.

Alan puts them on Zlata's frothy tongue.

The ambulance comes quickly. Two attendants rush in with equipment and a stretcher. They take her vitals and lift her onto the stretcher. "Who's family?"

"I'm her son."

"You come with us. The hospital will need all the information and history you can give us."

"Right." Alan turns to me with "hold the fort."

I feel so responsible for this. "I'm sorry, Zlata. You get better. You'll be okay."

"Come, a kiss." She waves a trembling hand for me to near as the attendants pack their equipment and strap her in. I bend low to her and she whispers, "Grab the bread."

Alan pulls his jacket on and holds the door as they wheel Zlata out.

The siren gets farther and farther away until we can't hear it. Solveig laughs, "She *did* remember."

We fiddle with the camera until we find ERASE ALL then head for the Metro Van.

URSULA'S GRAVE

WE DRIVE BACK TO THE CEMETERY and Ursula's grave.

I sit before the headstone and Solveig pulls up the grass and presses a hand into the dirt. It's dark brown and sandy. A dry mix of rocky rubble and petrified forests. She pulls up handfuls and fills our pockets.

Heinrich implores Solveig, "Komm mit mir to Kansas. Ich show you das man I become."

Solveig says, "Nein. Ich staying mit meiner daughter."

"Vergib mir, Solveig. I'm truly sorry," Heinrich says.

I can tell Solveig wants him to be quiet so I push past Heinrich. "We'll miss you, Solveig."

Solveig pats our heart with my hand. "Auf Wiedersehen, meine freunde."

"Good to know you, Solveig," Ruby says.

"Take it easy, but take it," reminds Dragon Lady.

We stand and Solveig pulls and pulls and we feel the stretch and—Jenny yanks her back.

"Jenny, was ist das?" Solveig asks.

"This is perhaps a delicate question. I hesitate to ask but find myself compelled. As I myself am not currently situated in a resting place with any form of family and don't foresee a change in that circumstance, I'd appreciate it if you would grant me permission to reside with you. I'd like to stay with someone I know and care for. Of course, I understand if you want to rest with only your daughter—"

"Bitte komm."

Ruby remarks, "Reckon we'll be at loose ends without you, Jenny. Seems like you are the tempered one."

"I have the utmost confidence in you. Goodbye, all," says Jenny.

Solveig pulls and Jenny pulls with her and they stretch us and then snap away. Their foggy specters appear. Solveig wears a ragged '40s-era dress. She looks older than her sixteen years and severely emaciated. Her eyes are sunken but lively. Jenny is thirty and has long white hair. She's in an institutional dress of the early twentieth century. Jenny and Solveig take each other's hands. A blur of another woman coalesces. Ursula. She looks to be in her forties. Even in this dim form, I can see she has one blue eye and one brown. She smiles at Solveig and Jenny and the three specters swirl and disappear.

We head back to the van, but Heinrich stops short. "Ich stay."

"Solveig's gone."

"Ja, but—" Heinrich nods to the red graffiti swastikas on four gravestones.

After a little brainstorming, we change out of my ripped shirt and, tying it to a straightened wire coat-hanger, slip the fabric down into the Metro Van's fuel tank. The gas-soaked fabric works well at removing the paint. Heinrich scrubs furiously, not resting until all the defaced stones are clean.

In a while we're on the road again, silent, each in our own thoughts. It's just Dragon Lady, Ruby, Heinrich, and me. I don't know how to stand the emptiness.

SALINA, KANSAS

AS WE DRIVE THROUGH NEW JERSEY and Pennsylvania, I feel my lips and tongue shifting. Jenny's mouth is gone and mine feels —I don't know—less tense. Less ready to revolt or fight. Less looking for confrontation. Crossing Ohio and Indiana I feel the heavy-hearted pain in my chest dissipate. Solveig was centered there. Illinois and Missouri, I feel the sorrow of Heinrich. He's missing Solveig.

We drive deep into Kansas. None of us has ever seen anything so flat before. The world is divided by a straight line—cloudless sky above and featureless ground below. The van moves forward, trying to reach the distant vanishing point of road, but it never does. Heinrich seems distressed. "Frankfurt ist mit forests und lakes und beauty. Dis ist ein erased land. Why Ich comme here?"

None of us know the answer.

We drive on and reach the small flat city of Salina. Most of the old buildings are two-story and the tallest structures are the cement grain silos. There's a desolation about the place. The streets are on a grid, no doubt because there's no reason to curve in such a flat land. The roads are wide because—why not? There is nothing but space.

We drive a tree-lined street of older homes, looking for the address of Heinrich Neuffer III. The house is a two-story building that looks about a hundred years old. There's a rusty pickup truck in the drive. Dead bushes in the yard. Missing shingles at the edge of the porch.

Dragon Lady puts the van in park but Heinrich doesn't move.

"Ich denke nicht. Das ist rotten. Ich nicht allow das bad home."

"You've been dead many, many years."

"Meine kinder wouldn't let happen."

"Maybe they don't live here anymore. These people might know where they went."

Heinrich agrees and we hop down and walk toward the house.

A bearded man of about forty in a dirty t-shirt and shorts opens the storm door and leans out. "Help you?"

"Yes, please," I say, trying to channel Simon's gracious politeness. "Sir,—"

"Let me see your hands." The man squints at me.

Dragon Lady holds hers up and I hold up what used to be Simon's.

"You ain't got no papers. Not here to serve or nothing?"

"Serve?"

"Serve me court papers. I won't accept and it don't mean shit if you even set it on the porch. Has to hit my hands, and it won't, so don't even try."

"Okay. But I'm not here to serve court papers."

The man studies me. "So what you want?"

"I'm looking for a relative of Heinrich Neuffer. I'm a distant relation. I'd like to meet his relatives and find out what he did in life. If he is buried here, I'd like to visit Mr. Neuffer's grave."

"*Mister* Neuffer," the man snorts. "Come on in." And he steps back inside the house but holds the storm door open for me. The interior looks like a black hole and suddenly this man with his dirty t-shirt and shorts and expectation of being served court papers makes me wonder if going in is a good idea. Heinrich insists it is and pushes us past the man and into the dark house.

The place is cluttered. There's way too much furniture and every bit of furniture is covered with stuff. Boxing gloves, plastic dishes, hammer, fly swatter, flip-flops, clothes, cereal box, sewing kit, baby shoes, mounted trout...

"What's your name, girl?"

"Elizabeth."

"I'm Heinrich Neuffer the fourth. But call me Hank. Changed it early so kids in school wouldn't call me Heiney."

My left leg trembles. "Do you mind if I sit? I got a little dizzy driving so long."

Hank leads me into the kitchen. It's cluttered like all I've seen so far. He lifts a tower of boxes from a chair for me to sit. There are packing supplies covering the kitchen table. "Got me an eBay business. Ship, ship, ship, that's all I do. But it keeps the lights on. Soda pop or sumpin'?"

"Water, please."

He fills a pink plastic cup from the sink. There are bite marks all around the rim.

"Salina had a big German influx after the war. Got to be a few Heinrichs in town. How you know we's the right family?

"The Heinrich I'm talking about lost his left leg in the war."

"Bingo. Hoppin' Granddad Heiny."

Heinrich spasms at the name. I try to cover by shifting in my chair. "What did he do here? What can you tell me about him?"

"He raised five kids. My daddy bein' one of them. Taught my daddy everything he knew."

A glow of pride rises from Heinrich.

A woman enters carrying a toddler. "Hey, Hank, why you ain't tell me we got company? Anymore, I would put out cookies. Hon, I'm Ellen, you want some cookies?"

I know what Simon would say, so I say it. "Yes please, ma'am. And what a cute little baby. How old is—he?"

"Phillip is two. Real handful like his daddy." Ellen kisses Hank IV on the head and he swats her rear as she goes to the cupboard for cookies.

Remembering Simon, I jump in with, "I'm forgetting my manners, ma'am. I'm Elizabeth. Izzy for short. Hank, you were saying he taught your father—"

Ellen puts a saucer of 'Nilla Wafers on the table. "Who you talkin' about anyhows?"

"Grandad Heinrich."

"That gosh-darn-so-n-so. Pardon my French. Whatchu—"

"Izzy is kin."

Ellen puts her hand over her mouth in mock embarrassment. "Oopsidaisy. Didn't I just step in it. Sorry, but that old man was nothing but steel wool and battery acid. Never a nice word to a soul. And goll-dern, I've heard the stories of his belt."

Heinrich starts trembling. Ellen and Hank both notice. "Too much coffee," I say. "Gives me the jitters. But, about Grandfather Heinrich—what did he do for work—a job—"

"Had lots of them and you know what that means." Ellen does a gesture like pouring a bottle down her throat. "Didn't leave home without it, and pretty soon didn't leave home at all. Stuck all day in the front room, railing at the television in German."

"Granddad seemed to think since he lost his leg and that was painful, everyone should feel pain." Hank takes the baby from Ellen and jiggles him on his knee. "That's lots of what he taught my daddy. And what my daddy taught me. With the strap. But I'm not teaching none of their lessons to my son. He didn't get the name and he won't get the hell."

"Your father beat you?"

"'Til he succumbed to the drink like Granddad and drove a telephone pole 'tween his eyes."

I'm afraid to ask, but in case this man's opinion is just a fluke, I ask, "Did your granddad Heinrich have other children? Any aunts and uncles?"

"Thing about abusive childhoods, it brings everyone together as allies or makes them all scramble apart. Those five scattered the minute they could. Anymore, alls I get are court papers from them trying to get me to pay a share for that man's grave. That's the papers I thought you might be bringin'. Damned if I'll pay a cent t'ward anything for Horrible Heinrich."

Heinrich leaps up, knocking me out of the chair and I fall, landing hard on bags of packing peanuts, and the white styrofoam squiggles explode across the room. "Oh no! I'm so sorry!"

Hank helps me up and dismisses my insistence to pick up the mess. I sit again, crossing my leg over Heinrich's to keep him still.

Ellen shakes her head with sympathy. "Hon, this has got to be a shock. You want to know about your relative's life and get horror stories. Hank, think of some good story, I'll get the picture album."

Hank looks like he's trying to think of something that would be a nice story. He shrugs and smiles at me apologetically.

Ellen returns with a vinyl photo album. She flips through— There's Heinrich with five kids and a wife. Everyone but Heinrich looks scared as they try to smile. There's older Heinrich at what could be this table, a bottle of beer and flaming birthday cake in front of him. There's Heinrich even older, squinting at the camera as if he's said, "Take das damn picture!"

I turn away. "Thank you."

"I'm sorry you didn't get what you wanted."

"Me, too. Is his grave nearby?"

Hank reaches around his son, pulls a mailing sticker from a pile, and draws a map. "I'd take you there, but I vowed I'd never set foot near him and I don't break vows."

Hank hands me the map and I stand. Heinrich is so wobbly I'm not sure I'll be able to walk. I smile at Hank and Ellen. "Could I hold Phillip for a moment?"

Hank passes the baby to me. He's really heavy! The kid looks in my eyes. I can tell Heinrich is right here, looking at his great-grandchild. Phillip's big blue eyes widen and then he LAUGHS LOUD! I squeeze his pudgy hand and laugh with him. We all laugh, Hank and Ellen, Dragon Lady, Ruby, and even a painful sobbing laugh from Heinrich.

Phillip is passed back and, using Simon's lessons once again, I say, "Thank you. I'll see myself out."

And I do.

Fifteen minutes later, we're at the cemetery looking down at a small plaque on the ground.

HEINRICH NEUFFER JR.
1923-1999 BORN GERMANY

"Das ist alles?!" Heinrich cries.

HEINRICH — FRANKFURT, GERMANY — 1927

SMASH! A BOTTLE OF SCHNAPPS crashes against the dark flowered wallpaper. I dart under the dining room table. Papa chomps on his cigar, rips the chairs aside and tries to kick me, but I keep moving.

"Come out and take your punishment like a man, Heinrich."

"Mama," I whimper.

Papa grabs the edge of the table and heaves it up. It rises high and flips, booming upside down behind me. Exposed, I crouch lower.

"DID YOU CALL FOR YOUR MAMA!?"

He grabs the leather shoulder straps of my lederhosen and yanks me up, my feet dangling in the cigar-heavy air.

"You got my name but you're no Neuffer. You're a coward. A worthless cockroach!"

And he flings me to the floorboards. My left shin slams into the edge of the upturned table. There's a crack inside me and a flood of pain. Tears form and I try to blink them back in.

"Crawl like the bug you are!"

I roll slowly to do as he orders but there's glass all over from the schnapps bottle and I don't know how I'll miss it. Sounds of the belt unbuckling. I crawl forward, with shards in my palms and bare knees, and the something broken in my left leg. The pain burns up my side but I crawl across the glass-covered dining room floor. In the kitchen beyond, I see Mother's sturdy shoes hiding behind the door. A *whoosh* and the leather strap snaps across my back, the buckle curling around to punch me in the stomach.

"Papa, please. I'm sorry."

A *whoosh* again and I don't know why but I lurch backward and the strap whips around my neck instead and the buckle snaps under and slices across my chin, digging deep. I scream, clutching the wound, and Papa pushes me over with his boot and peers down at me.

"Take your hand away."

I'm afraid to move my hand in case it's holding my chin on, but I know I must. I lift my palm slowly, blood sticky and dripping from it. A flap of flesh dangles.

"Got your first good scar, Heinrich. Tell Mother you fell on the stairs."

I cover the wound with my hand as Papa opens the wooden credenza and pulls out another bottle of schnapps. When he puts his overcoat on and stomps out the door, Mama hurries in and I collapse, sobbing in her arms.

HEINRICH'S GRAVE

HEINRICH STANDS OVER THE PLAQUE crying, "Why none help me? Ich hate Papa und ich become him. Why no one rescue me?" Heinrich kicks at the earth around the marker, digging his heel in, pounding out a ditch. Crickets scatter.

"Ich was beaten and abused and I lost my leg!" He keeps digging. A heel-full at a time. "Why no one help?!" Heinrich yells. "Ich died and Ich was hated! Why?" Heinrich drops and we all drop. "Ich hate you alle!" He screams.

"I get ya," Ruby says. "Reckon I'm a barrel full of hate."

"Me too. Trauma causes hate," Dragon Lady says. "Your father must have had trauma to have hated so much."

Heinrich sobs deep, wrenching wails from our gut.

We all slide a bit to give him space. Flashes of memories course through us and finally we lie, face in the grass, smelling the earth.

Heinrich breathes in slowly. "Das ist gut Solveig nicht come mit me here. Nicht see the bad man Ich become." He lifts us up. "Maybe Ich stay und be a geist—a ghost. Haunt mit good things. Das amends?"

"That sounds good, Heinrich," I say. "It's worth a try to be a good ghost and try to make amends."

"Ich learn a lot from all in you. More than this Heinrich," he says, kicking the grave. "Danke." And he pulls himself out of us with a swift *yank*.

Heinrich stands before us as a blurry young soldier, missing his left leg. With a goofy boyish grin, he waves, then disappears into the soil.

"I'm sorry, Heinrich," I say as I scoop up pocketfulls of the soil and shake my left leg. It's a lot lighter.

WHO'S THIS?

BACK IN THE METRO VAN, I put Heinrich's grave-soil in a jar.

I feel so very different. Only Ruby and Dragon Lady left.

As I sit in the driver's seat and fire up the engine, Ruby looks at us in the mirror. "All female now. The men are gone."

Dragon Lady whispers, "I'm not so sure about that."

We drive on the 70 across the flat land of Kansas.

"First, we'll cross the Rockies and get to Bodie, California to see if we can find Ruby's resting place, then—"

Uh—

Yuck. I feel weird. Like sick and worn out and agitated. There's an exit for a town called Hays and we swerve onto the ramp and I don't have to pee so I'm not sure why we're exiting, but we're always doing shit I don't know the reason for, so I accept it.

Into the tiny town. Same Taco Bell and McDonald's and Sonic and we pull over to the curb behind a sheriff's car.

"What're we doing now, Dragon Lady?" I ask.

"I don't have any idea. Ruby?"

"Ain't fixin' to venture a guess," says Ruby.

I get a sinking feeling we're not alone.

My left hand slides the van door open and I step out. Only it's not me stepping out. And I know it's not Heinrich, or Solveig, or Jenny, or Simon, or Kelly.

"Who is that? Who are you?"

There's a low laugh inside me. Not a nice one. One of ridicule and disdain.

We're heading for the sheriff's car.

Fuck.

Dragon Lady! Ruby! Turn me around!

But I keep walking. Up to the sheriff's car and my left hand knocks on the window.

FUCK!

The Sheriff rolls down his window.

My mouth is usurped. "I'd like to report an escape." The voice is somehow very familiar—and chilling.

"Yeah?" the Sheriff says as he texts on his phone.

HELP! I scream inside. Dragon Lady and Ruby both attack the being in my mouth and I cough and cough and get a tiny crack to squirm into and slide into my own mouth—"I've got an escaped cat."

"Jeeze, girl, put some signs up but don't bother law enforcement."

The Sheriff rolls up his window and drives off.

I drag myself back to the van. Once inside, I scream, "Who the fuck are you and what do you want?"

My left hand moves on its own and shifts the rear-view mirror so it shows my face. The eyes are square and cold and instantly familiar. Philip Gaston. My father.

I've wondered about not having DNA personalities from my mother and father, but figured it was because they hadn't had traumas, so they weren't part of my mix. I figured wrong.

"You stayed hidden all this time?"

"Had to be patient. Now that the men are gone, I'm ready to assert myself."

"Oh, I remember. Your big lesson 'Deliberation, Patience, and Timing dictate Action.'"

"Sounds like pompous drivel."

"What do you want?"

"I don't want you running around sullying the Gaston name. You need to be locked up in that nuthouse. And this time, I'll see you stay there."

"We won't let you do this. Not me, not Dragon Lady, not Ruby."

"You got a real gang of toughies. A nutcase, grease monkey, and whore. Female DNA can't match me."

Dragon Lady growls, "We don't intend to match—"

"—we fixin' to overpower," Ruby finishes.

"Shove him in what was Simon's pinkie!" Dragon Lady orders. "Shove every bit of him in and I'll chop it off!"

"I don't want to lose my pinkie!" I yell.

With my left hand, Father grabs a fist full of my hair and bashes my forehead against the steering wheel. Ruby is stunned.

The cruel voice rises in my mouth. "You're a loser and a fuckup and I hope you die."

The hand yanks my hair, tilting my head back to look into the rear-view mirror. Those reflected eyes are wild with glee. "That's it, I'll kill you. It'll be the sad suicide of an ugly worthless girl."

And Philip bashes my head again and starts the van. We pull away from the curb and drive north. Away from the highway. Away from town.

Dragon Lady, Ruby, and I try to think of what to do as the last of the fast-food joints gives way to flat empty land. A vast nothingness. There are no trees, no houses, and the unchecked wind pushes hard against the van. We drive for miles and turn off onto a smaller road. And a smaller one. This isn't even the middle of nowhere, it's the *edge* of nowhere.

Philip turns off the engine.

I look in the mirror and see such hatred. "I understand now," I say to the reflection. "If I ever thought I was ugly or disfigured, it was the *you* in me."

"Go ahead and make excuses. Won't change a thing. You'll be dead soon."

"Father—"

"Don't call me father. I'm not your father. There's a sappy old Philip Gaston who is, but I'm a fucking twenty-five-year-old Wall Street marvel."

"So you're twenty-five. What was your trauma back then?"

"I don't have traumas. I've got everything anyone could want. Money, sex, car..."

"Ah—I saw your trauma. You were in a terrible car crash on a country road in Maine. You swerved to hit a possum and—that woman with you was killed. I bet that was the terrible lesson Father learned. Who was she?"

"Who cares. That was my new Maserati. Completely fuckin' totaled."

I can't believe this creep. He's disgusting and he's been in me my whole life.

Dragon Lady yells in my head. *Where is he centered? We'll push him out.*

"I can hear you, bitch. I'm not centered anywhere. I'm everywhere!" And Philip punches Dragon Lady's arm with my left fist.

He stands us and walks us into the back of the Metro Van. *He really does have control of my body!*

My head moves slowly and I know he's scanning—the beds, the built-in cabinets, the kitchen space—looking for something. Something to kill me with.

This can't be how my story goes!

My left hand reaches into the table drawer and pulls out my chopping knife! Dragon Lady grabs the wrist and my two arms wrestle with each other. Father's hand bashes Dragon Lady's wrist against the table over and over.

He raises the knife toward my neck, as Dragon Lady tries to keep it back.

"STOP!" I scream.

The arms freeze.

"Please, all I ask is that you let me choose the method. I know men might favor certain ways, but females don't like to make messes. We don't go for guns or knives. Please let me choose the method."

Philip growls. "You're not taking pills. I won't know if it is successful. It's got to be real fuckin' death."

"Okay. Real fuckin' death."

REAL FUCKIN' DEATH

I HAVE NO IDEA WHAT TO USE, but I need to do something that won't hurt. I look around the van's interior, feeling Philip's impatience growing. There's rope. Could I even figure out how to make a noose? With Ruby here, I'm sure she could make a knot. But what would I attach it to? My eye passes the towel rack. If I tied the rope to that, would I be able to choke myself?

"Could you drop the knife? Just for a while. So you can check the strength of that towel bar?"

Philip sets the knife down and grabs the towel bar. He yanks it hard and one edge pulls from the wall. The towel whips off and flutters against the pile of carefully folded plastic bags Finn and I made. Seeing them chokes me up. I'll never see Finn again. But what he left behind—

"I've chosen my method, Philip."

"And?"

I slide myself into Dragon Lady's arm and lift the top plastic bag.

Inside, I feel Ruby and Dragon Lady revolt. They don't want any part of this.

Philip makes my mouth grin. "Works for me."

I turn to the mirror mounted over the toiletry area. A younger and angrier version of my father's face stares back at me. "What are you waiting for?" he asks.

I don't know what else to do, so I put the bag over my head.

"Sit down, so you don't collapse and lose the bag," my father suggests.

I sit on the bed and Philip grabs the edges of the bag and twists them tightly around my neck. I breathe and the bag moves in and out with each breath. The writing on the bag is backwards seen from the inside but I know it says. *This Bag is Not a Toy.* No, it's not.

It happens fast. There's not enough air and it's making me dizzy. The bag is sucked toward my mouth and out again and in and there really isn't any oxygen left for me to breathe. My eyes are blurry. I'm dizzy. I'll not last long.

"I always hated you, Elizabeth," Philip says without any air.

NOW! I shout in my head and Dragon Lady shoves and Ruby shoves and I shove and we try to force him out like the others that pulled and stretched from us but he's struggling and—he's immovable!

PUSH HARDER! And we all strain, but there's no air and we're weak and he's stronger and—

Some new force joins us! We all push together and SHOVE him out of us and into the bag!

Dragon Lady whips the plastic off our head and Ruby twirls the end and knots it tight and we all gulp dry Kansas air.

And there's a wispy, angry swirl in the bag. A misty, distorted, younger version of my father struggling to get out and cursing us. He pounds and kicks and bites but he's just vapor and has no power.

Ruby gets the Igloo cooler from under my bed and we put the bag inside and Dragon Lady gives the furious figure the finger and we close the lid on his rage and seal it with duct tape and then rope.

Dragon Lady grabs the shovel and we carry the Igloo prison outside. The wind is fierce and buffets us, but it's invisible as there's nothing to bend out here. No fields. No trees. What a perfect spot for Father. No one is going to be plowing up the ground around here. It's all rocks.

I get to digging and after a while, Ruby takes over and after her, Dragon Lady finishes. We go down deep enough that there'll be no chance of a flash flood or earthquake dislodging this. Put the Igloo in the pit.

"Fuck you, asshole," I say, and toss in the first shovelful of dirt. It makes a satisfying THUMP.

MELTING POT BODY

I DON'T KNOW WHAT HAPPENED. Philip was immovable, but suddenly an extra force came in, and together, we shoved him out.

"Hello? Is anyone there?" I ask.

"Yes," answer Dragon Lady and Ruby.

"I know that, but someone else. The one that helped push out Father. Hello?—Hello?"

No answer. Maybe there are others in me that want to stay hidden. That's scary. How are they affecting me? How do I even know if I'm acting in *my* interest or someone else's? Is it a *really* distant ancestor? A Neanderthal who can't speak? Or could I have some residue of Simon, Kelly, Jenny, Solveig, or Heinrich? I don't know.

We drive out of Kansas and into Colorado and keep driving until we're within the Rockies. Mountains rise all around us and it's a welcome hugging feeling after the flatness. We pull into the first motel, step outside, and get shocked by the air. It's cold and sharp.

The room is nice and the rugged view is great, and I should find a place to eat dinner and take a walk in the invigorating air, but I go to bed.

I dream of our building in New York City. I dream of the Vision Books and that they are reverse-burning, that the ashes are falling instead of rising and are coalescing and the flames are changing the pictures from burnt-black to slickly-vibrant. And the pictures are all of Findley. Findley in fancy cars. Findley in front of Mansions. And Father is laughing over and over and—

I wake screaming.

Blue crisp light pours in the open drapes. The morning mountain view greets me. I sit up and check myself.

"Ruby?"

"Here."

"Dragon Lady?"

"Yep."

"Anyone else?"

There is no answer. Maybe we'll be okay.

I stand and stretch. There, across the room, I'm in the mirror. And I'm *so* different. Things have shifted, moved, and blended. Kelly's ochre leg color has spread over all of me, so I'm slightly darker than I was. Simon's arm has lost all its width in the wrist and muscles. And even after just one day, Heinrich's leg has changed. The sculpted athletic muscles are now more smooth. The thigh scars are gone. I'm finally getting stirred. My melting pot is finally melting. I even think—get ready—I'm kinda pretty. Maybe having that father-asshole out of me allows me to see myself differently.

Nothing has changed with my remaining companions. Dragon Lady's still her sinewy strong sun-weathered arm and Ruby's spiderweb scar still shines on my forehead. I smile at them, glad we have each other.

"Shall we hit the road?" I ask.

BODIE

WE DRIVE THROUGH the Rockies. The Metro Van has trouble going up the steep inclines, but Dragon Lady knows when to shift gears. Thank god she's still in charge of driving or I'd be petrified as we swirl down the mountains.

As the rugged terrain lessens, Ruby sniffs the air. "Reckon I c'n smell home gettin' closer. The West."

It does smell different. And look different. Another place I've never been. It's exciting.

We leave Colorado and the world becomes a weird moonlike rocky place in Utah, flat again but more deserty than Kansas. Six hours of driving and we pull over in a town called Oasis that is nothing like an oasis and sleep in the van. Heat wakes us early in the morning and we trek on and on and on until we're out of Utah and into Nevada where we get more desert, scrubby plants, cactus, Joshua Trees, and Casinos. Eight hours later, we finally hit California.

It's afternoon when we make the turn toward Bodie, Ruby's last known location. "Bodie's a big city. Ten thousand folk. Reckon we can find someone who knew someone who knew someone that knew me."

We drive on, following the GPS and atlas, and get onto a dirt road. Climb higher, past the tree line. A sign says Bodie State Park. Ruby snorts, "Reckon Bodie t'aint no place for a park. Got harsh winters. But nowadays I 'spect they got electricity and heat and all the newfangled luxuries."

We drive 'round the bend and Ruby gasps. Ahead is a smattering of decayed wooden buildings. Not a thriving metropolis. We drive to the park Visitor Center. Inside are brochures for Bodie Ghost Town. We pay the admission price and step outside again.

Ruby walks us toward the remains of the town. We come upon a cemetery and Dragon Lady starts to move in that direction—"Maybe we can find your headstone"—but Ruby keeps us moving onward. "If I died in Bodie, you wouldn't find me there. Reckon I'd be buried in an unmarked grave out with the gunfighters, thieves, whores, and other undesirables. But I hope I didn't die here. I hope I got me gone."

I look at the brochure as Ruby walks us down Main Street. We wander past an ancient wooden shack. "That was the McMillan house. It was bright white. All the buildings were painted, not this worn wood, all decaying and leaning."

We walk up another dirt road. "Here's Bonanza Street. Folks called it Virgin Alley and Maiden Lane. Reckon they found that funny." Ruby leads us to a spot and stares at the dirt. "My crib shack. Where I lived and set out the lantern for my trade."

Past more leaning buildings. Worn wooden wagons. Tourists taking pictures. We step up to an area at the far edge of town. "This was Chinatown. Full of people. Big ol' Mercantile store for the Chinese. Upstairs—upstairs—"

Ruby stares, and Dragon Lady and I feel her dizziness.

RUBY – BODIE, CALIFORNIA – 1877

I PUT A PALM TO MY SWELLIN' BELLY but can't feel no child kickin' back. Too early maybe. Don't reckon folks c'n guess yet. I should leave a'fore they get wise to my condition. This damn town ain't good for babies, with winters so cold they kill most little things—but 'specially ain't good for babies that might look like this youngun's Papa. Wonder if Chan would go with me?

It's late and I'm plum tuckered. I step to the door of my shack and open it onto the frigid night. Put my hands together and blow. Coo-coo-coooooo.

The call comes back. Chan will go back to his bunk in the Chinese part of town. I lift the glass of my lantern and blow out the flame. This gal is closed for business.

I shut the door and begin to undress. There's a soft knock. Does Chan think he won't be seen knocking on my door? People won't accept him coming to me.

I open the door to tell him this—and a young man steps inside.

He kicks the mud off his boots in a shy, self-conscious way. "I seen your light and riding to it when you done blowed it out. Hope I ain't too late."

I look past him out into the darkness. Chan would do that dove call again if he was still watching. I hear nothing but the wind pressing on these boards. Reckon without Chan watchin', might be smart to turn this fella away.

I hear the snort of a horse 'side of my crib. That means the fella rode, so probably ain't from here. Workers at the Standard Mine walk to come my way and I do declare, I end up with a mighty share of those men's wages. But this one, I reckon he's a cowhand or trapper. Smells of horse sweat and snow.

The man takes off his hat. He ain't but a kid—maybe fourteen at most. Probably the first time. He'll be nervous and wanting to do right. Safer for me that way.

I laugh and close the door, pointing to the wash basin. "Use plenty of soap." Greenhorn kid probably doesn't need this harsh lye treatment, but I don't need to share my good soap with him.

He clomps in with the jangle o' spurs. Better remove those if he wears his boots to bed. I ain't stitching another pair of sheets.

Fella faces the basin and makes appropriate sudsing and splashing sounds.

"You can take off your coat. Get comfortable."

The kid doesn't turn to me. "Done got froze riding in. Keepin' it on."

Maybe he knows he looks like a kid and he feels bigger with it on. Hope it ain't that he got boils or pox some disease that's cetchin'. I pull back the blanket but not the top sheet. No sense messing two sheets. This kid prolly ain't washed in weeks. I get in my pose on the bed.

When he turns to face me, he coughs but doesn't move.

"Something particular you want?"

He points toward the mirrored vanity. "Stallion-style there— so I can watch at the same time."

I was wrong. 'taint the fella's first time. I saunter over and position myself so I'm leaning, palms down on the vanity and smiling at his reflection in the mirror in front of me. He steps in behind me and once he pushes his way in, there's a moment of pause, then he rams hard and my forehead crashes into the mirror, shattering it in a web pattern with blood in the center, and I try to move away but he slams again and my head impacts with the mirror over and over and I see the gleeful look in his face—in the many tiny reflections—and now my eyes can't see through the blood and I struggle to get away, but he has me pinned and he keeps ramming me—the mirror falls apart and— my head is about to do the same—and he moves a hand to press in me harder and I blink the blood away—reach for a mirror shard, arch my arm back and stab at anything, aiming high— glass cuts in something soft and I feel him jolt and recoil—I lunge to the side, hoping to break off his piece in me—he bellows and I spin enough to see him reaching for something in his coat and I fling the wash basin at his head. He bats the bowl away but the soapy lye water hits his eyes and he screams. I dive to the floor, crawling toward the bed and BOOM! he's shooting! BOOM! his gun shatters something. I flatten myself to the floor and inch forward trying to keep silent. BOOM! wood shatters and he gotta be firing blind because that was across the room. I can't see a thing with the blood pouring from my scalp. BOOM! Reach the bed and feel along the mattress for the pocket. BOOM! My hand touches cold metal and grab it and raise my head over the edge of the bed, can't see—try to wipe the blood from my eyes, see the blurred figure turn my way, gun up—BOOM!—my Colt jolts my arm—and there's a thud. I freeze—can't see, the blood from my head ain't stoppin'—smell of gunpowder all around.

Sounds of a door opening and a gasp comes with the blast of cold. "You alive, Ruby?" Lotte's voice. A flood of relief.

"For now. The fella?"

"He's done."

I hear her move around the room and I blink up at her shadow over me.

"Lord, you look 'bout done y'rself." More sounds. "Water picher's all busted. You wait." Moments later, she bends and a rush of pain and cold stuns my forehead. "Snow'll wash it some." As she rinses the blood, Lotte whispers, "Got a baby brewing, don't you?"

I "mm-mm" a yes.

"You know who's?"

"I been careful except for one."

"The Chinaman?"

I nod. *Oh!* Movin' hurts an' gets my head reelin'.

"You be still. If y'r skull ain't broke, reckon this'll leave a right peculiar scar. Let's get you dressed, 'cause you best be gone. Killin' ain't no stranger t' Bodie but people been talkin' 'bout you and the Chinaman. They's laws 'gainst mixin' races. You don't want no excuse t'get them comin' for you."

Lotte outfits me in warm clothes. Can't tell up from down. Wonder if that fella broke my skull. As she pulls my boots on, I hear footsteps. The door opens again. Please don't be the law.

Wafts of that smokey musk swirl in with the cold. The smell of opium. "Chan?"

"So sorry I not here. So sorry. Are you—"

Lotte hushes him. "No time for that. Ruby's got to git."

Chan helps me into my warm coat and wraps my bleeding forehead with a towel as Lotte loads my clothes and whatnots in a blanket. The kid on the floor is lying in a puddle of blood, a hole in his chest and his neck sliced. I don't feel sorry.

"Where's y'r stash, Ruby?"

I point to the chamber pot. She lifts it and retrieves my stocking of jangling coins.

She tucks the stocking of my savings into my blouse. "Horse tied up a'side y'r crib. Reckon yonder fella won't miss 'im. Time to git."

Lotte helps me to the door. Chan lifts the blanket bundle. I want to ask if Chan will leave with me, but I'm afraid to hear the answer.

Outside, the street of small cribs has only a few lanterns glowing. There is a snort and in the frosty moonlight a puff of horse-breath glows. Chan loads the blanket bundle and helps me up in the saddle.

"Try Bridgeport," Lotte says. "Better weather than this hell and things grow there. Even got trees and grass. Place to raise a baby."

"You want anything in my crib, take it," I say.

Lotte nods. "I'll take the crib. Now git."

Chan steps to the horse's head and grabs the reins. He leads the horse slowly down Bonanza Street, toward the Chinese mercantile building. There, we stop. I reckon this is where he says goodbye.

He flips the reins over the rail, whispers, "I get you something," and disappears inside. The warm glow of the second floor tells me where he's gone. Get me something. A parting gift. I don't want to say goodbye.

He returns with the smoky odor riding off him. Opium again. "This help pain," he says, holding up a packet. "But later."

He steps beside the horse and reaches up. A handshake? That's it?

"You make room," he says and pulls himself up behind me. All my fears drop away. "You rest. I get us away. Bridgeport?"

"Bridgeport."

BRIDGEPORT

"CHAN RETURNED WITH THE SMELL OF OPIUM all over his hair and clothes. He'd gotten it for me. I'd forgotten all this."

"So, onward to Bridgeport," Dragon Lady says.

We drive north and reach the small town of Bridgeport. It's not much more than a main street with a few tangential side streets. The usual pizza joint, drug store, retro motel, two ancient hotels probably from Ruby's time, and a large ornately decorated Victorian Court House.

"Where do you want to start, Ruby?" Dragon Lady asks.

"Reckon I can't say. Ain't got memories from here. I didn't even recollect leaving Bodie. Maybe I died from a cracked head."

"That couldn't have happened," I say. "I'm here, so you lived long enough to have a baby and pass on your DNA."

"This might be a place to get the low-down," says Dragon Lady as she parks the Metro Van in front of a small white building with the sign *Mono County Museum*. We go inside. It's a cluttered place, looking like an unsuccessful antique store. An elderly woman sitting at a desk smiles at us eagerly. "Good day. Admission is only two dollars." She's so excited we feel obligated to stay rather than just ask questions. I pass her a twenty. The woman shakes her head saying, "I'm sorry, we don't have change."

"It'll be my donation to the museum."

"Thank you, sweetheart. We're much obliged. You take your time."

As we wander the rooms, Ruby peers intently at everything. A dress. Old receipts. Indian pottery and baskets. She comes to a series of photographs. One is of this building but the caption says it was the first schoolhouse. There's a blurry figure in the front by the door—the school teacher, Mrs. Rose Scarlett. Ruby leans closer. "I think that's me."

We step to the old woman. "Do you know anything about the early inhabitants? Any information or rumors or anything? Like this teacher Mrs. Rose Scarlett?"

"Funny you should ask. That woman did have rumors about her. There was a little newspaper published in town and it had weekly news so we have quite a lot of the local gossip. And Rose Scarlett is written about in our book." The woman lifts a thin paperback from the desk: *TIMES GONE BY- A Historical Account of Bridgeport.* "I can let you have this because of your donation. Let's see if I can't find the section. Here it is. *Mrs. Rose Scarlett arrived last Wednesday with a head injury. Doctor Fletcher treated the wound, which Mrs. Scarlett said was caused by being thrown from her horse. She was accompanied by a Chinese man-servant.*" The woman taps her nose. "And that's what the paper prints, but you'll see there is more. Here is the section from what might be called hearsay. I quote: *As for Mrs. Scarlett's marital status, she seems quite adamant on remaining single, saying that when her recently-departed husband died, she'd had her fill of matrimony. Still, there is quite a bit of talk about her spending so much time with her Chinese man-servant.* And it goes on... *the newborn arrived in the world with his mother's red hair, but a slightly oriental look to the eyes. Perhaps there is more to the servant relationship than is customary.*"

Ruby smiles slightly. "Do you know what happened to them?"

"She was a school teacher for years. I don't know about the Chinese fellow."

"And the baby?"

The old woman shrugs. "It was hard times back then. Many babies didn't make it."

Well, we know one that did or I wouldn't be here.

We thank the woman and leave. Ruby wants to look for the cemetery but I'm hungry and sticky hot. It's been days since I've had a shower and it's time for a celebration. We get a room in the Bridgeport Inn. The clerk says it was established in 1877. Probably where Ruby stayed when she first arrived, with Chan relegated to the livery with the horses.

I take a shower and go downstairs to the bar. The place is empty, so I sit at the counter. Haven't had a drink since the one with Micias. I order a beer on tap and am glad not to be asked for I.D.

A clip-clopping sound makes me look out the wide window to see a woman in a cowboy hat dismounting from a speckled horse. She flips the reins around a post, pushes open the bar door, and nods hello to the bartender, who puts another draft on the counter. The woman drinks several long swallows, then sets the glass down with a long exhale.

"Beautiful horse," I say.

The woman smiles. "That's Betsy. She's a looker but ornery as a hornet's nest."

The bartender leans to me conspiratorially. "Sam gets all the ornery critters. She collects them."

Sam gives the bartender a fake evil eye. "Someone's got to tame the world." She pulls a leather glove off her hand. "Sam Pocket."

I shake her hand. "Izzy. Pocket—that's a great last name."

"Thanks. I chose it for the sound—pocket—and that it's a place you can keep things hidden or close."

"You chose it?"

"Yep."

I've gone from Elizabeth to Izzy, but I'm inspired to change my last name as well. That'll be fun to think about.

We spend a while talking and Sam is interesting and kind and attractive in her rough cowboy look. A clock over the ancient fireplace mantle rings six times. Sam stands. "Better go and see to Betsy. The sun's hitting her pretty hard and I gotta get her somewhere she can have water."

Ruby pipes up. "Mind if I visit with yr' Betsy?"

"C'mon out."

We pay and head out to the hot sidewalk where Betsy is tied. Ruby rubs the horse's muzzle. It's soft and I'm afraid of the teeth, but Ruby has no fear. She runs a hand along the smooth neck and down.

"You've been around horses," Sam says.

Ruby smiles for us. "Truth told, last time I rode were prit' near one hundred and fifty years ago."

Sam laughs and pulls herself up onto Betsy's back. "You up for getting back on?"

"Reck'n so."

"Alright then. I'll take the back way, you drive on up 395 for 2 miles and take the dirt road to the left. There's no sign but it's right after the historic marker. I'll meet you at the end of the road."

She slides on her leather gloves, turns Betsy, and trots off.

We're on an adventure!

Ruby hurries us to the van and we drive the two miles and see the marker and make the left. It's a rough dirt road. I hope the Metro Van won't mind. Dragon Lady reminds me we've done this before. Oh yeah. We're experts now. "You're an expert. You drive," she suggests. It's been a while since I've taken the wheel. In fact, I'm not sure I've driven at all since Ricardo's auto lot with Finn. I made such a mess of it that Dragon Lady took over. My hands at ten-and-two, I'm not as sure-armed as Dragon Lady, but I keep us going. It's fun!

We come to the end of the road and Sam stands by Betsy as the horse drinks from a galvanized tub. There are several buildings scattered about. One barn. Some shed-like things. A trailer with a built-on room addition.

When I step down from the van, Sam nods. "That's quite a vehicle. I liked you from our conversation, but now I know you're a humdinger."

My cheeks flush and I get all flibbity inside. It surprises me.

"Come. I'll introduce you to Sasha."

We head for the barn. Sam leads me to a stall with a horse with large patches of brown and white.

"That's one right pr'dy pinto," Ruby exclaims.

"Beautiful *and* smart," Sam replies.

Is she talking about me or the horse? The horse *is*, but Sam's looking at me. Is she flirting?

Sam lifts a saddle from a wooden stand and swings it onto Sasha. I'm getting nervous as she puts the bridle stuff in the horse's mouth. She leads Sasha out of the stall and turns to me. "Let's ride."

I stutter, trying to figure out how to explain my reluctance and fear, when Ruby grabs the saddle horn, puts a foot in the stirrup and swings us up, the other leg swirls over, and plop—we're on the horse!

Sam exits the barn and Ruby clicks our tongue and kicks our heels and the horse is put into drive!

Sam starts Betsy trotting so Ruby gets Sasha trotting and it's very fast and bumpy and we're moving over tall grass and Sam puts Betsy into higher gear and Ruby gets us going faster and it's like thunder with the hooves and wind and Ruby is laughing and laughing and we l-e-a-p over a ditch and land and we stay on and Ruby's steering us to race beside Sam and she's so happy. We l-e-a-p over several streams. Dragon Lady is laughing as well and I figure we probably won't be thrown and break our neck, so I relax and the laughter bubbles up in me. And Sam howls and hollers and we all do, making echoes in ourself and also with the mountains.

We slow as we approach a cluster of cottonwood trees by a stream. Sam dismounts and lets Betsy drink. Ruby gets us down without me mucking it up and leads Sasha beside Betsy.

The wind caresses our hair. Smells of moist grass and earth rise. Hawks circle and call a greeting over the remains of a stone fireplace standing in the shade of the tall rustling cottonwood trees. It's an idyllic spot.

"What is this valley?"

Sam laughs. "Very odd name. See You Water Valley. No idea where they came up with that."

Ruby half-laughs and half-cries. "See You Water. We lived here!"

Sam looks at me strangely. "Who lived here?"

"My ancestors," I say. "Ruby, also known as Rose Scarlett, and her lover, Chan. He called her *Joy of Mine* in Chinese. When she tried to pronounce it, it sounded like See You Water."

Sam and I sit on the stone hearth and lean against the cool rocks.

Ruby presses her palm on the moist dirt. She scoops up a handful. Dragon Lady and I know what this means.

Ruby, we can't do this now, I think to her.

Ruby scoops up another handful of dirt.

Better to come back later, adds Dragon Lady.

Ruby slips the dirt into our shirt pocket. Sam watches.

How would we get back here? The van can't cross all the streams and ditches. We're here and I'm staying, Ruby insists.

But maybe you're buried in the Bridgeport graveyard, I argue.

A smell rises from the earth. It's a musky scent. Somewhat floral, but dense and exotic. Ruby smiles. *I'm staying here.* And she starts pulling away.

I turn quickly to Sam. "Do you mind giving me just a little privacy? It—it's—I don't know—"

Sam touches my lips with her finger and quickly stands and walks out of the shady shelter of the cottonwoods toward the two horses.

Ruby whispers inside, *Take care of yourselves.* She cups our hands together and brings the formed chamber to our face and blows—-Cooo-cooo-coooooo—the sound of a dove.

The call repeats in front of us.

"See You Water?" Ruby whispers.

And the smell gets stronger. Ruby whispers "opium" as the misty vision of a man rises from the earth. He's got strong, intense features and a mischievous smile. A long black braid of hair hangs down his back. Simple loose clothes. He puts out a hand and Ruby instantly pulls herself from us. And there she is! A young woman with long auburn hair, a web of scars across her forehead. She wears a simple dress and laced boots. She leans against Chan's shoulder and they both laugh as if they've not been separated. Ruby turns to us, mouthing *See You Water* and blows a kiss. Chan points at me, points at his heart, smiles, and they disappear.

I collect more dirt and step out of the shade toward Sam. She smiles at me. "All good?"

I nod. "Except, I can't ride. My designated driver has departed."

"I'm not catching your drift."

"I'm willing to try, but I don't want to ride fast and you'll have to help me up on the horse and tell me how to steer."

Sam looks at me a bit sideways. "You want me to be the one in charge?"

I'm not sure, but I think this is more flirtation.

I give a kind of shrug, since I don't know what I'm agreeing to.

Sam threads her fingers to create a platform for me to put a foot on and boosts me up. It's hard to do but after three tries I get onto Sasha, then get a lesson in steering with the reins and how to hold my feet in the stirrups. Sam suggests that I let the horse follow Betsy and try not to do much steering. It's a much slower ride, walking instead of galloping. I feel sad and lonely with Ruby gone and nervous that I don't know what the evening will bring.

Dragon Lady, I'm confused about Sam. Is she flirting? Am I feeling attracted to her or is it someone else inside me that's feeling attracted?

Dragon Lady asks, *You mean me? I'm the only one left.*

What is your sexuality? You were married, but it seems like you may have wanted to be a man.

Be a damn fool not to. Especially back then. All the exciting people were men. What do you call them? 'Role-models.' All men.

292

They were competent, skilled, brave, powerful. If a lady wanted to be competent or powerful, we had to act like a man.

Maybe you were transgender back when it wasn't spoken about. I suggest.

Maybe. But you're asking about Sam. What do you hope happens with her?

I don't know. I can't tell what I feel.

Welcome to life.

It's after dark when we get back to Sam's place. She has me brush down Sasha and give her oats. It's a soothing moment.

We head inside the trailer. It's packed with Western stuff. Ropes, Indian blankets, cowboy hats, lariats. Sam heats leftover homemade chili and we share that with wine.

After dinner, Sam pats the seat next to her on the horse-blanket-covered couch. I sit. My heart is thumping.

Sam leans toward me and, like with Micias, I stop myself from jerking away. I let her lips touch mine. It's gentle and makes me tingle all over. But I don't know—

"I don't know," I say. "I'm a messed up person who is only just becoming less full of lots of other people and I can't tell what is mine or theirs or leftovers or fear or wants or anything. I like that kiss, but I can't do more. Not until I find out what part of me is me."

Sam smiles, "Okay, Iz. You take your time. If you figure that out and want to drop by again, you know where I am. There're cushions here for a pillow and more blankets if you need 'em on that chair."

And she kisses me again and slips out of the room. I lie awake wondering if it's me that Sam likes or Ruby or Dragon Lady or—?

Someone's shaking my shoulder. I wake up and look around the dawn-lit room. No one's there.

My shoulder is jostled again. Dragon Lady's shaking me. "Time to get up. We need to get moving."

Huh?

"It's my turn," Dragon Lady says. "Onward to Los Angeles!"

LOS ANGELES, CALIFORNIA

I LEAVE SAM A NOTE OF THANKS and we head out. We drive through Yosemite National Park. It's beautiful and I'd like to stop but Dragon Lady owns the wheel and gas pedal and isn't relinquishing control. As we drive, I think. *I wonder if I'm gay. Sam was attractive to me. But so was Micias. Am I bi? How will I know? Maybe when every ancestor leaves me, I'll know who I am. Or maybe I'm nothing without them.*

"Maybe you should stop worrying," Dragon Lady suggests.

Once we get on the other side of the park and down into the flatlands I take my turn at the wheel. Dragon Lady dreams of the next steps. "When we reach Los Angeles, we'll go to see the Pacific Ocean. I always wanted to see that."

"What else did you always want?"

"I always wanted to sit in an outdoor cafe at the edge of the ocean and look at all the wild and crazy people who lived in that bohemian place where everything seems possible."

"Okay. Let's do it."

We drive for nine hours straight, taking turns, and get into the city and it's pure chaos. The highway is many, many lanes wide on each side and everyone's charging ahead. Thank god Dragon Lady has the wheel, but I pray for the proverbial LA traffic so we can slow down.

The air glows hazy and the highway has tall walls so there's no view. We drive into the haze and take another freeway that points to Santa Monica and the road loses lanes and we head for a low tunnel and curve into it and there's glare ahead and the van's too big for this small tunnel and the glare gets worse and we burst out and we're NEXT TO THE OCEAN! It's got palm trees all along the road and we want to get out but there's no left turn allowed and a barrier's up to stop us even trying and we drive on and on and finally there's a turn lane and we swirl into a parking lot and Dragon Lady brakes just before a surfer crosses in front of us and we pull into a spot and shift to *park* and Dragon Lady has to GET OUT NOW!

We hop out and the air is cooler and smells of ocean and the sun is bright and everyone is in shorts and colors. We run toward the ocean. I've never seen Dragon Lady like this. She's focused on getting to that water. We pass volleyball nets and a lifeguard stand and then flat wet sand and—water! The waves rush over our feet and it's cold and wonderful. Dragon Lady raises our arms high and screams, "I MADE IT!"

We get a room in a hotel in Santa Monica a few blocks from the shore. Hungry, we walk to the waterfront businesses. A pelican flaps across the horizon. A pelican! This place is so exotic!

All around us is a mixture of different types. Long-haired retro-hippies. Bikers. Musclemen with no shirts. Women that look like models. White-haired ladies with walkers. Homeless men pushing shopping carts. Loungers on benches drinking from brown bags. It's a menagerie of people. A place as diverse and mismatched as I was.

We find a restaurant and eat outside watching the orange ball of sun sink 'til it disappears behind the line of the sea.

MAX

WAKE UP TO THE SOUND of traffic and seagulls. A quick bagel and tea in the hotel lobby and we're on the road, driving through the morning throng. The streets are never-ending but not like New York City. There aren't skyscrapers everywhere. The buildings are low and many of them are covered in stucco and painted in light pastels. It looks wonderful in the morning light. Like TV show neighborhoods.

On Blackburn Avenue, we pull to the curb in front of a mid-century three-story apartment building. Each apartment has a small balcony, so it may have been cool once, but it doesn't look in the best repair.

We walk to the front door and look at the apartment names on the buzzer. M. Dragon is in 206. The door is wide open so we don't buzz, just go upstairs.

The hall carpet is dirty and smells of mildew. The wall has swaths of paint in different colors, like someone covered graffiti but didn't bother to match the original paint.

We come to 206 and I'm scared. This may be the last person, for the last ancestor—

Dragon Lady is not having any more delays. She knocks forcefully on the door. We hear shuffling, a series of lock clicks, and the door pulls open with smoke wafting out. Behind the smoke, a hunched old man squints at me. He's got short-cropped white hair and a tough, no-nonsense look. And I've never seen Dragon Lady in person but this man has the unmistakably confrontational demeanor of that person I know.

"Go away. I ain't buying."

"I'm a relative of yours and—"

The door slams shut.

"Mr. Dragon, please, hear me out. I know about things. Know about Dragon Lady and Beau—"

The door opens again and the old man snarls at me. "Who are you and what do you want?"

"I'm Izzy Gaston. I just want to talk. Learn about your life. I'm related to you."

"Jive ass bullshit. No one's related to me. Git your ass—"

Dragon Lady rams my left palm against the door to keep it open and raises her arm—ready to punch. "Maxine, you let us in or you'll be seeing stars."

The old man spits on the floor between us and laughs. "You and what army?" he says, shuffling into the apartment. Is that an invitation? We follow him inside.

The room is dense with smoke. A cigarette in a standing ashtray curls more into the thick air. There isn't much furniture—a small table by the balcony sliding doors, a deeply sunken recliner, TV, footstool. But the walls are full. Trophies on shelves, ribbons, photos, newspaper clippings—all about Max Dragon, the racer.

Max drops heavily into his recliner as Dragon Lady moves around the room. She peers at a trophy. "Unbelievable! And the All-State in 1978? Who was the race against?"

Max can't help but puff out his chest. "Aaron Pemrose."

"Damn! Right on, man! This is so impressive! Laguna Seca! You jivin' me? Made it through The Corkscrew?"

Max tries to hide his smile. "I was pretty good."

Dragon Lady looks more intently, searching for something, flitting from one trophy to the next. "Where is it? Log Race trophy of 62?—Second place they gave—but I won."

Max stares at us. "What do you mean, *you* won?"

"Maxine. Dragon Lady. That's me."

Max takes a long drag on the waiting cigarette and glares at us defiantly. "The fuck you are, girlie. Lemme see your ID."

"Huh? I don't—I didn't bring it—it's in the van." *That was stupid. He'll tell me to go get it.*

"Bullshit. No ID. You a runaway? Leave a sad little midwestern town and come out to LA to strike it rich, but becoming a star didn't work, so you hit up old folks, pretending to be a relative to sucker us out of our savings? Got news for you —I won races, but the money's gone. Live on social security. Count my pennies. Can't get nothing from me 'cause I ain't got nothing."

"I'm not here for your money." I say and Dragon Lady adds, "I'm here to find out how I ended up in a dump like this—"

I put my hand over my mouth. Dragon Lady bites me! I yell at her inside—*Shut up! He doesn't see you, he sees me—an eighteen-year-old that looks nothing like you. Let me do the talking!* I feel her back down, slinking into her arm, but she's whirling. I step to the kitchenette just to move. "I'm sorry, Mr. Dragon. I have had a really bizarre time of late and sometimes my words come out mixed up."

"Welcome to the club."

In the kitchen sink is one cup, one glass, one plate, and one bowl. The ancient linoleum is worn from the entrance, to the fridge, to the sink, and out. I feel Dragon Lady's depression sink into me but keep talking. "Sir, I'm not here to swindle you. I'm not here for nefarious reasons."

Dragon Lady is furious seeing this place. *All these trophies and history of races won, why live in this seedy depressing apartment?*

"How long have you lived here, Mr. Dragon?"

"Shot here in the seventies. Groovin' place then. Hellcat life. Now, can't leave 'cause the place is rent controlled and I got my ancient rate. Fuck all who try to come to LA these days."

I step out of the kitchenette to the table near the balcony window. There's only one vinyl yellow chair. I sit. The chair is sticky. The walls are the color of mustard. Is this patina from cigarette smoke?

Max coughs. "What's your name again?"

"Izzy. Elizabeth. Gaston."

"How old are you?"

"Eighteen."

He snuffs out the cigarette and squints at me as if trying to see inside. Can he see Dragon Lady? "Talking 'bout the '62 Log Race. How you know that shit?'

"Research. Internet genealogy sites led me to your sister Luella and I met with Beau and he admitted everything about the rape and burial, and how you climbed out and, you know, the gender change idea came when you were picked up after walking so far when the guy called you 'buddy' and so I looked for Max instead of Maxine and here I am."

Dragon Lady and I hold our breath.

Max pulls a Lucky Strike pack from his shirt pocket, jerks it just right so one cigarette pops up, slides it out with his teeth, and lights the end with a bronze lighter. I feel Dragon Lady yearning for a hit. Max inhales sharply and exhales smoke-infused words. "Bullshit. I was alone when that man picked me up and called me buddy. No one knows what went on in my head. I didn't talk about it and there is no way you could know." Max leans forward in his recliner and glares in what I imagine is a typical Dragon Lady threatening way. "So what the fuck is going on, girlie?"

I glare back. "Alright. Here it is. You had a baby—from Beau's rape—that you put up for adoption and put out of your mind. That baby had a baby and on until me. All the trauma that happened to Dragon Lady, right up until the baby was born, was seared into her DNA and put in me! That's how I know. She's with me. So say hello to Dragon Lady." My right arm rises and points to Max and points back to my chest.

"I'm old, but I ain't a fool," Max says.

Dragon Lady holds up her palm to him. What's she up to? *Don't give me more trouble*—but she's got my mouth. "Asshole, I haven't had a Lucky Strike in half a century. Toss me the pack and a light."

Max tosses the pack, Dragon Lady catches it, jerks it just right so one pops up, slides it out with her teeth, and moves her hand an inch to catch the thrown bronze lighter. She looks at the B.T. engraving. "Still got this after all these years. The one I stole from Beau Tompkins at the campground."

As Dragon Lady lights her cigarette, Max takes a slow puff of his but can't hide his fingers shaking.

A tsunami of cigarette smoke is pulled into me and it tastes like garbage burning and I feel my lungs rebel and want to vomit and—at the same time—I feel a drop into a BLISS from Dragon Lady. She better not get me hooked!

Dragon Lady tosses the lighter back with the same rough flick and Max catches it as if he knew its trajectory before it was thrown. He shakes his head through a cloud of smoke. "You know a lot of odd information that you can't know. But I don't buy it. Tell me what this supposed lineage is from me to you."

I take over. "My mother and father, Evelyn and Philip Gaston, had two kids. Me and Findley, my little brother."

Dragon Lady chimes in, "He's a cool kid."

Max snorts. "Evelyn and Philip and Findley Gaston. Sound like rich fuckers."

"They are. Both rich—and fuckers. Except for Findley, I think I stopped that by kidnapping him."

"You kidnapped your brother?"

"We don't need to get into that."

Max whacks his palm on the recliner arm. "We get into what I say or you'll be the one seeing stars! You kidnapped your brother?"

"They got him back."

"But now you're on the run."

Shit.

You should have guessed I'd be smart, Dragon Lady says in my head.

"You should have guessed I'd be smart," Max says.

I ignore them both and continue, "Mother's father was Grandpa Wheeler. Grandpa was your baby. My mother said that Grandpa only found out he was adopted on his wedding day. His parents never told him until then. That day they gave him the key from his birth mother."

Max shudders. "Key?"

"I saw it taped in the photo album. An old metal key. Not a very impressive present."

"Did the key have writing on it?"

Dragon Lady jumps in before I can speak, "Briggs and Stratton. It was the key to my Indian motorcycle. Wanted to give that kid some spirit of adventure and speed."

Max shakes his head vehemently. "I don't buy it. You know lots of shit but I know what I see. All my wild genes get passed on and end up reduced down to—," Max gestures to me dismissively, "—this little girl? That's fucking—"

We leap across the room, grab the arms of Max's recliner and loom over him, breathing hard in his face. Dragon Lady roars, "You don't know shit about Izzy! She is the most courageous person I ever met and if you say one more word about her, I'll bury your cock in a shoebox like a dead hamster."

Max stares at me, eyes spinning with fear or rage. "Fuckin' get a new line, bitch!"

Dragon Lady leans closer. "Bitch? You gonna talk like you're one of them assholes?"

"Maybe," Max says and coughs. The smoke and spit hits me in the face and I back up.

Max coughs several times and looks groggily at the spiraling smoke from his cigarette. Another cough. Then again. A slurry of deep rasping coughs interspersed with gasps for air. I hurry to open the balcony sliding door but he, coughing, waves no. He stands—coughing—and lurches to a closet and wheels out a green oxygen tank on a dolly, opens the valve and puts the mask over his face, breathing deeply between coughs.

"Come back tomorrow. I need rest," Max coughs out weakly. "Not before eleven. Go."

Dragon Lady doesn't want to leave. "You fucking with us?"

Max shakes his head, inhaling the oxygen. We step out.

A second later, there're the clicks of locks. And no more coughing.

I imagine it's a lot to process, I think.

Yeah, but I imagine if using oxygen is a common occurrence, you don't keep it in the closet.

So you think he faked that coughing fit?

I faked a lot in my time. Can't imagine I've changed.

STINKING OF CIGARETTE SMOKE, we head back to our hotel, but with the whole day ahead of us, Dragon Lady wants to see LA. The hotel has several brochures and we end up taking a bus tour starting at the Santa Monica pier. We ride through Beverly Hills, Rodeo Drive, The Grove, pass Sunset Strip, see the Hollywood sign, the sidewalk stars on the Walk of Fame, the foot and hand prints, and people dressed up as Marilyn Monroe, Charlie Chaplin, and Spiderman. It's exhausting. A sensory overload. I don't know how people can live here, but maybe it's not so tiring if you're not doing tourist stuff. I wonder where the locals go. Maybe we can ask Max tomorrow.

When the tour ends, we walk along Hollywood Boulevard and stop at an old building. Old enough that Max might have gone there. The Roosevelt Hotel. Inside it's cool and the lobby is high and wide, with the second level overlooking the shiny ceramic-tile floor, leather furniture, fountain, and chandelier. Everything looks like it's out of a movie. And it probably is. I expect men to be in suits and hats and women to be in tailored jackets and skirts. It would be cool if we could go back in time.

Don't you do that already? With all our lives in you?

I guess I do.

I sit in a comfortable club chair and a woman approaches me. "Can I get you something to drink? Our happy hour menu is in play."

I order blackened Brussels sprouts against Dragon Lady's wishes and a glass of white wine. Luckily, Dragon Lady is shocked at how far Brussels sprouts have come since her day.

We watch people come and go and eventually take a taxi back to our hotel. A little time on the beach to watch the sunset and we're both ready for bed. A shower gets rid of the cigarette smell until tomorrow. Wiping off the fogged mirror, I'm amazed to see Ruby's spiderweb scar on my forehead has disappeared. Also, my different types of hair have blended into something quite unique, and, I gotta admit, kinda great.

SURPRISE

DRAGON LADY HAS SPENT THE NIGHT thinking about questions for Max. I hope we can make it through them all without him having another coughing fit. I wonder what Dragon Lady intends to do if she doesn't have a grave to go to. Could she end up staying inside me forever? As we knock on Max's door in the musty hallway, she says, *I know what you're thinking. I don't have any idea what I'll do yet. Okay?*

With the clicking of the locks, the door opens. Max nods at me and steps back into the room and as I enter and turn to close the door, a different smell hits me. Something familiar. When I walk toward Max by his recliner, he glances at the kitchenette and I know something's wrong. Sounds shift behind me but before I can turn, a figure steps from the kitchenette. Mother.

And behind me, a male clears his throat to let me know he'll be stopping any attempted escape. I turn to him. He's obviously trying for the classic private dick vibe. Suit, tie, and jaded alcoholic look. Not a big man, but without all those beings inside me working my parts like they used to, I doubt I'll be any more than a fly in his ointment.

I nod hello and he doesn't.

"Elizabeth. You look good."

"Thank you, Mother, so do you." Mother looks more brittle than I remember her. Could my disappearance have weighed on her?

"Seriously, Elizabeth, you really do look good. Something has changed. You're more—of one piece."

That's certainly corroboration that my visage has melded with each departing person, but not the issue at hand. "What are you doing here?" I ask.

"Mr. Dragon had a suspicion you were on the run and was kind enough to notify me of your appearance. Mr. Dragon, as we discussed in our call, I greatly appreciate you contacting me and have written a check."

Dragon Lady and I both glare at Max. "You turn in your own flesh and blood for cash?"

Max gives me the finger. Mother steadies herself with a touch to the small table but quickly removes her fingers from that sticky surface. "I'm taking you back with me, Elizabeth. You escaped from the—institution, and will return there."

Dragon Lady turns to Max, "If you sell your own self out for money, you are worse than those fuckers who took my first place in the Log Race!"

The man behind me puts a paw on my shoulder. *This again— Do I have to tell you, you don't have the right to touch me?*—I drop and spin and my left leg swirls and lands in his crotch and my forehead bashes his nose as he crumples and my left hand grabs his thumb and twists it back against his wrist and my right heel rams down on his foot and Dragon Lady spins to put us behind him and his thumb-wrist is raised high up his back and my right foot kicks the rear of his knee and he drops hard and I reach for the oxygen tank and yank the clear tube off and create a loop and it's around his free hand and pull and swirl, swirl, swirl and knot both wrists behind his back and knee him to the ground.

"Elizabeth!" Mother says with a mix of horror and awe.

I put my left foot between the man's shoulders and turn to her. "It's Izzy."

Philip Marlow isn't happy on the ground and if he can escape my Ruby-inspired bonds, I'm not sure the next fight will be to my advantage.

"Mother," I say quietly. "I'd be much obliged if you would call off your bulldog and ask him to lie peacefully. I'd like to discuss things without any more interruptions."

Mother shifts uncomfortably.

Dragon Lady looks at Max. "Log Race. You were first place and everyone knew it. But you let them take it from you. Don't do it again."

Max turns to Mother. "Let's hear what she has to say, Mrs. Gaston."

Mother turns to the man on the floor. "Uh, Mr. Valanzuela—"

"Velázquez," the man beneath me mumbles.

"Mr. Velázquez, if you would be so kind as to not struggle or fight back at this time, I'd appreciate it."

"Mmm," the man says and lets his tension go.

"Eliz—Izzy," says my mother. "Do go on."

EVELYN – SYRACUSE, NEW YORK – 1998

"DO GO ON," PROFESSOR SCHWICK says in a mocking tone.

The class giggles.

The blood goes to my face and I can't even remember what it was I was saying.

"Please, Miss Evelyn, we're all waiting for your insight into what Cervantes was 'doing' via Don Quixote."

"It's just—to me, it reads more like a comedic parody than this supposed tragic epic of idealism."

Professor Schwick's eye twitches. "'Supposed tragic epic of idealism,' this ever-so-smart girl says with her nose in the air."

"I didn't—"

"Miss Evelyn thinks she knows all from her sophomoric perch. Enlighten us. Do go on."

I know I have more to say, but my mind can't focus. Everyone is staring at me. Professor Schwick laughs and waves for me to take my seat. I drop heavily, staring at the stupid cover with the stupid Picasso drawing of the stupid characters of this stupid book.

"Never mind. Miss Evelyn is obviously channeling the deep recesses of Mr. Quixote and his delusions. No windmills here, young lady!"

The class roars with his fuel.

"That's today. Next week, bring in an essay of 1000 words exploring contemporary instances of 'fighting windmills.' Class dismissed. Not you, Miss Evelyn."

It's not fair. Ridiculed in class and now he'll ridicule me after?

I stay in my seat.

He packs his leather satchel, wipes down the board, puts on his tweed jacket, and steps toward the door. His hand on the light switch, he turns to me, saying, "Coming?" And the lights go out.

I follow him down the emptying halls up the stairs—

"Professor Schwick—"

He holds up a finger to me for silence without turning around. We go downstairs, along the empty halls, to his basement office. He unlocks the door and ushers me inside ahead of him. It's a narrow room with bookshelves taking up both walls. Hardly enough room for two people. The fluorescent light buzzes overhead. I don't know where to stand and he's at the door. He smiles and maneuvers past me to sit in the only chair at his desk.

"I'm going to have to fail you, Evelyn."

"What?"

"You're a disruption to the class and I can't see a way to give you a passing grade."

"No, professor, I'm sorry I spoke—"

"Come. Sit." He points to his lap.

I don't move.

"You will come here. If you don't, you will fail."

I dart in the opposite direction and grab the doorknob. The door's locked.

"You don't have a choice. I make the rules. You can fight windmills but you can't win. Any ideas of repercussions are futile. The whole class saw your shame. They will understand any aspersions you cast my way will be trying to get revenge for being shamed. No one will believe anything you say, so let's get on with the lesson."

Professor Schwick stands and in two steps he's against me. He smells like wet wool. He shoves me violently against the metal file cabinet, his hand on my breast, the other up my skirt, ripping down my panties. I struggle but he is really strong and is skilled in his ability to hold me from escaping.

"Professor, please don't."

His hand moves from my breast to my neck and squeezes with just enough force to make me fear for my life. He unzips and forces himself into me. His grunting grows louder in my ear and the thrusts more painful. My tailbone is slammed into the metal handle of the file cabinet again and again. I'll be black and blue.

Across the narrow room is that famous Picasso print of Sancho Panza and Don Quixote. I watch them jerk back and forth in my vision. And then it's over. He pulls out, zips up, and wipes his hand on my skirt.

He doesn't look satisfied or happy. What was that all for? Did I challenge him and hurt his ego, so this was his only recourse?

He steps to the door and unlocks it. "Tidy yourself and go," he says as if I disgust him. "You'll pass."

MAX, MOTHER, AND DRAGON LADY

"I'M SO SORRY ABOUT WHAT HAPPENED with you and your Cervantes teacher, Mother. That was horrible," I say.

Mother drops into the yellow vinyl chair by the table. Her hands tremble as she whispers, "What?"

I shrug. "I didn't know that I had you in me, but I do. I had Father, as well. Maybe you helped push him out?"

"What?"

Max turns to my mother. "Your daughter believes she has ancestors' traumas in her. She thinks she has mine, but you said she escaped from a loony bi—"

"I never told—you can't know," Mother says, her eyes tearing.

"I do know. The embarrassment in class, the office, the threats, and the rape. That trauma was planted in me with your genes."

Mother starts sobbing. I've never seen her sob. It breaks my heart. I go to her and put my arms around her shaking shoulders. "Mother, what happened to you was terrible, but not unusual. And never think it was your fault."

Max nods sadly. "It's true, Mrs. Gaston. Never your fault. This hell happens more than anyone knows."

I glance up and Mr. Velázquez is watching us from the floor. He has tears in his eyes. I raise my eyebrows to him in a *You okay?* He nods, pressing his mouth tight to hold back any escaping emotions.

"Mother, I can't go back to the institution. I'm not crazy, I'm just full of ancestors. Or was. Max, I can go on and on with things you never told anyone. Jack hitting you with the flaming branch, dancing to Elvis, mixing martinis in the thermos lid, olive jar, and a used Chock Full o' Nuts coffee cup. I really do have Dragon Lady in me."

Max squints at me, "Take it easy."

"But take it." Dragon Lady says.

Max nods. "Hello, Maxine."

My mother shakes her head. "You're saying really strange things, Izzy. You sound crazy and sane at the same time. But, don't you think you need help?"

"Mother, I've had help. So much help. I know shit that you can't imagine—from Nahrungssuche, also known as foraging, to driving, to compassion, to politeness, to standing up for my rights, to—" I glance at Mr. Velázquez on the floor—"defending myself. I'm a much wholer person than I was."

Mother's hands flit about nervously.

"You said I look better. That's because I get more integrated as each ancestor leaves. They learn about their lives—"

Max jumps in, "They leave? Dragon Lady is leaving you?"

Dragon Lady waffles. "I don't know, Max. Everyone else in Izzy, when we found where they'd lived, they were long dead. I'm here now—but you—me—you're alive. I don't have a grave to go to. I don't know what to do."

Max stands and shuffles over to us. He puts his bony hand on Dragon Lady's arm. There's a jolt in us with that touch. He must feel it as well because his eyebrows jump in surprise. Max squeezes that arm. "Dragon Lady, I'd like you to stay with me."

Dragon Lady wobbles our head. "And do what? You know I like getting into things. Mashing it up. Interacting. I can't sit in this damn gloomy room for the rest of my life."

Max nods slowly. "I understand."

"Wait a minute," Mother says. "Who is Dragon Lady, and why would she stay with Max?"

"Dragon Lady was Maxine, a woman motorcycle racer. She was a little too opinionated and a little too strong and a little too accomplished—" I watch Max puffing up as I say this—"and a little too ballsy and a little too excellent, so the intimidated men called her Dragon Lady. And rather than pushing the name away, she made it her official moniker. But after her horrible trauma of a violent rape and burial alive—" I look at Max.

He continues the story. "I gave up my baby for adoption—

"Grandpa Wheeler," I add.

Mother's eyes widen.

"—and changed my name from Maxine Fredricks, aka Dragon Lady, to Max Dragon. And from that moment on, I've been a man. I raced as a man. Finally able to win as an equal. I think I'd always been a man inside, and when I survived what was meant to kill me, I wanted to be true to myself for the rest of my life."

Mother looks awkwardly at Max. "You're—transgender? Did you—do the—operations?"

"Whether I did or not is irrelevant. I was a woman. Now I'm a man."

We stay in silence for a moment until Mr. Velázquez clears his throat. Mother has me untie him and she gives him a check that makes him smile. He shakes my hand and hands me his card, saying, "Si alguna vez necesitas algo, llámame." And damn if I don't understand. I must have learned a lot of Spanish from Yasmina when she carried me, or—there must be more lives in me than I am aware of.

After Mr. Velázquez leaves, my mother looks at me and Max. "I'm proud to have Dragon Lady as my ancestor."

"Me too, Mom."

Mom gets tearful again. "You called me Mom. You never have before. Always Mother."

"You never were a mom before."

"Izzy, I would like it if—now that we've started—we could keep talking. I'll contact the hospital and make it clear you were released on my—on your *own* recognizance. You don't have to run anymore."

"Thanks, Mom. Nor do you."

Mom blinks several times, like it's a weird concept to absorb.

Max coughs. "I could try."

"Try what?" I ask.

"I could try to get out and paint the town and do things. Exciting things. How old are you, Dragon Lady?"

"Twenty-eight."

"I'm seventy-eight. But I still got gumption. Could you stay and get me back to living?" Max asks quietly.

"I have waited forever to get to Los Angeles. I want to experience it all."

"I'll be your guide," Max says.

"Damn straight." Dragon Lady and Max clasp hands and I see they are meant for each other. Either that or they'll be so opinionated and challenging, they'll drive each other crazy.

I don't know what to do now. Should I leave Dragon Lady here and—

She hops to my mind. *No, You and me need to be alone.*

I tell Max and Mom that we're going out for a bit and that they should stay and get to know each other. Dragon Lady and I leave before they can protest and a minute later we're in the Metro Van weaving through the traffic, heading for the beach.

BEACH WALK

DRAGON LADY AND I walk on the sand for a long time and my left hand holds my right hand. I'm feeling sad and know this is goodbye, but I'm scared. I've never been alone. Soon I'll be just me. Just Izzy. No protection or advice or skills or help or companionship or empathy or—

Stop. You're digging a pit of despair. Sit.

I sit on the moist sand.

You know you are much bigger than you think. Remember what I said way-back-when? "You can't defend yourself. Can't drive. Can't fuel up the van. Can't make a plan..."

Yeah, I'm a dumb-fuck, rich kid with no experience and no skills and I'm way outta my depth.

Not anymore, girlie—Izzy. You have so many skills and they don't disappear. Just because your ancestors are leaving doesn't mean your DNA is changing. Your genes are what they have always been. You're not losing your innate abilities or traits. You're just losing the yammering.

But who will I be without you all?

You'll be Izzy. You'll do like everyone else does. Find out who that person is. Find out, experiment, change your mind, move on... all that living shit.

I dig my fingers into the sand. Dragon Lady's hand joins me.

Yeah, let's get some of this. I want my soil contribution to be Pacific Ocean sand. Fill your pockets.

We fill every pocket to the brim, and even get a lot of extra sand in our shoes.

FORMOSA CAFE

AFTER RELIEVING OUR CLOTHES of their sandy collection, we change into a clean outfit and drive back to Blackburn Avenue.

Mom looks relieved when we return. Bet she thought I'd skip out and she'd wonder if she needed to hire Mr. Velázquez again. She's in the vinyl chair beside the recliner. Max has a scrapbook across his lap, showing clippings and programs of all his races. I'm sure that's the other reason for Mom's relief. I'm disrupting an endless litany of triumphs. Dragon Lady is about to protest my thinking but Mom interrupts her. "We just realized that Max is my Grandfather—and Grand*mother*. I've learned all about his family and his great-grandparents were in the rodeo circus with Buffalo Bill and Annie Oakley!"

I step up to them. "I'm hoping my Great-Grandma Dragon Lady and I can take you and Great-Grandpa Max out for dinner. He'll have to suggest the place as we're novices to this city."

Max steps into his bedroom to change and I sit beside Mom. I see her so differently, especially knowing what that asshole did to her and how she hid it for so long.

"Uh, Mom, if you want to visit that jerk Professor Schwick anytime, I'm game. I know a thing or two about scaring the shit out of perpetrators."

Mom looks into my eyes. In a slow, low voice she says, "Thank you. That might be something for the future."

Max returns dressed in a very snappy suit that looks like it's from the musical *Guys and Dolls*. We walk through the city up to the Formosa Cafe. The restaurant is dark and full of red leather and photographs of early movie stars. There are oriental lanterns but I know they aren't what Chan would consider authentic. Probably not the food either.

Max glows as he ushers us into a curved booth. "This is old Hollywood. The booths that Bogart and Bacall sat at. Maybe there's some ancestor here as well. Luckily, we can still get them from the movies. There are ancestors everywhere, even if they aren't direct lines."

Max orders a dirty gin martini. Dragon Lady lifts her hand for another. Mom gives me a look of shock. I shrug—"Dragon Lady wants one." Mom smiles and puts up her hand for another.

My god, my mother is really not who I thought she was!

After we toast each other carefully with the to-the-brim martinis, I sip and cough at the salty turpentine flavor, but Dragon Lady relishes the taste.

An old-style crooner sings over the speakers.

Dean Martin, Dragon Lady tells me.

How am I going to know these things when you leave?

You learn. Pay attention. You can also ask.

I turn to my mother. She's sipping her dirty martini in a way I've never seen. She's relishing it. "Do you know who is singing, Mom?"

"Dean Martin. My father loved him."

"I know so little about Grandfather. Or you. I'd like to know more."

My mother puts a hand up to her lips to stop what might be a sob. Her eyes tell me it was.

"Mom, I'm gonna take some time for myself, but don't you think it would be good to get Finn out to meet his great-grandfather? He knows Dragon Lady already, so Max won't be a stranger. Give him a few months in California."

"He's too young to travel alone—"

Max puts his hand on Mom's. "You both come. I can get some blow-up mattresses."

Mom smiles at him. "I think that's a fine idea. Findley—*Finn*—he prefers that now—would love to meet you, Max." She looks at me and I see honest respect for the first time. "Izzy, Finn never said where you traveled but he told me all the wonderful memories of camping and weird food concoctions and swimming and foraging—and he loved it. Every minute."

That makes me glad, but I wonder if it will stick. I can only hope something will.

We have egg rolls and noodle dishes and wonton soup and things in spicy sauce but we don't pay attention to any of it. We play with the chopsticks and tell jokes from different generations and have more dirty martinis and sing along to the old crooners and open the cookie fortunes and everyone insists I take the *Obstructed paths clear. Be open to adventure.*

Mom's phone rings and a look of dread crosses her face. "Your father's ringtone."

"Don't answer it," I suggest.

She sighs and puts the phone to her ear. "Yes." The dread leaves and joy sparkles. "Go on video." And she hands the phone to me as Finn's face fills the screen. He looks much more mature and still has long hair!

"FINN!" I yell.

"IZZY!" he yells back. "You look so different! Like—like—pretty! I mean, sorry, Miss. Not that you weren't before, but—what happened? All those great people in you aren't gone, are they?"

"Not if I can help it. As long as I remember them, they'll always be with me." Dragon Lady pats my arm.

"Ja! And I reckon with me as well, lass!"

We talk a bit more but Finn can't stay long as he's on his way to pick up his phone he left—at CULINARY CLASS! I promise him I'll get in touch soon and we part with a lot of nonsense and Max, Dragon Lady, me, and Finn yelling, "Take it easy, but take it!"

Gosh, it feels good to see him so wild and free and different. I guess my whole adventure was worth it.

The check comes and when I give Mom a glance, she graciously lets Max pay. It brings tears to my eyes and gets Max going too. We're all crying 'cause Grandpa's paying.

The streetlights glow orange as we walk back. The night is cooler and things feel oddly peaceful. Mom turns to Max. "Do you mind if I slip ahead, Max?"

"I know I walk slow, go on."

"No, it's not that. I just want to speak to my daughter."

Those words choke me up. My daughter. She really is accepting me. I'm hers!

Mom pulls us ahead a few paces and takes my hand. She's on what was Simon's side so that hand is all me now. We never did this. She always avoided touching me. It feels so very good to hold her hand.

"Izzy, I've got a lot to tell you. This last year or so has been rough. Finn's kidnapping, and your father freaking out about it nightly, and the stress of that, and afterward you in the institution, and I didn't know how to help, and then you escaped, and suddenly, I kept picturing you traveling and staying in motels or under bridges—meeting people, having adventures. I think all these things—Finn's descriptions of camping and—your travels —I was seeing places in my mind that weren't those familiar Central Park West walls. I saw the possibility of something else and, I'm sorry to tell you, your father and I are getting a divor—"

"YES!" I scream.

"I guess that means you're okay with—"

"YES! A million times, yes! Get out and get free! Find out who *Evelyn* is!"

Mom squeezes my hand. "Thank you. I will. Finn and I are moving out and—I have to say, California looks very inviting."

"You do it, Mom. Leave the old ways behind."

We slow down our walking to let Max catch up, then walk arm in arm with me in the middle—Max on Dragon Lady's arm, Mom on my other. It's wonderful.

At Max's building, Mom pauses. "I'll take my leave now. It has been an incredibly—joyous day, and Max, I'll be in touch very soon about Finn and I staying with you." She kisses Max on the cheek. "Grandfather."

Max starts to speak but stops himself. The fact is, he was a woman and, even if he no longer is, he knows when to be silent so someone else can have their moment.

Mom turns to me and kisses one cheek, "Grandmother," and the other cheek, "Incredible Izzy."

And as Mom turns and steps away, there's a tugging in me, a pull, and a snapping out, and before me swirls a figure I recognize as young Evelyn when she was in college, and she shrugs and smiles and blurs off to catch my mother, and I'm not sure what is her or wisps of Los Angeles smog as she disappears. This will be what will happen to us all some day, my mother will be a wisp, Finn will, and so will I.

I feel another tug in me and a pull and I'm yanked and she's loose. Dragon Lady stands before me. What a tough cookie! Leather motorcycle jacket, wild ragged short hair, muddy jeans, and laced boots. She smiles at me, winks, and mouths *Take it easy, but take it.*

I touch my heart to say she'll always be there and Dragon Lady pops me a thumbs up and then slips her arm over Max's and he straightens like a proud escort and, blowing me a kiss, leads her up the steps and inside.

It's all good. They're where they need to be. Home with each other. But my arm is empty. My whole being is empty. I'm completely and utterly alone.

KIN

I WALK ON THE BEACH again. It's cool and dark and the ocean shimmers with moonlight. I don't know if it is safe to be out here —not too many people are on the beach—but I don't care. Right now I feel a deep, overwhelming loneliness. How can I become my own person? I've never been without them all. My whole being feels like a wound.

Sit on the beach. Listen to the *shhhh, shhhh* of the waves. But the sound is no comfort. Nothing will ever fill me. I should go back to the hotel but it'll make me even more lonely. I'd rather sleep in the van. At least it has memories of being full of people—

even if they all inhabited one body. But now it'll be even more lonely and—

"Hey babe."

A man drops onto the sand beside me. It's dark so I can't see much of him except he has a beard and no shirt on.

"You alone, sweetheart?"

I don't need this. Especially now with my ancestors gone—

"Give me a kiss," the man says, leaning closer—

I put my palm up directly in his face and the words come out un-rushed and strong. "No. I suggest you get up RIGHT NOW and get the FUCK away from me before you experience MY FORMIDABLE WRATH."

The man scrambles backwards, hops to his feet, and hurries off without a word.

I'm shaking, from adrenaline and fear and my own power. I did that. I was there for myself. Maybe I'll be okay after all.

I head up the beach toward the boardwalk and the familiar warm home of my Metro Van. I lock the door and sit, letting my nerves settle.

The sand from the beach is in a large yogurt container. I label it *Dragon Lady Pacific Ocean* with a Sharpie and put it beside the other collected soils. They're all stuck in disparate vessels. To-go containers, plastic bags... Not what they should be in. Something important and honoring. Something...

The thought comes in and I move everything off the built-in table. Fill a bowl with water and line up all the samples in front of me. I dump Dragon Lady's sand on the tabletop. Pour the rocky, twiggy, dark brown from Jenny and Solveig's Levittown. The rich earth from Kelly's meadow sticks to its to-go-carton. The soil from Heinrich's has a yellower color and small pebbles. Simon's Mississippi is heavy red clay. Ruby's Bridgeport is dense with rich organic decay. I dip my hand—it's entirely my hand now—in the bowl and sprinkle water on each pile. The colors darken and become bolder. Wet both hands and lay them over everyone gently and get mixing. Solveig into Ruby. Simon into Dragon Lady.

Pacific sand into Kansas prairie. Mississippi muck into Eastern Sierra runoff. Glacier alluvium from Long Island into Pennsylvania meadow. I kneed and fold and press and turn, melding the soils. Melding the ancestors. The colors blend— swirls of ochre, beside umber, beside sienna. As I mix it, my right arm changes. It loses the weathered skin, the tough sinewy muscles. My body is finally homogenous, as is this earthen mixture. All my disparate bits have integrated. I've been stirred.

My tears moisten the mass. I form the torso, the head, arms and legs. It's like a mud doll or a large gingerbread cookie that needs flattening. The clay really works to hold it together. I'm no sculptor, but I make a figure that has my proportions and even without detail, it looks a bit like me.

I stand the figure up. It makes me smile to look at it. Feels like I'm not alone.

"Hey, Solveig and Ruby and Kelly and Simon and Heinrich and Jenny and Dragon Lady and Mom and all you other ancestors I don't know about. I am who I am because of you. I've learned to drive and forage and fight and ride horses and speak up for myself and demand my rights and give compassion and care for people and be polite and kiss and a lot more. I will never forget any of you and what you've been and given me. But I won't carry your traumas anymore. That's your baggage. I'm separate from you. Your trauma is tragic, but it's not mine. I will hold you close, but I'm not you. Now it's my turn. I'm sure there will be more traumas. Hopefully not as bad as some of yours, but they'll be mine and I'll try to heal them."

I touch the face of that figure.

"I will never lose you, but I'm not you. I'm me. Izzy."

I turn off the light and go to sleep with the figure staring at me.

The morning light streams in. The clay figure is still standing, looking happy.

I step out into the parking lot. There's a homeless man pawing through the dumpster. He looks up at me. I wave and he smiles and goes back to his work. A young woman skates by on rollerblades talking into her phone. I wave and she nods. An overweight man in a greasy white apron and chef hat opens a back door and hands the homeless man a to-go container, then looks at me. I wave and he waves back. These could all be my kin. Who knows who I share DNA with. If you go back far enough, we're all related. These people *are* kin. That mother jogging behind the baby stroller. That skinny dude with the pants hanging below his crotch. That woman in the hijab. That one sleeping on the sidewalk. My ancestors populated this country. Some thrived, others were subjugated and marginalized. I don't know all about them, or what they did, but I do know they all had sex and I see ancestors in every face. On the TV and in the parks and bodegas and juke-joints and congress and native pueblos and universities and prisons and hospitals and kitchens and bedrooms and boardrooms and classrooms. Everywhere I look, I see kin. Guess it's time to meet the family.

I hop in the Metro Van, get it rumbling, and start the rest of my life.

THE END

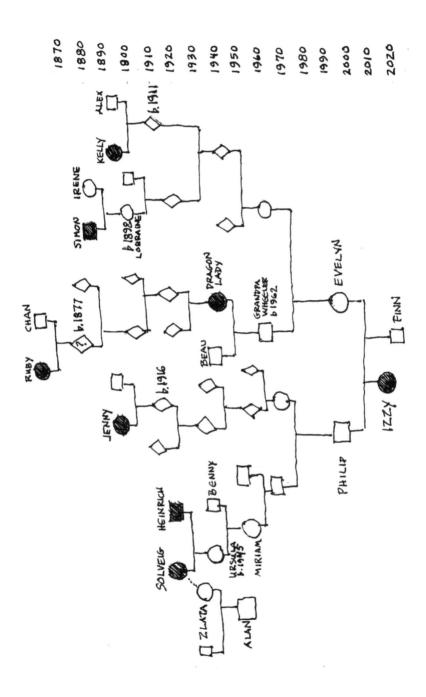